ɔk of
ɔ fantasy
$ 11.95

D0285813

Comic Fantasy

Also available

The Mammoth Book of 20th Century Ghost Stories
The Mammoth Book of Arthurian Legends
The Mammoth Book of Astounding Puzzles
The Mammoth Book of Battles
The Mammoth Book of Best New Horror 11
The Mammoth Book of Brainstorming Puzzles
The Mammoth Book of Bridge
The Mammoth Book of British Kings & Queens
The Mammoth Book of Cats
The Mammoth Book of Chess
The Mammoth Book of Comic Fantasy
The Mammoth Book of Comic Fantasy II
The Mammoth Book of Dracula
The Mammoth Book of Erotica
The Mammoth Book of Eyewitness History
The Mammoth Book of Fairy Tales
The Mammoth Book of Fantastic Science Fiction
The Mammoth Book of Gay Erotica
The Mammoth Book of Gay Short Stories
The Mammoth Book of Heroic and Outrageous Women
The Mammoth Book of Historical Detectives
The Mammoth Book of Historical Whodunnits
The Mammoth Book of the History of Murder
The Mammoth Book of Humor
The Mammoth Book of International Erotica
The Mammoth Book of Jack the Ripper
The Mammoth Book of Killer Women
The Mammoth Book of Lesbian Erotica
The Mammoth Book of Lesbian Short Stories
The Mammoth Book of Life Before the Mast
The Mammoth Book of Love & Sensuality
The Mammoth Book of Men O'War
The Mammoth Book of Modern Science Fiction
The Mammoth Book of New Erotica
The Mammoth Book of New Sherlock Holmes Adventures
The Mammoth Book of Nostradamus and Other Prophets
The Mammoth Book of Private Lives
The Mammoth Book of Pulp Fiction
The Mammoth Book of Puzzle Carnival
The Mammoth Book of Sex, Drugs & Rock 'n' Roll
The Mammoth Book of Soldiers at War
The Mammoth Book of Short Erotic Novels
The Mammoth Book of Sword & Honor
The Mammoth Book of Symbols
The Mammoth Book of Tasteless Lists
The Mammoth Book of Terror
The Mammoth Book of the Third Reich at War
The Mammoth Book of True War Stories
The Mammoth Book of the West
The Mammoth Book of True Crime (revised edition)
The Mammoth Book of Unsolved Crimes
The Mammoth Book of Vampires
The Mammoth Book of Victorian & Edwardian Ghost Stories

THE MAMMOTH BOOK OF

Awesome
Comic Fantasy

Edited by Mike Ashley

CARROLL & GRAF PUBLISHERS, INC.
New York

Carroll & Graf Publishers, Inc.
19 West 21st Street
New York
NY 10010–6805

First published in the UK by Robinson,
an imprint of Constable & Robinson Ltd 2001

First Carroll & Graf edition 2001
Reprinted 2001

ISBN 0–7867–0867–0

Printed and bound in the EU

CONTENTS

COPYRIGHT AND ACKNOWLEDGMENTS

ANOTHER INTRODUCTION

Mike Ashley

I'm delighted to be able to compile a third volume of comic fantasy.

Oh hell, not another introduction!

What?

Who reads introductions, for God's sake?

What do you mean?

People don't want to read your waffle, they want to get on with the book.

But this is where I say what the book's all about and what's in it and thank people.

We know what the book's about – you've already done two of them.

Yes, but . . .

Come on, cut the crap. Get on with it.

But I need to thank people.

Thank them on that acknowledgements page. No one reads that, either.

And what about revealing some of the hidden treasures here, like the rare stories and forgotten gems, and that there are thirteen brand new stories specially written for this book, and that we've got a mixture of . . .

We'll find out. We'll just read the book.

Yes, but, this is my only spot in the whole book . . .

Thank God for that. Right, I've had enough. I'm off to the first story. Who's coming with me?

But there's all that about my broad definition of fantasy, and something for all tastes, and all types of humour . . .

Goodbye!

Oh, go on then. Have fun. Don't worry about me . . .

HAPPY VALLEY

John Cleese & Connie Booth

What can one say about the genius of Monty Python *and of the brilliance of John Cleese and Connie Booth, the creators of* Fawlty Towers, *that hasn't already been said time and again? This story featured in one of the later episodes of* Monty Python's Flying Circus *and gets this book off to a suitably silly start.*

Once upon a time, long long ago, there lay in a valley far, far away in the mountains, the most contented kingdom the world has ever known.

It was called Happy Valley, and it was ruled over by a wise old King called Otto, and all his subjects flourished and were happy, and there were no discontents or grumblers, because Wise King Otto had had them all put to death along with the Trade Union leaders many years before. And all the good happy folk of Happy Valley sang and danced all day long, and anyone who was for any reason miserable or unhappy or who had any difficult personal problems was prosecuted under the Happiness Act. (See, for example, R. *v.* Schlitz (1251). S, a carpenter, was heard moaning quietly contrary to Section 2 of the Cheerful Noises Act (1208); also admitted being depressed with malice aforethought under Section 1 of Happiness Act. Plea in mitigation that S's wife had died on previous day; S sentenced to be hanged by the neck until he cheered up.)

And, while the good people of Happy Valley tenaciously frolicked away, their wise old King, who was a merry old thing, played strange songs on his Hammond Organ up in the beautiful castle, where he lived with his gracious Queen Syllabub and their lovely daughter Mitzi Gaynor, who had fabulous tits and an enchanting smile, and wooden teeth which she bought in a chemist's in Augsberg, despite the fire risk. She treasured these teeth which were made of the finest pine and she varnished them after every meal. And next to her teeth her dearest love was her pet dog Hermann. She would take Hermann for long walks and pet and fuss over him all day long and steal him tasty titbits which he never ate, because sadly he was dead and no one had the heart to tell her because she was so sweet and innocent that she knew nothing of death or gastro-enteritis or even plastic hip joints. One day, while Mitzi was taking Hermann for a pull round the Royal Gardens, she set eyes on the most beautiful young man she had ever seen and fell head over heels in love with him, naturally assuming him to be a prince. Well, as luck would have it, he *was* a prince, and so, after looking him up in the *Observer's Book of Princes* to discover his name, she went and introduced herself and the subject of marriage, and, in what seemed like the twinkling of an eye, but was in fact a fortnight, they were on their way to see King Otto, to ask his permission to wed. What a perfect couple they looked! Mitzi, resplendent in a delicate shell-pink satin brocade and some new bulletproof mahogany teeth, and Prince Kevin, handsome as could be, drawing many an admiring glance from some randy old closet queens in the vestibule.

Soon they were at the door of the Kingdom-Ruling Room. And then, trying to control their excitement, they were ushered into the presence of the King himself, who sat at the Royal State Organ singing his latest composition, the strangely discordant "Ya bim dee bim, thwackety f'tang stirkel boo bum". And when the King had finished, some hours later, and the courtiers' applause had died down, Mitzi presented Prince Kevin, who bowed gracefully and asked the wise old King for his daughter's hand in marriage.

"Is he in the book?" asked the King.

"Oh yes, Daddy," cried Mitzi.

"And do you love my daughter?" he queried, penetratingly.

"I do, sir!" replied Prince Kevin, and a ripple of delight passed round the room for already Kevin's princely bearing and sweetness of nature had won the entire court's approval.

"Good! But first, before I can grant permission, I must set you a task that you may prove yourself worthy of my daughter's hand."

"I accept!!" cried Kevin gallantly.

The old King's face grew grave. "At nine o'clock tomorrow morning," he explained, "you must go to the top of the highest tower in this castle and, armed only with your sword, jump out of the window."

And so, early the next day, the brave young prince, dressed in a beautiful gold and white robe, and armed only with his magic sword, plummeted three hundred feet to a speedy death. How they all cheered! How funny the royal remains looked!

"Can we get married now, Daddy?" cried Mitzi, for as we know she knew nothing of death.

"No, daughter, I'm afraid not," answered the wise old King, although he was himself a necrophilia buff. "He simply wasn't worthy of you."

"Oh dear," said Mitzi. "Will he have to go in the ground like all the others?"

And so most of Prince Kevin was buried alongside the remains of Prince Oswald (page 4 in the book) who'd had to fight an infantry division armed only with a copy of *The Guardian*; and Prince Robin (p. 19) who'd gallantly attempted to extinguish a fiery furnace by being thrown in it; and Prince Norbert (p. 36) who'd had to wrestle a combine harvester; and Prince Malcolm (p. 8) who'd had to catch a VC 10, but had dropped it; and all the many other princes who'd been a touch unlucky in their quests.

So, the moment that Kevin's coffin had been laid to rest on the traditional huge black-edged Whoopee Cushion (for as Kevin was a prince, he had been granted a State Fancy Dress Funeral), Mitzi was off once again to the Royal Gardens, dragging the faithful Hermann behind her, to see if she could pull another prince. But alas, although most of the good folk of Happy Valley were there, the Carpenter and the Blacksmith and the Secret Policeman, and the Candlemaker and the Window-Dresser and his friend, and the Hangman and all his little apprentices, and the Writer-Performer and the Chartered Agent Provocateur, not a prince was to be seen. For princes had become extremely scarce; as rare, indeed, as an Australian virgin.

So Mitzi set off along the river bank, hopefully kissing frogs, until she was almost half-way to the Magic Scampi Provençale Bush when – all of a sudden! – she spotted the slightest glint of gold from beneath a Giggling Willow Tree and running forward, espied – sure enough! – a prince. He was rather thin and spotty, with a long nose, and bandy legs, and nasty unpolished plywood teeth, and a rare foot disease, but, thought Mitzi, a prince is a prince, and she fell in love with him without another thought.

And after a time, or a few times anyway, he, too, fell in love with her, and a few hours later they were on their way to ask wise King Otto's permission to wed, as this latest prince didn't read the newspapers any more than any of the others did, decadent, dimwitted, parasitic little bastards that they were.

But as they made their happy way through the stately corridors that led to the Royal Chambers, by chance they came across Queen Syllabub being laid by a coloured gentleman.

"Hello, Mummy," cried Mitzi, "this is Prince Walter."

"Hello, Prince Walter," cried Queen Syllabub graciously, slipping on her bra, "how nice to see you."

"Hello, Mummy's friend," cried Mitzi.

"Don't stare, darling," smiled the Queen, "this is Dr Erasmus, my new Algebra teacher."

"I guessed you were a doctor," cried Mitzi gaily, for she knew nothing of gynaecology. "Mummy, we're going to ask Daddy's permission to get married."

"Ah," muttered Queen Syllabub, "I want a word with him about that. I'll see you about the Binomial Theorem at eight o'clock, Doctor Erasmus."

"OK, Queen," boomed her tinted mentor, "I'll bring the baby oil."

"Now, Mitzi," continued our gracious Queen, hevelling herself, "is Walter kosher?"

"Page twenty," cried our sweet heroine, proffering the trusty tome. And then, "Does Daddy like Doctor Erasmus?"

"Best not to mention anything, darling," explained her mother. "Daddy's a little funny about darker people."

"I know nothing of racial prejudice," said Mitzi wistfully, for she knew nothing of racial prejudice.

"Now, you two just wait here a moment," ordered Queen Syllabub, "I want a word with your father." And she strode forward into the Kingdom-Ruling Room, where, rudely interrupting the King's golden oldies ("Ni ni ni ni ni ni ni ni ni ni ni ni ni ni ni ni ni ni ni *NI*!!" 0001 on the HMV label) she explained in no uncertain terms that as Mitzi was rapidly running out of acceptable fiancés, Otto had better set this latest one an easy task or else.

"Is he in the book?" asked the King, surlily.

"Yes, Daddy," cried Princess Mitzi, delightedly.

"Do you love my daughter?" queried the wise old King.

"Could be," allowed Prince Walter, nasally.

"Do you," continued the wise old King, "want her hand in marriage?"

An uneasy silence fell upon the assembled courtiers, for none of them much cared for Walter's looks, not even the Lord Chancellor, who was extremely gay.

". . . Yeah, all right."

"In that case," said the King, pursuing his line of thought

most doggedly, for he knew full well that Queen Syllabub's first spouse had met with a mysterious end, "I must set you a task to prove you worthy of my daughter's hand."

"Why?" came the bold reply.

"Because she's a fuckin' Princess, that's why," explained the King, scarcely controlling his rage. "And your task is that you must, quite unaided and unarmed, go down the town and get me twenty Rothmans."

"What, now!?" exploded Walter.

"Not necessarily," cried the King weakly, smiling round the court with all the easy spontaneity of a chat show host. "I'll think about it."

Well, soon the day arrived when Prince Walter was to meet his challenge. In fact, it was very soon, as it was the next day. The whole of Happy Valley gathered in the village square in great expectation. The King, Queen Syllabub and Princess Mitzi in all their finery sat on the gaily decorated scaffold surrounded by all the Royal Guards (except Brian Freud who was indisposed).

Suddenly the assembled throng fell silent as the commanding figure of Prince Walter slouched into the square and approached the royal party. With a few brief words the King stated Walter's task for all to hear, Queen Syllabub added the royal blessing and Princess Mitzi presented a pair of royal panties for him to carry on his quest as a token of her undying love and to ward off evil spirits.

With the tumultuous cheers of the excited crowd ringing in his ears, and the surge of the drum rolls echoing through the square, Walter, single-handed and armed only with half a pound, strode off on his quest. Yard after yard he walked, foot after foot, inch after inch, on and on, resolutely thrusting forward each leg in turn in the orthodox way, undeterred by the pebbles in the street and the birds flying overhead, on and on, and on and on, and on, ever forward, never looking back or at least not very often. Once perhaps, as Walter turned into Exceptional Crescent, the hordes of Happy Valley folk, and all the guests that had been invited from far and wide to witness the spectacle, and everyone else who had got tickets, sensed a moment's hesitation, a fleeting infirmity of purpose, as Walter seemed to falter, but it was only to scratch his crotch, and seconds later he was off again, beckoned ever forward by the glittering but forbidding prospect of the Splendido Tobacconist Shop, just two doors down from the butcher's.

On and on he marched, pace upon pace, stride upon stride, until, at last, he stood before the portals of his Holy Grail, his improbable dream, his cherished target, as it were. The great shop lay before him!

A sudden stillness fell upon the crowds clustering the pavements, thronging the windows of all the houses and inns and spilling over from all the tiny side streets. This was the moment of truth! It was now or not for a bit! Slowly Walter stepped towards the door, paused, gripped the doorknob and, with one expert twist, turned it and thrust the door towards the tobacconist. The crowd gasped as he disappeared into the Splendido's murky depths.

Minutes passed. The crowd held their breath. Many fell unconscious as a result of this unintelligent behaviour. But then! The ring of a cash register! The sound of the doorknob turning and there was Walter! Standing victorious in the doorway, arm thrust proudly aloft and in his clenched fist – Yes! The twenty Rothmans, nestling effortlessly in their magnificent packet, the priceless cellophane glinting in the dazzling sunlight!!!

A joyous cry rang out throughout Happy Valley, and the crowds surged forward to salute the conqueror. Walter stood one moment, savouring the acclaim, and then, turning, started to retrace his steps, pace after pace, yard after yard, his feet alternating deftly, very much in the way already described when he was travelling in the opposite direction earlier. But not for long! For the rejoicing crowd, unable to contain themselves further, surged forward and, sweeping their hero upwards, carried him shoulder high, back through Exceptional Crescent, into Anti-Depressant Street and round into the main square, setting him down in front of the royal platform just before the photograph was taken. How the square echoed and re-echoed with cheers! How thunderously the cymbals crashed! How joyously the old bells of the cathedral pealed forth! And as Walter proudly presented the fruits of his quest to King Otto, it almost seemed as though the birds on high filled the air with their purest rhapsodies while the flowers below opened their very blossoms in sweetest celebration.

"Where's my change?" queried the King.

"I've given it you," said Our Hero.

"I gave you ten bob," stated the King, for this was many many years before decimalization. "How much were they?"

"Shut your gob, Otto," muttered the Queen, waving graciously. "And give him Mitzi's hand."

"Halt!" cried a mysterious voice, lilting and musical, yet strangely strong and masculine, like an inspired newsreader.

All eyes in the square swivelled to the source of the voice described in the line above and lo! There before them, astride a magnificent Arab stallion, sat a princely figure, more beautiful than Apollo, more commanding even than Richard Attenborough, more royal than the Duke of Kent himself.

"Halt, I prithee!" cried this apotheosis of young manhood. "Gentle King, pray halt!"

"Who are you?" demanded King Otto, quite bewildered.

"I am Prince Charming of the Kingdom of the Golden Lakes," cried the godlike creature, as his attendants wheeled the magnificent stallion forward. "Page five in The Book. And I claim the hand of your beautiful daughter Princess Mitzi!"

A gasp of astonishment rose from the village square.

"You're too late," shouted Prince Walter.

"What?" cried the butch vision.

"I got her, Charming," snarled our former hero. "Now buzz off!"

"Wait a minute!" The Queen was on her feet. "Mitzi is not betrothed yet!"

"What?" screamed Prince Walter. "The King said if I got him twenty Rothmans I could 'ave her."

"Got him *twenty Rothmans*?" repeated Prince Charming, in astonishment.

"I had to go into the town."

"For this priceless treasure," cried the gallant Prince Charming, indicating the beautiful Mitzi Gaynor, who had risen to her feet and was now eyeing this golden princeling with something approaching pure lust. "For this most perfect of God's creatures, for this finest and most delicate flower in the whole of this geographical area, I will face in mortal combat that most dreaded of all creatures . . ."

"An emu!!" gasped the crowd.

"No, no, no," cried Prince Charming. "A dragon!"

"We accept," cried the Queen.

"We accept," cheered the villagers, to a man, or to a woman, as the case may have been.

"Where's he going to get a dragon from?" squealed Prince Walter.

Prince Charming favoured him with a gracious smile.

"I provide my own."

It was a beautiful Spring morning, the excited crowds were milling around the unused dog track where the Dragon Fight was to take place. Hermann had died, you see, the day before the dog track was opened, and as Mitzi had registered Hermann as an entry in all the races, and as he would have run last (on account of his being dead) and as royal pets must not fail, under the Constitution of Happy Valley the races were cancelled; but as Mitzi continued to enter Hermann whenever new races were announced, these races too were always being cancelled at the last minute. (Due to expected rain.) This had been going on in Happy Valley for over six years. The Editor says this is not relevant but I wanted you to know anyway, just for background.

Anyway . . . everyone was there, clustered round the edge of the specially erected ring, jostling for the best views, chattering excitedly, and laughing merrily at the antics of some of the high-spirited youths who had clambered into the arena and were now roasting an immigrant, on a spit wittily improvised from a flagpole borrowed from the Royal Stand. Suddenly an outburst of ironic cheering and catcalls announced that the Royal Family were taking their places in their Special Box, King Otto leading the way and playing selections from Bizet on his new Japanese wrist organ, Mitzi close behind accompanied by the Lord Chancellor, then Queen Syllabub and Archduke Harry, the Lord Chief Justice and the Archbishop, and Field Marshal Spratbanger and Admiral Spam-Willoughby-Spam, followed by all the courtiers and attendants carrying the ceremonial crates of brown ale and cheese-and-onion rolls. Soon they had reached their places, and they stood a few moments waving to the crowd while the Lord Chancellor argued about the tickets with the Royal Usherette. Then they were seated, and, almost immediately, a great cheer erupted from the crowd as it espied the heart-quickening figure of Prince Charming and his fine stallion being wheeled into the arena. Excited applause broke out and a chant of, "Char-ming . . . Char-ming . . . Char-ming" on the Kop was taken up by the record 22,407 crowd (with the single exception of Prince Walter, sitting in the middle of the East Stand sporting a Dragon rosette, who whistled derisively and apprehensively picked his nose with great abandon).

Prince Charming halted, and paused a moment, his golden hair reflecting the rays of the sun and his broad, manly shoulders visibly expanding in the heat, while his attendants moved the ladder into position, and then, gracefully, delicately, firmly, confidently, tenaciously, boldly, deftly, commandingly, irrefutably, yet poignantly, he descended, and bowed low in the direction of the royal box. At this very moment, there rang out over the arena the most terrifying roar, the most utterly blood-curdling bellow that Happy Valley had heard in a thousand years. It was, to make no bones about it, bloody loud, about 12,000 watts at a guess, and it was a sound of such indescribable strangeness that it cannot be described.

The crowd, quaking and trembling, shrank back in sheer

horror and, awestruck, stared aghast in the direction of the huge pantechnicon drawn up at the edge of the ring. A second hideous screech followed the first and before the crowd could even gasp, the side of the pantechnicon fell open revealing to their awestruck gaze . . . the dragon !!! A single sheet of solid flame flashed forth and with one bound, the fearsome creature sprang into the ring, baying a third grotesque, spine-chilling shriek. Even Prince Charming, for one fleeting moment, seemed frozen by this appalling sight and from the East Stand floated Walter's solitary chant . . . "Ea-sy, Ea-sy!"

For a second the dragon stood poised as though bemused by his surroundings. Charming measured his frightful adversary. As its massive jaws gaped he could see the red-hot tongue flicking viciously inside, the glitter of the razor-edged teeth, the foul sacs of venom hanging from the armoured neck, the macabre ears, the baleful bloodshot eyes, and the positively alarming hairs up its nose. And what a ferociously shaped body!! Spiked ribs of poisonous thorns ringed its scaly slimy back, and great ironclad plates clustered round its private parts. Its feet were pretty frightening too. And as for its tail! It had a curl in it that would have put the wind up Muhammad Ali. The whole ghastly nightmarish beast could not have been an inch less than one foot long and in height nearly as high as a rabbit.

Charming's jaw tightened. With one thrust of his golden shoe he was on his way toward the dragon, moving lightly across the sun-dried sand, cautious yet determined, with all the smooth power of a panther, the poise of a matador, and the grace of God. Still the dragon waited, roaring hideously into its throat-mike and breathing great jets of flame three-eighths of an inch long. Thirty feet, twenty feet . . . ten feet! The tension was at breaking point! Five feet . . . four . . . three . . . Charming checked his stride for one brief moment, a single bead of fear glistening on his brow and then, as the dragon drew back its head to charge, he drew his trusty Luger and blew its tiny brains out.

"Foul!!!" cried Walter, but his appeal was swallowed up in

the thunderclap of emotion that greeted this mighty feat! How the arena echoed and re-echoed with cheers! How thunderously . . . (see page 8 for further details).

And so Prince Charming and Mitzi were married that very afternoon and went to live at the Royal Palace of the Kingdom of the Golden Lakes with King and Queen Charming, and when King Charming died they took over the Royal Toy Dragon farm and bred many new varieties and made a packet and lived happily ever after. And Walter soon got over it, and settled down, and became an accountant and did very well for himself, really, and married a very very nice girl, a little plain some people said but very nice, and bought a second-hand Rover and a little house in Watford. They had a little boat too and they used to go to Majorca for their holidays. Walter often suggested going to Happy Valley instead but Brenda felt they wouldn't really fit in there now so they never did.

ATTACK OF THE CHARLIE CHAPLINS

Garry Kilworth

You might know Garry Kilworth better for his wonderful animal fantasies, such as Hunter's Moon *(1989) and* Midnight's Sun *(1992). Or maybe his horror books, like* Angel *(1993) or* Archangel *(1994). Or his children's books,* The Wizard of Woodworld *(1987) or* The Rain Ghost *(1989). Or his historical novels set in the Crimean War, starting with* The Devil's Own *(1997) under the pen name Garry Douglas. Or – well, anyway, you get the picture. Garry Kilworth is prolific but his work is hard to define as he is always varied and original. So, although you might not automatically associate him with humorous fiction, it's yet another of his many talents. Just sample the following.*

SCENE 1

A subterranean bunker somewhere in South Dakota. Feverish activity is taking place within the confines of the bunker. In the centre of it all a middle-aged general is musing on the situation which unfolds before him.

Reports are coming out of Nebraska that the state is under attack from heavily armed men dressed as Charlie Chaplin.

My first thought was that a right-wing group of anti-federal rebels was involved. It seemed they were using irony to make some kind of point. After all, Charlie was eventually ostracized to Switzerland for having communist sympathies.

As more accurate reports come in, however, it becomes apparent that these are not just men dressed as Charlie Chaplin, they are the real McCoy – they are he, so to speak.

"It's clear," says Colonel Cartwright, of Covert Readiness Action Policy, and the Army's best scriptwriter, "that these are aliens. What we have here, General, is your actual alien invasion of Earth. Naturally they chose to conquer the United States first, because we're the most powerful nation on the planet."

"Why Nebraska, Colonel?" I ask. I am General Oliver J.J. Klipperman, by the way. You may have seen my right profile next to John Wayne's in *The Green Berets*. I was told to look authoritative, point a finger in the direction of Da Nang, but on no account to turn round and face the camera. I have this tic in my left eye and apparently it distresses young audiences. "Nebraska isn't exactly the most powerful state in the Union. Why not New York or Washington?"

Cartwright smiles at me grimly. "Look at your map, General. Nebraska is slap bang in the middle of this great country of ours. It has one of the smallest populations. You get more people on Fifth Avenue on Christmas Eve than live in Nebraska. You simply have to wipe out a small population and you control this country's central state. Expand from there, outwards in all directions, and you have America. Once you have America, you have the world. It's as easy as that."

I nod. It all makes sense. Nebraska is the key to the control of the US of A. The aliens had seen that straightaway.

"What do we know about these creatures?" I ask next. "The President will expect me to sort out this unholy mess and I want to know who I'm killing when I go in with my boys."

The colonel gives me another tight smile. "These creatures? Nothing. Zilch. But we have a trump card. We've been preparing for such an invasion for many, many years and our information is voluminous."

"It is?" I say. "How come?"

"Hollywood and the Army connection," says the colonel. "Army money, personnel and expertise have been behind every alien invasion movie ever made."

"It has?" I reply. "I mean, I knew we had fingers in Hollywood pies – I've been an extra in over a dozen war movies – but every alien invasion movie? Why?"

[Zoom in on colonel's rugged features.]

"Training," the colonel says, emphatically. "Preparation. If you cover every contingency, you don't get surprised. We've been making films of alien invasions since the movie camera was first invented. We've covered every eventuality, every type of attack, from your sneaky fifth-column stuff such as *Invasion of the Body Snatchers* to outright blatant frontal war, such as *Independence Day*. We know what to do, General, because we've done it so many times before, on the silver screen. We know every move the shifty shape-changing bastards can make, because we've watched them in so many films. *Alien, War of the Worlds, The Day the Earth Stood Still, Close Encounters of the Third Kind*, you name it, we've covered it. On film." He pauses for a moment, before saying to himself, "That speech is a little long – I'll have to think of some way of cutting it when we make the actual movie of this particular invasion."

[Back to middle-distance shot.]

Something is bothering me. I put it into words.

"Weren't they friendly aliens in *Close Encounters*?"

"No such thing, General. What about those poor guys, those pilots they beamed up from the Bermuda Triangle in December 1945? They kept them in limbo until their families were all dead and gone, then let 'em come back. Is that a friendly thing to do?"

"I guess not. So, Colonel, we've had all these exercises, albeit on celluloid, but what have we learned? What do you suggest we do with them?"

"Blast them to hell, General, begging your pardon. If there's one thing we've learned it's that if you give 'em an inch, they'll take a planet. They've got Nebraska. That's almost an inch. We need to smash them before they go any further. Blow them to smithereens before they take Kansas, Iowa or Wyoming or, God forbid, South Dakota."

I always err on the side of caution. That's why I'm still a one-star general, I guess.

"But what do we actually know about these creatures? I mean, why come down here looking like Charlie Chaplin?"

The colonel's eyes brighten and he looks eager.

"Ah," he says, "I have a theory about that, sir. You see, we send crap out into space all the time. I don't mean your hardware, I mean broadcasts. They must have picked up some of our television signals. What if their reception had been so poor that the only thing they picked up was an old Charlie Chaplin movie? What if it was one of those movies in which he appears on his own – just a clip – and, here's the crunch, they thought we all looked like that?"

The colonel steps back for effect and nods.

"You mean," I say, "they think the Charlie Chaplin character is representative of the whole human race?"

"Exactly, sir. You've got it. We all look alike to them. They came down intending to infiltrate our country unnoticed, but of course even most Nebraskans know Charlie Chaplin is dead, and that there was only one of him. The dirt farmers see a thousand lookalikes and straightaway they go, 'Uh-huh, somethin's wrong here, Zach . . .'

"So they did what any self-respecting Midwestern American would do – they went indoors and got their guns and started shooting those funny-walking little guys carrying canes and wearing bowler hats."

"I see what you mean, Colonel. They're 'not from around here' so they must be bad guys?"

"Right."

"Blow holes in them and ask questions later?"

"If you can understand that alien gibberish, which nobody can."

"I meant, ask questions of yourself – questions on whether you've done the right and moral thing."

"Gotcha, General."

I ponder on the colonel's words. Colonel Cartwright is an intelligent man – or at least what passes for intelligent in the Army – which is why he is a senior officer in CRAP. He has obviously thought this thing through very thoroughly and I have to accept his conclusions. I ask him if he is sure we are doing the right thing by counter-attacking the aliens and blowing them to oblivion. Have they really exterminated the whole population of Nebraska?

"Every last mother's son," answers the colonel, sadly, "there's not a chicken farm left."

[Gratuitous shot of a dead child lying in a ditch.]

"And we can't get through to the President for orders?"

"All lines are down, radio communications are jammed."

"The Air Force?" I ask, hopefully.

"Shot down crossing the State line. There's smoking wrecks lying all over Nebraska. Same with missiles. We were willing to wipe out Nebraska, geographically speaking, but these creatures have superior weapons. We're the nearest unit, General. It's up to us to stop them."

"How many men have we got, Colonel?"

"A brigade – you're only a brigadier general, General."

"I know. Still, we ought to stand a chance with four to five thousand men. They . . . they destroyed our whole Air Force, you say?"

[Zoom in on TV screen showing smoking wrecks.]

The colonel sneers. "The Air Force are a bunch of Marys, sir. You can't trust a force that's less than a century old. The Army and the Navy, now they've been around for several thousand years."

There had never been much call for the Navy in Nebraska.

[Back to half-frame shot.]

"Are we up to strength?"

"No, sir, with sickness and furlough we're down to two battalions."

"Okay," I state emphatically. "We go in with two thousand, armour, field guns and God on our side."

"You betcha!"

[Enter Army corporal carrying sheet of paper.]

"Yes, Corporal?" I say icily, recognizing her as the extra who upstaged me in the remake of *The Sands of Iwo Jima* by obscuring my right profile with her big knockers. "I'm busy."

"I thought you ought to see this message, sir." She offers it to me. "Just came through."

"From Washington?" I ask, hopefully.

"No, sir, from the alien."

"The alien?" I repeat, snatching the signal. "You afraid of plurals, soldier?"

"No, sir, if you'll read the message, sir, you'll see there's only one of him – or her."

The message is: YOU AND ME, OLIVER, DOWN BY THE RIVER PLATTE.

"Looks like he's been watching John Wayne movies, too," I say, handing Cartwright the piece of paper. "Or maybe Clint Eastwood."

The colonel reads the message. "How do we know there's only one?" he asks, sensibly. "It could be a trick."

"Our radar confirms it, sir," the corporal replies. "He's pretty fast, though. It only looks like there's multiples of him. He seems to be everywhere at once. He's wiped out the whole population of Nebraska single-handed."

"Fuck!" I exclaim, instantly turning any movie of this incident into an adult-rated picture. "What the hell chance do I stand against an alien that moves so fast he becomes a horde?"

"Fifty per cent of Nebraska was asleep when they got it," says the colonel, "and the other half wasn't awake."

"What's the difference?"

"Some of 'em actually do wake up a little during daylight hours."

"You think I stand a chance?"

The colonel grins. "We'll fix you up with some dandy hardware, sir. He'll never know what hit him."

"But can I trust him to keep his word? About being just one of him? What if he comes at me in legions?"

"No sweat, general," says the colonel. "This baby—"

[Close-up of a shiny gismo with weird projections.]

"—is called a shredder. Newest weapon off the bench. One squeeze of this trigger and it fires a zillion coiled razor-sharp metal threads. Strip a herd of cattle to the bone faster than a shoal of piranha. You only have to get within ten feet of the bastard and you can annihilate him even if he becomes a whole corps."

"Can I hide it under my greatcoat?"

"Nothing easier, sir. And we'll wire you with a transmitter. He's only jamming long-distance stuff. You can tell us your life story. Oh, and one more important thing."

"What's that?"

"We have to give him a nickname, General."

I stare at the colonel. "Why?" I say at last.

"Because that's what we're good at. We always give the enemy a nickname. It demeans them. Makes them feel self-conscious and inferior. It's our way of telling them that they're the lowest form of human life."

"Or, in this case, alien life."

"Right, General. So we have to give him a humiliating nickname – like Kraut, Slopehead, Raghead, Fritz, Dink or Charlie . . ."

"We can't nickname him Charlie, he's already called Charlie."

"Okay, I take that on board. How about we call him Chuck?"

"Doesn't sound very demeaning to me. My brother was called Chuck."

"Depends on how you say it, General. If we're talking about your brother, we say 'Chuck' in a warm kind of tone. But if we're talking about Chuck, we use a sort of fat, chickeny sound – Chuck – like that."

"I think I understand, Colonel. Well, let's get me armed and wired. It's time I taught Chuck a lesson."

Stardom, here I come. A part with lines. My part. A lone, courageous part, if they let me play myself in the movie – providing I live to rejoice in it, of course.

SCENE 2

Somewhere out on the plains of Nebraska. A man is walking down towards the River Platte. The night is dark but studded with bright stars, giving the impression of vast distances and emphasizing the insignificance of the brave lonely figure. The brave lonely figure is apparently talking to himself.

Are you listening, back there in the base? The moon is gleaming on my path as I reach the banks. Here in the humid Nebraskan night I wait for my adversary. Single combat. *Mano a mano.* The old way of settling differences in the American West.

Hell, what am I saying, we didn't invent it. The old, old way. The chivalric code of the knights. A tourney. A duel. An affair of honour. Rapiers at dawn. Pistols for two, coffee for one.

[Aside: We're kind of mixing our genres here with Westerns and Science Fiction, but I think we can get away with it since the two have always had a close relationship, being drawn from the same source – the conquest of frontiers by American pioneers.]

And I am ready. You didn't send me out unprimed, Colonel. You made me submit to brainstorming. Masses of data has been blasted into my brain in the form of an electron blizzard. Every extraterrestrial invasion movie ever filmed is now lodged somewhere inside my cerebrum, waiting to be tapped. Any move this creature makes, I'll have it covered. Hollywood, under secret Army supervision, has foreseen every eventuality, every type of Otherworlder intent on invading and subduing us Earthlings. They're all in my head.

[A solitary charred and wounded chicken crawls silently across the landscape.]

Swines! Uh-huh. More movement up there.

Chuck's coming up over the ridge! Thousands of him doing that silly walk with the cane and twitching his ratty moustache. This is really weird. A swarm of Charlie Chaplins. Did he lie? Is he going to come at me in hordes? Boy, can he move fast. They're all doing different things. One's swinging his cane and grinning, another flexing his bow legs, yet another pretending to be a ballet dancer. Multitudes of him, pouring over the ridge now, like rats being driven by beaters.

"Don't let him get to you with the pathetic routine," you warned me, Colonel. "You know how Chuck can melt the strongest heart with that schmaltzy hangdog expression. Don't look at him when he puts his hands in his pockets, purses his lips, and wriggles from side to side." Well, don't worry, I hate Charlie Chaplin. That pathos act makes me want to puke, always did. If he tries that stuff, I'll shred him before he can blink.

He's getting closer now, moving very slowly. He's suddenly become only one, a single Charlie Chaplin. I can see the white of his teeth as he curls his top lip back.

My fingers are closing around the butt of the shredder. I'm ready to draw in an instant. The bastard won't stand a chance. Wait, he's changing shape again. Now he's Buster Keaton. I never liked Buster Keaton. And yet again. Fatty Arbuckle this time. I detest Fatty Arbuckle. Someone I don't recognize. Now Abbot and Costello. Both of them. The Marx Brothers.

Shit, he's only eleven feet away, and he's changing again. He's gone all fuzzy. He's solidifying. Oh. Oh, no. Oh my golly gosh. God Almighty. It's . . . it's dear old Stan Laurel. He's got one hand behind his back. I guess he's holding a deadly weapon in that hand.

"Hello, Olly."

Did you hear that, Colonel? Just like the original. He . . . he's beaming at me now, the way Laurel always beams at Hardy. And I . . . I can't do it. I can't shoot. He's scratching his head in that funny way of his. Of all the comic actors to choose. I loved Stan Laurel. I mean, how can you shoot Stan Laurel when he's beaming at you? It's like crushing a kitten beneath the heel of your boot. I can't do it. The flesh may be steel, but the spirit's runny butter.

Tell you what I'm going to do – I'll threaten him with the shredder. That ought to be enough for Stan Laurel.

Oh my gosh, he's burst into tears.

"Don't point that thing at me, Olly. I don't want to hurt you. I just want to be your chum."

I've put the weapon away. He's smiling again. He's offering me a cigar. Hey, you should see this, Colonel. He's done that trick, you know, flicking his thumb out of his fist like a lighter? There's a flame coming from his thumbnail.

He's still smiling. He's friendly after all, though he's still got one hand hidden from me. Maybe he's realized he's made a mistake? I have to show willing. I'm taking a light for the cigar. Hell, he could be a really nice guy.

I don't know what this thing is, but it's not a Havana cigar. Tastes kinda ropy, like the cigar that producer of a low-budget B-movie once gave me, when I played Young Ike. What was his name? Ricky Hernandez, yeah. Good movie that. Pity it was never released.

Jesus, this thing is playing havoc with my throat. Can you still hear me? It has a familiar smell – now where did I – oh yes, in the Gulf. Shit, it's nerve gas! The bastard has given me a cigar which releases nerve gas into the lungs.

Oh fuck, oh fuck – I'm getting dizzy. I feel like vomiting. There's blood coming from my mouth, ears and nostrils. He's reaching forward. He's taken my weapon. I'm . . . I'm falling . . . falling. Oh God, my legs are twitching, my arms, my torso, my head. I'm going into a fit spasm. I'm dying, Colonel. I'm a dead man.

Wait, he's standing over me. I think he's going to speak. Are you listening, Colonel?

"You're supposed to say, 'Another fine mess you've gotten me into, Stanley', and play with your tie."

Hollywood, damn them. He's speaking again. Listen.

"I suppose you think I lied to you, Olly?"

Yes I do, you freak, you murdering shape-changing bastard. I *do* think you lied to me.

He's giving me one of those smug Stan Laurel smiles, showing me his other hand, the one he's had behind his back all the time. He's . . . he's got his fingers crossed.

"Sorry, Olly."

Hollywood covered every contingency except one. In all the alien-invasion movies they ever made, the attacking monsters are always as grim as Michigan in January. As I lie here dying, the joke is on you and me, Colonel. There's one type of extraterrestrial we didn't plan on. An offworlder just like our own soldiers.

An alien with a sense of humour.

FADE OUT

MOTHER DUCK STRIKES AGAIN

Craig Shaw Gardner

I am a dedicated fan of the adventures of the apprentice Wuntvor and his master, the wizard Ebenezum, who is allergic to magic. I have reprinted two of their tales in the previous two anthologies, and I don't apologize for presenting a third. If you want to track down the full corpus of Ebenezum and Wuntvor then you'll need to find six books: A Malady of Magicks *(1986),* A Multitude of Monsters *(1986),* A Night in the Netherhells *(1987),* A Difficulty with Dwarves *(1987),* An Excess of Enchantments *(1988) and* A Disagreement with Death *(1989). In* An Excess of Enchantments, *from which the following episode comes, Wuntvor has travelled to the far Eastern Kingdoms in search of a cure for Ebenezum's allergy but has fallen foul of the witch, Mother Duck, who robs Wuntvor of his memory and casts him into a series of fairy tales, of which this is the first.*

Once upon a time, a young lad named Wuntvor travelled far from his native land, seeing the sights and having many adventures. So it was that he came over a hill and saw a bright and verdant valley spread before him. Brilliant sunlight shone down on green trees and golden crops, and Wuntvor thought that he had never seen a place as beautiful as this in all his travels.

He left the hilltop and began his descent into the valley. But he had not gone a dozen paces before he saw a hand-painted sign hanging from one of the beautiful, green trees. And on that sign, in large red letters, someone had painted a single word:

DANGER.

Wuntvor paused for a moment, and stared at the sign. Was someone trying to warn him? But danger of what? And where could any danger be on such a fine day as this?

So Wuntvor continued upon his way, whistling merrily as he studied the wild flowers that bordered the path on either side. He came to a broad field of wild grass and clover, and saw that on the far side of that field wound a lazy blue river.

Wuntvor looked along the trail he followed, and noted that in the distance it led to a narrow bridge that crossed the wide expanse of water. *Well then*, he thought to himself, *that is the way that I must go.* But he had not walked a dozen paces before he found that a giant boulder blocked his way. And on that boulder was painted a single word, in red letters three feet high:

BEWARE.

Wuntvor paused for a long moment to regard the message on the boulder. This was the second warning he had received since he had entered the valley. But what were these messages trying to tell him? What, or whom, should he beware of?

At length, Wuntvor decided that it was much too fine a day to beware of anything. *Let the fates do what they must*, he thought. On a sunny afternoon like this, he could best whatever was thrown in his path!

And with that, Wuntvor skirted the boulder and continued down the trail to the bridge. He had not gone a dozen paces, however, before a large man stepped out from behind a concealing hedge. Wuntvor studied the newcomer with some surprise, since he was the largest man the young lad had ever seen, being massive in girth as well as height. The large fellow was dressed in a bronze breastplate, which was somewhat dented and tarnished, and wore an elaborate winged helmet on top of his massive head. He raised a giant club above his head, and uttered but a single word:

"DOOM."

Wuntvor took a step away, being somewhat taken aback by this new turn of events. Was this the danger that the first sign spoke of? Was this what he had to beware of, as the boulder had cautioned? Yet the large man did not attack. Instead, he simply stood there, the giant club still raised above his massive head.

"Pardon?" Wuntvor said after a moment.

"What?" the large man asked.

"I beg your pardon?" Wuntvor expanded.

"Oh," the large man answered. "Doom."

"Yes," Wuntvor prompted. "But what kind of doom?"

"Oh," the large man answered again. "Down at the bridge."

Wuntvor smiled. Now he was getting somewhere! "What about the bridge?"

"Doom," the large man replied.

But Wuntvor wasn't about to give up. "At the bridge?" he prompted again.

The large man nodded his head and lowered his club.

"That's where the danger is?" Wuntvor added. "That's where I have to beware?"

The large man continued to nod.

"But what is the danger?" Wuntvor insisted. "What do I have to beware of?"

"Doom," the large man insisted.

Wuntvor began to despair of ever getting any real answers out of the large fellow. He gazed down the path at the distant bridge. It certainly looked peaceful enough. Just what was this big fellow trying to warn him about? Wuntvor decided he would try to gain a definite answer one more time.

"Indeed," he began, for there was something reassuring to Wuntvor about beginning sentences in this way, "you tell me that my doom waits on yon bridge?"

The large fellow nodded again, smiling that Wuntvor had understood his plea.

"And yet," Wuntvor continued, "there is no way that you might explain to me what that doom is?"

The large fellow shook his head sadly.

"Doom," he agreed.

"Why not?" Wuntvor demanded, upset with this turn of events.

The large fellow looked all around. When he was convinced they were all alone he spoke to Wuntvor in a voice barely above a whisper.

"I am here as a warning," was all he said.

Wuntvor bit his lip so that he would not scream. After he had regained his composure, he asked:

"But can't you at least inform me what you are warning me about?"

"Doom," the large fellow replied sadly.

"Why?" Wuntvor demanded.

"Because that is the way fairy tales work," the large fellow answered.

Wuntvor blinked. Fairy tales? What was this about fairy tales? The lad felt some faint memory stirring at the back of his brain. A word floated toward his consciousness. *Mother.* Mother what? Of course, now he remem—

"Once upon a time." Wuntvor's lips moved, saying words he could have sworn he never thought. "Once upon a time."

He shook his head violently and stared at the large man again. "Can you tell me nothing about the bridge?"

"Doom," the immense fellow pondered. "Perhaps I can ask you a question or two. Would you by any chance have a good deal of gold?"

At last! Wuntvor thought, *I shall get some information.*

"No," he answered. "I am but a penniless traveller, out to seek my fortune in the world."

"Doom," the other responded. "Still, all is not yet lost. Are you good at riddles?"

What was this large fellow talking about? "Riddles?" Wuntvor demanded. "What do riddles have to do with anything?"

"Doom," the immense one replied, nodding to himself as if he had confirmed something he'd known all along. "I suggest you turn around and go the other way, unless you fancy yourself as troll fodder."

And with that, the large fellow turned and disappeared behind a sizeable hedge.

"Indeed," Wuntvor mumbled to no one in particular. Somehow, he did not feel he had gained much information at all.

But after a moment's thought, Wuntvor decided to go to the bridge anyway. After all, hadn't he left his native land to seek adventure? He had the feeling that this bridge he was approaching, as small and innocent-looking as it was, might contain so much adventure that he could return home immediately after crossing it.

He was not a dozen paces from the bridge when he heard a voice.

> "Ho, young traveller!
> We have advice:
> If you want to cross,
> You will pay a price."

And with that, a horrible creature leaped from beneath the bridge and landed less than a dozen paces away from the startled Wuntvor. The creature's skin was a bright shade of yellowish green, but that was nowhere near as startling as the horrible fact that it wore clothing filled with purple and green checks, not to mention that it held a brown, smoking thing between its teeth.

The creature removed the brown, smoking thing (which was quite foul-smelling besides) from between its jaws, and spoke again.

> "Now that you're here
> You won't get old,
> Unless you give
> This troll some gold."

"Indeed," Wuntvor replied. So this, at last, was what he was being warned about. Wuntvor thought, somehow, that he should feel more cheered by finally learning the truth. The truth, though, left something to be desired.

The hideously garbed creature smiled with even more teeth than a creature like that should have, and sauntered toward the lad. Wuntvor decided that what he mostly wished at this precise moment was that the large fellow he had so recently spoken with had been more specific in his details of the danger's exact nature, so that Wuntvor might be currently pursuing his adventures in an entirely different location from where he was at present.

The creature pointed at Wuntvor. More specifically, its sharp yellow claws pointed at Wuntvor's belt as it spoke again.

> "Gold need not be
> My only reward,
> I'll take instead
> Your meagre sword!"

Wuntvor looked down at his belt. He had a sword? It came as a total surprise to him. Shouldn't a person remember if he was wearing a sword?

Well, he reasoned, as long as he had a sword, he might as well defend himself.

"What are you doing?" the sword screamed as Wuntvor yanked it from the scabbard.

The sword spoke! Wuntvor almost dropped the weapon. He definitely should have remembered a sword that could talk. The lad frowned. *Something*, he thought, *is not as it seems*.

"I would like an answer," the sword insisted. "As your personal weapon, I think it's the least I deserve."

"Indeed," Wuntvor responded, wishing to grant the magic sword's wishes. "I was merely drawing you forth to slay yon horrible creature."

"Merely?" the sword began, but whatever it had to say next was lost beneath the creature's new rhyme.

> "Ho, young traveller,
> Your valour growing.
> Sad to say,
> I must be going."

And with that, the garishly garbed creature dived under the bridge.

"Merely?" the enchanted blade repeated.

Wuntvor glared at the sword. "Who are you, anyway?"

"Is that a trick question?" the sword responded, a suspicious edge to its voice.

"Nay," Wuntvor insisted, although he doubted, under the circumstances, that he would know a trick question even if he spoke it. "I fear I am under a spell of forgetfulness, and hoped that a magic sword might know the truth."

"Why didn't you say so?" The sword brightened perceptibly. Wuntvor had to shield his eyes not to be blinded by the glow.

"That's exactly what we magic swords are for," the blade continued. "My name is Cuthbert, and I'm a first-class example of sorcerous weaponry. What else do you need to know? Your name is Wuntvor. You do remember that? Good. Do you recall that you are on a quest for your master – Hey!"

The sword screamed as it fell from Wuntvor's hand, which had gone suddenly numb. But the lad had no more thought for his discarded weapon. All he could think of were the words upon his lips.

"Once upon a time," he said. "Once upon a time."

And, as if in answer, he heard a second voice come from beneath the bridge.

> "Ho, young traveller,
> No need to fiddle!
> You'll simply die
> If you miss this riddle."

And with that a second creature leaped onto the path, less than a dozen paces from Wuntvor, who was nowhere near as startled this time, having come somewhat to expect such occurrences. The second monster was a bit different from the first, a tad shorter and more of a putrid grey-green in colour. Its clothing was more conservative as well, as it wore dark, almost monastic-looking robes that ballooned around its short body in great folds.

"Riddle?" Wuntvor inquired. This must be the second thing the large fellow had warned him about. A riddle that, according to this creature, he could simply die from. Wuntvor suspected the creature was not speaking metaphorically.

The sickly green thing smiled broadly and pulled a piece of parchment from beneath its robes. It read in a clear, high, annoying voice:

> "With this riddle,
> The seeds are sowed:
> Why did the chicken
> Cross the road?"

The monster licked its chops, obviously intending a quick and tasty meal. The lad had a difficult time even thinking about the riddle.

Wait a second. Wuntvor stared hard at the riddling horror. A chicken crossing the road? That wasn't difficult at all. His aged grandmother had told him the answer to that one a thousand times.

"To get to the other side!" Wuntvor shouted triumphantly.

"Get to the other side?" the green thing mused. "Well, I suppose that's possible. Just a moment." The creature reached within its voluminous robes and pulled forth a sheaf of parchment.

"No, no, I'm afraid the answer is as follows—" It cleared its throat and announced portentously:

"A newspaper."

What? Wuntvor thought. What was a newspaper?

"It is not!" the lad insisted angrily. "Everyone knows that chickens cross the road to get to the other side!"

The creature shook its head sadly, reaching within its robes with its free hand to draw out a knife and fork. "Perhaps that sort of thing happens wherever you come from," it answered as it scanned the sheaf of parchments. "I do remember seeing that answer somewhere. Ah, here it is: 'To get to the other side.' I'm afraid though, that it's the answer to another riddle entirely. Uh – here it is – 'What's black and white and read all over?'"

"What's black and white and red all over?" Wuntvor repeated.

The creature nodded triumphantly. "To get to the other side!" It paused, waiting for some sign of recognition from the traveller. "You see now, don't you?" it prompted at last. "You see, because it's black and white and read, it has to cross—" The thing paused and stared for a moment at the parchment. "Well, perhaps it is a little difficult to explain. It has to be correct, though. I assure you, Mother Duck uses nothing but the very latest equipment. So there's no chance for a mistake." The thing blinked, as if it couldn't quite believe what it was saying. "Well, not that much of a chance."

Mother Duck? The lad frowned. Where had he heard that name before? And why did he have an almost uncontrollable urge to say "Once upon a time?"

"Other side?" the thing said, more to itself than to Wuntvor. "What kind of stupid—" The creature stopped itself and, after a moment, coughed discreetly. "Well, perhaps, in the very slight chance there was an error, we should give you another opportunity. It's your life at stake, after all." The green thing riffled through the pile of parchment. "Oh, here's the old chestnut about four legs, two legs, three legs. She's got to be kidding. There must be something with a little more verve than that." The creature turned the page. "Let's try this one."

The monster cleared its throat and spoke in a loud, even more annoying voice: "How many elephants can you get into a Volkswagen?"

It paused, staring at the parchment in disbelief. "Where did she get these questions, anyway?" The creature flipped another page, frowning as it quickly read the text. "Let's see. I don't suppose you have any idea what a – 'light bulb' is? I thought as much."

The thing crumpled the parchment in its green claws. "I'm sorry, this is ridiculous. What am I doing in a stupid fairy tale, anyway?"

Fairy tale? Wuntvor remembered the Brownie. And that woman the thing had mentioned. What was her name? Mother something. It was on the tip of his tongue. Mother—

He had it!

"Once upon a time!" Wuntvor cried in triumph. Wait a second. That wasn't the point he was going to make. Was it?

"Once upon a time," he said again for good measure.

And again, as if in answer, a third voice, far gruffer than either of those that spoke before, came from beneath the bridge.

> "Ho, young traveller,
> Not yet beaten;
> Prepare yourself now
> To be ea—"

But instead of completing the rhyme, the third creature began to sneeze.

"Are you just going to leave me here?" the sword demanded.

The sword? The sword! He looked down to where he had dropped it. Somehow, Wuntvor had forgotten all about the magic weapon again.

"Yeah!" the green thing shouted at Wuntvor. "And just what are we doing in this stupid fairy tale when we're supposed to be on a quest?"

A small brown fellow appeared by the lad's foot. 'I couldn't agree more! Fairy tales! Just think how much better it would be if it were a Brownie tale!"

The green thing had recoiled at the very sight of the little fellow. "Don't ever agree with me!" he shouted, then looked back to Wuntvor. "There are simply certain things I cannot cope with."

"I suppose I'm just going to lay in the dust for ever," the sword moaned, "left here to rust, forgotten by my owner—"

The checkered monster was suddenly in their midst. "Are you tired of your lot in life, enchanted sword? Well, come with me, and I'll offer you foreign sights, adventure—"

"It's ruined! It's ruined!" a woman's voice called from somewhere far up the hill.

Wait a second, Wuntvor thought.

There was something about all this chaos that was disturbingly familiar. He looked around and remembered that the robed creature was Snarks, a demon who was forced to speak nothing but the truth, no matter how unpleasant that truth might be. And there, in his checkered suit, was Brax the traveling Salesdemon, purveyor of previously owned enchanted weapons, "Every one a Creampuff!" And the sword was Cuthbert, a weapon that was unfortunately a bit of a coward. And he had seen Tap the Brownie during his last fairy tale.

His last fairy tale?

That's right! He was a prisoner of Mother Duck, who was currently storming down the hill toward them, pursued by a hairy fellow who looked rather like a wolf standing on his hind legs, sporting a green cap. Hadn't he seen this fellow before somewhere, too? Wuntvor shook his head and wondered what else he didn't remember.

THE BLACKBIRD

Jack Sharkey

Since the death of Jack Sharkey in 1992 his work has become all but forgotten, which is a great shame as he was a gifted writer, especially of short stories. In fact, he spent the last twenty or so years of his life working in the theatre, writing over eighty stage plays and musicals, so his output of fiction was curtailed. So far as I know, none of his short stories has been collected into book form, so here is another rare and forgotten treat.

THE Turk, true to traditions established by writers of Arabian adventure stories, was a giant. The villagers of East Anchorville – named from its geographic relation to the larger town of Anchorville – were sure from the moment he'd first appeared in town that no good would come of it. No one would admit to being actually afraid of him, but everyone was of the mind that caution was the prime consideration when dealing with him. So it was only natural that, when the horrors began, all minds should arrow like iron filings to the magnet of the Turk's mysterious nature.

The horrors began in the autumn, when the dry leaves clogged the irrigation ditches of the hinterlands, and cold grey dust sifted underfoot on the nubbly dirt roads about the town, and nightfall was an occurrence to be watched from inside one's home, with door bolted and fireplace glowing with burning logs.

Harriet Cord, the belle of the village (and bane of the womenfolk) had gone out for a buggy ride with Marvin Sply, son of the late village blacksmith, toward sundown. Old folks in the town could be seen to purse their lips and cluck their tongues as the couple clattered out of town on Marvin's buckboard, an heirloom from his father, Marvin with one hand on the horse's reins and the other quite definitely on Harriet.

Two hours later, Marvin had come back into town alone, his eyes wild, clothing awry, and lips spouting a dreadful tale. The rattle of the buckboard entering the main street with the horse at full frantic gallop had brought out a curious crowd, including the town sheriff, who, on hearing Marvin's hysterical tale, had turned at once into Grogan's Saloon to round up some help, and was seen no more that night.

Villagers, men and women alike, had gotten aboard wagons, horses, and into the few automobiles the town boasted, and taken off for the scene of the crime, for such they were already convinced it was.

It was a terrible sight that met their eyes.

Harriet lay by the side of the road, stone-cold dead, her face for ever frozen into a bewildered sneer. There was not a mark upon the body, but clutched in the left hand they found a single black feather, large and shiny . . .

The coroner's verdict was, "Death of an unknown and mysterious nature, at the hands of person or persons unknown."

Suspicion immediately fastened upon the Turk.

His landlady, who "ran a respectable place," was of a mind to put him out at once. Mrs Balsam didn't want "no truck with monsters" in her boarding house. But she somehow felt that walking up the three flights to his attic room alone was not the easiest of tasks, and could find no one to accompany her upstairs – her husband suddenly decided to mow the lawn although the grass was yellowed and sere, and "didn't ask to have that fellow room there in the first place" – so she thought she'd bide her time and wait.

Thelma Bracy, her next-door neighbour, was of the opinion that Mrs Balsam should dope his food and call the police to take him, and it was then for the first time that the odd fact came to light that the Turk had never taken a meal in Mrs Balsam's establishment, though dinner and supper were included with the room rates. Within an hour after Thelma heard this bit of information, the word was out all over town, and the even more amazing fact came to light that no person in the town had *ever* seen the Turk take a meal, anywhere.

The sheriff (who had eventually arrested Marvin Sply for want of any other suspects) was informed of this turn of events at once. Or, rather, as soon as he was located, in Grogan's Saloon. And he informed Mrs Balsam that the best thing to do under the "circumstances" – the Turk was seven feet tall and about 250 pounds – was to wait and watch.

Marvin, when he awoke the next morning in his cell at the East Anchorville jail, had demanded that he be let out at once, denying any knowledge of the means or motive of Harriet's death. His story was that they'd taken a stroll across a field, and it had grown too dark for Harriet to navigate the field back to the buckboard without turning a well-turned ankle, so Marvin had cut across to the other side of the field after their transportation, and driven the buckboard back to where she should have been standing. He'd at first thought she'd gone, till he espied a pale white hand upon the edge of the roadside ditch, and, on investigating the hand, located Harriet on the other end of it.

The sheriff was adamant. Marvin was there; no one else was. So Marvin did it. The sheriff was quite positive in his accusation, and determined to keep Marvin in jail till he rotted. And he probably would have done so, had not a group of the sheriff's constituents – irritated because their horses were losing shoes like mad, and wagon spokes were falling out, and fenders needed undenting – insisted that Marvin be released to his blacksmith duties. The sheriff gave in, albeit grudgingly, but made Marvin promise to return to the jail at nightfall, which promise was given with alacrity.

The townsfolk were shocked that afternoon to learn that Marvin, on the pretext of going to Anchorville for supplies of some sort, had instead boarded a westbound express for San Francismo, undoubtedly never to return.

The sheriff was about to put out a national alarm for the fugitive when a panicky farmer dashed into the sheriff's office to announce the second horror.

Abel Stanley, the town's leading hog-raiser, had been found dead in his pigpen, his noble heart for ever stilled, his terrified blue eyes staring sightlessly into a trough of swill. And stuck into the brim of his hat was a shiny, blue-black feather.

And even as the sheriff was running toward Grogan's saloon for deputies, Tom the Barkeep came running out to meet him with news of horror number three.

Edward Forbes – who, while not the town drunkard, was next in line for the office – had been discovered under the bar at Grogan's, his open mouth beneath the spigot of an emptied whisky keg, with a shiny black feather in his buttonhole, completely deceased. But this time the barkeep – under the clear-sighted direction of the sheriff (from the far end of the bar) – found a *mark* on the body; a strange-hued star-shaped discolouration beneath the left armpit. But on the coroner's report that this was a birthmark, the town threw up its hands in despair.

The panic began to spread through the heretofore placid village. Thelma Bracy's significant remarks about the Turk began to take their toll of credible people. Mothers in the town, hoping to discourage the apparently passionately neat killer, began to belt, whip and otherwise mar their children, as a safety measure. "Bruise 'em or lose 'em!" became the battle cry.

The Turk – and not strangely at all, since he was not on speaking terms with any of the villagers – had not yet, on this the third day after Harriet's demise, heard a thing about the horrors. So it was not strange that he dared to show his face in the town square, striding along mightily toward Gulby's Drugstore. He thought it unusual that the town children, whose wont it was to dog his patient footsteps while chanting some abominably rhymed ballad about cranberry sauce and people from Turkey, did not do so this day. Indeed, they all vanished into houses, up trees, and around corners as soon as the measured clump of his heavy boots announced his imminent arrival at the town square.

As he ducked his prodigious torso enough to permit passing his head through the door of the store, all the customers turned and stared at him, white-faced and speechless.

Gulby the Druggist, who was the excitable type, blurted out, "It's *him*!! The *fiend*!" and made his short speech memorable by collapsing upon the toothpaste stand, his paunchy frame carrying the hapless display to the floor, where the weight of his body pressed resolutely downward, causing him to sag amid a spreading wiggle of fluoridated dental cream.

"Evil eye!" screamed the villagers in the store, and, covering their eyes with one hand, outstretched the other like stiff-arming football players and rushed pell-mell from the drugstore.

Now the sheriff was really on the spot. An angry body of citizens came to his office and demanded that he arrest the monster (for who could it be but the Turk?) at once, or they'd put their democratic powers of recall into immediate effect and elect a new sheriff.

That settled him. Bolstering up his courage for an hour at Grogan's Saloon, he proceeded to Mrs Balsam's boarding house, up the stairs, called out the Turk (who came along amiably enough), and ensconced him in the cell so recently vacated by Marvin Sply. When the sheriff became sober enough to realize the enormity of what he'd done, he headed for Grogan's at once, to try and blot out the memory.

Well, the fat was in the fire.

With the arrest made, there had to be a trial.

The whole village perked up at the news. Ladies all went out and bought new dresses, new bonnets, new shoes, and new coats, and men all went over to Grogan's to discuss the facts of the case.

The sheriff was there, as usual, and as the men talked, and the conversation became more uncertain and faltering, the horrible truth came out that no one at all knew *anything* about the case.

Immediate action had to be taken.

The sheriff's brother, who was also Assistant District Attorney, was the editor of the town paper. A quick phone call from the sheriff, and the Contest came out in the next issue of the *East Anchorville News*. The good word spread throughout Massachusetts.

Entries, mostly from women, started pouring in.

BE A WITNESSS! proclaimed the paper. ENTER NOW!

Testimonies were chosen on the basis of thought, creative imagery, and knowledge of the English language. Thelma Bracy's was by far the best – due, she admitted freely, to a correspondence course she'd once taken in Novel Writing – and the town knew it had a star witness in Thelma

Excitement was at its zenith. It was like the good old days of witch-hunting all over again.

The sun rose and set and rose again, and it was the day of the trial.

Everyone in town was packed into the narrow courthouse. People from neighbouring townships had driven all night to get there for the gala event. Popcorn, cotton candy and cold beer – to the annoyance of the local clergy – were sold on the steps of the courthouse, and the judge, who owned the local brewery, was out there pushing the sales along until almost time for the trial to begin.

The widows of the deceased men – Gulby had passed away during his sensational tumble into the toothpaste, leaving the bereaved widow with her memories and thirty thousand dollars' Life Insurance – sat well up in front, waiting to see justice done. To ensure a fast pyrotechnic trial and a verdict of "guilty", they'd been careful to have the DA (the town's sharpest lawyer, and the brother-in-law of the local editor) send off to Anchorville for three of the greenest lawyers that could be found, fresh from Anchorville U. Law School, and from the three the widows had picked what they hoped was the dullest one.

Thomas Bit, their choice, now sat with the silent Turk, fingering his collar nervously and sharpening his pencil every five minutes. The eyes of the eastern seaboard were upon the courthouse that day, and he'd be an overnight success if he could bring in a verdict of "not guilty".

He wished that the town had been a little larger, for it had been impossible to get anyone on the jury who didn't seem to be either a relative of one of the dead men or a good friend of Harriet Cord. As far as that went, *all* the people seemed to have known Harriet Cord. Had she been the only victim, and had he been able to select a jury of the local women . . . Thomas Bit sighed.

His Honour, wiping a bit of foam off his chin, hurried up the aisle toward his chambers, vanished within them, then the court clerk called everyone to order, and the judge appeared in his solemn black robes, lurched up the steps to the bench, and sat with a loud thud, his eyes somewhat glazed and lips smiling inanely.

Thomas Bit noted this and groaned in his soul.

His Honour rapped sharply for order, dropped the gavel accidentally upon the bald pate of the court scribe, had it recovered and handed back to him, rapped again, and the trial was on!

Ervin Burns, the DA, approached the nervous Mrs Balsam, his grey eyes steely and stern, and manner impeccably modelled after a movie he'd once seen of an infamous trial. Mrs Balsam, no bantamweight by any stretch of the imagination, still managed to shrink to a more compact size as he loomed over her, pince-nez held between right forefinger and thumb.

"You are Nettie Balsam?"

"I am Nettie Balsam," she answered, after a thoughtful pause.

"You run the boarding house where the murderer lived?"

"Objection!" yelled Thomas Bit, springing to his feet. "The guilt of this man is what we are here to prove!"

The laughter in the courtroom was deafening until His Honour raised a tolerant hand and waved it to a chuckling murmur. "Please, Mister Bit, you must not interrupt Mister Burns at his work, if you wish the same consideration when she is *your* witness. Then you will have your chance."

Abashed, Thomas Bit sank shakily into his chair. "It looks pretty hopeless," he whispered to the Turk. The Turk merely shrugged his great shoulders and remained stolidly silent.

"You run the boarding house where the *alleged* murderer lived?" asked the DA.

Thomas Bit sighed, softly, and chewed his nails.

"I do," said Mrs Balsam. "I run a respectable place!" she added.

There were a few cheers from the front row, where some of her other boarders sat. Mister Balsam hadn't come that morning. He was at home, asleep.

"And did you ever note anything . . . *mysterious* . . . about this man?"

"Yes," said Mrs Balsam severely. "He never ate any of my cooking."

"Nothing mysterious about *that*!" came a *sotto voce* comment from the rear.

The DA cleared his throat, and stared the impertinent one into red-faced silence. Then he smiled at Mrs Balsam.

"And why is that odd?"

"Because the meals're included in the room rates. Seems funny a man'd spend money for something and then not use it."

The DA smiled and nodded wisely. "Very funny, indeed. What, in your opinion is the reason for this?"

"Objection!" Thomas Bit was on his feet. "We're here to get facts, not opinions!"

The judge gave him a baleful stare. "Oh, *come* now!"

Thomas Bit sank into his chair, completely defeated. "This is awful," he said to the Turk.

The Turk shrugged again and scratched the back of his head.

"In my opinion," she said, shuddering, "he didn't eat or drink anything because he lived on human blood! . . . Or *worse!*" she added, darkly.

Thomas Bit hid his face in his hands and manfully resisted bursting into tears.

"That will be all," smiled the DA. "Your witness."

Thomas Bit composed himself as best he could and approached the witness stand. Mrs Balsam looked at him warily, like a duck watching a woman stitching up a new pillowcase.

"Mrs Balsam . . ." he began.

"Objection!" thundered the DA.

"Sustained!" said the judge.

In the rear row, the editor of the paper smiled happily and wrote furiously in a small pad on his knee. Things were going indeed well, and it was an election year, too.

"Er . . ." Thomas Bit faltered, then tried again. "You *are* Nettie Balsam?"

"Yes," she said.

"Has the accused ever given you any trouble as a boarder?"

"Well, no . . . but—"

"Has he ever done anything positively unusual?"

"He didn't eat my cooking!"

"Then why—" Thomas Bit leaned forward, narrowing his eyes, "did you charge him for it?"

Nettie Balsam faltered. This was a side-issue the DA hadn't covered in rehearsals. "Because—Because with the extra money, I could buy more food for the other boarders!"

"Then," said Thomas Bit, pressing his point home, "you never *did* cook any meals for the Turk. I'll bet if I were to subpoena your boarders, it would turn out you never even set a place at the table for him! Is that correct?"

Nettie Balsam burst into tears. "Well, I did at first, for the first week he st-stayed at my place, b-but when I saw he wasn't going to eat, I j-just used the extra money." She broke into uncontrolled sobbing at this point and couldn't go on.

Thomas Bit paused until the flood had abated somewhat, then said in a more kindly tone: "Then the loss of this man as a boarder – if he is convicted – is taking money out of your pocket?"

Nettie's tear-blurred eyes widened at this insidious aspect of the thing, heretofore unconsidered. "Why . . . you're right!"

Thomas Bit took a step back and indicated the Turk, sitting unperturbed at the table before the bench. "Then do you think this man had anything to do with the horrors?"

Before the shaken DA could object, Nettie Balsam shouted, "*No!* A thousand times no! He's innocent as a babe, and, when this is over, he'll have his own little room waiting for him same as always . . ." She hesitated. "At the same rates, of course."

"Of course," said Thomas Bit. "You may step down."

Nettie Balsam did so, quite contented with herself. In the back row, the editor gnashed his teeth in impotent fury. And the three widows were frozen in stony hatred. Who did this young upstart think he was? The first good murder case in years and he's making out that the killer is innocent! One of them even wished, momentarily, that her husband were still alive.

The DA, fairly recovered from the near-mortal blow dealt him, called Thelma Bracy to the stand. A hush fell over the room as she waddled proudly up to the small railed-in witness seat. After all, she was something of a celebrity, the star witness whose picture was all over the front page of the local paper, looking knowing and wise.

She immediately crossed one knee over the other. Her knees were not visible, due to the wide slats of the railing, but she crossed them anyhow.

"Your name?" the DA was unctuously charming.

"Thelma. Thelma Bracy." She looked out to where reporters from neighbouring towns were clustered, pencils poised over notebooks. "T-h-e-l-m-a B-r-a . . ."

"Miss Bracy—" the DA interrupted swiftly, "will you please tell the court where you live?"

"I live at 115 West Pike – P-i-k-e – right next door to the house where the *murderer* lived!"

All eyes in the room turned instantly to Thomas Bit, who now had his chance to louse things up. He sighed, shrugged, and shook his head. A murmur of relief went up, and one of the widows even smiled a little. Things were looking up.

"Would you please tell us," continued the DA, "exactly what you saw on the night of the late lamented Harriet Cord's demise?"

A profound hush settled over the room, and all eyes riveted on Thelma, who cleared her throat carefully and began her tale.

"It was hard upon the hour of midnight," she said, almost in a whisper. Even Thomas Bit was magnetized by her tone. "Chill was the night, but fain did I long for a current of air to relieve the unwonted stuffiness of my bedchamber. Went I then toward my casement, to ope my room to the night air . . ." She paused, and added, less studiedly, "My window's right across from the side of Nettie's boarding house . . ."

The hush grew more profound.

"The window of *that man's room!*" She stabbed a finger dramatically and accusingly at the Turk. "It was closed, but *lo!* there was a flickering light inside. I, of course, do not make it a practice to look into the windows of men with whom I am hardly acquainted, so I was about to turn back to my bed, when suddenly—" Her face went blank. "When suddenly—" she repeated miserably, looking at the DA, who had closed his eyes in exasperation.

Thelma drew back a pace in her monolgue, and tried taking a running start to get over the hump. "I-was-about-to-turn-back-to-my-bed-when-suddenly . . ." She brightened. "When *suddenly*, the window flew open, banging the sash quite loudly, and that man—" some of the folks in the Turk's vicinity edged away from him furtively "—peered out in a very suspicious fashion, then stepped he back from the window.

Frozen to the spot by nameless apprehensions, waited I there, and then— Something big and black and horrible flopped onto his windowsill from within his room."

The DA – albeit having heard the tale at rehearsals – had still to moisten dry lips before speaking. "What was it?" he asked, his voice shaky.

"A giant blackbird!" said Thelma.

(Careful research on her part into Arabian customs and history had unearthed the fact that the raven was considered an almost sacred harbinger of dire things by the Arabs and Turks, and she'd changed the name of the bird into a species conforming to her listeners' experience.)

"It flapped its great black wings, rose into the air, and then, as though sensing something, it flew away."

"Which way—" the DA made the question assume great importance by his tone, "—Which way did it fly?"

Thelma paused dramatically, then looked upon the Turk with the eye of a basilisk, rose to her feet and said, "Straight east!"

A furore broke out in the room. The body of Harriet Cord had been found almost due east of the Town; in the minds of the townsfolk, the guilt of the Turk was as good as written on the court record.

Thomas Bit shook his head. There was nothing to do but sit tight and wait for his turn at Thelma.

She hadn't finished. "Something made me stay there, watching, for almost a quarter of an hour. Finally, it had grown too cold to stand by the window, so I closed it. And just as I did, the blackbird flew back, and it heard the window closing, because it turned and looked at me. And suddenly I was terribly afraid, and I ran back to my bed and did throw myself under the blankets!"

"And then?" asked the DA.

". . . I fell asleep," she finished lamely.

"Your witness," said the DA to Thomas Bit.

Thomas Bit took a deep breath to steady his nerves and approached the stand. "Miss Bracy," he said, "are you aware that it was early evening when Marvin Sply went out with Harriet Cord on her ill-fated ride?"

"Of course," she said. "Everyone knows that."

"And are you further aware that he was back in a matter of hours?"

"Sure," she said.

"Then how could there possibly be any connection between the blackbird you claimed you saw and Harriet Cord's death, if the blackbird's nocturnal flight was shortly after midnight?"

Thelma drew herself up, proud and confident. "A supernatural creature is not bound by the ordinary laws of time and space," she replied.

There was considerable applause from the spectators, which the judge indulgently permitted to die down of its own accord, while Thomas Bit gritted his teeth to keep from breaking down and sobbing.

"Supernatural!?" he said, fiercely. "Do you expect a court of law to recognize such a statement?"

"Son," said the judge, not unkindly, "this is the State of Massachusetts . . ."

Approaching despair, Thomas Bit tried one more query.

"Would you kindly tell the court just what you think this 'blackbird' of yours did to cause the deaths of Miss Cord and the three men, Stanley, Forbes and Gulby?"

"Certainly," said Thelma. "That man is a werebird!"

"A *werebird?*"

Thelma nodded. "Human by day, feathered fiend by night. Flying the countryside after sundown, in hideous unnatural guise, sucking the souls from helpless people that cross his gruesome path!"

"Your Honour," said Thomas Bit, "I move that this testimony be stricken from the record as irrelevant, fanciful, and just plain ridiculous."

"Overruled," said His Honour.

Shoulders drooping, Thomas Bit said, "No further questions," and returned to his seat, beside his client.

"I call Herbert Hoskins, MD, to the stand," said the DA. The town corner arose and made his way to the witness seat.

As Thomas Bit doodled hopelessly on a pad of paper, hardly listening to the testimony of the coroner, a hand fell lightly upon his shoulder. He looked up into the face of a stranger, a sporty-looking fellow with a pink-tipped nose and thick muttonchop sidewhiskers. The stranger winked his eye.

"Having a bit of difficulty, eh?" he smiled.

"Who are you?" asked the lawyer.

"Wallen's the name, son. Wilbert Wallen. I'm sort of a specialist in rare diseases. That's why I'm here."

Thomas Bit cocked an eyebrow at the stranger. "I'm afraid I don't see—"

"You will, son, you will," said Wilbert Wallen, seating himself beside the young lawyer. "I'm your star witness."

"My *what*?" said Thomas Bit.

Wallen began to explain, in a low, urgent whisper. As his meaning became clear to Bit, the lawyer's eyes grew round, and the subtle beginnings of a smile touched his lips for the first time that day.

"You're kidding!" he said to Wallen.

"Scout's honour," said the specialist. "Soon's I read about the case in the papers, I got to East Anchorville fast as I could."

"Zowie!" said Thomas Bit, reverently.

Burns, the DA, finished with Hoskins.

"Your witness," he said.

"No questions," said Thomas Bit.

"Not giving up, are you?" asked the DA with a tiny simpering smile.

"I call Wilbert Wallen, *MD*, to the stand," said the lawyer. The courtroom buzzed, and the DA and the judge exchanged looks, raised eyebrows, and shrugs as Wallen took the stand.

"Your name?" asked Thomas Bit.

"Wilbert Wallen."

"Occupation?"

"Pathologist. My specialty is rare diseases."

The room grew strangely quiet.

"Can you perhaps throw some light on these four deaths which the accused is supposed to have brought about?"

"*Light?*" Wallen chuckled. "I can tell you exactly what caused them!"

"Would you please do so . . . ?" said Thomas Bit.

"Well . . ." Wallen cleared his throat, loudly. "I have just come from the Ogilvy Funeral Parlour, wherein Miss Cord, and Messieurs Gulby, Forbes and Stanley are lying in state. It seems as if the employees of that establishment were all over here at the trial – in fact, this whole burg looks like a ghost town today – so I took the opportunity to examine the four."

"That's against the law!" thundered the judge. "Without a court order, bodies of deceased persons may not be subjected to—"

"Your Honour," Thomas Bit interrupted smoothly, "in this case, there was no time to await a court order."

"No time?" said the judge. "What do you mean, no time?"

"For the sake of the town – which includes Your Honour, of course – Doctor Wallen had to move quickly."

The spectators murmured, louder and louder, until the judge rapped for silence. "Mister Bit! Are you implying . . . There's something *ominous* in your tone."

"If Your Honour will hear Doctor Wallen out?"

"Most irregular . . ." His Honour hedged. Then his curiosity got the better of his jurisprudence, and he nodded. "Very well. But it better be good."

"I found," Wallen continued, "that Miss Harriet Cord was what you might call a 'carrier'. A sort of Typhoid Mary."

The judge's face paled. "A carrier of *what*?" he said, in a hoarse whisper.

"A very rare disease, known in the trade as *Leprosis Arboris*, a sort of cross between Jungle Rot and Chestnut Blight. The victim's innards turn to sawdust. It's more or less painless.

There's no approach in this disease, no warnings. One moment you're full of vigour, the next moment . . . '*Foosh*'."

"*Foosh*?" asked the judge.

Wallen nodded. "All the internal organs crumble into a nice oaken dust." He sighed, and scratched his nose. "It's rather painfully obvious what happened. Somehow, those unfortunate men came in contact with Miss Cord—"

The three widows stiffened and gasped in unison.

"—And they were goners."

All over the courtroom, men were losing colour, and wives were narrowing eyes. The judge, his face the colour of buttermilk, asked, with a break in his voice, "Is – is there any cure?"

"Oh, certainly." Wallen smiled. "Rose petals."

"Rose petals?" A note of hope had crept into the judge's voice. He had a rosebush on his estate, and he was certain the autumn cold had spared a few tiny buds.

"Yup," said Wallen. "No processing, either. Just pop one in your mouth like candy, chew it, swallow it, and presto! – you're as good as new."

At the rear of the room, a man slipped toward the door, then another man, and another. His Honour's eye caught the motion, and he remembered that his rosebush was near the roadside where everyone in town must have admired it.

Judge, DA, coroner, sheriff, editor and every last townsman in the room clawed, punched and kicked his way out the door.

When the thundering died down, and the dust began to settle, Thomas Bit shook Wallen's hand.

"I guess the case is dismissed," he said. "You've made me a success. I've won my first case. Is there anything I can do for you? Can I buy you a beer, take you to lunch, pay for your transportation to your home?"

Wallen laughed and clapped Bit on the back, shaking his head. "No, thanks, son. Don't drink beer, brought my lunch, and my transportation's arranged for."

He picked up a small bag, tied with twine, and began to undo it. The Turk, smiling happily, sat down beside Wallen. "Thanks, Uncle Wilbert," he said, fondly.

"Least I could do." Wallen smiled. "You being my sister's boy, and all."

"You're related?" Thomas Bit gasped.

"Well, of course." Then Wallen frowned. "Gad, son, don't tell me *you* fell for that mumbo-jumbo on the stand?"

"I—" Thomas Bit sank weakly onto a bench. "You mean it wasn't true? The disease and all?"

"Heck, no," said Wallen. "Made the whole danged thing up outta my head. Good, wasn't it? . . . Gosh, boy, I ain't even a doctor."

Bit's heart sank slowly into the quicksand of dread that oozed into his breast. "But all those people – out in the cold – eating roses!"

"Won't hurt 'em none," said Wallen, smiling. "Fresh air'll do 'em good."

"But why'd you *do* it?" asked Thomas Bit.

Wallen finished unwrapping his lunch, and indicated the Turk with a tilt of his head. "Couldn't let him down. My only sister's boy, you know. She died. I brought him up."

"You brought him up . . ." Thomas Bit mumbled blankly.

"Sure," said Uncle Wilbert. "Raised him from an egg."

As icy horror began to tickle Thomas Bit's frayed nerve-endings, Uncle Wilbert leaned over to him in a friendly manner and extended the box of lunch.

"Have a worm?" he asked.

PALE ASSASSIN

James Bibby

*James Bibby is the author of the Conan-like spoofs set in
Midworld that began with* Ronan the Barbarian *(1995).
He has also been a frequent contributor of jokes and sketches
to many television series including* Not the Nine O'Clock
News *and* Three of a Kind. *The following story, specially
written for this anthology, brings to the fore one of the
hitherto minor characters in the Midworld saga, the re-
doubtable Inspector Heighway. Any similarity to Inspector
Morse is, of course, just a remarkable coincidence.*

It was a typical midwinter's day in the city of Koumas. The
muddy, litter-strewn streets were packed with carts, wagons
and drays. Traders, shopkeepers and barrow boys bickered
and haggled with their customers. Children squabbled and
shouted. The pavement taverns echoed to the laughter of
warriors, merchants, travellers and even the occasional dwarf
or elf, all sitting on wooden benches beneath the rain-spattered
canvas awnings, drinking wine or beer from pewter tankards
and swapping stories of daring deeds in far-off places. The
clatter of hooves, cursing of draymen and the squeaking of
wooden axles filled the air, and the clamour of a thousand
voices spiralled up towards the leaden skies. It was like Bedlam, only it was louder and it smelled worse.

In his tiny office on the top floor of the main police station, Inspector Heighway was trying to do the crossword on the back page of the *Koumas City Chronicle* and finding it hard going. It wasn't that he was bad at word games; on the contrary, he could usually finish the difficult crossword in the *Lampa Sanda Times* inside ten minutes. But there were three factors conspiring against him today.

Firstly, the sheer tumult of noise pouring in through the window was making it difficult to concentrate. Secondly, he knew from experience that the crossword's current compiler wasn't exactly the most literate person in the world. In fact, the guy couldn't spell to save his life, and Heighway had spent ten minutes trying to think of a three-letter word for a wriggly fish beginning with *o* before realizing that the compiler must have spelt six across *schewl* instead of *school*. And thirdly, Heighway was being "helped" with the crossword by his assistant, Sergeant Raasay, a man completely unencumbered by even the merest hint of intelligence.

"Fifteen down," Heighway muttered. "Digging tool. Six letters."

"Pickaxe?" suggested Raasay.

"*Six* letters. And if the compiler has spelt 'mince' like I think he has, it begins with an S."

"Spade?"

Heighway sighed and laid his newspaper down on the desk. He had learned to be tolerant, especially since the time when the sergeant had been writing a report and had blacked out whilst trying to spell "misappropriation". But there were moments when it became a little wearing.

"I need a break," he told Raasay. "You stay here and hold the fort while I nip downstairs for a spot of lunch." Bracing himself for the ordeal of a trip to the canteen, Heighway left his office, his stomach rumbling hungrily.

At first, he thought he was in luck. It was blissfully quiet as he trotted apprehensively down the police station's rear staircase, and the only sound that could be heard was the *tup, tup, tup* of his feet on the stone steps. But then, all at once, a series of agonized screams came hurtling up from the basement dungeons, the desperate sounds of a human in mortal agony. The shrieks echoed around the stairwell and set Heighway's skin crawling like a tankful of cockroaches.

Taking the last flight of stairs at a run, the inspector burst through the double doors and strode along the corridor leading to the canteen, his hands over his ears. But it was too late. Once again, his appetite had disappeared without trace, to be replaced by a vague queasiness and a desire to take up a kinder, more honourable profession than being a member of the Koumas City police force. Slave-trading, perhaps, or possibly assassination.

Heighway had always thought it was a big mistake to have the police canteen on the ground floor, directly above the Department of Interrogation. He couldn't understand how anyone could enjoy the canteen food when it was accompanied by the distant sounds of someone having their fingernails forcibly removed.

But then, he couldn't understand how anyone could eat the canteen food, full stop. The current cook was a half-orc whose idea of cuisine was to boil food fiercely for several hours until it gave up. The only reason Heighway came here at all was because the superintendent had banned him from visiting taverns during working hours.

Pessimistically, Heighway pushed open the canteen door and wandered across to the servery. The table here was liberally strewn with cracked and stained serving dishes that held congealing piles of unidentifiable grey items that might once have been recognizable as food. Behind it, Ratshagger the cook was on patrol, a food-encrusted serving spoon at the ready in one hand, the other wedged down the front of his pants, absently scratching his scrotum.

Heighway stared down at a bowl of round, pallid objects that huddled together in a pool of black gravy and realized with a shock that they were meant to be dumplings. He prodded one doubtfully with a knife and decided that he'd seen softer, moister granite.

"You want dumpling?" asked Ratshagger, eagerly. Extracting his hand from his pants, the half-orc picked up one of the items in his grimy fingers and offered it to the inspector. "'Ere, you all right?" he added. "You gone funny colour . . ."

Heighway shook his head and gestured weakly as a wave of nausea swept over him. The sight of a coarse and suspiciously wiry hair poking out of the dumpling had caused the last few traces of his appetite to melt away, leaving him feeling as though he would never eat again. He could still hear muffled screams coming through the floor from the basement, and for a moment he wondered whether some poor soul was being forcefed some of Ratshagger's cooking.

"Afternoon, Inspector Heighway . . . sir," growled a familiar and detested voice, and with a sinking heart Heighway turned to find the vast, loathsome bulk of Sergeant Hogman standing behind him, idly cleaning dirt from behind one of his fingernails with the tip of his dagger.

"Ah . . . Sergeant. Good afternoon." Heighway tried not to stare at the dried blood on Hogman's hands. "I thought that had to be you at work in the basement."

"Ah, that." Hogman paused as more screams filtered through the floor. He listened with his head on one side, his piglike eyes unfocused and a faint smile on his lips, as though he was savouring the sound. "No," he continued, after the screams had died away. "That's Constable Zaglin, or 'Fingers', as he likes to be known. He's just joined us from the Lampa Sanda force. A very promising boy. Looks like being an excellent interrogator."

"Why is he known as 'Fingers'?" Heighway asked, then immediately wished he hadn't.

"He likes to keep a memento of all his . . . customers," leered the sergeant. "He's got quite a collection. It's started a bit of a trend amongst the lads downstairs."

Heighway winced. All at once he understood why the members of the Interrogation Department had recently taken to calling Hogman "Knackers" . . .

"He keeps himself in shape, too," added the overweight

Hogman, with obvious admiration. "He's got us all on a bit of a health-and-fitness kick . . ."

Heighway was about to mutter something devastatingly cutting about ill health and fatness but then the screaming started afresh and, suddenly, he couldn't stand it any more. He felt that he had to get away from the barbarity of Hogman and his cronies and, even though the superintendent had expressly forbidden it, Heighway knew that only the soothing atmosphere and the finest beer of some friendly hostelry would calm him.

So, pushing past Hogman and ignoring his scornful sneer, the inspector headed away from the horrors of the basement dungeons and the canteen food, and out onto the teeming streets, in search of the blissful peace and relaxing atmosphere of his favourite tavern.

Two hours later, Heighway was sitting in The Green Manticore, his third tankard of Old Organs bitter in front of him, a bowl of hot chicken stew inside him and his crisis of conscience behind him. The good food and the smooth, creamy beer had produced their usual soothing effect, and the inspector was feeling a great deal happier.

After all, he thought, there were plenty of positive aspects to the job. The work was varied and interesting. And in a world where a sizeable proportion of the population consisted of large, muscle-bound warriors with short tempers and long swords, there were more than enough murder inquiries to go round.

Heighway also liked the fact that he was getting quite a reputation as a bit of a maverick amongst the other detectives. They were amused by his insistence on trying to find the real perpetrator of a crime by discovering clues, questioning witnesses and using his brain, but the fact that he frequently succeeded elicited a grudging respect. And on those rare occasions when the superintendent considered it vital to find the actual criminal, as in the recent blackmail case at the Pink Centaur Club, it was always Heighway who was put on the case.

Picking up his beer, Heighway downed half of it in one long swallow. He was just thinking that maybe life wasn't that bad after all when the distant shouting of a familiar voice reminded him of yet another negative aspect to his job. Sergeant Raasay.

"Inspector Heighway! Inspector Heighway, sir!"

The shouting was coming from outside the door of the tavern. Heighway sipped his beer and waited for the sergeant to enter, but the door remained closed. Instead, the shouting seemed to be moving along the outside of the tavern towards a nearby window, and showed no signs of stopping. If anything, it was becoming more agitated.

"Inspector *Heighway! Sir!*"

Sighing, the inspector stood up and crossed to the window, which was closed and shuttered against the heat, the noise and (most particularly) the smell of the city. Unlatching it, he thrust the stout wooden shutters outwards, catching Raasay neatly on the forehead in mid-shout.

"Inspector HeighwOUCH!" yelled the sergeant.

"For the sake of the gods, man!" muttered the inspector. "You obviously know I'm in the tavern. Why don't you just come in?"

"Can't do that, sir. My Uncle Billy . . . erm, I mean, Superintendent Weird has ordered me not to go into taverns during working hours, sir."

"I know that, Raasay, but *I*'m ordering you to come in."

"Yes, sir."

Raasay took a hesitant step towards the door, then halted, locked into immobility as his brain struggled to sort out the conflict caused by two contrasting commands from his superior officers. Heighway watched with fascination for a moment before taking pity on the sergeant.

"Raasay, listen. The superintendent ordered you to stop *drinking* in taverns while on duty. He didn't say you couldn't come in to deliver a message, or whatever you've come down here for."

"Coo, yes, sir," said Raasay, brightening. "I'll be right in, sir."

He trotted off towards the tavern's door, and Heighway went back to his seat. To be honest, he felt responsible for the trouble Raasay had got into. He was painfully aware that the sergeant had developed a touch of hero-worship and had started imitating many of his habits, convinced that they would help him become as good a detective. But whereas a few lunchtime beers relaxed Heighway and helped him to think, Raasay usually got so relaxed that he couldn't stand up and needed to be carried back to the police station to sleep if off under his desk.

Heighway drained his tankard and looked up as his sergeant sidled uneasily across to the table.

"Inspector Heighway, sir . . ."

"The superintendent wants me back at the station right away."

". . . The superintendent wants you back at the station right away, sir."

There was a pause, and then a look of awe began to spread across Raasay's broad face like the tide creeping in across a long, flat beach.

"It wasn't that difficult to work out, man!" Heighway told him. "After the bollocking you got last week, the only thing that could have forced you within fifty yards of a tavern is a direct order from the superintendent himself."

The sergeant flinched at the memory, and Heighway wasn't too surprised. Only the fact that he was the superintendent's nephew had enabled the sergeant to hold on to his job (and to a couple of other things, for anyone else who had thrown up all over Sergeant Hogman's boots would have been singing falsetto in the police choir by now).

"Come on," Heighway continued, "we'd better get back and see what your Uncle Billy wants. Let's hope I'm not in too much trouble, eh?"

Clapping the sergeant jovially on the shoulder, he led the way out of the tavern.

Half an hour later, the inspector was feeling anything but jovial. They had found Superintendent Weird in his office, but after a quick (and unusually benign) "Dragged you out of the pub again, have we?" to Heighway, he had gestured to a chair, ordered Raasay to "go and do something useful, like topping yourself" and had then followed the sergeant out, leaving the inspector to become more and more apprehensive.

It was his superior's air of quiet preoccupation that Heighway had found unsettling. Usually, the superintendent had an in-your-face, no-nonsense manner that was, at best, forthright and, at worst, downright insulting. But today there was an untypical thoughtfulness about him that Heighway found deeply worrying. Something was seriously wrong, and the inspector could only hope that it was nothing he had done.

By the time the superintendent returned ten minutes later, Heighway had convinced himself that he was about to be fired. He fidgeted in his chair as Weird sat down behind his desk, and waited for the blow to fall. But his boss seemed to be having trouble in getting started.

The seconds piled up into minutes as the superintendent sat staring into space, all the while tapping unrhythmically with one fingernail on the desk's polished surface. And then, all at once, he spoke.

"Avago, we've got a problem," he said. Heighway blinked, taken aback at the rare use of his first name. Whatever this was about, it was very serious indeed.

"I'm putting you on the case," the superintendent went on, "because it calls for qualities that none of my other officers possess." He paused and looked at Heighway quizzically. "How can I phrase this without hurting your feelings? Well, let's put it this way. You may be an uncooperative miserable old git who drinks far too much, but you're a *talented* uncooperative miserable old git who drinks far too much."

"Don't worry about sparing my feelings, sir," muttered Heighway. "Give it to me straight."

"And you're honest. Well, for a policeman, anyway. I can trust you, as long as it's not to do with keeping away from taverns. And you've got brains in your head."

"Thank you . . ."

"Let's hope you manage to keep them there."

"*What?*"

The superintendent smiled humourlessly.

"Somebody," he said, "is murdering my best officers. Three have died in two days. I want you to find the murderer before he finds you. Or anyone else. Or, more importantly, me."

The lifeless body of Constable "Fingers" Zaglin of the Department of Interrogation lay on the flagstoned floor of one of the gloomy basement torture chambers where it had been discovered. Even in the dim, flickering light of the single burning torch wedged into a nearby sconce, it was plain that his death had not been easy, for his body was contorted and twisted, and his face was resting in a pool of vomit.

Heighway grimaced and looked away, feeling his own stomach threatening to rebel. Behind him, Superintendent Weird was pacing restlessly up and down, occasionally pausing to examine one of the unpleasantly sharp implements that rested on a table beside the interrogation chair. Nearby, Sergeant Hogman leaned against the wall, looking ill. Shock had drained his skin of what little colour it had contained, and the muscles beneath the pendulous jowls had sagged completely. His face looked like a wax mask that had been left too close to a fire.

Taking the torch in his hand, Heighway lifted it from the sconce and examined the corpse reluctantly. The eyes were wide and staring, but there were no signs of wounds to the body that he could see. The vomit contained what appeared to be a mixture of raisins, nuts and oats.

"So what's he been eating, then?" Heighway muttered. "Horse food?"

"No, that's muesli," said Hogman. "It's good for you. Fingers swore by it. Ate it every morning."

"Doesn't seem to have done *him* much good." Heighway raised the torch again, scanning the stone floor around the body. In the dim light he could just make out a series of faint but familiar chalk marks.

"I see the police pathomancer's been down here, then," he added, straightening.

"Yes," nodded the superintendent. "Madam Min had a look at him half an hour ago."

Heighway scowled. Although the witches and wizards of the Pathomancy Department undeniably came up with useful information on occasion, he couldn't help feeling that there must be a more scientific method of examining a corpse than drawing a pentangle around it, muttering an incantation and scattering a bit of fresh chicken-blood about.

"So what conclusions did the mad old bat come to?"

Superintendent Weird stopped his pacing and glared at the inspector. Turning to Hogman, he gestured towards the corridor with his thumb and waited for the distraught sergeant to shuffle out of the room. As the door closed he turned back to Heighway.

"The Chief Pathomancer," he said, giving Madam Min her official title, "has provided us with important information."

"Has she, now?"

"Yes. She succeeded in making contact with Constable Zaglin's spirit. She says he was poisoned."

"Brilliant. Who'd have thought it?" Heighway wedged the burning torch back into its sconce and turned his back on Zaglin's corpse. "I don't suppose she was able to tell us who did the poisoning?"

"Well, no. Min said the spirit was extremely agitated. Apparently it turned up in the afterlife only to discover a lot of other spirits with one finger missing that wanted a word with it. She says she might find out more when it's had time to calm down a bit."

"How long will that take?"

"Ah." Suddenly the superintendent couldn't meet Heighway's gaze. "About two hundred years, apparently."

"You what?"

"Madam Min says time is different in the afterlife."

"With respect, sir, Madam Min is a complete basket case!"

"She happens to be an extremely powerful and talented witch."

"Then she's a wicca basket case."

"That's enough, inspector!"

"Sorry, sir." Heighway rubbed at his face with his hands, wondering where to start. He felt tired and stale. "I'll get Raasay to start questioning everyone in the station. Did they see anything unusual, when did they last see Zaglin, that sort of thing. And I suppose I'd better have a look at the other two victims as well."

Once again, the superintendent seemed to be having problems in meeting Heighway's gaze.

"Er, that might be . . . difficult," he mumbled.

"Oh? Why's that?"

"Well . . . Sergeant Vaedrl and Constable Matsaran were both single men with no next of kin, dedicated to the job . . . you know how it is when someone has no life outside the force."

"They become our responsibility then, don't they, sir? We give them a proper send-off, an official funeral and all that stuff . . ."

"Yes, yes, yes . . . in theory, laddie, in theory . . ." The superintendent was twisting his fingers together nervously and had the air of an eight-year-old who has just been caught using his father's best sword on the cat. "But all that costs money, and it's difficult enough already trying to stretch the budget to cover everything. I mean, you have to realize that in their case there was no one left to care what happened to them. And it's not as if we knew they'd been murdered then . . ."

"What's happened to their bodies?"

". . . Because Vaedrl died at home, you see. You know how much he drank, we assumed it was natural causes. And then we thought Matsaran must have had some kind of fit. It was only when we found Zaglin today that I realized they'd all died in exactly the same way . . ."

"*Sir!* What's happened to the bodies?"

Superintendent Weird sighed heavily. He was looking about as happy as an orc in a tavern at closing time.

"I asked Sergeant Dendril of Race Relations to . . . dispose of them," he muttered.

"Dendril?" exclaimed Heighway, unbelievingly. "By the gods, you know what *he*'ll have done with them, don't you, sir? He'll have sold them to one of his orc contacts! And you know what that means!"

The superintendent nodded tiredly.

"Only too well," he muttered. "Only too well."

"So what we're saying here," Heighway continued, "is that vital evidence, in the shape of the first two bodies in a murder investigation, has almost certainly been skinned, boned, diced and marinaded, and is probably at this very moment being served up in some seedy orc restaurant as the dish of the day?"

"That's about the size of it," agreed the superintendent.

"Good grief!"

Heighway turned away and stared down dejectedly at Zaglin's lifeless body. It was fair enough, he supposed. That was all you were after your spirit had flown the coop – meat on a slab. Why should it matter what happened to the meat? There was no one to miss or to mourn the two dead policemen. They had both been unmarried, with few friends and sad, lonely lives outside the force. But all the same . . .

"Not much of a send-off, is it, sir?" he said, eventually. "Main ingredient in an orc's lunch. Not quite the ceremony you'd like to mark your passing."

"Oh, it's not so bad," responded the superintendent, as they turned and walked to the door. "You can get quite stylish service in some orcish restaurants these days. The waiters can be *very* posh. And they give you a lovely garnish . . ."

Heighway found Sergeant Dendril in his ground-floor office. He was fast asleep in a chair, his feet propped up on his desk, his hands clasped across his stomach, and his wide-open mouth was emitting a sound like a pig snorting through a megaphone. Heighway woke him by the simple expedient of slamming the door hard, at which Dendril made a noise like a pig choking on a couple of cabbages and fell backwards off his chair to disappear behind the desk.

As he waited for the sergeant to pick himself up, Heighway glanced around the office. It wasn't too difficult to work out that it belonged to the Race Relations boys, for there were souvenirs of all the free races of Midworld scattered about the office. An orcish drinking-skull stood on the desk next to a beautifully-moulded elven wine goblet and a carved-quartz bottle of *vlatzhkan gûl**. On top of the filing cabinet was a dwarven helmet that was disfigured by a large dent suspiciously similar in size and shape to a standard-issue police truncheon. And leaning against the wall was a cave-troll's war club: a swollen lump of rock-hard wood six feet long with a fifteen-inch nail sticking through it.

Heighway smiled to himself nostalgically. Whoever had taken that away from its owner had either been incredibly brave or incredibly stupid. He'd once seen a troll making such clubs by the simple method of holding the nail against the wood with one hand and whacking it hard with the other. And he'd also once seen the body of an orc who'd been punched in the face by an angry cave-troll. His head had been the shape of an ice-cream scoop, and his nose had been sticking out of the back of his skull.

Groaning noises from behind the desk brought the inspector back to the present and he watched with satisfaction as Sergeant Dendril dragged himself upright. The sergeant was an open, cheery man who people instinctively liked and trusted on sight. Which just goes to show how misguided people can be, for Heighway knew that he could trust Dendril about as far as he could throw a hill-giant.

The man was, it had to be said, ideally suited for the task of dealing with the different races that inhabited the teeming city. He got on equally well with them all, partially because of

---

* *vlatzhkan gûl* — an orcish liqueur that is somehow actually stronger than pure alcohol. The name, literally translated, means "removes lining of stomach in seconds".

his open, friendly disposition, but mainly because he had an orc's appetite for alcohol, a dwarf's appetite for gold and, most especially, an elf's appetite for sex. Indeed, when it came to race relations, Dendril liked to boast that he'd had relations with members of every intelligent race in Midworld. And several other species as well.

"Inspector Heighway!" the sergeant beamed, sounding as though there was no one he'd rather have seen come into his office. "What a pleasant surprise. Do you know, I was only saying to Constable . . ."

"Cut the crap, Sergeant," Heighway broke in. "This is a murder inquiry now. Vaedrl and Matsaran . . . you got rid of their bodies. I need to know where they went."

"Me? What makes you . . ."

"I said cut the crap. The superintendent asked you to dispose of them, and we all know your usual methods of dealing with a nice, fresh corpse."

"I really don't know what you mean," Dendril murmured, carefully reseating himself. His open, smiling face seemed to be saying that he'd just love to help Heighway, if there was only some way that he could.

Heighway sighed.

"You may be unaware," he said tiredly, "but this afternoon a third officer was murdered. Constable Zaglin."

"Zaglin, eh?"

"Yes, Zaglin. Sergeant Hogman's protégé. And the sergeant isn't feeling too happy about it. He wants to know who's responsible. In fact, he's very, very keen to find out, and if he discovers that anyone is withholding information, they're quite likely to find him paying them a little visit and inviting them to try out his basement entertainment suite . . ."

Heighway paused. Dendril's smile had started to fall off in large chunks, and his ruddy complexion had turned the unhealthy, pallid colour of a maggot that doesn't get out of the house much.

"So I'll just tell him you don't want to help us, then," finished the inspector, and turned to open the door.

"No, wait!"

All of a sudden, Dendril's voice was shrill and filled with panic. Heighway waited, his hand on the doorknob, his features carefully composed into an expression of polite enquiry, while the sergeant tried to wrap himself in the shreds of his dignity. It was like someone trying to wrap themselves in a very tiny flannel when surprised in the bathroom.

"I, er . . . I passed them on to a friend of mine who had kindly offered to, um, to make suitable arrangements for the two dead officers," Dendril told him.

"This friend of yours wouldn't happen to be an orc, would he?"

"Why, yes. Chancre is an orc, yes."

"And he wouldn't happen to work in an orc restaurant, by any chance?"

"Now you come to mention it, I do believe he did once mention that he was a chef, or something of that nature . . ."

"Which restaurant?"

"The Long Pig Grill-room, on Bile Street."

"Thank you."

Heighway opened the door, then paused to look back at Dendril, who was already reaching for the bottle of *vlatzhkan gûl* with a shaking hand.

"Oh, by the way," he added with relish. "You might not have heard, but Constable Matsaran was transferred to the Department of Interrogation two days before his death. Sergeant Hogman might not have known him well, but he's very loyal to his own. I wouldn't be too surprised if he paid you a little visit anyway."

The bottle fell from Dendril's nerveless fingers to shatter on the floor. Tendrils of smoke began to drift up as the liqueur ate into the floorboards. Inspector Heighway closed the door with a satisfied smile and went in search of Sergeant Raasay.

The Long Pig Grill-room was, by the standards of most orcish restaurants, a very high-class establishment indeed. Although the tables were encrusted with old food, there was very little

on the walls and none on the ceiling. Most evenings there were
only four or five fights, and Heighway knew for a fact that no
one had been killed there for at least ten days. The orc waiters
were trained to a remarkably high standard; somehow, the
owner had managed to instil in them the basic tenet that, no
matter how severe the provocation, you *never* massacred the
clientele.

After ordering Raasay to stay on guard outside (for it was
never wise for a human to disappear into an orcish establishment without some form of back-up), Heighway pushed open
the door and went inside. The restaurant was full of orcs, all
plainly on their best behaviour, for the noise was merely
deafening and it was possible to dodge between the bits of
food being thrown around.

Brushing his way past an ineffectually gesturing waiter who
he guessed was of the *shashlik* tribe*, Heighway strode to the
back of the restaurant, where the *maître d'hôtel*, a much larger
uttuk, was snarlingly surveying his domain and occasionally
reaching out to give one of the scurrying waiters a ringing
clout around the back of the head.

Wordlessly, Heighway held up his police ID card, and the
maître d' surveyed it impassively.

"Yeah. Right. Well, what can I do for you, Inspector?" he
growled.

Heighway was impressed, for it wasn't often you came
across an orc who'd bothered learning to read. In fact, he
was relieved he'd remembered to bring his real ID. On those
frequent times he forgot it, he usually showed orcs his membership card for the Pink Puss-Cat club instead, and it would
have been very embarrassing to show that to an orc who could
recognize it for what it really was.

"I believe you bought in a couple of corpses yesterday from

---

* The two smallest breeds of orc are the *shashlik* and the *bazhakûl*. Both
are about five feet high, with grey scaly skin, green pointed fangs and
yellow slits for eyes. Usually, the only way a human can tell the two
breeds apart is by smell, for *bazhakûl* smell like a rotting skunk that's
been dipped in a vat of liquid manure, whereas *shashlik* smell far worse.

our Sergeant Dendril," he said. "I don't suppose there's anything left of them?"

"Ah! A human being of discernment!" It was the orc's turn to be impressed. He turned and clicked his talons, summoning one of the cowering waiters across. "If the inspector would care to take the table in the corner . . ."

"No!" Heighway was horrified. "You don't understand! I don't want to sample them! It's just that we've discovered they were murdered, and I was hoping to examine their . . . remains, to see if there was any evidence of how or why they were killed."

"I see. Well, you'd better have a word with the chef, then. Come with me."

The *maître d'* turned to lead the way through a swing-door into the kitchen beyond, and Heighway followed apprehensively. The only orcish kitchen he'd previously experienced had looked like a pigsty that had just hosted a particularly bloody massacre, but he was relieved to find that this one was actually cleaner than some human kitchens he'd seen. In the far corner, a small, scowling orc in a mucus-green chef's hat was chopping up onions. Heighway guessed that this was Chancre.

"Chef?" the *maître d'* called across the room. "There's gentleman here from the police force. See if you can help him. He's investigating a murder and he'd like to know if we've got any remnants of the two policemen we bought yesterday."

Chancre paused to wipe his brow with the back of one taloned hand.

"The two policemen, eh?" he snarled. "Hang on. Lemme think. The *noisettes de gendarme* have all gone. Same with the *filet de flic avec champignons* and the *brigadier bourguignonne*. And all the trimmings went in this morning's stock. Apart from one piece. That's still in the meat larder over there."

He jerked a thumb in the direction of a battered wooden cupboard that was sprawled against the wall.

"One piece," repeated Heighway.

"Yeah."

"Just the one?"

"You got it."

"Oh, great. Er . . . do you mind if I . . .?"

"Nah, go right ahead," Chancre told him. "Help yerself. I don't want it. Nasty spotty-looking thing."

The orc chef turned back to his onion chopping, and Heighway wandered reluctantly across to the cupboard, desperately hoping that this one remaining piece wasn't going to turn out to be the piece he thought it was. If so, it was going to be downright embarrassing having to produce it in court as evidence. Mind you, on the plus side, it would be a laugh watching Madam Min trying to carry out an autopsy on it . . .

Heighway gripped the handle of the rickety door, watched impassively by the *maitre d'*. Pausing to take a deep breath, he closed his eyes and pulled open the door. For a moment he stood there, eyes screwed tightly shut, and then he forced his right eye open a fraction and squinted nervously into the larder. And found two eyes staring back at him.

Constable Matsaran was spotty, all right. Years of fatty junk food and little exposure to sunlight had left him, when alive, with a complexion that had been more spot than not. In death the skin of his face and neck looked like a very old chopped-tomato pizza. For all Inspector Heighway knew, maybe the rest of his body had looked the same, but there was no way of telling, for all that was left of Matsaran was his head, neatly severed above the Adam's apple and resting on a plate.

Heighway winced and was about to turn away when something caught his eye. Bending, he peered closely at Matsaran's open mouth for a few seconds. Then he reached into his inside pocket, pulled out a pencil and used its finely sharpened point to prise a couple of tiny items from between Matsaran's decay-ravaged teeth.

Turning to face the light, the inspector examined the two items. One appeared to be a flake of oatmeal, the other a piece of nut. He gazed at them for a while, occasionally turning them this way and that with his forefinger, and a slow smile spread across his face.

"I wonder," he muttered to himself. "Could it possibly be . . .?"

Straightening, Heighway beckoned to the orc *maitre d'* and pointed to Matsaran's pathetic remains.

"That head is now evidence in an official police inquiry," he said. "Find some sort of a bag to put it in, would you, and then take it outside to my sergeant?"

The *maitre d'* frowned.

"I'm afraid it's not really my job . . .," he began, but Heighway cut him off.

"Of course it is," he said. "You're the *head* waiter, aren't you?"

And, chuckling happily to himself, he left the kitchen. At last, Inspector Heighway was starting to enjoy the case.

All the way back to the police station, Sergeant Raasay kept throwing fascinated glances at the weighty leather bag that the *maître d'* had given him. He was dying to know what was inside, but the inspector had told him not to open it and was now lost in one of those reveries of concentration that Raasay knew meant they were close to cracking the case. So he just trotted contentedly along behind his superior and said nothing.

After a while, Heighway spoke.

"I just can't make the connection," he murmured, almost to himself. "Why would Vaedrl be killed? He was nothing to do with the Interrogation lot."

"Well, he *was* a mate of Sergeant Hogman, sir," ventured Raasay, and immediately had to take sharp evasive action in order to avoid colliding with the inspector, who had stopped dead and swung round to stare at him.

"*Was* he, now?"

"Oh, yes, sir. Old mates, they were. Well, they'd been in the same group at cadet school, sir, years ago. They used to go out once a month and get drunk together, sir."

"Well, I never knew that." Heighway thought for a moment. "So if Hogman had some new fad he was dead keen on, he'd have told Vaedrl all about it?"

"Oh, I should think so, sir."

Heighway grinned and clapped the surprised Raasay on the back.

"Good man, Raasay. Well done. Now, let's get back before another member of the Interrogation Department dies a horrible, lingering death . . ."

But they were too late. When they arrived at the police station, the place was in uproar. Three burly constables were on guard outside the main entrance, their swords drawn and at the ready, their eyes scanning visitors suspiciously. Inside the entrance foyer, people were scurrying hither and thither, and the air was filled with a confused babble of voices.

Raasay stared about him, bewildered, whilst Inspector Heighway sighed and leaned against the wall, his shoulders slumped in dejection.

"We were too slow, Sergeant," he muttered. "Some other poor sod has copped it. We should have run back . . ."

"Heighway!" Superintendent Weird's voice rang out across the foyer. Looking up, Heighway saw his superior beckoning from an office doorway.

"Ah, well," he said to Raasay. "Better let your Uncle Billy know what's been going on. You wait here, and don't let anyone else see inside that bag."

He walked wearily across the foyer through all the hubbub, like a ponderous beetle wading through scurrying ants. The superintendent beckoned him into the office and shut the door behind them.

"There's been another one, Inspector!" he burst out.

Heighway nodded resignedly.

"Who is it this time?" he asked.

"Hogman."

"Hogman?" Heighway was stunned. There had been something unpleasantly permanent about the sergeant. He'd given the impression that, like death and taxes, you couldn't escape him.

"By the gods, Heighway, where's it going to end? How do we find this killer?" The superintendent took time out to punch a nearby filing cabinet in frustration, then yelped with pain and scowled at his throbbing knuckles. "If I could only get my hands on the person responsible . . ."

"That won't be too difficult, sir," said Heighway, quietly. The superintendent swung round and stared at him with new hope.

"You mean you've cracked it?"

Heighway nodded.

"If you come with me, I think I can show you the killer, sir," he said.

They walked out into the foyer. On the far side, near the door, Raasay was flat out on the floor, unconscious.

"What's happened to him?" asked the superintendent.

"Raasay? Oh, he's probably just fainted. He must have looked in the bag."

"Eh?"

"I'll explain later, sir."

They climbed the stairs to the canteen in silence. Heighway pushed open the doors and led the way into the dining area. It was deserted, save for Ratshagger the cook who was sitting at a table eating something black and crunchy that might have once been a chicken leg. He leaped to his feet at the sight of the superintendent, an apprehensive look on his leering features.

"Superintendent!" he gasped. "What brings you . . ."

"We want to see the ingredients you use when you make up muesli," interrupted Heighway.

"What?" Ratshagger looked baffled.

"Come on, man, it's not a difficult concept to understand. Muesli. Ingredients. Us. Look at."

Frowning, the cook led them into the kitchen. He ambled across to some chaotically stacked shelves at the back and pulled down three small sacks. Heighway opened each in turn. One contained shelled mixed nuts, one raisins, and one dried apple slices. There seemed to be nothing remotely suspicious about any of them.

"What exactly are we looking for, Heighway?" the superintendent asked him.

"Constable Zaglin ate muesli as part of his healthy-diet thing, sir. Hogman and the others admired him. I think they all tried the same healthy diet . . . and it killed them. Listen, Ratshagger, muesli has oats in it. Where do you store them?"

"Oats?" The cook's eyes flickered nervously from Heighway to the superintendent and back again.

"Yes. Oats. Come on!"

The cook scowled, then reluctantly jerked a filthy thumb at a door in one wall.

Heighway crossed to it, followed by the superintendent, and pulled it open. Inside was a storeroom about twelve feet long by six feet across. It was filthy-dirty and neglected, with grimy sacks and barrels piled along one side. Opposite, the wall was lined with ramshackle wooden shelving that was liberally covered in dust, spider webs and rat droppings. And at the far end of the room, beneath a closed and shuttered window, was a large barrel with PORIJ OTES written on it in Ratshagger's near-indecipherable handwriting.

Heighway winced at the assault on his nostrils, for the room smelled worse than a *shashlik* orc with a gangrenous leg. He strode forward and, as he did so, a large rat scrambled out of the PORIJ OTES barrel and quickly disappeared into a hole in the floor-boards.

"Something tells me this might be it, sir," said Heighway. He stepped gingerly forward, opened the window's shutter to allow more light in, and then peered into the barrel. And almost retched at the sight that met his eyes.

The barrel was half full of damp, mouldy, greenish oatmeal, liberally interspersed with rat droppings, mealworms, maggots, weevils and cockroaches. It was so infested that it seemed to be seething with constant motion. And if the sight was bad, the smell was a thousand times worse.

"There's your answer, sir. There's probably more germs in

that barrel than on a dead rat. In fact, judging by the smell, there may well be a dead rat in there too. Hogman and the others weren't murdered – it was the oats in their muesli that killed them."

"But loads of officers eat the canteen porridge," insisted the superintendent. "Why haven't any of *them* died?"

"You know how Ratshagger cooks things, sir. He probably boils the porridge for about two hours. Even this amount of germs couldn't survive that. But the thing about muesli is that you don't cook it."

They stared at the heaving mass of infested, infected oatmeal.

"Surely someone would have said something," muttered the superintendent. "I mean, that must have tasted appalling!"

"Zaglin had a bad cold in his first week here. He probably couldn't taste a thing. And the others had never eaten muesli before. They knew it was meant to do them good, like medicine. They probably thought that the worse it tasted, the better it was for them."

"So after all that, it was only food poisoning," said the superintendent with a faint smile. "Well, well."

"We'd better arrest Ratshagger for manslaughter," said Heighway, "and then I think we should announce—"

"No, I rather think we'll hush this one up," cut in the superintendent, quickly. "No point in damaging police morale. No, we'll have a quiet word with Ratshagger about his hygiene standards, then issue a statement about a food-poisoning outbreak, source traced to, ooh, let's say that nasty little Southron restaurant in Flensing Lane."

"With respect, sir, four people have died because of that insanitary little—"

"My mind's made up, Heighway," the superintendent cut in again. "We're hushing it up."

A sudden flash of insight hit Heighway.

"You hadn't been on at Ratshagger about cutting back on the canteen budget, had you, sir? Ordering him to spend less on food, use up all the old supplies, that sort of thing?"

"I've no idea what you mean, Inspector." Superintendent Weird stared coldly at Heighway. "Nor do I think you'd be wise ever to repeat such a strange theory. Still, I must say you've done an excellent job in tracking down the cause of the deaths. You deserve some time off. Why not take a couple of days' leave and relax in a few nice taverns, eh? And leave me to straighten out this mess . . ."

There was no mistaking the order in the superintendent's voice, or the threat implicit in the tone. Heighway nodded.

"Very well, sir. I'll leave it to you."

Mustering what dignity he could, he walked out of the canteen, down the stairs, and out of the police station. There was nothing he could do about the cover-up that would now take over. That was a reality of life in the police force. He would just have to take pleasure in the fact that he'd been able to crack the case so quickly. But it was a shame that his fellow officers would never find out that he'd solved it.

Still, it was best to look on the bright side. And so, with a smile on his face, Inspector Heighway went off to find a nice tavern and celebrate in style. For it wasn't every police officer who had the satisfaction of knowing that he had just tracked down the city's first-ever cereal killer . . .

THE STRAWHOUSE
PAVILION

Ron Goulart

*Ron Goulart has been writing stories about the occult
investigator Max Kearney for forty years. You'll find some
of the stories collected as* Ghost Breaker *(1971). He's
written a lot else besides. His more recent books include a
series featuring Groucho Marx as a detective, starting with*
Groucho Marx, Master Detective *(1998), and the beau-
tifully illustrated* Comic Book Culture *(2000).*

The second time the kitchen caught on fire Wendy Mayer
didn't rise from the living-room sofa.

"Bert?" she called toward the distant door the smoke was
billowing through.

Her husband appeared in the smoke, a tall slightly stooped
young man. "Do you have a five dollar bill, Wendy?"

"Another fire?" asked middle-sized Max Kearney, who'd
run for the fire extinguisher in the hall closet.

"It's out already. I'm sorry, Max," said Bert Mayer, "to
keep you jogging back and forth with that thing. Can I get you
a fresh drink, Jillian?"

Max's slim auburn-haired wife was on the window seat, her
back to the tree-filled acres outside. "I can wait."

"Bert," asked Wendy, a tall, pretty girl with no make-up, "why did you want five dollars?"

Bert blinked. "Excuse me for not mentioning it." He grinned over at Max. "Just smoke now, Max. It was the chafing dish. When I was opening the back door for the delivery boy the chafing dish fell into the salad and the dressing and the denatured alcohol started a fire."

"What delivery boy?" asked Wendy.

"From the Cala market," explained Bert. "The last fire ruined the steaks. I'm sorry. So I ordered some frozen fish. You can't get meat after six o'clock. I hope that's okay with everybody."

"Won't they take a cheque?" said his wife.

"Not after I knocked him down," said Bert.

"How'd that happen?"

"He drove over the petunia beds out behind the patio and I thought it was the raccoons again come to steal the garbage cans and I ran out," said Bert. "And, I'm sorry, I sort of fell into him. Because the patio lights are on the fritz again. Even after I helped him up the stairs he stayed surly. Max, we sure seem to have trouble with delivery boys. It was the same when we lived near you folks in San Francisco."

Wendy said, "Bert trips a lot."

"I do," agreed Bert. "Can't help it. I'm sorry."

A motor started up outside and they heard a truck driving away. "He didn't wait, I guess," said Wendy. "Max and Jillian, I hope you'll forgive us. Here you are, the first time we've had you to dinner at the house we inherited, and the meal is getting all fouled up."

"They're used to that," said Bert. "We gave dinners like this before we moved to Marin County."

"Bert, why don't you make us all fresh drinks and I'll fix up something quick," said his pretty wife. "An omelette or something."

Bert shook his head. "No, Wendy. When we moved in here last month we made up a schedule. Now that I don't have to work any more, I can give a lot more help with the house. And,

I'm sorry, but according to the schedule, it's one of my nights to cook. You can understand, Max, our wanting to stick to a schedule and keep ourselves organized."

"It's your mansion and you can run it any way you'd like," Max scratched the very top of his crew-cut head. "Though maybe things would go faster if you just sent out for pizza."

"Those pizza places," said Bert. "They never understand my instructions on how to get here. They always send anchovy even if I ask for salami. No, we're always having trouble with pizza people, Max." He grinned at Jillian. "Anyway, here's Jillian who's a food consultant to your ad agency, Max. She isn't going to eat a pizza in my house. I'm sorry." He noticed that the kitchen had stopped smoking. "I'll whip up something quick. Wendy, come on and get the fresh drinks."

When they were alone in the living room Jillian asked her husband, "Well, is he?"

Max moved to her, rested his forefinger on the nape of her neck. "Haunted? I don't know. Bert's always been sort of a screw-up. Sometimes when you approach thirty it starts to accelerate."

"What about that first fire?" asked Jillian. "Could a ghost have done it?"

"His cigarette lighter fell into a pan of cooking oil," said Max. "Maybe something supernatural nudged his hand."

"It's my father," said Wendy, behind them. She put a tray of drinks on a marble-top coffee table. "That's who it is. He won't leave Bert alone. He hasn't since we got married sixteen months ago."

"Your father's ghost, you mean," said Jillian.

Wendy returned to the sofa, sat, nodded. "My father was, as I remember him and he died eight years ago when I was seventeen, he was an exceptionally competent man. He had to be. He was, you know, in the music business most of his life. Led his own dance band from the 1930s to late in the 1950s. King Challens and His Musical Jacks. Not as well known as Benny Goodman or even Anson Weeks, but we always lived well."

Max picked up a Scotch and ice. "What makes you think the ghost is him?"

"It plays all his arrangements."

"Oh, so?" said Max. "There's music."

Wendy shrugged slightly. "Since we moved here anyway, Max. My father was a very careful, efficient man and he did all his own arrangements. I know his versions of *Harbor Lights* and *Laura*."

"Where'd you hear the music?" asked Jillian as Max handed her a glass.

"Well, in the dance pavilion."

"Dance pavilion?"

"Yes, it appears out on the front acre. Where there's mostly grass," said the girl. "It's the Strawhouse Pavilion, where dad played so often in the forties. I've got photos of it in my scrapbook upstairs."

Max asked, "The whole ballroom shows up to haunt you?"

"And the parking lot. The real Strawhouse Pavilion was torn down, in Sacramento it was, ten years ago," said Wendy. "It's appeared out there some six times now. In fact, the neighbours have begun to complain. We're next door, about three acres from, to the Psycho/Technocratics Foundation, you know. They have all those quiet retreat weekends and I guess hearing *Tuxedo Junction* from a twenty-four piece swing band spoils their mood. Bert and I have both apologized."

"Wait now," said Max. "You told Jillian that you felt Bert's been haunted for much longer than just the month or so you've lived here in Marin."

"Sure," said Wendy. "Really, Max. He wasn't like this before we got married. He maybe wasn't as heads-up and efficient as my father, but he wasn't always setting fire to kitchens and falling over delivery boys, either."

"Why is your father supposed to be haunting him?"

Wendy ran her tongue over her upper lip. "It's sort of a joke, I guess. Dad always used to kid me I'd never find a husband like him. Now I think he's exaggerating Bert's clumsiness and forgetfulness, making extra things go wrong, to point up the contrast between Bert and himself. You don't always want to marry somebody just like your father anyway."

"Whatever your father's ghost was doing before," Max said, "he didn't bring his ballroom with him then."

"There wasn't any space," said Wendy. "That third-floor flat we had was charming but small. Bert could hardly ever even find a place to park our Volkswagen. Where would you have put a dance pavilion?"

"All the evidence, the real evidence, of a ghost," said Max, "has shown up since you got here."

"The signs my father is haunting us are more obvious now, yes," admitted Wendy. "I'd like you to investigate this, Max, and find out exactly what's going on."

Max turned away from her, watched the dark grounds beyond the high wide windows. "The occult investigating, Wendy, has never been more than a hobby. Jillian and I are on our way up the coast to Wollter's Bay for a week, as you know. For a vacation."

"Max is reluctant about the ghost detective business," said Jillian in her faintly British voice.

"Couldn't you investigate after your vacation? Next weekend, maybe," said Wendy.

Max said, "What does Bert feel about this?"

"About what?" asked Bert, coming into the big beam-ceilinged room with a bottle of red wine in his hand. "I'm sorry, Max, I didn't catch what you were saying. The ghost stuff, was it?"

"Wendy's told us about the problems you've been having with what might be her father's ghost," said Max. "She asked me to investigate, but I won't unless you agree."

Bert was pumping the wooden handle of the corkscrew which seemed to be stuck in the cork of the wine bottle. "I like to open the wine early, give it time to breathe. Excuse me a second." He twisted the bit of the corkscrew and the cork plopped down into the wine. "That keeps happening. I have a trick with a fork and a drinking straw that usually gets it out.

What were you asking me, Max? Oh yeah, the ghost. I don't know. I think Wendy is making too much of the situation. Still, if you want to."

From out in the darkness came the sound of automobiles driving across gravel and parking. Yellow and orange light, throbbing, grew up in the night. "It's him," said Wendy. She hurried to the front door and out onto the elevated sun deck that looked down on the front acre of the estate.

Max and Jillian followed.

The grass and some of the trees were gone and a bright wood-and-glass building rested on a wide stretch of gravel. The building was white, octagonal in shape, with a great thatched dome and stretches of lattice work all over it. The cars in the parking lot were bright and new, none newer than 1940. The name Strawhouse Pavilion flashed gold and below it were the red neon words Dine & Dance. An oilcloth banner, painted red and gold, stretched across the space above the wide arched door and announced the appearance inside of King Challens, his piano and his orchestra. Laughter and light came from the pavilion.

"That's some ghost," said Jillian, holding Max's hand tight.

The band began to play. "*One O'Clock Jump*," said Wendy. "That was one of his favourites." Her waist was pressing against the porch railing.

"I'm sorry," said Bert, joining them. He had red wine blotches on the leg of his tan slacks. "There's our mysterious phenomenon, Max. You'd think, since I inherited this place from my uncle, that the ghost would be from my side of the family."

"Be quiet a minute," Wendy said without looking at him. Her head moved gently in tempo with the music. "It's hard to see inside the pavilion. Why is that, Max?"

The windows glowed with light but it was a hazy light and you couldn't see anyone inside the pavilion. "I don't know, Wendy." Max touched his wife's hand and let go, moved down the porch steps toward the yard. The summer night was still warm. Max had walked twenty feet toward the Straw-

house Pavilion when he noticed several people on the grounds.
They were staring up at the pavilion.

"We've warned them about this," said a dark-suited man
with a shaggy moustache. He was carrying an unplugged
mixer. "How can you have a Psycho/Technocratics weekend
and play appliance games when this lousy rotten noise is going
on." The cord of the electric mixer swung with his angry
gestures at the noisy ballroom.

"I take it from your clothes," said Max, "you're not a 1940s
ghost."

"You bet your lousy dingbat," said the moustached man.
"My wife and I are novices second class at the foundation. My
suit is from Lew Ritter in Westwood."

"Connie," said his wife, a blonde woman with a blender
under her arm, "don't let your anger spoil all your fine
progress."

"What kind of lousy progress am I making when a lousy
rotten anachronistic honky-tonk can upset me?" He threw his
mixer at the ghost pavilion. "As for you, Dr Wally, I quit. I
demand a refund. I want a lousy rotten refund from you.
When I pay for silence and beatific solitude I don't want lousy
rotten jitterbug music."

Gliding silently across the grass was a tall, slender man of
about fifty. He had hair like a Midwest poet and a gap between
his front teeth. "The fervency of your reactions, the vehe-
mence of your furor, the sufusion of fervid emotions, Mr
Conners," the tall man said, "add nothing to an already
pungent situation."

"Listen, Wally," said Conners. He grabbed the blender
from his wife and threw it in Wally's direction.

Dodging the flung appliance, Wally asked Max, "Are you
an intimate, a confrere, a compatriot of Mr and Mrs Mayer? I
am Dr E. Phillips Wally, founder of the Psycho/Technocratics
Foundation and pioneer in appliance therapy."

"Yes, I'm Max Kearny. I'm a guest at the Mayers'," Max
told him. "Why are you and your disciples carrying appliances?"

Dr Wally smiled. "You haven't read, haven't pored over, haven't studiously regarded my book, which is called *If You Like Machines, You'll Like People.*"

A dark woman of forty was at Wally's side now. The pavilion was playing a slow waltz. "Don't waste time, Phil. What would this shmuck understand about establishing rapport with the deep forces of machinery?"

"My wife, Charlotte," said Dr Wally.

"You look to be some kind of public relations simp like your friend Bert Mayer."

"Advertising, art director," said Max. This thin dark-haired woman looked vaguely familiar. Max pointed a thumb at the pavilion. "What do you know about this?"

"Only that we want it to stop," Dr Wally told him. "The noise, the increasing frequency of the noise, Mr Kearny, is disrupting, desolating, and laying waste to the important silences my work and my therapy call for."

"What's this boob know about tranquillity?" said Charlotte Wally.

The music of King Challens's big band, the shuffling of feet on the dance floor, all the sounds of the pavilion began to grow dim. The image of the ballroom was becoming less distinct. For a few seconds the sound and look of the place flared full again, then it was gone. There was grass again, trees. Mrs Wally gave a small grunt and gathered up the two appliances Conners had flung. She and Dr Wally walked away toward the pines and redwoods at the edge of the estate, up the gradual incline and into the woods. Their disciples left with them. Max went and paced the area where the Strawhouse Pavilion had stood. He found nothing. From the three-storey Mayer house came a mild explosion. Max ran back to the porch and Jillian met him on the steps. "Bert again?"

Jillian nodded yes. "Looks like we'll all be going into Tiburon for dinner."

"I'll drive," said Max.

*   *   *

Seagulls were walking in single file along the warm sand toward Max. He squinted slightly in the bright noon sun and watched them. On the hillside behind him underbrush rattled and crackled. Max stretched up off his towel and saw Bert Mayer tumbling, fully clothed, from the edge two hundred feet above. When he hit the white sand of the beach Bert rolled over twice more, sat up. He held part of a flowering bush in his right hand.

"I'm sorry," said Bert, getting to his feet as Max approached. "I guess I ruined your flowers."

"You okay?"

"I suppose," said Bert. "I should have tried the stairs but I had a bad experience with old rickety weather-beaten stairs like that once and I decided to try the hillside, except I tripped over something."

"What brings you?"

"That's what Jillian asked," said Bert. "I saw her up at the cottage. She's really gotten a tan in the three days you've been here." He started to hand Max the bush, decided to throw it away. "I hate to bother you, Max, but that ghost, well, things are much worse. The ghost of Wendy's father is showing up every night now. The pavilion is really bothering the Wallys. You know, he was trying to buy our place just before my uncle died and left it to me. I suppose Wally'd like us out of there entirely."

"He would, huh? What else is worse about the ballroom?"

"Wendy," Bert said. "Wendy seems to be getting more and more fascinated with the place, with the idea her father's ghost is playing in there. She used to just stand on the sun deck and watch. Last night she started walking up to the place." He shook his head. "Mrs Wally told me it would be dangerous if Wendy went right in there."

Max said, "Charlotte Wally, Charlotte Wally," and tapped his bare foot three times in the sand. "Of course she'd say that."

"I'm sorry, I don't understand."

"I thought she looked familiar," said Max, grinning. "She wasn't always in the psychoelectric business. Eight or nine years ago, when I was first getting interested in occult detecting, I went to one of her seances."

"Seances? She was connected with ghosts?"

"Right," said Max. "A very good medium and very good at summoning up all kinds of spirits and spectres." His foot tapped the sand again. "I'll have a talk with the Wallys."

"Good. Maybe that'll help. I hate to see you cut your vacation short but this is an emergency."

"It's your emergency," said Max. "Jillian and I will be at your place on Saturday."

"This is Wednesday, Max. Suppose she goes inside the ghost pavilion before Saturday?"

"You'll have to keep her from doing that."

"How?"

"Hold on to her if you can't talk her out of it."

"I don't know. I guess I can." He put his hands in his pockets. "One other favour, Max."

"Which?"

"My car got stuck in the sand off the road up there. Can you help me tow it out?"

Max said, "Okay, Bert," and led him to the stairs.

The branches of the willow tree flicked against the bow window of the study and Dr Wally turned his head away from the refrigerator. He noticed Max. "I can tell you nothing of consequence, nothing of significance, nothing of great moment about the unfortunate, and much too loud, haunting our neighbours are suffering. If you'd like to sit down and meditate you're welcome."

There was an electric toaster on the only other chair. "No, thanks," said Max. He stepped around a portable dishwasher and a clothes dryer. "Your wife used to be a successful spirit medium. In fact, you used to put on a turban and run the check room. A few days after the Mayers move in next door to you they start having ghosts."

"A coincidence, an accidental synchronism, an innocent concurrence," said Wally. He put his fingers on the smooth sand-coloured surface of the refrigerator and closed his eyes. "We gave up the spirit dodge years ago, Kearny, after I got my PhD. When I found how to establish rapport with machinery and how to translate it into the daily conduct of life, there was no more need for the other world."

Max leaned against a water cooler. "I notice you can communicate with machines even when they're not plugged in."

"You're not ready for that concept," said Wally. "You must work up. My advice to you, Kearny, is to try to understand your electric can opener, then perhaps work up to your power lawn mower."

"We live in a flat."

"If you could even relate to your wristwatch or understand your doorbell," said Wally, "it would be progress."

"I'd like to talk to your wife."

Wally shook his head. "Oh, you are not ready for that yet. Start with your wristwatch. No, Charlotte takes a long preparation." He shut his eyes, turned in his canvas chair and was with the refrigerator again.

Max stepped out into the hall, which was full of appliances and cardboard cartons. Two doors past Dr Wally's study, someone hissed at him. The doorway was partially blocked by a sewing machine. In the small room it led to was Charlotte Wally. "In here, boob."

Max slid the sewing machine aside, stepped over a carton of mixers. "I wanted to ask you some questions."

"That's all nitwits like you ever want." She was wearing a dark and narrow ankle-length lounging robe and her hair was done into two long braids. "Listen, rube. I need your help. Imagine that, turning to a peabrain for aid."

"You ought to have another talk with that sewing machine and get rid of some of your hostility," said Max. "You're responsible for the ghost of King Challens, aren't you?"

"Shut up and listen." Mrs Wally crossed to an electric stove and slid out the broiler drawer. "I have to hide my collection from the good doctor. He's a clunk at times himself. Here, coconut, this is the book I used."

Max took the proffered magic book. It was bound in cracked black leather. He read the title aloud. "Familial Ghosts And Various and Divers Ways To Summon Them."

"I'm going to loan that to you, stupe. Don't lose it. It's a first edition, besides being invaluable for the spells in it."

"You used this to summon up the ghost of Wendy's father. What went wrong?"

"I didn't expect the whole pavilion and all the noise," said Charlotte Wally. "My husband, and I was feeling sentimental toward the jerk at the time, had his heart set on acquiring that place of Mayer's. We almost had the old uncle convinced he should sell and then he died. As soon as your chums moved in I paid a courtesy call on the pair of dimwits. I found out all I needed to know." She smiled evenly. "She's got a thing about her father and he's a screw-up. I figure the ghost of her father would either break them up or scare them off."

"A common motive in ghost cases," remarked Max. "All the extra ghosts or whatever they are, the big band and the noise are hurting business here."

"I wanted to do this as a surprise for old nuts and bolts, my husband. Now I can't even admit I'm involved. That's where you come in, dodo."

Max asked, "Why can't you call off the ghosts yourself?"

"Turn to page 112, dumbell."

Max did and read the spells written there. "That's great. The only way to reverse the spell is to get the nearest kin of the haunted person to go up against the ghost and read a counter-spell."

"Kin to kin, a nice old-fashioned touch," said Mrs Wally. "I knew Bert Mayer, the nearest kin as defined by that spell, even if he found out what was going on, wouldn't be able to bring off the counter-spell."

Marking the place with his finger, Max said, "He'll have to."

"For a jerk, you've had some pretty good luck as a ghost breaker. You'll have to coach that boob."

"First," said Max, "you'll have to sign an agreement not to

hex or spell the Mayers in any way again. Otherwise I don't cooperate."

Mrs. Wally went to a front-loading washing machine and got out writing paper and a rattling little box of steel-tip pens.

Jillian came running into the guest room of the Mayer house. She stopped, hesitated, waiting for her breath, then said, "Max, it's out there and she's gone inside."

Bert Mayer jumped up out of the wicker easy chair. "The pavilion?"

"Yes, it showed up just a minute ago, while Wendy and I were setting the table out on the patio in back," said Jillian, two folded white cloth napkins still in her hand. "Wendy heard it, drifted off. I followed, couldn't stop her. She pushed me away and ran. Right inside the place."

The magic book slid out of Bert's hand. "Max, I figured it wouldn't get here for an hour or two."

Max was still sitting on the edge of the bed. "Bring the book and let's go."

"I'm sorry," said Bert. "What page was it again? I should have taken notes while you explained."

"Page 112." Max stood and walked out of the room.

Bert caught up with him in the hallway. "Are ghosts really that perceptive, Max? Would they absolutely know it wasn't me if you went in?"

"Yes." Max and Bert went out the front door, across the sun deck and down the steps. The Strawhouse Pavilion was sharp and clear, the band was playing *In The Mood*.

"I'll mess it up," said Bert. "Read it backwards."

Max said, "No, you won't. You'll go in and get Wendy out and do what you have to do and end this. Right?"

Bert said, "Okay." He left the real grass, hesitated just onto the gravel, then walked to the flashing pavilion and up the wide wood staircase and in.

Jillian joined Max, took his hand. "What do you think?"

"Watch," he said.

The band finished the tune and there was applause. They

went into *Sophisticated Lady*. The number was almost finished when the Strawhouse Pavilion exploded. It flashed
bright, expanded and was suddenly gone. The cars, the
parking lot, the sounds, the past. All were gone and Bert
and Wendy were in the field of dark grass. The sky was night-
clear and you noticed stars again.

Bert and Wendy walked to Max and Jillian. "Wasn't too
hard," Bert told them. He was shaking his head, half smiling.

Wendy said quietly, "I wonder if my father was always like
that. He didn't seem very much like I remember. Just a
middle-aged man, trying so hard to impress everyone." She
waved a hand at where the pavilion had stood, not turning.
"He willed all that, he said, kept it coming back. He was the
ghost and the rest of it he willed somehow. To impress me, to
have me see him at his best. I don't quite know how he did it.
He wouldn't talk about that, about himself that way. He told
me, 'You wouldn't get it, Wendy.' He always used to say that.
Why did I forget he did? He wanted to impress me. He
couldn't just come back. He had to bring a ballroom." She
stopped, touched Bert. "You handled the situation very well,
Bert."

"Wasn't too hard," he said.

A Bevy of Beasts

DRAGONET

Esther Friesner

*Esther Friesner is without a doubt the queen of comic
fantasy. Just check out her novels* New York by Night
(1986), Here Be Demons *(1988),* Gnome Man's Land
(1991) and Majyk by Accident *(1993) for a few examples.
Or her collections* Ecce Hominid *(1991),* It's Been Fun
(1991) and Up the Wall *(2000). Or her anthologies* Alien
Pregnant by Elvis *(1994) or* Chicks in Chain Mail *(1995)
and its sequels. Of course she doesn't just write humorous
stuff. But it's all fun. Try* Druid's Blood *(1988) or*
Yesterday We Saw Mermaids *(1991) for alternate views
of our history. I'm delighted to be able to include two stories
by her in this anthology. Here's a short piece to serve as an
entrée to the much longer one later on.*

This is the castle – Righteous Garde. Here over eight hundred
knights, ladies, lackeys, squires, toadies, and the odd monarch
live and work together in peace and harmony. Only sometimes
harmony's too much to ask. That's where I come in. My
name's Britomart. I'm a damsel. It's a dirty job, but someone's
got to do it.

AD 839. The Dark Ages were well under way, and most of
the ladies were counting the months until the Norsemen
showed up to carry them off. I was catching up on my tapestry

work. Just then, Helios came in. He's my partner. He's a unicorn.

"How's your latest maiden, Helios?" I asked.

"Eaten. Dragon."

"Sorry."

"Those are the breaks."

Helios is a good unicorn. You don't get many like him these days. I could see something was on his mind. "Spill it."

"We've got a 403."

I couldn't believe it. We hadn't had a 403 in years. Rogue mage. "You sure, Helios?"

"I'd stake my horn on it. Got it from a wood elf."

"Wood elves lie."

"Not this one. Mage changed him into a squirrel from the waist down. Hard to argue with that."

I put down the tapestry frame. "Let's investigate. We'll use the black-and-white."

I was proud of the black-and-white. Not many castles had one. Not many would. It was a bear. Not your ordinary bear, but a foreign model, imported all the way from the mountains of Cathay. "You have to move with the times, Britomart," the king had told me. "It doesn't pay to keep local bears any more. They put away too much food, then they're out of service for most of the winter."

We found the black-and-white in his stall, eating bamboo. He got up when he saw me and bowed. "Does Lady Britomart have use for this unworthy bear?" Can't beat these imports when it comes to style.

"We've got a 403."

"Rogue mage," Helios said for the bear's benefit. By the way, his name's Ch'a. It's a weird name, but someone's got to have it.

We hitched up Ch'a to the panda-wagon and headed for the Forest Perilous. Hard to believe that Righteous Garde, with all its beauty and intrigue, is less than a basilisk's spit from the Forest Perilous. It's a tough place. You've got your elves. You've got your moss-wives. You've got your wyverns and your sometime-trolls. When they can't make it in the big epics, they head for the woods. They're young, they're failed, and they're bitter. It doesn't pay to go there unless you're looking for distress. But distress is my business. Like I said, I'm a damsel.

Helios took us straight to the elf. If he'd been changed into a squirrel from the waist down, he'd also been changed into a squirrel from the neck up, years ago. Inside, I mean. That's the trouble with these wood elves. Wood alcohol. His tiny little eyes were so bloodshot, they looked like a pair of juniper berries.

"Lee' me 'lone," he mumbled. He wiped his slobbering mouth with the tip of his furry grey tail.

"Sober up, point-ear." Helios is tough. Tough, but fair. "We're here to help you."

"Huh! Castle folk! When you ever help us elves, huh? Ge' one look at one of us inside your damn' castle and call the 'sterminators." He belched loudly and sang something quaint. Quaint, but obscene.

"You get in the castle, you spend your time looking up the ladies' skirts, short stuff," said Helios. "You don't want this horn somewhere vital, you'll cooperate. This is the damsel Britomart. Tell her what you told me."

"Damsel?" The elf gave me a canny look.

"That's what it says on my card."

"If you're a damsel, I'm a—"

"Watch it!" Helios threatened the elf with one sharp hoof.

"Yah! Real brave, ain'tcha? When it's the little people you're stepping on. But wait until you hit that wizard, horn head! He'll turn you into unicorn on the cob and have you for lunch."

"What wizard?" I asked.

" 'What wizard?' she asks! Sure, I *always* run around this cockamamie forest with a craving for acorns! 'What wizard?' " The elf was ticked. Ticked elves aren't a pretty sight.

"Just the facts, elf."

"Oh, a tough honey. OK, you think you're tough, you go

down this path, turn left at the well of lost souls, double around the swamp of the hanging men, two grave-mounds on your right, and when a dragon eats you, you're there."

A real class neighbourhood.

"This wizard have a name?"

"Mildred." Like I said, ticked elves aren't your Mr Nice Guy.

The black-and-white got us there fast. I had to unhitch him from the wagon when we hit the swamp, though. Too boggy for wheels. No one said this was going to be an easy job. The dragon was waiting. He guarded the wizard's lair. He was big, but you learn fast that size isn't everything in this kingdom. He let out a roar when he saw us. It didn't faze Helios.

"Go ahead, worm," he said. "Make my day." The dragon charged. Helios slew him. He made a minor earth tremor when he hit the ground. The wizard came out of his den to see what was up.

"What have you done to Mildred?" He was one angry mage.

"Dragon gets out of line, dragon takes what's coming. Those are the breaks," I said. "We're here to investigate a complaint. You turn an elf into a squirrel?"

"Half a squirrel."

"You admit it. Why'd you do it?"

The wizard stroked his beard. I didn't like the way he looked at me. "Who wants to know?"

"If he doesn't like the report I bring back, maybe the king wants to know. Turning elves into squirrels is a felony. Turn him back, and maybe we can settle out of the royal court. Don't make it tough on yourself."

"Half a felony."

"A wise guy." Helios has a good sneer, for a 'corn. He lowered his horn at the wizard's chest. "OK, smart man. This is a forty-four spell unicorn's horn, the most powerful piece of *mana* known to sorcery. Now I can't exactly remember whether I've used forty-four of the annihilation spells in it, or only forty-three, so if you don't answer the damsel Britomart's questions real polite, maybe you can ask yourself, 'Am I feeling *lucky* today?' "

"You don't scare me," said the mage. He disappeared.

"Where'd he go?" Helios was baffled.

"Respectfully beg to point out presence of second large dragon," said Ch'a. This time, it was a fire-breather. This time, Helios was the one whose luck ran out.

The dragon grabbed me. Ch'a hid. Helios smouldered. He'd been a good unicorn. I was sorry to see him go. But right now I had other problems.

"That elf was small potatoes, sugar," the dragon said. "I'm taking over this kingdom."

"It's a fool's game and you know it, mage. Give yourself up. The king'll be lenient."

"The king will be *dead*! The whole kingdom will die, unless it submits to me!"

"Big talk. You two-bit thaumaturges think that just because you can take the hicks on market day with the old shell game, you can take the kingdom. I've seen your kind come and go. Mostly they go. And it's not a pretty sight when they do."

The dragon laughed. He was big, all right, big and golden, but he still had the mage's eyes. I didn't like them. "It won't be a pretty sight, my dear? Then you should be happy you won't be around to see it! Say your prayers, damsel, for you shall be the first to perish!"

"No prayers. Just let me say goodbye to the bear."

"Bear? What bear?"

Ch'a emerged timorously from the underbrush. "If the august and majestic dragon-king would not find it too great an inconvenience, this unworthy bear would be most grateful for the opportunity to bid his beloved Lady Britomart farewell."

"A touching last request. Granted." The dragon-mage set me down, but kept one paw on the hem of my dress.

"So long, Ch'a," I said. "Sometimes this business gets away from you. But you have to take the good with the bad."

"This humble bear is distressed beyond words," said Ch'a. He was crying.

"Don't cry," I said. "You'll serve other damsels. You've been a good partner. Go back to the castle." He turned to go. "Hey!" He stopped. I gave him a kiss for luck. "You be careful out there."

The black-and-white skin slipped off in my hands. A big man in strictly non-reg armour – black-and-white lacquerwork – stood in front of me. He pulled a sword and leaped at the dragon-mage. The dragon-mage laughed. Then his head fell off. Those are the breaks.

I made my report to the king. Things were back to normal in the forest. The squirrel-elf was disenchanted. Who isn't, these days? We'd need a new unicorn and maybe a new bear to pull the wagon. Ch'a introduced himself. He was a warrior from an island beyond Cathay, turned into a bear by one of those hotshot Eastern wizards. I'd broken the spell with my kiss.

"Good work, Britomart."

"Just doing my job, Sire."

I married Ch'a. You can't stay a damsel for ever. You can try, but it's a fool's game.

There are eight million stories in the Forest Perilous. This has been one of them.

THE DIPLODOCUS

Porter Emerson Browne

I like to take the opportunity when I can to reprint lesser-known stories, especially if they demonstrate that comic fantasy isn't new and has been with us a good long time. I found reference to this story in Everett Bleiler's incredible book Science Fiction: The Early Years, *and I am extremely grateful to Denny Lien, reference librarian at the University of Minnesota, who tracked it down for me from the long-ignored pages of* The New Broadway Magazine *of 1908. I was pleased to find it was every bit as amusing as it sounded, and surprisingly modern in tone. Porter Browne (1879–1934) was a popular American humorist of his day, best known for his work for the theatre, especially* A Fool There Was *(1909).*

HE looked up from his paper.

"This Burbank guy," he said, "is sure a wonder, ain't he?"

I nodded.

"I suppose before long he'll be grafting corn onto beans and getting succotash," he continued, speculatively. "And then he'll fix apple trees so's they'll bear pertaters, thereby saving all the trouble of digging 'em."

"I shouldn't be at all surprised," I assented. "The wonders that science each day unfolds are almost unbelievable."

He nodded profoundly at my very trite remark.

"Yes," he agreed. "And that same science is folding up a few wonders, too, that we don't never hear nothing about. Take my friend Vertigo Smith, for instance."

"Who was he?" I queried, interestedly.

"You never heard of him?" responded my vis-à-vis; as one who asks a question, knowing beforehand the answer.

"No," I replied.

"And you ain't lonesome," he observed. "Lots o' people never heard of him; and never will. But in his way, he had this Burbank party skinned a league. I'll tell yer about him if yer got time," he volunteered.

I had the time, plenty of it; and I so said. Whereat, taking a long draught from the glass at his elbow, and wiping his trailing moustache on the back of his hand, he began:

"Back in ninety-nine I was prospecting around through Californy, looking for gold but finding nothing but sore feet and a thirst. Fate was sure handing me out a deal from the bottom of the deck, and I was redooced at length to one burrer, loaded with a shovel, and the habiliments I was standing in. I retained said shovel and raiments only because I couldn't sell 'em and said burrer only because I couldn't give him away.

"Well, one afternoon I'm tramping along with despair in my heart and even less in my stomach, wondering weakly whether there's enough meat on the burrer to pay for mending the teeth I'm liable to break picking it off, when suddenly I comes to a turn in the trail and there before me spreads a vegetationous valley full of the most fullsome verdure that ever you see.

"In the middle of this valley there stands a 'dobe mansion and all around it the most amazing collection of sheds and shacks that ever you laid your lamps on. They was some high ones and some low ones and some long ones and some short ones. And what with the house, they all looks like a big Buff Cochin hen surrounded by a bunch of the most ill-assorted chickens that ever was.

"However, I ain't hypercritical. 'Where there's life, there's beans,' says I to myself. 'And if a party desire to deface the beauteous visage of Nature by sticking around on it a lot of five-and-ten-cent-store edifices, it ain't none of my funeral as long's I can get a handout. Git up, there, Gehenna,' says I to the burrer; and we prepares to teeter down into the aforesaid verdant valley.

"Halfway down the hill there's another bend in the trail. And as we comes around this, I stops short while the burrer does even better – for he turns a back somersault; and then sets there on the shovel too frightened to bat an eye.

"The one glimpse I has is plenty sufficient. I stands back to trying to make my convolutions convolute.

" 'I've heard about hunger bringing on hallucinations in a gent,' I thinks to myself, 'but never in a burrer. So maybe he sees all them delusions as well as me.'

"This thought gives me hope, and sufficient courage to look again; which I does.

"Before me, meandering saloobriously across the plain, is the worst looking collection of fauna that ever made merry in an Inebriates' Home. It was sure a psychopathic ward assemblage, and then some. Four-footed things with wings, and two-footed ones without, and birds with hair on 'em, and fishes with laigs – great suffering Jemima! It was sure enough to make a party pin blue ribbons on himself until he couldn't see out, and take up his residence permanent in the cellar of the headquarters of the WCTU.

"With my eyes bugged out so's you could 'a' knocked 'em off with a stick, I watched the procession out of sight and then turned to the burrer. He was setting there with a faraway look in his eyes, talking to himself.

" 'Come on, Gehenna,' says I, nudging him gently with my shoe spikes. 'Le's get a move on ourselves toward yon villa and put an end to this debauch of starvation that we've been on; for if we're seeing things like that today, tomorrow will behold us making suicide pacts and picking mud turtles out of each other's hair."

"Poor Gehenna has all he can do to get up on his pins, and we're a very shaky pair as we wends our way onward to the

Edison concrete villa aforementioned which looked as though it had been made in an ice cream mould and poured out before it had time to set properly.

"As we nears the colony of joovenile houses that I have before alooded to, I sees that they're all coops and cages of different kinds. Some of 'em has barred winders, some of 'em hasn't. Some of 'em's empty. Some of 'em's full. But I keeps my eyes resolutely to the fore; for I ain't takin' no chances. When a party has set on the edge of his bed for weeks at a time, throwing his boots at a blue jellyfish with pink wings and a plug hat, he learns that curiosity is a curse and he don't pay no attention to no zoölogical exotic until it trips him up. But the burrer, being denied the valyooable data that is mine, immediately begins to rubber like an up-Stater in a sightseeing truck with the result that he becomes so obsessed with terrifying fears that his laigs won't work, and I has to carry him the rest of the way. And as we comes around the corner, we sees, setting before the door, an old man teaching a large hornpout to set up on its hind laigs and beg.

"After focusing my already bugged eyes on this new spectacle, I begins to wonder if Gehenna himself is trooly reel. So I kicks him; and when he kicks me back, and I find it hurts, I'm delighted beyond words.

"So I smiles on the old party with deep sympathy and fellerfeeling.

"'That's right,' I says, encouragingly. 'Humour yerself. When you get 'em as bad as that, it ain't a particle of use to try to kill 'em. So jest set down and have a good time with 'em and byme-bye they'll go away.'

"'What's the matter with you?' asks the old man, sort o' peevish-like.

"'I don't know,' I says to the old party, 'whether it's stomachache or backache that's ailing me. All I can tell yer is that I ain't tasted food for so long that I've forgot even the smell of onions.'

"'Lie down, Lucy,' says the old man to the hornpout; and as the last named settles down comfortable with its head between its fore paws, the old party climbs up onto his feet. 'Come on in the house,' he says, 'an' I'll see 'f I can get a snack for yer.'

"Taking Gehenna under my arm for company, I follers him into the house.

"The old man watches me thoughtfully as I loads into my shrunken frame four dollars' worth of pork and beans and biscuits.

" 'I hopes my pets ain't frightened you,' he says, at len'th, apologetically, combing his whiskers with his fingers.

" 'Oh, not at all,' I rejoins, p'litely. 'I've had 'em myself, several times. They're unpleasant, but not necessarily dangerous. And if you'll swear off gradually, say cutting down half a pint a day at first, and then slowly increasing the stringency, it's surprising how quick you'll get rid of 'em.'

"He brushes my well-meant suggestions aside with an impatient wave of the hand and, stooping over, takes from the floor a long, bloo snake with green wings and three sets of laigs.

" 'Do you see this?' he says.

" 'Yes,' I replies. 'And I may as well confess that it's the first time I ever knowed delirium trimmings was contagious.'

" 'Feel of it,' he says. 'It won't hurt you.'

"I grins.

" 'I know it,' I says, 'and good reason why. It ain't there. I wore out three pairs of shoes and put my shoulder out of joint on two separate occasions finding out that simple fact.'

" 'Try,' he says, shoving the snake at me.

" 'Why, sure,' I says, 'if it'll please yer any.'

"I puts my hand out, confidently expecting it to go right through the snake and flat on the table. But it don't. And I gives a yell that sends Gehenna scuttling under the stove and falls plumb over backward in my chair.

" 'Easy,' says the old party. 'They ain't no danger.'

" 'Ain't, eh!' I says, a trifle peevishly, I fear, 'I know that well enough. But it's the strain on yer credulousness that I objects to,' and I goes back three steps to get a flying start.

" 'Well, set down and have a piece of prune pie,' he says.

"Jest at that juncshure, for a piece o' pie, prune or otherwise, I'd have set down in the middle of a school of gryphons and gargoyles and been glad of the chance. So I done it. And the old party, after slicing me out a wedge of the succulent provender aforesaid, sets down opposite me again.

" 'I,' he says, at len'th, impressively, puttin' down the snake and taking out of his vest pocket a creation that looked like a smallpox microbe magnified one million times, 'am Vertigo Smith.'

" 'I don't wonder,' I says. 'Was the name bestowed or acquired?'

" 'It was give me by my payrents,' he rejoins, 'who was well-intentioned parties, but sadly illiterate. They seen it in a almanac and, thinkin' it sounded good, they gives it to me.'

"He continues:

" 'I,' he says, 'am a second Burbank. Or ruther, I should say, Burbank is a second me. For he deals with senseless and inanimate things like flowers and trees and froot and cord wood and such futile and contemptible inyootilities, while I devote my tireless energies and unlimitless genius to the animile kingdom. Them,' and he waves his hand blithely at the snake and the smallpox germ, 'are some of my eggsperiments. This,' he goes on, patting the microbe gently, 'is the result of mixing the life blood of the scorpion with that of the cockroach, and again crossing the combination with the tarantula. I eggs-pect in time to be able to instil into this lovely little creature the instinc's and flesh of the sloothhound and finally of my cultivated rhinoceros, passing on my way through the lion, the tiger, the leopard, the grizzly bear, the rattlesnake, the Gila monster, and the panther.'

" 'That'll make a fine pet when you get it finished, won't it?' I queries. 'It'll be a nice thing to replace lapdogs with.'

"He ignores my untimely facetiousness.

" 'It will add greatly to zoölogy,' he asserts.

" 'And subtract greatly from anthropology,' I suggests.

" 'And it'll make a fine watch dog,' he says.

"'You're right,' I agrees. 'The burglar will immediately begin to hump the dodo for first place, and that's no lie.'

"'Among my other interesting eggsperiments,' he goes on, 'was crossing a cat with a mouse. But this wasn't entirely successful, being as when the resultant animile grew old enough to find out what it was, it chased itself to death.

"'I have also,' he goes on, 'intermingled the blood of the horse and the ostrich, thereby securing a maximum of speed with a minimum of weight; and I found that the feathers that you could get off'n the horse would pay for his keep; whereby I got Edison's newly discovered storage battery, that has been coming out sence I was a boy, beaten eighty ways for Christmas.

"'Also, by weaving my way around through the species of Gordon setter, cow, and giraffe, I have obtained a animile meek, intelligent, that gives milk, that will do simple little errands like fetching you yer gloves and shutting the door, and that as well can be used to double advantage in the cherry-picking season.'

"'If you could get a hen and a egg beater in that combination somewheres,' I ventures, helpfully, for I'm getting a heap imbued with his ideas by this time, 'and hang a bottle of good Four X around its neck, all you'd have to do would be to whistle and it would bring you an eggnog any time you was thirsty!'

"He ignores me. 'At present,' he says, 'I am much interested in parasites. A parasite is a zoölogical antidote. Cats is parasites for mice. Dogs is parasites for cats.'

"'I see!' I eggsclaims. 'Jest like drunkards is parasites for whisky, and panics is parasites for money.'

"'That's the idea,' he approves, 'except that you must stick to the fauna. Now,' he goes on, 'take mosquitoes for eggsample. You live, say, in Noo Jersey, or Pelham Manor, or some other badly infested State. Every time you go out on the piazza after four o'clock, you're kep' so busy slapping your laigs and neck that you can't converse in anything eggscept profanity. Now jest imagine what a wonderful, priceless relief it would be if you could have, say, half a dozen mosquitoe parasites to set around on the back of your chair, or along the welts of your shoes, and nail the mosquitoes as fast as they come! And then, when bedtime had arrived, they'd set on your piller beside your head and pop every dad-blamed stygomia that tried to tap a blood vessel.'

" 'Fine!' I agreed. 'Immense!'

" 'I think so,' he acquiesced, complacently. 'We can afford to sell 'em for a quarter a piece. They'll be self-supporting in summer and will hibernate all winter among your summer clo'es, keepin' the moths out of 'em and living on a small quantity of camphor.'

" 'It sounds fine,' I says. 'It sure does!'

" 'It *is* fine,' he says. 'But there's more money in big things. And the biggest thing of all is the diplodocus.'

" 'The what?' says I.

" 'The diplodocus,' he says. 'It's reptile,' he says, 'or a mammal, or a fish, or a bird, or something like that. I don't know what it is. But I'm going to find out or bust a suspender trying. Andrew Carnegie bought the skeleton of one the other day for twenty thousand, or fifty thousand, dollars 'r something like that. And if the skeleton is worth that much, the finished product ought to be worth a million. So,' he announced, impressively, 'I'm going to raise a herd of 'em for the home and eggsport trade. I figure that when I get 'em to multiplying right, I'll have a income of at least twenty or thirty million per annually. I'll work slow and secret at first, selling stuffed ones to the natural hist'ry mooseums. Then I'll branch out, taking in zoological gardens and circus menageries. And after they get all supplied, I can sell 'em for domestic animals. They'd be fine for moving houses or towing canal boats.'

"Well, to stretch a short story, the old gent took a great fancy to me; and I did to him. So when he offered me a job helping him with the speciments, I took it and settled down with him in the poured-out villa. And though I was nervous at first, it wasn't long before I got use' to it and didn't mind it no more'n if I'd always lived in a psychopathic ward. And

Gehenna he used to have good times, too, playing with the horsetriches and the kangaroosters.

"There was a lot of animales there that I hadn't seen. He kep' 'em in an immense corral, around the corner of the mountain. There was some elephants he was makin' over into mastodons and mammoths and behemoths and things, and a two-laigged rhinoceros that was as big as from here to yonder and back.

"We used some of this fancy stock to start our diplodocus with. We had one biped that was worked up through a penguin to a hippotamus that was a peach. And another creation that was composed of kangaroos, whales, and emus. And so on, by arduous, unreemitting, painstaking effort we began to get results, and after several years there came one day something that looked a whole lot like the desired fauna.

"When it got big enough to balance itself with having its head and tail resting on the ground, we stood around one day looking at it.

" 'There something wrong,' remarked old Smith, loogoobriously. 'It looks more like a cuspidor than a diplodocus. What's ailin', d'yer s'pose?'

" 'You can search me,' I says. 'It looks as though it had lost its last friend, and that friend owin' it money. I don't b'lieve it's got enough initiative to bite if you was to stick your finger in its mouth and make faces at it.'

"Old Smith brought his hand down on his knee so hard he like to split the cap.

" 'You've hit it,' he eggsclaimed. 'It's too mushy and meek and lowly and humble looking. All them things we bred it through was soft and lumpy animiles, like cows and hippotamuses and things. It wants a little bit o' fervor injected into it – some stamina and gumption, by heck. We should 'a' mixed in the rhinoceros and the rogue elephant. That would straighten it up and stiffen it out and make it a diplodocus and a diplodocus right!'

" 'That's so,' I agrees. 'We'll insert the requisite blood and sperit. This present disapp'inting speciment, though, will help us increase the stature.'

"Well, that was what we done. We got the old rogue elephant that was that cantankerous that he had to be handled with a derrick and dynamite, and the rhinoceros who was a natural-born misanthrope and a fighter from the word go, and 'way behind that, and proceeded to go back along the fambly tree of our diplodocus and grafted them on at what we deemed suitable intervals.

"You can magine we was some eggscited as we waited. Our first diplodocus wasn't no slouch. We'd had to build a special barn for it that was as big as the main tent of a three-ringed circus; it would take you ten minutes to walk around it and the longest ladder in the place wasn't long enough to reach to its ridgepole. So you can imagine that our second was going to be some pumpkins. Old Smith had it all framed up that he wouldn't let him go for a cent under half a million; and then only after he had a large fambly of descendants strewed over the valley.

"Well, he was right. That second diplodocus equaled, and even eggsceeded, our fondest hopes. He was so big that his skeleton would have made the one Carnegie bought look like an X-ray photograph of a dress form. It sure towered above its maternal ancestor like the Singer Building above the subway.

"To say that Vertigo and me was delighted is expressing it feebly. We was in transports of joy. Ecstatic happiness oozed out of us at every pore, and between, and all that morning we just took a hold of hands and danced around our new diplodocus. It was like playing Ring-Around-a-Rosy in a department store.

"Day by day we watched our creation grow and expand, both physically and mentally. Them big animiles, as a rule, are slow in machuring. But this one was right up to the speed limit. In less'n a week he could stand alone. He was weaned at three months. And after that it kep' me and Vertigo busy fourteen hours a day rustling enough provender to keep them two diplodocuses from starving to death.

"Le' me tell yer, it was some kind of a parlous job, was feeding them exotics. They had some dog in them somewhere, and from that the new one had a habit of wagging his tail; the old one was too puny. And Rover (we'd named the new one that) smashed the end of the house off one afternoon, in showing his gratitude for a couple of bales of hay we'd give him. Another day he knocked down three o' them giant redwoods and an orange tree. We found some o' the oranges four mile down the valley.

"Well, everything went along all right for about six months. Me and Vertigo was as happy as kittens under a stove and Rover was thriving to beat three of a kind. Not a cloud was upon our horizons. We dwelt in the soft sunshine of sweet content and wouldn't have swapped places with the Czar of all the Rooshias and some of the Rooshians.

"That's always the way, I've noticed. It's always serene just before something's doo to be handed to you in the place where it will hurt the worst. Whenever things is going along on castors, and you're liking yourself particularly well, and feeling particularly good, and beginning to believe that the Golden Rule might possibly not be a fake after all, you're doo for a bump.

"We got ours. It come in the night. It usually does.

"I had just rolled over on the other side and was getting nicely started away on the second lap of the Morpheus handicap, when I heard a noise that sounded like the end of the world.

"I come out of it, and fetched Vertigo a kick.

"'You're on your back,' I hollered in his ear.

"But then the noise come again; and I knowed I was wrong. And additional proof come in another minute; for the house was yanked right off from over me and I was gazing up into the starry heavens and wondering what had happened.

"And then it burst forth in all its fury. The air was filled with wild, discordant yells and yowls. The redwood trees was falling like grain before the patent reaper; and our D. T. menagerie could be heard in a little concerted specialty that sounded, however, feeble and unimpressive in comparison to the main noise.

"It come to me in a flash. It was Rover! We had injected too much elephant and rhinoceros! Our impetuousness had made us incautious. Alas! How true it is that careless work carries its own penalties.

"I lay there in the Californy midnight and my union suit thinking over these things when, all of a sudden, the diplodocus, who had just finished filling the middle distance with the contents of our coop of jackassowaries, got his lamps on me.

"Giving a wild shake of his head, and emitting a horrid snort, he threw the last jackassowary straight up at Cassyopeer's chair and charged at me.

"It took me less'n a fraction of a split second to leave the woven wire. Vertigo was already standing in the middle of what had once been the room, combing his whiskers with a shoe and staring helplessly about.

"'The horsetriches!' I yelled at him, as I flew past.

"A word to the wise, you know; and he was wise, all right, and getting wiser every minute.

"The barnyard was a sight. Rover had done a clean job. There was jest one horsetrich left out of all the strange creations of Vertigo's great genius. Even the diplodocus old lady was a contribution to the festival.

"I grabbed the horsetrich by one wing, and Vertigo he grabbed the other. We swung ourselves upon his back, me in front, and stuck our heels into its sides. It responded nobly to our encouragements and slid off down the valley at a rate of speed that would have had the Empire State Express looking like a traction engine.

"But did we lose the diplodocus? Never on your immortal life! He hadn't missed our steed's tail feathers by a foot when we started forth from the barnyard. As we passed what had once been our happy home, he was spreading himself for further orders, emitting the most blood-chilling yelps at every leap; and every third jump his kangaroo blood would assert itself and he'd slam his tail down on the ground, give himself a push, and hurtle through the air for a good ninety foot.

"The memory of that ride is with me yet, particularly after a bedtime snack of pigs' feet and ice cream, or mince pie and Welch rarebit. Often, in the still watches, I awaken the house with weird yells and the affrighted boarders come running to my room to find me astride of the radiator, urging it on to frantic endeavor, while the cold sweat runs down my pallid, somnambulistic visage in streams, by heck!

"As we flashed past the end of the valley, I could hear those frightful yowls coming nearer and nearer. I dared not look around. We were covering the ground at a rate of at least three miles per minute, and it required all my skill to keep my place.

"I clutched our faithful horsetrich around the neck. On we raced, and on, and on . . . I heard a shrill yell in my ear. Vertigo's hand suddenly slipped from the waistband of my union suit. Our steed (ours no longer, alas, but now mine alone) pressed on more swiftly; and I knew that Vertigo was gone. Poor Vertigo! . . . Poor, poor Vertigo! He come down three days later in San Antonio, Texas, and broke up one of the most successful revival services they'd ever had there . . .

"Another fifty or seventy-five miles, and I felt, rather than heard, the diplodocus again at our heels. I stole a hurried glance over my shoulder. Yes, there he was, his bared, glistening teeth not a yard away, his little eyes flashing venomously. He made a swipe for me – and missed. Another – and suddenly my poor horsetrich was yanked out from under me and I was going on alone, through the air.

"I lit in a small but well-ventilated hole in the ground that turned out to be the other end of the Mammoth Cave. It was too small for the diplodocus to enter. That is the only thing that saved my life.

"For three weeks I subsisted on fish. They were blind, and a cinch to catch; though much harder to eat. And at length I was found by a guide who was taking a party of school-teachers from Beebe, Indiana, through the simplest ramifications of the wonderful burrow. I was delirious, they told me, and sadly emaciated; and when they discovers me, I'm setting on a stalagmite, with a blind tadpole in each hand, singing, in feeble accents. However, I know nothing of all that myself; for I was out of my head for weeks."

He ceased.

"But did you never go back?" I queried.

He eyed me with squelching scorn.

"Did I ever go back!" he repeated. "Did I ever go back!" And then, "Say, what do yer take me for, anyhow, hay?"

I didn't answer his question. It would not have been polite. And, besides, he was much bigger than I.

NOTHING IN THE RULES

Nelson Bond

Nelson Bond has had a writing career stretching back over sixty years, since his first sales in 1935. He soon made a name for himself as a writer of weird and wacky fantasies, his first success coming with "Mr Mergenthwirker's Lobblies" in Scribner's *in 1937, which formed the title story for his first collection in 1946. He sold over two hundred stories during the next twenty years but when his main market,* Blue Book, *shifted away from light fiction, Bond turned to his other interests as a bookdealer and expert on philately. Several of his stories were collected as* The Thirty-First of February *(1949),* No Time Like the Future *(1954) and* Nightmares and Daydreams *(1968). Among his stories for* Blue Book *were a series of tall tales narrated by "Squaredeal Sam". For some reason the following story, the second in the series, has never been reprinted, so here's a chance to savour another rare treat.*

"Until next spring," said "Squaredeal Sam" McGhee, "or August at the latest. It ain't like I was astin' you to *give* me the money. It's just a loan, on an investment as sound as the Rock o' Prudential, so to speak—" He eyed me with hope.

I frowned at him severely. "And just why," I asked, "do you need three hundred dollars?"

"Well," said Squaredeal Sam, "it's a long story—" His gaze wandered to the box of cigars on my desk. I nodded; he took one, and lighting it, he leaned back, exuding wreaths of Havana fragrance.

Like maybe I sometime told you (Sam began), I'm the original hard-luck kid. Everything happens to me – most of it bad. For instance, just atter I signed a contract with Marty Kildare, the smoothest light heavy which ever flang leather in a squared circle, along come Pearl Harbor, an' Marty switched over to *another* manager named Sam for the duration.

Course, bein' an honest kid like he is, Marty sends me my right an' legal commission every month, but ten per cent of a private's pay ain't exactly what'll support me in the style to which I'd like to become accustomed.

So, since it looks like the boxfightin' game is all washed up till atter Hitler an' Hirohito is likewise, I began lookin' around for a job in some more essential war industry. The way I figger it, one o' the most essential war industries in these times is the racetrack racket. Guys can't squander their money on frivi-alities like silk shirts an' the etcetera if the bookies got it, an' that prevents inflation. So I ast a few questions an' pulled strings, an' come spring, I was in Florida with the gee-gee circuit.

Well, right off the bat I got a break. I hooked up with this guy name of Tom Akers – the owner of a small stable – which he was reclassified 1-A when his draft-board happened to find out he could see lightnin' an' hear thunder. So he'd been called up, an' he ast would I run his string till he got back. Which I would.

Atter we signed a contract, I seen Akers down to the depot, an' since the train was a couple hours late, I an' him sat around bendin' elbows to wild the time away. First Akers toasted me; then I toasted him, an' *vicey-versy* – an' to make a long story short, by the time the train arrove, we was both pretty well done on both sides. So I poured him into his car an' went back to the stables to have a look at the nags I was now manager of which.

Confidentially, they wasn't the classiest outfit of hay-burners I ever met up with. They looked less like racin' horses than fugitives from a black market.

Readin' from left to right in the stalls, there was Robin Hood, a geldin' with bow legs, a narrow forehead, an' a quiver; a colt named Runningboard, who done the first like he was the second; one named Pitiful, who was; one named Speedy, who wasn't; an' one named Willwin, who wouldn't.

The only likely-lookin' prospect of the bunch was a filly named Princess Sally, a two-year old maiden which Akers hadn't never raced yet on account of she was a bag of nerves. Accordin' to her test runs, she was greased lightnin', but she was scared of startin'-gates. Every time they put her in, she started kickin' like a front-row chorine.

To make matters worse, along with this accumulation of unground round-steaks, I'd inherited an alleged assistant by name of Dumbo, a tow-headed little squirt with oversized ears an' adenoids. He had five thumbs on each hand an' an impediment in his brain. He served as a combination trainer, swipe an' jockey for the Akers colours. Why? Your guess is as good as mine. Maybe the fact that Akers owed him seventeen months' back pay had somethin' to do with it.

He was in Princess Sally's stall, rubbin' her down, when I wandered by. I stared at him for a minute.

"Hi!" I said.

He looked up, noddin' an' flappin' his ears gently.

"'Lo!" he said.

"Jack an' game!" chimed in a voice from the adjoinin' stall. "Down two, doubled an' vulnerable. Wheeee!"

I started. "Who's that?" I ast.

Dumbo shrugged. "Oh, just *him*," he said. "Pretend like you don't hear him, an' he'll shut up. What can I do for you, Mister?"

"The name's McGhee," I told him, "an' I'll tell you atter I've had a look around. I'm your new manager. Your old boss has gone to war."

He gawked at me. "What for?"

"Because he had to. The Government called him up."

"They did?" said Dumbo. "Gee! That must have cost a lot of money, huh?"

"*What* cost a lot of money?"

"A telephone call all the way from Washington."

I glared at him suspiciously. "Now, looky here!" I said. "If you're tryin' to be funny—"

Dumbo wriggled, sort of embarrassed-like. He said: "D-did I say somethin' wrong, Mr McGhee? I'm sorry. Honest, I am. Seems like I'm always sayin' the wrong thing. I guess I better rub down the Princess." An' he started spongin' the filly again. But not for long. That voice from the next-door stall called him.

"Never mind her – come in here an' take care of me! I want my back curried!" The voice lifted in sudden raucous song: "*Curry me back to old Virginny*—"

"Hey!" I demanded. "What is this?"

Dumbo said: "I told you, Mister, he's a pest. Just let on like you don't hear him."

"But who's in there?" I said. "A talkin' horse? It ain't that Egbert Haw I read about in a magazine?"

The ears waggled negatively. "I don't know nothin' about no talkin' horses, Mr McGhee. But he ain't one."

"It's a man, then? But what in blazes is a *man* doin' in a horse's stall?"

"We-e-ell," said Dumbo dubiously, "he ain't exactly a man, neither. He's sort of – well, sort of peculiar."

I strode to the other stall. The door was shut. I opened the top half – an' jumped a yard. Leanin' with folded arms over the lower gate was a glinty-eyed little rascal with a fringe of chin-whiskers an' an impy grin. Or not exactly a grin – a *leer*, more like. An' no wonder. 'Cause as far as I could see, he didn't have a stitch of clothes on!

I yelled: "For cryin' out loud – what makes here?"

"*I* do," said the guy, "when I can. Hyah, chum! So you're the new boss?"

"Who are you?" I hollered. "An' what are you doin' in

there? An' where did you come from? An' for Pete's sake, go get some clothes on!"

"Nestros," smirked the stranger, "waitin' for something to eat, Thessaly, an' don't ask questions so fast. Did you say clothes? Nonsense! Garments are for stupid humans!"

Sayin' which, he swished a long bushy tail into my eyes, turned an' cantered around the stall proudly. I stared at him – an' moaned. He had the body of a man down as far as his floatin' ribs. From there on – he was a *horse!* . . .

An inch of ash tumbled from Sam's cigar to the rug. He said, "*Damn!*" and scrubbed it into the nap. I squinted at him dazedly. "Sam!" I said. "Are you crazy? Are you telling me you met a *Centaur?*"

"Centaur!" said Sam. "*That's* the word. I tried to remember it for weeks, but all I could think of was '*senator.*' . . . An' this guy was a front of a horse, too. Yep, a Centaur. That's what Nestros was."

"B-but," I protested, "centaurs were fabulous monsters who lived in ancient Greece! They don't really exist!"

"This one did," said Sam.

"Nonsense! They were wild woodland creatures, sly and treacherous, given to drink and mad orgies—"

"You're tellin' *me!*" said Sam.

Course I don't blame you (he continued) for not believin' me. It's a cockeyed set-up, I know. But there it is. An' I can prove it, too – I hope.

Naturally, the first thing I done was to holler for Dumbo. He came shufflin' in from the Princess' stall, an' ast me questions with his eyebrows.

I said: "Dumbo, am I in my right mind, or have I got delirious tantrums? Do you see what I see in there – a horse with a man's head?"

"Where?" ast Dumbo, an' looked at Nestros. Then he shrugged. "Oh, you mean *him?* Gosh, you had me excited for a minute. A horse with a man's head—"

"Well, ain't that what he is?"

"Shucks, no!" said Dumbo. "He aint nothin' only a man with a horse's body. I better go now. I got to rub down the Princess."

Nestros leered at him. "Give her my love, bud," he said.

Dumbo scowled. "Never mind that! You just let the Princess alone, that's all. The next time I catch you tryin' to kick down the p'tition between your stalls—"

"Aw, don't be such an old grouch!" said the Centaur sulkily. "It's no skin off your nose if me an' Her Nibs want to fling a little whoa."

"It'll be skin off your hide," said Dumbo grimly.

Nestros snorted. "Great Zeus! You think she wants to be a filly all her life?"

"As far as you're concerned," said Dumbo, "yes! Or you'll be a filly-mignon."

I stared at him. "For gosh sakes, Dumbo," I busted in, "how can you be so calm? Don't you realize we're lookin' at a real, live centaur?"

"I don't care," he sniffed, "if he's an All-America halfback. I'll comb his mane with a cobble if he don't leave the Princess be."

An' he stomped away. Nestros said glumly: "There's a killjoy for you! For two drachmas, I'd kick his ears off!"

"What's the matter?" I ast. "What do you want with the Princess, anyway?"

He grinned. "What do *you* think?"

"If it's companionship," I said, "there's six other horses in this paddock—"

"It's a moot question," said Nestros. "Sex of one, an' half a dozen of the other. Oh, well – this ain't gettin' us nowhere. The question is, when do I start to see a little action around here?"

"Action?" I repeated.

"Don't be a dope!" snorted Nestros. "This here's a racetrack, ain't it?"

"W-why, sure. Of course."

"Well, when do I make with the hoofs? I'm gettin' tired of standin' around here like a stuffed owl."

"You mean you want to *race*?"

"Why not?" he demanded. "For three weeks Akers has been stallin' me; if you do the same, I'm signin' myself up a new boss. So what do you say, chum? Do I run or don't I?"

"What I want to know," I countered, "is can you run or can't you?"

"Can I run!" he snorted. "Can I *run*? Listen, pal, I'm the fastest thing on four legs you ever saw. Why, I gave the Minotaur a ten-mile start an' beat him from East Phrygia to Peiraeus by the Marathon route. I'm Greece lightning. I run faster than a lisle stocking. Ever hear of the 'Trudgin' Horse'? I'm the one who made him look slow. I can outrace, outdrink an' outsmart any equine you ever heard of!"

"An' outbrag," I added, "any I ever heard, period. But okay. If the Commission'll stand for it, I'll play ball. Let's go see the racetrack papas."

An' I took him over to the track office.

Well, what his appearance done to them Florida lads was a caution! He threw them crackers into bedlam. The Head Steward, guy named McClannaghan, took one look at Nestros an' keeled over in a dead faint. The Wet an' Dry platforms split even on the deal: two onlookers signed the pledge, an' another two hit the corn like a hobnailed boot in a crowd.

There'd been eight guys – managers, track officials an' so forth – at the office when me an' Nestros appeared. A minute later there was only two left, the Track Commissioner an' a guy that you've prob'ly heard of – "Thick Nick" Pappalousas, owner-manager of the Vulcan stables an' the shrewdest tin-horn gambler which ever fumbled a form-sheet. The Chief was still with us because his piggies was *peet*rified; Nick was still on deck because his sense of direction was bad. He'd mistook an open closet for the THIS WAY OUT.

Nestros helped me lift Harkrader, the Commissioner, down offen the chandelier. He looked sort of scornful of the human race, which I don't much blame him. Atter Pappalousas' teeth stopped chatterin', I told the Chief what I wanted.

His eyes bugged out of his head.

"What!" he managed. "You want to enter *th-that* – I mean *him* – I mean *that* – in a race?"

"Why not?" I ast him.

"B-but he's not a horse!" said the Commissioner.

"No?" I said. "Then what is he?"

"Why, he's a – a human," said the Chief. "I think. Or, no . . . wait a minute! He's a—"

"He's a myth," broke in Thick Nick. "A myth out of the folklore of my homeland. That's what he is."

"Well, a myth," I told them, "is as good as a miler – especially when he's got four legs, like this one. I want to enter him in a race, an' I mean to. I been studyin' races since I was knee-high to a jockey, an' there's nothin' in the rules against it."

I had him there. The Commissioner leafed through a collection o' rule-books as bulky as an O.P.A. study on paper-conservation, an' he couldn't find no law against me enterin' Nestros in a horse-race. The only ruling which come anywhere close to applyin' was the one which says no six-legged horses or similarly improved models can run, on account of its bein' unfair to standard nags, an' therefore in restraint of trade. When I pointed out that Nestros' forelimbs was arms, an' that they couldn't reach the ground no how, he give in.

"Okay, McGhee," he said hoarsely. "Looks like he's eligible, so long as you pay the entry fee. What race do you want to enter him in?"

"If he's as good as he says he is," I said, "plenty of 'em. But for a starter, I'd like to run him in the Silver Stakes tomorrow."

Thick Nick started.

"Huh!" he said. "What's that? The Silver Stakes?"

"What's the matter?" I grinned at him. "You scared because you had that one figgered in the bag for your colours? Well, you might as well scratch Printer's Ink now, Nick. The race is as good as won. How about it, Nestros?"

Nestros leered up from the divan he was settin' on. "You

said it, chum. I aint goin' to show them punks nothin' but heels. Hey – what's that?" His eyes had suddenly lit on a decanter on the Chief's desk; he rose an' sniffed it eagerly. "Well, bless my withers, if it ain't four-star ambrosia!"

"Look—" I said.

"I ain't had a snort of this," said Nestros, "since I left the Old Country. How about it, Chief?"

He stared at the Commissioner hopefully, but I took the bottle away from him.

"Oh, no, you don't!" I said sternly. "Tomorrow I'll buy you all you want, but right now you're in trainin'. Come on, now. We got places to go an' things to do. See you guys later."

An' we left.

Squaredeal Sam paused, rubbing his chin. "All this talk about likker," he said, "sort o' dries me out around the gills. I don't suppose you'd happen to have—"

"Scotch," I asked him, "or rye? Or gin?"

"I ain't choosy," said Sam. "Just mix 'em." When he had finished four raw fingers in a gulp, he sighed genteel appreciation. "Now, that's what I call good stuff," he said. "Eighteen months old, if it's a day. It ain't often you taste that aged-in-the-wood stock any more. Ambrosia – that's what it is. Necktie an' ambrosia, like Nestros was always talkin' about."

"What – and – ambrosia?" I asked him.

"Necktie. He was a sort of a poetical guy, Nestros was. 'I ain't much on music,' he used to say, 'but firewater an' fillies is my dish. Give me the Princess an' a moonlight night, an' we'll sup necktie an' ambrosia together—'"

"Nectar," I said. "You mean nectar!"

Sam sighed again, sadly. "I'll say he did!" he declared. "But I was just gettin' around to that—"

Well (Sam said), what happened was my own darn' fault. I ought to of knew better than leave that centaur out o' my sight with the big race comin' up the next day. But of course I had preparations to make, like slippin' a few of the rival jockeys a few bucks an' bettin' a few centuries with my bookie pals before word got around how fast Nestros was. An' so I turned the centaur over to Dumbo for safekeepin'.

"Rub him down good," I said. "Give him his supper, an' see that he gets a good night's sleep tonight. Get it?"

"Yessir," said Dumbo. "What'll I do, Mr McGhee – pour ice-water on him?"

"Ice-water!" I yelled. "Are you off your button?"

"You said he was to get a good nice sleet tonight," said Dumbo.

"*Night's sleep*, you nitwit!" I told him. "Not *nice sleet!* He's runnin' in the Silver Stakes tomorrow. He's got to be in tip-top condition. I'll see you in the mornin'."

"Yessir," said Dumbo.

"So long, pal," said Nestros. "Bet your shirt."

Dumbo led him away. The last I seen of them, Nestros was hummin' *I'll See You in My Dreams* as Dumbo led him past Princess Sally's stall, with a good grip on the halter.

The next mornin' I got to the paddock early. An' a good thing, too. I arrove in the nick o' time, just as Dumbo come bustin' out o' the enclosure like a whirlwind with ears. He bumped into me, an' I grabbed him.

"Hey!" I yelled. "What's the matter?"

"Lemme go!" he howled. "Gimme a gun – a knife – an ax! Let me at him!

"Who?" I demanded, shakin' him. "What's wrong?"

"Wrong?" he sobbed. "Nothin' except that that darn' centaur got into the Princess' stall last night. Wait till I get my hands on him, the low-down—"

"Take it easy!" I soothed him. "You must be wrong. Everything seems to be okay. Come on, let's have a look."

But it was me that was mistook, not him. We walked over to Nestros' stall, an the closer we got, the stronger we smelled the aroma of alcohol. I flang open the top door, an' there sprawled the centaur, tight as a starlet's sweater, one mitt clenchin' an empty bottle. Half asleep, in a triumphant mumble he was croonin', "*Oh, the ol' grey mare, she ain' what she used to be—*"

"I'll murder him!" bawled Dumbo. "I'll chop him up into point rations—"

"You'll do nothin' of the sort!" I told him. "This drunken sot may be a heel without a soul, but he's our chance to get rich. I've bet every cent I own an' a few I don't own, on his winnin' today. How did this happen, anyway? How come he got out of his stall?"

"How should I know?" ast Dumbo.

"Well, you was here, wasn't you?"

"Not atter you sent word I was to go home."

I stared at him. "Me? I sent word? Who said so?"

"Thick Nick. He come down about twelve o'clock an' told me you said I was to go home an' sleep—"

"Thick Nick!" I repeated, understandin' everything now. "That dirty crook! He knew Nestros would run the pants offen his Printer's Ink, so he framed this. Well, we'll learn him! Come on! We got to get Nestros sobered up so he can run!"

Well, we done it. Don't ast me how. We worked out on that refugee from a sideshow with Epsom salts an' ice-water an' steam-baths till he was seepin' alky like a still.

By ten o'clock we had him standin' up without help; by noon he could walk a reasonably straight line; an' by two-thirty he was feelin' good enough to trot around the paddock. He had a terrific hangover, o' course, but that was to be expected. He was meeker than I ever seen him.

"I'm sorry, McGhee," he said. "I only meant to get a little edge on. But it's been so long since I had a snootful—" He shook his head ruefully. "Who was that guy gave me the ambrosia?" he ast.

"Thick Nick, the Greek," I told him. "He's entered a horse in the Stakes, too. He wants you out of it."

He nodded. "I might have knew there was a catch in it," he said. "Timmy O'Daniels, doughnuts forever—"

"Excuse me a minute, Sam," I interrupted. "Are you sure that's what he said?"

"Well, somethin' like that," said Sam.

"Are you sure he didn't say: '*Timeo Danaos et donœ fer-entes*'?" I asked. "That means, '*Beware the Greeks bearing gifts.*'"

"Could be," said Sam . . . Well, anyhow (continued Sam), the Silver Stakes was scheduled fourth on the ticket – around four-thirty that would be. One thing I'll say for Nestros: he had good recup'rative powers. By four o'clock he was fit as a fiddle an' ready for anything. I sent Dumbo on up to the tack-room to get dressed in his silks – he was our jockey, you know – while I saddled Nestros an' give him last-minute instructions.

I was just tightenin' the final cinch when into the paddock come Commissioner Harkrader an' Thick Nick. Nick was grinnin' like a cat in a creamery, but his smirk curdled when he seen Nestros. The Commissioner looked puzzled too.

He said, "I – er – there seems to be some misunderstanding, McGhee. Nick led me to believe you were scratching your entry."

"Unless he develops hives between now an' the post-time," I said, "Nick's wrong. Nestros is runnin', Chief."

Nick moaned, "I – I don't understand it! He was as stiff as a boiled shirt—"

Nestros chuckled. "A mere truffle, chum," he said. "Drop around tonight, an' we'll split another keg – on me, this time."

Harkrader turned to Nick. "Well, Pappalousas – you were wrong. Apparently this – er – horse is quite capable of run-ning, and eligible too. I'm afraid there is nothing more we can do to stop him."

"No," said Thick Nick. "I guess not—" He paused sud-denly, his eyes lightin' on Nestros' hoofs. "Hey! Wait a minute!" he yelled. "There *is* somethin' else! This horse *is* ineligible!"

"Why?" demanded me an' Harkrader together.

"Because," pointed Nick, "he aint shod! Accordin' to the rules of horse-racin', no horse can enter a race which aint properly equipped with horseshoes! He ain't got none!"

I took a quick look. The Greek was right. Nestros didn't have nothin' on his pedals but grass-stains.

I groaned. Nestros looked puzzled. "Horseshoes, chum?" he said. "How long does it take to get them?"

"Too long," I told him. "There's a blacksmith here on the track, but it would take him a half-hour, at least, to shoe you. An' the race starts in less than thirty minutes."

"Half an hour," said Nestros thoughtfully. "That's not so bad. I think I can fix it. They delay the race if it rains, don't they?"

"Yes," I told him. "Long enough to see if it's goin' to clear up again or not. Why?"

"Why, because," said the centaur, "I think I'll let it rain a little." He lifted his head an' started whisperin' something in foreign words. The sky, which had been as clear as a crystal ball, all of a sudden started gatherin' wisps of cloud. They got thicker an' heavier an' darker by the minute – an' before you could raise an umbrella, down come the rain in a regular cloudburst!

Nick howled like a kicked pup, tossed one horrified look at Nestros, an' ran. Harkrader lit out too. You see, what Thick Nick had forgot to take into consideration was the fact that centaurs, in addition to bein' legendary creatures, is also – demi-gods!

In a tight spot, Nestros had turned on a miracle!

But there wasn't no time to waste. I grabbed aholt of Dumbo, who had just returned from the tack-room.

"Quick, kid!" I yelled. "We've got a thirty-minute lease on life, liberty, an' the pursuit of filthy lucre. Not a minute to waste. Hurry Nestros down to the smithy an' have him shod!"

"Huh?" said Dumbo, gawkin'. "You mean it?"

"Of course I mean it! Get goin'!"

"Sure, Mr McGhee!" he said. "Yes-sir! Right away, Mr McGhee!" he said. An' he grabbed Nestros' reins, an' off they went.

I should of knew right then. I should of seen that he was too anxious, too willin' to help. But I was too eager to get goin', too wrapped up in my own thoughts . . .

First hint I had that anything was wrong came a few minutes

later when I heard somethin' like an auto backfirin'. The minute it sounded, the rain stopped. I was just thinkin' to myself how funny this was, when Dumbo appeared, exposin' a mouthful of molars in a grin that stretched from the nape of his neck to his tonsils. He was carryin' Nestros' saddle an' gear. I stared at him.

"What are you doin' back here?" I demanded.

He nodded happily. "It's done, Mr McGhee. I done it myself."

"Already?" I gasped. "You mean to tell me you shod a horse in less than five minutes? Dumbo—"

His jaw dropped. "*Shod!*" he said, "*Sh-shod!* Gee, Mr McGhee – I thought you said to take him away an' have him *shot!*"

"So," said Squaredeal Sam, "that's all. I told you I'd bet everything I had on Nestros. I maybe forgot to say I also bet everything Akers owned. Which is why his stables is bein' auctioned off next Sattiday."

I stared at him dubiously.

"This has all been most entertaining, Sam," I said, "but it still doesn't explain why you want three hundred dollars. An investment, you said—"

"That's right," nodded Sam. "I got to buy Princess Sally at that auction. I may be wrong – but from what I know about centaurs, it looks to me like there's still a chance to hit the jackpot. Like the fellow says, 'There's no foal like a young foal.'"

BAD DAY ON MOUNT OLYMPUS

Marilyn Todd

Marilyn Todd has a wicked sense of humour, as anyone who has sampled her Roman mystery stories, which began with I, Claudia *(1995) will know. I was sure that she could also turn her talents to comic fantasy and the following is her first venture in this field. I'm sure it won't be her last.*

The meeting was going well. Boring, but hey. They only come round once a year. Who's going to quibble about the odd satyr too fond of his own voice to relinquish the floor? Or some nerd of a faun who's all presentation-this/flip-chart-that? Let it ride, that's what I say. If these guys get off on pie charts and graphs, who am I to begrudge them their fun? Not everyone's idea of a good time is free-flowing wine and the chance to get to know one another afterwards.

By which, of course, I mean sex.

And lots of it.

Also, you get to catch up with the gossip. After all, Cupid's still a kid. Not every shot is on target. Some really interesting alliances can result. *Plus* – a real bonus, this – we get to see who's been turned into what animal, tree, bug or whatever. Naturally, this year's big story was Io. *Apparently* (and you didn't get this from me), but *apparently* Juno walked in on Jupiter relieving Io of the rather cumbersome burden of her virginity and . . .

Look. Let's just say the wife wasn't any too pleased at the picture, OK?

Well, we all know what a bitch Juno can be when she's mad. Look what she did to me. I'm her friend. Anyhow, Jupiter's thinking he'd best get in first, if he's looking to protect the girlfriend, so . . . Spotting a herd of cows on the hill, quick as a flash, he turns Io into a heifer. Find her among *that* lot, he smarms to the wife. But this was the thing, see. Juno didn't *want* to go looking for Io. "Who needs it?" she says. "Didn't I always say she was a scheming little cow?" (Incidentally, Io's apologies for absence at this AGM have been duly noted.)

Anyways, like I said, the meeting's going well. After a few millennia you get to know the pattern and this was the point on the schedule when whichever river god was spouting off this time would begin to run out of steam. Happens every year. Someone, somewhere, gets fed up with what he's doing and wastes hours of precious drinking time by making out a lengthy case for changing course. The response from the rest of us is the same each year, too. We let the old windbag make his speech and then say yes. The reason we don't say yes straight off is that then some other windbag would get up and start making demands. So we let it run and then pretend to vote according to our conscience. Of course, the reason we *all* say yes *every* time is that if we didn't, we'd lose even *more* drinking time during the debate. This is democracy, see. It's the only way to do business.

So we vote. The motion's carried. Some little stream in Arcadia (or was it Thrace?) will change course and the river god, bless his sediment, duly gets his change of scenery. Tedious or wot? But any minute now Sagittarius, half-man, half-horse who's chaired the last three hundred meetings, will start to wind things up. We'll get the usual jeers of Sagittarius always wanting to be the "centaur of attention". Some wag will ask Pan, doesn't *he* want to, ho ho, "pipe up" with a question. And someone else will accuse Orpheus of "lute behaviour" in a public place. The usual stuff. Old as Olympus. And call us sad, but we still find it funny.

By the time our equine chairman was rolling up his scrolls and murmuring "Any other business?" Bacchus was already on his cloven feet, heading for the wine. We almost missed the voice that boomed out "Yes" from the back . . .

Yes? You could have knocked me down with a feather. (Well, you could have, if I'd had a body to blow down).

"Er." Sagittarius stamped a hoof, whinnied a bit, and you could see what was going through his head. Nothing like this had ever happened before on Mount Olympus. "Did someone say yes?"

See, after him asking "Any other business?", there's always the same short silence, when everyone *pretends* they're trying to think up a question (most of us being more polite than Bacchus). Then we shake our heads, like how we'd all have *loved* to raise a point or three but since the meeting covered everything on *our* agenda, boy, were we stumped. At this point, when Sagittarius pronounces the AGM closed, a cheer goes up loud enough to cause a landslip in Crete, followed by a stampede to the wine. Hey! It's not called the "Amorous Gluttonous Massing" for nothing, you know.

Except now someone was spoiling the fun.

"Me," the voice said. "I have a point I'd like to raise."

Necks craned for a better view. Who was this party pooper? we all demanded. And couldn't someone tear his damned head off or something?

The reason we couldn't see him was that, until now, he'd been sitting down. Wise move. Had we noticed him beforehand, we'd all have guessed he'd be trouble and taken the necessary countermeasures to keep him quiet. Like sit on him or something. Because no one wears the full lion's pelt on a sweltering hot day like this without courting *some* kind of disaster.

"Ah. Hercules."

I don't *believe* it! Sagittarius, the knucklehead, was inviting him up to the front. At the same time, I noticed a lot of eyes turn longingly towards the wine jugs. Not least Bacchus's. Although, in fairness, I have to say most of Hundred-Eyed Argus's gaze was directed straight down the bosom of that little wood sprite from Corinth.

Swinging his olive-wood club as though it weighed no more than a sunbeam, our doughty hero stepped onto the stage. "Mister Chairman," he drawled, flexing his pecs. "Fauns, satyrs, nymphs, dryads, maenads—"

"Gonads!" yelled a heckler from the crowd, and you can see where *his* thoughts were headed. OK, so we all know that sex isn't everything. But come on. There's more than enough hanging around in between as it is.

"—And all my fellow Immortals." It was satisfying to watch the sweat pour down Hercules' face under the heavy lion's head. Not so good that he produced a thick wad of notes from somewhere deep in its pelt. "For some considerable time," he read, "there has been an awareness among each and every one of us that all is not well on Mount Olympus. Morale has never been lower—"

How swiftly the mood of the crowd changed! With each bass syllable that carried across the clearing in the woods, they forgot about the wine, the partying, the reason they'd come here in the first place. Ears pricked up. Backs straightened. Lips pursed in concentration. At last they were not forced to endure some nebulous whinge, a trivial piece of planning that needed approval, an excuse for self-congratulation and praise. This speech embraced them all. *Their* needs. *Their* hopes. *Their* ambitions, *their* prospects. A breathless silence descended as Hercules proceeded to outline the riches he felt the Immortals deserved. What rewards they should reap.

Page after page turned in the big man's hand until, having raised them right up, having lifted the crowd to the very summit of spiritual aspiration, cleverly he began to trawl through their grievances. He listed the niggles that had eroded their confidence over the years. The petty bureaucracies imposed by the gods that stood in their way. I felt, rather than heard, the rumble that surged through the clearing. An emotion pitched somewhere between approval, fear and excitement . . .

Couldn't they see what he was planning? *Didn't they care?* With each fervoured agreement, each enthusiastic nod of the head, each vociferous "Hear, hear!" that fell louder and louder from their lips I myself grew that much colder.

"So I put it to you, brothers, that the gods – those men and women who laughingly refer to themselves as our masters – have not only grown lacklustre and idle, they have become spiteful and careless, abusing their powers. Moreover, brothers." Hercules paused. "These presumed masters, these so-called invincible beings, have not only lost interest in the running of mortal affairs on Earth, I say they have proved themselves *incompetent* here on Olympus."

Oh, shit. There it was, out in the open. An overthrow. A coup. A takeover. Revolution.

"Incompetent," he repeated forcefully.

You can say it six times over, *brother*, but this is not for me. I am out of here . . .

"By way of example, take little Echo here."

"Here!" I protested. Oh, I do *so* not want any part of this—

"Look at the spiteful way Juno punished that poor little nymph."

Well, that bit was true. Juno's revenge *had* been harsh. But hell, I knew the risks when I took them, keeping her talking time and again while Jupiter made his getaway from whichever pretty young thing he'd been seducing. I knew full well what would happen if she ever found out. She'd deprive me the power of speech – and for ever. Only Jupiter's intervention left me with some kind of voice. The gift, if that's what it is, of repetition.

"Not once did Juno punish the poor creature," Hercules said, "but little Echo was made to suffer twice over. What a bitch! What a spiteful, malicious bitch. And this, brothers, is supposed to be justice under the rule of the Queen of Olympus, the one and only Mighty Juno!"

"No!" I cried out.

Not true. Juno played no part in my doomed love for Narcissus. But, alas, no one could hear me . . .

"Not content with robbing Echo of her voice," our muscled hero was saying, "she takes the poor kid's body away, too."

"Ooh," I protested.

Unfair. Hercules knows damned well I pined away out of love. That was my choice, my decision. You can't pin that one on Juno. If I could not belong to Narcissus, I would not belong to anyone else. And I tell you something else, *brother*. I've never regretted that. Not for an instant. But Hercules had his audience right where he wanted them. Which meant he wouldn't let a little thing like the truth get in the way . . .

"When Juno saw Narcissus waiting for Echo at the pool, she couldn't resisting adding insult to injury. She made him fall in love with himself."

"Sylph," I corrected firmly.

No one but me and Narcissus knows what happened down there by that pool. Being dormant right now, Narcissus can't tell and I sure as hell won't. Some things are personal. But I won't have it bandied around that Narcissus fell in love with his own reflection. That just wasn't true. And frankly it bothers me that if Hercules goes on repeating that rumour, that's how it will end up being believed.

Look how he was playing them now! Not a dry eye in the clearing, and that included Hundred-Eyed Argus. Hell, I know everyone's a sucker for that somebody-done-some-body-wrong shit. I just didn't approve of Hercules using *me* to win his audience over. To show them that the deities on Olympus weren't as intelligent or as resourceful as they'd have us believe.

And now he was about to muscle in and oust them, with the backing of this gullible band! I looked round at my comrades. Wood nymphs and fauns, gorgons and sirens, cyclops, titans and sibyls. Over there, Arachne, turned by Pallas into a spider for no better reason than having woven a better tapestry than the goddess. Lycaon, changed into a snarling, howling wolf for doubting Jupiter. Midas, given the ears of an ass for siding with Pan against Apollo. Atalanta turned into a lioness by Venus just (would you believe!) for consummating her marriage, poor cow.

Up they surfaced, though. Grudges that had festered over the centuries. Rancour that had grown more bitter with each passing millennium. Centaurs, bacchants, fountain nymphs, muses, harpies, furies, those unfortunate men and women turned into stone – all began to dredge up their resentment. For most, though, the prospect of power was simply too tantalizing to resist . . .

"No more tyrants!" Hercules cried, thumping his fist into the palm of his hand.

"No more tyrants!" came the rallying chorus.

"Democracy for Olympus!" he roared.

"Democracy for Olympus!" they cried, and I thought, *Yeah. Io isn't the only one stuck in a herd.*

"In place of Jupiter and Juno," Hercules said, "I propose a triumvirate."

Took him long enough to get round to it, eh? The tyrant is dead, long live the tyrant. But the baying mob cheered him on.

"Are you with me?" he urged. "*Are you with me?*"

Back came the predictable roar, the applause, the tumultuous stamp of approval.

"Then I propose three men at its head – myself, and the heroic twins. What do you say, Immortals? What do you say to democracy led by Hercules, Castor and Pollux?"

I knew what I had to say.

"Pollux!" I said. And I sighed. Dammit, *someone* had to put paid to this midsummer madness.

I just wished that someone didn't have to be me . . .

Don't get me wrong. I'm no fan of the gods, I don't fawn and flatter them like some I could mention. Well, all right. Who I *will* mention. Ganymede, for one, the oily little oik. OK, so he was a shepherd boy plucked from obscurity to become cupbearer to the gods, but does he really have to suck up to them in the repulsive way that he does? Then there's Janus. He's not two-faced for nothing, you know—

But you're right. This is not the time to start bitching. We'll go into that later, once we've got this revolt bedded down. The problem was, of course, *how* to stop Hercules toppling Jupiter from his throne.

Now it's not as though I personally believe the gods are infallible. Hercules made many valid points and I'd be the first to admit there's ample room for improvement. The Olympians *have* grown indolent. Mistakes *have* been made. They've become careless, underhanded, ethics have gone out the window and if ever there was a time to wheel out the clichés this was it. Power corrupts, blah, blah, blah. But! And this is the thing. *The same would be true if Hercules and the twins took control.*

Within no time they, too, would become self-serving tyrants. Who would notice the difference? Find me an altruistic politician and I'll show you glaciers on the equator. Oh, and cut the crap about doing it for the Good Of The People. Hercules performed Twelve Labours all right, and magnificently so, I might add. But they were not for the Good Of The People. He mucked out stables and slew lions and hydras and wot-have-you for his own ends, remember. That this son of a mortal might himself become a god.

And you can forget Castor and Pollux. One's a wrestler, the other's a boxer – sporting heroes without doubt. But have you spotted a single brain cell between them? Keep looking! No, in Hercules' book these brawnballs were nothing more than walking, talking advertising hoardings. "You are safe in our hands" was the message. The Immortals flocked to their feet.

So what was *my* problem, you ask? If one order is the same as another, why not go with the flow? We-ell. Ask yourself this. Would you want *your* destiny in the hands of a group of drunken revellers who yawn their way through their own AGM and who change sides at the first bit of oratory? I rest my case.

The problem was, where to start. Jupiter was off on one of

his wenching sprees, and who knew what disguise he'd adopted this time. Swans, showers of gold, husband impersonations, there was no telling – and certainly not enough time to find out. Hercules wasn't stupid. He knew full well that he was carrying the Immortals along on the tide. He intended to strike before they changed their minds. So who did that leave? Neptune? Uh-uh. Too busy whipping up storms and sinking the ships of some little Greek island he felt had neglected him. Apollo? Still driving his fiery chariot across the skies over our heads. As for Mars, well, damn me, hadn't he turned himself into a ruddy bull again? (After Io, I'll bet!)

This, then, looked like being a job for the girls.

After a hard day's chase through the forests or a bit of post-prandial nookie, there's really nothing quite like unwinding over a good gossip with friends. OK, so I use the term loosely. Maybe the girls meet up more for the mutual massaging of egos than friendship, but who cares? On this particular occasion I hit lucky. It was the A-Team splashing about under the waterfall.

Diana, needing the usual reassurance that she was the swiftest. Venus, bragging about Adonis, so everyone knew she was the fairest. Minerva, head in a book. (Like we didn't know she was the brainy one!) Plus, of course, Juno, angling for sympathy now that everyone knew Jupiter was out playing eeny-meeny-maenad-mo again.

Diana was practising her javelin stance in the water's reflection. "Where's Cupid today?" she was asking his mother.

"That little pest!" You could never accuse Venus of suffocating Cupid with maternal instincts. "I sent him off to practise in the butts."

An order, believe me, that Cupid takes literally. And it's bloody painful, I tell you, when that arrow hits home. I heard Adonis couldn't sit down for a week and Vulcan says his scar *still* won't heal.

"I don't know what he sees in these mortal women," Juno was saying. "Strumpets, the lot of them."

"Ahem," I said. It invariably takes an age to catch some-one's attention. You have to wait for just the right moment.

Bugger. This wasn't it.

"Well, you know what they say about husbands, darling," laughed Venus. "They're like fires. They go out if you neglect them."

"*Ahem!*"

"Are you suggesting I'm not stoking Jupiter's passions, you bitch?"

Oh-oh. This wasn't going the way I had hoped. They were too busy starting a cat fight to listen to echoes round the edge of the pool. Briefly, listening to the squabble break out, I was tempted to call it a day. Let Hercules *lead* his taggle-taggle band to glory.

I slipped away at the point where Venus was offering to give Juno lessons in techniques of the bedchamber. I was willing to bet that, at this rate, the next time I saw Venus, she'd have her fringe combed over one eye to hide the shiner.

What do do, what to do . . .

Back in the clearing the Immortals were drunk with both power and wine. Not so much ambrosia and nectar for them, I thought. More like lotus eaters. One taste and everything else is forgotten. I looked at them. Sons and daughters of mortal women rising up against their own parents. Even Hercules, son of Jupiter and fostered by Juno at one stage, was prepared to overthrow his own father and that, I thought, told the story. That was what separated men from the gods.

Olympians might throw tantrums.

Mortal men yearn only for violence.

That's why Hercules would never be King of the Gods. OK, Jupiter has his faults. Serial adultery by no means the least. But was Hercules – indeed, were *any* of the rabble massed in the clearing – genuinely interested in the welfare of ordinary people? Did they see them as anything other than pawns in their own selfish power game?

Back at the pool, Juno and Venus had joined forces to turn on Diana.

"You can shut your trap," Juno was saying. "The day I take advice from virgins about sex is the day my husband turns celibate."

"How dare you!" Diana snarled. "I value my virginity—"

"Rubbish," Venus sneered back. "No man will have you, you prissy little cow. That's why, after all these millennia, you're still a virgin. You're frigid."

"*Frigid?*"

Diana's spluttering drowned the splash of the waterfall and, since it was turning into a right old scrum over there, I left the three of them to it. It was Minerva I focused on. You notice she hadn't uttered a squeak about Jupiter's philanderings or Diana's chastity bent? (Told you she was the brainy one.) I waited until she came to the end of the scroll she was reading – or at least pretending to read, take your pick. Because I know which I'd have sooner been watching, kiddo. Three top goddesses at it hammer and tongs or a dull old page of poetry? No contest. Anyway, as Minerva reached down, I gave the signal.

With a groan that cut through to the marrow, my old friend Boreas, the north wind, spread out his feathers, beat his grey wings and scattered Minerva's scrolls to all points of the compass.

Everyone shivered at the unexpected drop in temperature. Even me. It had been ages since I'd dallied with Boreas; I'd forgotten how icy his embrace could be. But Boreas whipping up Minerva's papers was the signal for Daphne to start. The distinctive rustle of her leathery leaves echoed round the wooded glade, a cue for Myrrh to begin weeping thick, sticky ooze from her bark. Suddenly, all my other friends descended. Ceyx and Alcyone, whose wish to become seabirds had been granted, swooped out of nowhere. Snakes rustled among the long grasses. All those gentle creatures who had asked – yes, *asked!* – to be changed from human shape descended now round the pool, calling at the tops of their voices as Boreas kicked up a din of his own.

"What the hell's up?" Juno was forced to shout over the

racket of birdsong and animal sounds and the wild woodland echoes.

"Up!" I yelled back.

"It's that bloody AGM," Diana snapped, rubbing the goose pimples on her arm. "Happens every time we leave them alone. Something always goes awry."

"Wry," I said, fixing hard on Minerva.

"What the blazes does Apollo think he's playing at up there?" Venus said, glancing up at the sun, still blazing brightly in its innocence. "I'm bloody freezing."

"*Zing!*"

"Did you hear that?" Juno sniffed. "Even scatty little Echo has got in on the act."

Ooh, you don't know how much I wished she'd said something that I could have replied to at that!

"Sssh," said Minerva, and the other three goddesses swung round on her, ready to lay into Jupiter's favourite daughter. (You notice how quickly they change sides, these girls. Loyalty changes hands faster than coins in a pickpocket gang.)

"Don't tell *me* to shut up, you bossy cow—"

"No, listen," Minerva said, and there was a tone to her voice that made everyone shut up, not just the three squabbling beauties. The glade plunged into silence. Even the tears of the cataract seemed to fall softly. The laurel stopped shivering. The bird calls ceased. The serpents stopped writhing. Only Myrrh's resin continued to weep.

"All of you, listen to Echo," Minerva ordered.

Oh, bless you, Minerva. You're not the Goddess of Wisdom for nothing! I let my repetitions echo into the still summer air.

"Up," I repeated. "Wry. Zing."

"Do you hear that?" Minerva reached for her armour.

"Up. Wry. Zing," I said, softly now. Hurry up, ladies. I was running out of zing here myself.

"By the heavens!" Diana thundered, strapping her quiver onto her back. "We hear you, Echo. By all the gods, we hear what you're telling us. Trust me, you'll find the Olympians grateful!"

No one ever accused Juno of being quick on the uptake, but finally the bronze penny dropped.

"*UPRISING?*"

Oh-oh. I recognized *that* tone from the Queen of Olympus. Someone, somewhere was going to pay.

For once, I was thankful that that someone wouldn't be me!

I won't bore you with the details. No coup is bloodless, and suffice it to say that there are a lot of wild bears and boars and snakes running about who'd far rather have remained river gods, satyrs and fauns. Especially now the hunting season's nearly upon us.

But there you go.

For my part, I'm pleased with the outcome. One day, perhaps, men *will* take over from the gods and that will be a sad day for mortals. It is the nature of men to always want to war with one another – and who will be there to quench the fires of hatred, if not Jupiter, Juno, Minerva, et al?

My only regret was that Hercules was taken out of circulation before he could retract his scurrilous lies about me and Narcissus, but what the hell? My lover and I might be condemned to false history, but the truth of our love shows itself every spring. And don't tell *me* some bloke called Wordsworth or Jobsworth or whatever won't want to write a poem in the future about the fruits of our ardour!

As for Hercules, he and the twins didn't disappear entirely. Being a son of Jupiter, his Twelve Labours were given a positive spin in the history books, while at the same time any mention of this little episode was duly deleted. Ditto Castor and Pollux. The gods, being gods, wouldn't kill them, of course. That's not in their nature. So, if you care to tilt your head upwards on a clear night you can see them. Up there in the heavens.

Only you and I know the real reason the three of them have been placed in the Constellation.

And I, of course, am not telling.

At least. Not unless you top up my glass . . .

HOW MUCH WOULD YOU PAY?

Craig Shaw Gardner

Yep, it's Craig Shaw Gardner again. I certainly don't apologize for including an author twice in this volume, especially when it gives us a chance to have both a Wuntvor episode, as we did earlier, and now a brand new story, written specially for the book. It doesn't feature Wuntvor or Ebenezum, but is rather chillingly closer to home than that.

Earl just hoped there was something good on. After the kind of day he'd had, he needed a little relaxing. He tipped the barcolounger back at just the right angle and pointed the remote across the room.

Click.

"Bigger! Brighter! Bolder! Better!"

Click.

"If you think for one minute that being the head of this hospital prevents you from accepting responsibility for this child inside me—"

Click.

"Now! For a limited time only!"

Click.

"Exactly! Why *can't* society accept transsexual nuns? After all, it's not as though all of us are lesbians—"

Click.

Ah, this looked interesting. One of those old-fashioned fantasy films. The screen was a wash of red, with everything in flames. Everybody screaming, too. And look at those devils with their twitching tails. Their pitchforks positively gleamed! Pretty good production values. Earl chuckled. With computers these days, you could do just about anything.

"Welcome to Hell," intoned a voice deeper than that of James Earl Jones. "And have we got a surprise for you!"

Something crashed upstairs. His wife yelled up at Brian, their fifteen-year-old son. Earl sighed. Just another quiet evening at home.

"That's right!" the on-screen voice rumbled on, "You've tuned in just in time to receive our exciting offer."

The bass line boomed down through the ceiling above. Brian had fired up his stereo to the usual ear-splitting volume. Earl punched a button to turn up the TV. He didn't want to miss a word of this.

A body in flames screamed as it fell across the screen.

"Just one of the unfortunates who didn't take advantage of this exciting television offer," the voice continued with the slightest chuckle in his voice. "Don't you get burned, too!"

So this was a commercial? Earl felt a little disappointed. Well, at least it was different. What they wouldn't do to get your attention these days. His wife yelled something from the other room. She knew he couldn't hear her when the TV was on. Earl decided she wasn't worth hearing anyway.

He looked back to the screen.

The announcer continued: "And now a word from Mephistopheles!"

A face filled the screen, round and smiling, with a pair of horns at the top and a pencil-thin moustache in the middle. To Earl, it looked like a pinker version of Don Ameche. Don Ameche grinned. The light in his eyes seemed to come from within. "What have we got? Bargains, bargains, bargains! Stay tuned for the sweetest deals of your life – and your afterlife."

Something crashed upstairs. Something else crashed in the kitchen.

His wife bustled out to the base of the stairs to yell at Brain. His son stomped out of his room, an amazing amount of noise for someone who only weighed 140 pounds, and stood at the top of the stairs so he could yell back. Brian used a four-letter word. Earl's wife replied with some four-letter words of her own. And where, she added, had he learned that language in the first place?

The conversation continued in the usual circles. Earl didn't have to hear every word. He could fill in the rest. Too bad, Earl thought, his family couldn't be as clever as these infomercials.

He looked back at the set, and realized he was actually a little disappointed that he had missed a bit of the commercial.

The announcer said, "This is just one small sample of what you'll get with your entertainment package, the latest from Hades Sports Central!"

A man, dressed in rags, his body covered by scrapes and scabs, was giving his all to push a good-sized boulder up a steep slope. A half-dozen words were superimposed over the bottom of the screen: "BOULDER ROLLING COMPETI-TION – ALREADY IN PROGRESS".

A pair of announcers spoke in hushed voices.

"You've got to give it to old Sisyphus here, he's a real competitor," the first remarked.

"I think he's really got a fighting chance this time around," the second replied.

The ragged man strained and sweated, pushing the great boulder with his back, digging his bare feet into the rock-strewn soil. It looked nearly impossible, but, inch by inch, this Sisyphus guy was pushing the big rock up the hill. Earl had to admit, this was a real man's sport. It reminded him of a Scottish games sort of thing, like caber tossing, or that bit they did with a sheep's stomach. It was a real change from all those bass-fishing shows you'd usually see around dinnertime.

"This could be particularly meaningful for our competitor," the first voice said. "He's been pursuing this goal for a really long time."

The second voice laughed. "It seems like he's been doing it for an eternity."

Earl became aware of the noise of a crowd behind the action, shouting now, rather than screaming.

"Listen to those fans!" the second voice exclaimed.

"The home team can get you over that hump," the first enthused. "Sort of like that extra player."

"And Sisyphus needs it now! He has to give 110 per cent!"

But Sisyphus was having trouble. The angle of the hill appeared to grow steeper the higher he got, and the boulder moved more and more slowly. Earl watched for a long, agonizing minute as the great rock seemed not to move at all. With a strangled cry, the ragged man fell to one side, barely avoiding being crushed as the boulder crashed back down the hill.

"Oh! So close!"

"Better luck next time, Sisyphus! What a trouper! He just never gives up, no matter how long it takes."

"It does seem to take for ever." The second voice chuckled again. "This could be almost as bad as the curse of the Bambino. We'll be back shortly, to watch Sisyphus try again. But stay tuned for an important message!"

Earl had had just about enough of this. Maybe there was something good on the Playboy Channel. He punched the remote. It didn't do a thing. The TV still showed the bright red infomercial.

What now? Hadn't he just changed the batteries in this thing a month ago? Earl shook the remote and punched it again.

The first announcer's voice took over: "Well, we'll check back with you fellows later, after we tell our viewers about this exciting offer."

The remote wasn't doing squat. Maybe he'd actually have to get up and change the channel on the cable box.

The camera panned across a sea of miserable-looking people, some dressed in rags, the rest totally naked. "You already know the story," the announcer continued. "Expenses are up everywhere. Hell is feeling the crunch just like everybody. But you can help. We want to contact every living soul. That's right, Hell needs you."

The pinkish Don Ameche grinned on-screen again.

"No," Don added, "we're not talking about our special contracts, although if you're interested, simply call the number at the bottom of your screen."

1–800–DAMNATION appeared in white letters as he spoke.

"But what about the rest of you?" he continued. "Do you ever think of the fiery pit? Because the pit thinks about you. And now you can let a little bit of Hell into your life for an amazingly low price!"

Earl's wife appeared in the door from the kitchen. "What the hell are you watching?"

It had to be something special to get Gladys's attention. Earl guessed this qualified. He waved the remote towards the set.

"It's one of those infomercials – probably for one of those dot-com things."

His wife's bitter expression grew more sour still. "Now you're watching infomercials while I'm out slaving in the kitchen? It's not like you do anything around here."

Earl wasn't going to get into a fight over something like this. "Well, I think I've had enough of it, too." He raised the remote and pressed the "off" button.

"Ow!" His thumb leaped from the remote as the shock almost jolted him off the couch.

"We won't do that again, now will we?" Don Ameche asked happily. "Not until you've heard the rest of our amazing offer!"

Gladys stared at the screen. "Is the TV talking to us?"

"You, and everybody else in your miserable excuse for an existence," Don replied with a laugh. "But I digress." He pointed directly at Earl. "So you aren't ready to give your all for Hell? Perhaps you need a bit more . . . persuasion. And, rest assured, long, slow persuasion is our specialty. We'll find a way to get you to open your wallets and give till it hurts – because that won't hurt as much as this." Don looked off-screen. "Hey, Beeze! What have we got for these nice folks?"

"A real charmer today," the announcer's voice replied. "Disco pig calling."

"I'm not going to watch this!" Gladys announced. But she didn't move. It was as if her feet were nailed to the floor. Earl thought he saw a trace of panic on her frowning face.

A very fat individual in a broad-brimmed hat appeared on-screen.

"*Sooooooweeeee!*" *Thump thump thump.* "*Sooooweeeee!*" *Thump thump thumpity thump.* And so on. The fat fellow would scream, followed by disco drums. It went on for quite some time. Earl thought about turning it off. Not that the devils would let him. But he couldn't tear his gaze from the screen. "*Sooweeee!*" *Thumpity thump thump.* It was like watching an automobile accident – you know you shouldn't watch it, but your head just won't turn away.

Don Ameche took the fat fellow's place. Earl breathed a sigh of relief.

"Thanks to our first contestant," Don said. "Only 4,682 more disco pig callers to go!"

Another, perhaps even more obese individual in an even larger hat appeared on-screen.

"Dad!" Brian crashed down the stairs. "Something's really wrong. All my stereo will play is music with accordions!"

Earl glared back at the TV.

"We adjust to the circumstances," the announcer's voice replied proudly.

Gladys actually smiled at this. "But our musical tastes are so different. How could they possibly find something that – unusual – for all of us?"

The announcer only hesitated for a second before announcing: "Disco pig calling with a polka accompaniment!"

A chorus was added to the repetitive noise issuing from the

TV. "In Heaven, there is no beer . . . *Soooweeeeee!" Thump thump thump thumpity thump.*

This seemed to go on even longer than before. The entire family was transfixed.

"That's why we drink it here . . . *Soooooweeeeee!"*

"For the love of God, turn it off!" Gladys shrieked. But she didn't look away.

Thumpity thump. Oompahpah. Thump.

Brian covered his ears. "Okay, Dad! You win! This time I really will go upstairs and do my homework!" But he stared at the screen, open-mouthed.

Earl couldn't take any more. He didn't care about the consequences. He thumbed the power switch.

This time, the shock hit all three of them. The whole family screamed as one.

"We can stop this," Don said softly.

"How—" Gladys gasped, clutching at her chest.

"By giving you control of the Hades network. And for a special low price! How much would you pay for this fine programming—" As he spoke, the screen flashed on the boulder-rolling, the pig-calling, the people screaming and falling, and lots and lots of flame. "—Or even better. How much would you pay to be able to turn it off?"

Don's grin grew even wider. "Think about it. The power of Hades at your command, for only $19.95 a month. That's right! Only $19.95! And we won't change that price until we decide to make it higher!"

Earl shook his head. This wasn't the time for some extra expense. They were pretty maxed out already. "But our credit cards—"

"Now, now," Don chided. "There's still some room on your Discover, isn't there?"

Earl glanced to his wife. She nodded her head all too eagerly.

"So you agree?" Don nodded. "Done! If only everything was as simple as a devil's bargain!

"You've just made Hell a happier place that hopefully,

you'll never have to visit. We now return control of your television – well, you know the routine. But now you can see the best of Hell every single day! And, so long as you keep up your payments, you'll never hear from us again – at least until our next financial difficulty. You have the word of the devil on that one!" Don glanced downwards. "But, if you ever need us, you now know where to find us!"

A logo appeared on the bottom corner of the screen – Channel 666.

The whole family breathed a collective sigh of relief as Earl changed the channel.

"Well," Gladys said as Earl flipped past another dozen cable offerings. "That was certainly – different."

"Yeah," Brian agreed. "Disco pig calling – wild!"

Earl realized the family wasn't screaming at each other for a change. His thumb paused before he could click the remote one more time.

What was this?

The room was filled with golden light. The light was coming from the TV. Earl was surprised the set could give off that much illumination.

The room was filled with the sound of an angelic choir.

Images of blue skies, with perfect white clouds, appeared upon the screen. Then that dissolved to a new view, showing row upon row of perfect angels, all with their wings spread, all lifting their voices in song.

Well, Earl thought, this was certainly a more peaceful image than the last channel. Of course, anything would look peaceful after what they'd been through.

The choir continued to sing. Earl sat there, waiting for something to happen.

"We just thought you'd like to get a little look at Heaven," a soothing voice said at last. The angelic choir kept it up in the background. "But even Heaven has its problems. Like everything these days, our expenses have increased dramatically."

Maybe they'd lower their expenses if they didn't hire so many singers. Earl glanced down at the remote.

"So we've come up with a whole range of programming that's just – heavenly. A special package, especially for you. Just see what Heaven has to offer. Here's a little bit of our uplifting drama series, 'A Slice of Heaven'."

The scene shifted to three people – all in heavenly robes – glowering at each other, their fists raised.

The person on the left frowned, and lowered his hands. "You know what? I don't want to argue any more."

The other two looked at each other, and put down their fists as well.

"No, you're right," the second fellow said with a smile. "Let's talk, and solve our problems.

"We'll be friends for ever!" the third agreed.

The soothing voice returned: "Or how about a bit of 'Heavenly Messages', our topical talk show that raises all the important issues we have up here."

A man in heavenly garb stood before half a dozen others in similar attire. The first man – Earl guessed he was the host – spoke into his microphone.

"I don't know when I've felt this good. How about you?"

The words PEOPLE WHO FEEL REALLY GOOD were superimposed over the bottom of the screen.

"You know," one of those seated agreed, "I feel even better!"

"Yeah, we all do!" a third chimed in as the others nodded their heads.

The choir kicked back in as the soothing voice continued:

"All this fine programming, and more! Think about it. You may hope you'll be coming here. But who can be really sure to get off on the right foot from that mortal coil?"

The choir sang for another moment before the voice added: "Why not help out the worthiest of causes? It's sure to put in a good word where it counts the most. After all, by helping Heaven, you're only helping yourself."

More of the choir. At last the picture had gone back to the sky and clouds. Earl glanced at the remote one more time.

"We won't stop you from changing that channel," the

soothing voice continued, "but think what might happen if you do. Keep the shine on those pearly gates! Give generously—"

Earl looked over to his wife, then to his son. Both of them nodded.

Earl turned the TV back to Hell.

He wished all the family decisions were this easy.

THE DEVIL TIMES THREE

Fredric Brown

Fredric Brown (1906–1972) was a brilliant writer of science fiction, fantasy and crime fiction. He could write serious stuff – as anyone who has read his horror story "The Geezenstacks" or his science fiction story "Arena" (later adapted as an episode of Star Trek) *will know. He could write very tense, hard-edged books, as in his first mystery novel* The Fabulous Clipjoint *(1947). But if he's remembered for anything it will be for his clever, sardonic vignettes. At one stage he was known for having written the shortest of all stories, "Knock", arguably the only story to be ever regularly quoted in full. Here are three examples of his wit.*

NASTY

Walter Beauregard had been an accomplished and enthusiastic lecher for almost fifty years. Now, at the age of sixty-five, he was in danger of losing his qualifications for membership in the lechers' union. In danger of losing? Nay, let us be honest; he had *lost*. For three years now he had been to doctor after doctor, quack after quack, had tried nostrum after nostrum. All utterly to no avail.

Finally he remembered his books on magic and necromancy. They were books he had enjoyed collecting and reading as part of his extensive library, but he had never taken them seriously. Until now. What did he have to lose?

In a musty, evil-smelling but rare volume he found what he wanted. As it instructed, he drew the pentagram, copied the cabalistic markings, lighted the candles and read aloud the incantation.

There was a flash of light and a puff of smoke. And the demon. I won't describe the demon except to assure you that you wouldn't have liked him.

"What is your name?" Beauregard asked. He tried to make his voice steady but it trembled a little.

The demon made a sound somewhere between a shriek and a whistle, with overtones of a bull fiddle being played with a crosscut saw. Then he said, "But you won't be able to pronounce that. In your dull language it would translate as Nasty. Just call me Nasty. I suppose you want the usual thing."

"What's the usual thing?" Beauregard wanted to know.

"A wish, of course. All right, you can have it. But not three wishes; that business about three wishes is sheer superstition. One is all you get. And you won't like it."

"One is all I want. And I can't imagine not liking it."

"You'll find out. All right, I know what your wish is. And here is the answer to it." Nasty reached into thin air and his hand vanished and came back holding a pair of silvery-looking swimming trunks. He held them out to Beauregard. "Wear them in good health," he said.

"What are they?"

"What do they look like? Swimming trunks. But they're special. The material is out of the future, a few millennia from now. It's indestructible; they'll never wear out or tear or snag. Nice stuff. But the spell on them is a plenty old one. Try them on and find out."

The demon vanished.

Walter Beauregard quickly stripped and put on the beautiful silvery swimming trunks. Immediately he felt wonderful. Virility coursed through him. He felt as though he were a young man again, just starting his lecherous career.

Quickly he put on a robe and slippers. (Have I mentioned that he was a rich man? And that his home was a penthouse atop the swankiest hotel in Atlantic City? He was, and it was.) He went downstairs in his private elevator and outside to the hotel's luxurious swimming pool. It was, as usual, surrounded by gorgeous Bikini-clad beauties showing off their wares under the pretence of acquiring suntans, while they waited for propositions from wealthy men like Beauregard.

He took time choosing. But not too much time.

Two hours later, still clad in the wonderful magic trunks, he sat on the edge of his bed and stared at and sighed for the beautiful blonde who lay stretched out on the bed beside him, Bikiniless – and sound asleep.

Nasty had been so right. And so well named. The miraculous trunks, the indestructible, untearable trunks worked perfectly. But if he took them off, or even let them down . . .

ROPE TRICK

Mr and Mrs George Darnell – her first name was Elsie, if that matters – were taking a honeymoon trip around the world. A *second* honeymoon, starting on the day of their twentieth anniversary. George had been in his thirties and Elsie in her twenties on the occasion of their first honeymoon – which, if you wish to check me on your slide rule, indicates that George was now in his fifties and Elsie in her forties.

Her dangerous forties (this phrase can be applied to a woman as well as to a man) and very, very disappointed with what had been happening – or, more specifically, had *not* been happening – during the first three weeks of their second honeymoon. To be completely honest, nothing, absolutely nothing had happened.

Until they reached Calcutta.

They checked into a hotel there early one afternoon and after freshening up a bit decided to wander about and see as much of the city as could be seen in the one day and night they planned to spend there.

They came to the bazaar.

And there watched a Hindu fakir performing the Indian rope trick. Not the spectacular and complicated version in which a boy climbs the rope and – well, you know the story of how the full-scale Indian rope trick is performed.

This was a quite simplified version. The fakir, with a short length of rope coiled on the ground in front of him, played over and over a few simple notes on a flageolet – and gradually, as he played, the rope began to rise into the air and stand rigid.

This gave Elsie Darnell a wonderful idea – although she did not mention it to George. She returned with him to their room at the hotel and, after dinner, waited until he went to sleep – as always, at nine o'clock.

Then she quietly left the room and the hotel. She found a taxi driver and an interpreter and, with both of them, went back to the bazaar and found the fakir.

Through the interpreter she managed to buy from the fakir the flageolet which she had heard him play and paid him to teach her to play the few simple repetitious notes which had made the rope rise.

Then she returned to the hotel and to their room. Her husband George was sleeping soundly – as he always did.

Standing beside the bed Elsie very softly began to play the simple tune on the flageolet.

Over and over.

And as she played it – gradually – the sheet began to rise, over her sleeping husband.

When it had risen to a sufficient height she put down the flageolet and, with a joyful cry, threw back the sheet.

And there, standing straight in the air, was the drawstring of his pajamas!

THE RING OF HANS CARVEL
(retold and somewhat modernized
from the works of Rabelais)

Once upon a time there lived in France a prosperous but somewhat ageing jeweller named Hans Carvel. Besides being a studious and learned man, he was a likeable man. And a man who liked women and although he had not lived a celibate life, or missed anything, had happened to remain a bachelor until he was – well, let's call his age as pushing sixty and not mention from which direction he was pushing it.

At that age he fell in love with a bailiff's daughter – a young and a beautiful girl, spirited and vivacious, a dish to set before a king.

And married her.

Within a few weeks of the otherwise happy marriage Hans Carvel began to suspect that his young wife, whom he still loved deeply, might be just a little *too* spirited, a little *too* vivacious. That which he was able to offer her – aside from money, of which he had a sufficiency – might not be enough to keep her contented. *Might* not, did I say? *Was* not.

Not unnaturally he began to suspect, and then to be practically certain, that she was supplementing her love life with several – or possibly even many – other and younger men.

This preyed on his mind. It drove him, in fact, to a state of distraction in which he had bad dreams almost nightly.

In one of these dreams, one night, he found himself talking to the Devil, explaining his dilemma, and offering the traditional price for something, *anything*, that would assure him of his wife's faithfulness.

In his dream, the Devil nodded readily and told Hans: "I will give you a magic ring. You will find it when you awaken. As long as you wear this ring it will be utterly and completely impossible for your wife to be unfaithful to you without your knowledge and consent."

And the Devil vanished and Hans Carvel awakened.

And found that he was indeed wearing a ring, as it were, and that what the Devil had promised him was indeed true.

But his young wife had also awakened and was stirring, and she said to him: "Hans, darling, not your finger. *That* is not what goes *there*."

FAIR-WEATHER FIEND

John Morressy

In the previous volumes I have reprinted two of John Morressy's stories featuring the wizard Kedrigern and his odd retinue of acquaintances – "Alaska" and "A Hedge Against Alchemy". Here's a third. If you want to sample further stories you can check out the five Kedrigern books: A Voice for Princes (1986), The Questing of Kedrigern (1987), Kedrigern in Wanderland (1988), Kedrigern and the Charming Couple (1990) and A Remembrance for Kedrigern (1990). John Morressy is a retired US professor of English, and is working on further Kedrigern stories.

Midnight had come and passed. Princess had nodded off to sleep over her spelling book. Spot was working at something in the cellar, from which thumps and clinking sounds arose at intervals, interspersed with clatters and clanks. Kedrigern was struggling against weariness as he reached the last pages of a spectacularly gory chronicle. All without the house, and all within – save Spot's muted industry and Kedrigern's turned pages and smothered yawns – was silent.

Suddenly, without preamble of any kind, three knocks sounded at the door, and Kedrigern was alert at once. Princess stirred and sighed, but did not wake. The knocking had been no peremptory battering, but a soft, almost surreptitious, series of taps. Kedrigern waited a moment, listening, and it came again, no louder than before, but this time doubled: three quick taps, a pause, and then three more.

Spot's huge head appeared at knee level in the doorway. "Yah?" it enquired softly.

"Good troll, Spot," said the wizard, rising. "I'll get the door. You stay close, just in case."

"Yah, yah!" the house-troll whispered.

There had been no heavy footsteps or flapping of wings; the caller was most likely an ordinary mortal, then. But neither had there been hoof-beats – and what ordinary mortal would walk up Silent Thunder Mountain in the dead of night? And who, having the courage and determination to find his way to a wizard's abode, would tap so timidly at the door? A thief or assassin would not knock at all; a lost traveller would pound and shout in mortal terror; a friend would rap with assurance. As he made his silent way from the cosiness of the hearthside, Kedrigern pondered the mystery, but could not puzzle out a solution. The only thing to do was to answer the door and ascertain the visitor's identity by ocular evidence. He worked a short-term security spell on himself, the cottage, and all within. That, plus Spot's formidable strength, he deemed sufficient protection.

Directing the house-troll to a handy place of concealment, Kedrigern drew the latch and eased the door open. He saw no one. In his most authoritative voice, he demanded, "Who knocks? Answer, or I close the door!"

"Master Kedrigern?" whispered a voice near at hand.

"I am Kedrigern. Who speaks?"

"A messenger from Tarpash, King of the Valley of Misgivings. I come on a matter of utmost urgency," said the voice.

"Where are you?" Kedrigern asked. The night was overcast. He could see nothing more than the vague outline of the treetops, dark against a lesser darkness.

"Here," whispered the messenger.

"Are you invisible?"

"I am veiled, masked, and cloaked. My horse is shod in felt. Mine is a mission of the utmost secrecy as well as the utmost urgency."

Kedrigern raised his medallion to his eye and peered through the Aperture of True Vision in the direction of the voice. He saw a human form, lithe but sturdy, clad head to foot in black. He breathed a sigh of relief. There was no magic in any of this, nothing out of the ordinary, only typical royal self-importance. That was kings for you: a splinter in the royal thumb, and everyone for leagues around was expected to drop what they were doing and weep over His Majesty's injured digit. With a gesture, Kedrigern said, "Come inside."

The figure did not stir. "You really are a wizard, aren't you? I can deal only with the wizard Kedrigern."

"I told you who I am. What do you want for proof – shall I turn you into a toad?"

"Oh, no, no! That will not be necessary. I believe you. It's just that . . . well, you don't look like a wizard," said the messenger.

Kedrigern sighed. He heard this from everyone, including Princess, and had grown accustomed to it without growing to like it. He had no long white beard; he dressed in ordinary homespun tunic and breeches and comfortable, well-worn boots, and did not look to be anywhere near his 170th year. He did not look young, except when he laughed; nor did he look old, except when he was deep in memory and a certain look came into his eyes. He looked like a merchant, a scholar, a great man's steward, perhaps a goldsmith or a carver of delicate designs in ivory. He looked like anything but a wizard, and was content with the situation. It made his life simpler.

"I am Kedrigern the wizard," he said slowly and distinctly. "Take my word for it, or leave my door."

"I believe you, Master Kedrigern! Truly, I do!"

With an impatient, grumbling grunt, Kedrigern stepped inside and dismissed Spot with a silent gesture. The troll bounded off to the cellar, to resume its exertions.

"Well, come in," said the wizard.

Once inside, the messenger doffed his cloak and broad-brimmed hat. He retained the mask that covered his face. A veil depended from the mask, but did not conceal the reddish gold beard of the wearer. He was a tall man, well formed, and he spoke with assurance in a mild, cultured voice.

"I will be brief, Master Kedrigern: the king is sore afflicted. Only a wizard can help him."

"What is it? A curse? A spell? Did he open something he shouldn't have opened? Provoke a witch? Insult a fairy?"

"The details are obscure, and even the little I know, I cannot reveal."

"Then how do you know that King Tarpash needs the services of a wizard and not a physician?" snapped Kedrigern irritably.

"The Royal Physician was summoned immediately. He examined His Majesty and declared that only a wizard or an alchemist could—"

"An alchemist?" Kedrigern cried. "What is he trying to do to the poor man? An alchemist couldn't help a sick rat!"

"We are desperate, Master Kedrigern."

"You must be, if you can consider calling in an alchemist. Tarpash always had a good head on his shoulders. He would never have—"

A sob burst from the messenger, silencing Kedrigern. When the man had composed himself, he said in a subdued, but no less urgent, voice, "The king must be helped at once. If he is not, the marriage cannot take place!"

"What marriage? Tarpash is happily married – has been for thirty years."

"His son's marriage. Prince Middry is to marry Belserena of the Dappled Dales, the sweetest, loveliest, most adorable woman in all the world. Her hair is spun gold, her eyes twin pools of violet, her lips a rosebud, her form divine. Flowers of indescribable fragrance spring up where her dainty foot caresses the ground – oh, happy ground! – and her very voice perfumes the air," the messenger rhapsodized. He paused to draw breath so that he might continue his litany of adoration, but Kedrigern raised a hand to silence him.

"It's all right, Prince Middry. You can take off the mask and tell me the whole story," he said.

The messenger stood thunderstruck for a moment, then tore away mask and veil to reveal a reasonably handsome, rather pallid face and red-rimmed eyes. "How did you know? My disguise was impenetrable!"

Kedrigern smiled inscrutably. "I am a wizard, my son. I know all sorts of things."

"Then you must help my father! The wedding is set for nine days hence!"

"Come in by the fire, Prince Middry. Sit down, put your feet up, and tell me everything."

By this time, Princess had been awakened by the sound of voices. She welcomed the visitor, and listened with profound attention to his account. It was depressingly short. The King of the Valley of Misgivings had lost his wits. No one knew how, or why, or precisely when or where the tragedy had occurred, and no one had the faintest idea of a remedy. The approaching wedding added urgency to the gravity of the situation. It would be socially unacceptable, and politically disastrous, to have the father of the groom insist on a game of pat-a-cake, or pull off his boots and start playing with his toes, in the middle of the ceremony; and yet to postpone the wedding, or call it off entirely, would create a diplomatic crisis, as well as desolate the betrothed couple.

Much as he abominated travel, Kedrigern recognized his obligations as a wizard and an old acquaintance of the royal family. Princess was pleased by the prospects of a visit to a royal court, albeit a distraught one. She spoke cheerfully of a nice little trip, as Kedrigern had known she would. "A nice little trip," he reflected unhappily, was Princess's term for any journey short of a decades-long mass migration fraught with perils beyond imagining.

★   ★   ★

This trip, if not exactly nice, was at least short and free of mishap. They left Silent Thunder Mountain at first light, yawning and uncommunicative, and covered the distance in less than four days' hard riding.

Dusty, travel-sore, weary, and faint with hunger, they were conducted at once to the presence of Queen Yulda. In her youth she had been known as Yulda of the Dovelike Voice, and praised in the conventional forms for her beauty; but her youth was now a remote memory. Yulda had changed. She was now a large frowning woman with hair the colour of wood ash and a jaw like a nutcracker.

Her manner suited her appearance. Without so much as a glance at her exhausted son, she speared Kedrigern with an angry question. "Who is this woman?" she demanded of him in a voice more corvine than dovelike.

Princess had concealed her wings under her cloak. Though as tired as the others, she was still spectacularly beautiful, perhaps too much so to be taken for a wizard or a wife. Her black hair gleamed; her blue eyes glowed; and at Yulda's question, her white teeth clenched.

"This is my wife. She is a woman of royal blood and my fellow adept. We work together," Kedrigern replied.

"I require your services only," said the queen.

With a low bow, Kedrigern said, "We work together, Your Majesty, or we do not work at all."

Queen Yulda glowered on them both, and cast a quick, angry scowl at her son. "You are presumptuous in your speech, wizard," she said.

"Those are my conditions, Your Majesty."

She pondered for a time, frowning mightily, then said, "Only five days remain before the wedding. Can you help Tarpash? Be truthful, wizard."

"I'll have to see His Majesty before I can answer that."

"You're supposed to be a great wizard – can't you work a spell, or a counterspell, or something like that? Something quick?"

"I *am* a great wizard, Your Majesty. And precisely because I am, I do nothing in haste. A great wizard never disenchants or despells until he knows what kind of enchantment or spell he's dealing with. May I see the king?" Kedrigern replied patiently.

"His Majesty is asleep, and I do not wish to have him disturbed. He played very hard today, and missed his nap," said the queen.

"Then perhaps you will provide what information you can. I must know precisely what happened."

Queen Yulda glanced surreptitiously around the chamber, then beckoned Kedrigern closer. Lowering her voice, she said, "We don't know. His Majesty was fine at breakfast. By midday he had lost his wits."

"Where did His Majesty spend the morning?" Kedrigern asked.

"The king was in the countinghouse."

"Counting out his money?"

"Certainly not. The Treasurer's men do that. The king goes to the countinghouse to relax."

"Was anyone with him?"

"He never takes anyone with him. He likes his privacy. He stayed in the countinghouse for a time, then went out to sit under his favourite tree. It was a beautiful sunny day. Not a cloud in the sky."

"I see," Kedrigern murmured, stroking his chin in a thoughtful gesture. In truth, he saw nothing. A thick mist of fatigue lay over his mind. His stomach felt like an abyss, his bones ached, and he was ready to collapse from exhaustion; but he did his best to preserve a wizardly façade. "Where were you and the prince?" he asked.

"I was in the parlour when I received word of the tragedy. I had just finished a light repast," said the queen.

"Bread and honey, I presume," Kedrigern said confidently.

"Currant cake and sweet wine," Yulda corrected him, with an expression of genteel disgust. "Bread and honey is not a suitable snack for one of royal blood. It is very common."

Princess, who enjoyed the occasional bit of bread and honey, gave the queen a black glance, but said nothing, being too bone-weary to dispute over any matter less than life-threatening. She merely yawned.

"And where were you, Prince Middry?"

"I spent the morning with my tailors. It was such a lovely morning, too. Perfect for riding. But they insisted on a fitting," said the prince, pouting.

"And how did you learn of . . . the incident?"

"Mother sent the messenger directly to me."

"Yes, of course," said the wizard, nodding. He turned to the queen. "Do you recall the messenger's exact words?"

"No. He babbled. When I finally got him to pull himself together, he told me that the king was sitting under the oak tree near the counting-house, eating a worm. I perceived at once that something was amiss. When I arrived at the scene, Tarpash had pulled a boot over his head and was trying to put his gloves on his feet. I was greatly distressed."

Middry, after a wide, audible yawn, said, "Mother, one must not overtax oneself. Let's continue this in the morning."

"I am not overtaxed. Every minute is precious."

"But, Mother, *I* am overtaxed. I've been travelling hard for days. I've been in the saddle since dawn."

"Think of the kingdom, boy! Think of the wedding. Think of your father. Pull yourself together," said Yulda severely.

"Your Majesty, we are all overtaxed. Disenchantments always work best when one is fully rested and one's mind is keen. Fatigue can be hazardous to the enchantee," said Kedrigern. He emphasized his words with a yawn.

"Delay can be hazardous to the kingdom, wizard," Queen Yulda growled.

"We still have five days, Your Majesty."

"If you wait until morning, we will have only *four* days."

"Trust me, Your Majesty," Kedrigern said. After a great yawn, which was immediately reprised by Princess and Prince Middry, he went on, "I will confer with the Royal Physician first thing in the morning, and then examine His Majesty – if he is awake."

Yulda glowered at all three of them in turn. At last, grudgingly, she said, "Very well. You are dismissed. I will have you roused at the first crowing of the cock, wizard – you and your fellow adept."

Princess did not speak until they were alone in their chamber, to which she strode with lips compressed and eyes narrowed. When the door was closed, she rounded on Kedrigern, saying, "That woman deserves a curse on her own head, and I'm ready to provide it! I never met such a surly virago in my life! If she thinks I'll lift a finger to help—"

"My dear, Yulda's upset. We're not seeing her best side," Kedrigern said in his most soothing voice. He opened his arms to embrace and comfort Princess, but she would have none of it. Taking wing, she flew to the mantelpiece, where she perched with cold eye and folded arms. "Best side? Hah!" she said with a contemptuous toss of her head.

"Think of the strain she's under. Her husband's wits gone, her son's happiness in jeopardy, her kingdom—"

"A lot she cares about Middry's happiness. Did you see the way she treated him?"

"Yes, but—"

"No wonder he's so fearful of the wedding's being called off. He can't wait to escape from this place and that monstrous woman!"

"I'm sure Middry really loves Belserena. He spoke glowingly of her at every opportunity."

"Talk. Nothing but talk. He only wants to get away. It's hard to blame him, actually," said Princess. She flew down and stood by the open window.

"Then we must do all we can to help King Tarpash. To help him is to help Middry."

Princess paced up and down before the window, fluttering a short distance every now and then as was her habit when deep in thought. She stopped abruptly and said, "What about the poor girl? It's all very well to help Middry, but Belserena will wind up with that gimlet-eyed fishwife for a mother-in-law. And no great prize for a husband, either."

"Presumably the young lady knows what she's getting herself into, my dear. She may be in love. Perhaps she's doing it for her kingdom. I don't think we ought to meddle in private affairs."

Princess was unconvinced, but she and Kedrigern were by this time too weary to dispute further. A servant brought them a tray of bread, cheese, and fruit, which they consumed with great appetite before turning in, to fall asleep at once.

A pounding at the door awoke them just as the first light appeared in the eastern sky. A cock crowed near by.

"All right, all right! We're getting up! We're up!" Kedrigern groaned. "Stop hammering!"

"The Royal Physician attends in his chamber," a voice outside the door announced. "I will conduct you to him."

Peevish and puffy-eyed, Kedrigern and Princess dressed in haste and followed the servant up several broad staircases, down three long corridors, and along a gloomy passageway until, having climbed one final narrow, winding staircase, they came to a tower room. A portly, bald man with a bushy, grizzled beard stood in the doorway, yawning.

"The wizard Kedrigern," the servant announced.

Princess gave a flutter of her wings, hovered before the servant at eye level, and said sternly, "Announce us properly, young man. It's the wizards Kedrigern and Princess, and don't you forget it."

"My lady flies!" the servant whispered, hoarse with astonishment.

"That's not all she does," said Princess, gliding to Kedrigern's side. "Well, go ahead. Announce."

"The wizards Kedrigern and Princess," said the servant, his voice cracking slightly on her name. Dismissed, he sped off.

"Very nice. So you're the wizards. Mind if I have a look at those wings?" said the physician.

"I am not here to be examined," Princess said with dignity.

"Just a quick look, my lady. I want to see how they're attached."

"They are not *attached*; they are *mine*. It was all done by magic."

"Look, about the king . . .," Kedrigern said.

"Can't help you there, I'm afraid," said the physician, not taking his eyes off Princess. "Yours, you say? Growing right out of your back?"

"We have to learn what's happened to King Tarpash!" Kedrigern cried in exasperation.

"Well, don't look at me. I'm not going to make a fool out of myself."

"How can you make a fool out of yourself by telling us what you found?"

"I didn't find anything. It's none of my business, anyway. You're the wizards – you help him."

"If you didn't find anything, why did you tell the queen to send for a wizard?" Kedrigern demanded.

"Because it's all magic, that's why! It has to be! If you tell them what happened, they'll believe you, but if I – Never mind. Just leave me out of this."

With a little flirt of her wings that captured the physician's attention at once, Princess said, "If the king doesn't recover, Queen Yulda will rule. Won't that be nice?"

The physician's expression clouded. He licked his lips nervously, but said nothing.

"She'll make a wonderful ruler. So strong-willed. So determined," Princess said, smiling.

Taking a cue, Kedrigern said, "She'll stand for no nonsense, that's certain. She'll make people toe the mark. Heads will roll."

"You must promise not to tell anyone I said this," the physician blurted.

"My dear fellow! Of course we promise," Kedrigern warmly assured him.

Lowering his voice, looking furtively around the room, the physician said, "Lightning. The king was struck by lightning."

"Lightning?" Princess repeated in disbelief.

"But it was a lovely day. Everyone said so!" Kedrigern objected.

"It was a gorgeous day. Best all year. I know. I sat by the window, looking out over that very oak tree, for a full two hours. I heard no thunder. I saw no lightning."

"Yet you say His Majesty was struck by lightning."

"Definitely. I know the signs."

"So you suspect magic."

"Of course. Don't you?"

"It certainly looks that way."

"I've never been comfortable about lightning. It comes out of the heavens, after all. That puts it outside my line. And when it comes out of a clear blue sky . . . well, I just don't want to get involved," said the physician. He appeared to be uneasy even talking about the subject.

"Understandable. Can you tell us anything more?"

The physician shook his head and spread his hands in a gesture of utter helplessness. "The king was struck by lightning. Only, he couldn't have been struck by lightning. There *was* no lightning. What more can I say?"

"Nothing, obviously. Thank you for your help," said Kedrigern.

"I want to see the king recover. We all love His Majesty. But if I tried to tell them . . ." The physician shrugged. Brightening, he asked, "Now can I look at those wings?"

Lifting out of reach, Princess called down, "We'll talk about that when the king has his wits."

Unaccompanied, undirected, Kedrigern and Princess made their way down to the kitchen, where they beguiled the cook into preparing them a quick breakfast. Afterward they inspected the oak tree under which Tarpash had been found witless. Princess flew up into the branches and examined everything carefully while Kedrigern studied the ground and lower trunk. They found no traces of a lightning strike.

"That physician is up to something," Kedrigern said grimly.

"He's harmless," Princess said, dismissing the suggestion with a smile.

"Don't be so sure. He had alchemic equipment in his

workroom. I saw a cupel and a flask and a very pretty set of balances."

"That doesn't make him an alchemist. Physicians use those things, too."

"He had alchemic texts on his bookshelf," Kedrigern said, with the air of one clinching an argument.

"So do you," Princess pointed out.

"But I need them! I have to know what the competition is up to."

"Maybe he does, too."

They sat under the tree in deep and thoughtful silence for a time, and at length, Princess said, "I don't trust Middry. What if he doesn't really want to marry Belserena? This could be his way of getting out of it."

"He sounded very sincere to me," Kedrigern said.

"Men always do."

Silence returned. After a time, Princess said glumly, "I just can't figure out how. I wouldn't put anything past Yulda, and it wouldn't surprise me if Middry had some plot going, but neither one seems capable of magic."

"They're not. I checked them out," Kedrigern said, holding up his medallion and displaying the Aperture of True Vision at its centre. "The physician, too. But he could still be an alchemist."

"Alchemists can't work magic. That's why they're only alchemists," Princess reminded him.

Silence once again. Then Kedrigern snapped his fingers and gave a little laugh. He sprang to his feet and held out his hand. "Come. We're going to ask the queen a few questions," he said, smiling with anticipation.

Princess bounded up. "So you agree with me; that stringy-haired shrew is behind the king's affliction!"

"I think it's something far more subtle than that, my dear, but Yulda may be able to help us clear it up."

The queen received them without delay, but before they could speak, she raised a peremptory hand and said, "His Majesty is playing in the royal sandbox and cannot be disturbed."

"Is His Majesty wearing the same clothing he wore on the fateful day?" Kedrigern asked.

"Certainly not. If you must know, he is wearing a yellow sunsuit and a broad-brimmed straw hat – to keep the sun off his head."

"Then we may not have to trouble His Majesty at all. May we see everything the king was wearing when he was found?"

The queen gave a command. Two servants hurried from the chamber. Yulda drummed her fingers on the arms of her chair, frowning impatiently.

"Had His Majesty any enemies?" Kedrigern asked.

"What a ridiculous question! Of course he had enemies. He was a king!"

"Have any of the king's enemies been seen near the castle recently?"

"No. Things have been quiet. Very quiet." Yulda heaved a deep, nostalgic sigh and shook her head sadly. "We're all getting too old for feuding. We're not enemies any more, not really. We're all survivors now."

"Have you been reconciled with all your old enemies?"

She nodded. "Nothing official. No pacts or treaties or anything of that nature. We've lost interest in the old quarrels, that's all. Half the time we can't remember why we quarrelled in the first place. We're content to stay in our castles and keep warm and dry. Leave the bashing and the glory to the young, if they care for that sort of thing." She glanced sourly at her son, who sat by the window fingering a lute. "Some do, and some don't," she concluded.

"Then there's no visiting back and forth?"

"Can't spare the time, wizard. We have our kingdoms to run. Besides, it's too uncomfortable. But they've all been invited to the wedding, and they've all sent lovely presents. Three-quarters of them can't attend, but they all sent presents."

"Aren't presents usually sent to the bride's residence?" Princess asked.

"Not when she marries *my* boy," snapped the queen.

"These presents are all in the countinghouse, I presume," Kedrigern said.

Yulda and Princess both looked at him with sudden curiosity. Before either woman could speak, the servants returned bearing a pile of royal clothing. Under Kedrigern's direction, they laid it out in orderly arrangement on the floor. Yulda and Middry joined the two wizards around the display.

"Is this exactly what the king was wearing when he was discovered under the oak?" Kedrigern asked.

"Yes. I remember very clearly," said the queen, and the prince nodded in agreement.

"Nothing missing? No rings, amulets, brooch, torque, or other bit of jewellery?"

"Tarpash didn't like such things. The only jewellery he wore was a gold ring that had been handed down in his family for generations," said the queen.

"And his crown, mother," Middry pointed out. "Father liked to wear a crown. He said it made him feel kingly."

Pointing to the display, Kedrigern said, "The ring and the crown are not here."

"The ring is on his finger. Hasn't been off it since before we were married. The crown . . ." Yulda paused, scowling fiercely in the effort to remember.

Cautiously, Middry said, "He was wearing it at breakfast that morning. I'm sure he was."

"Yes! Yes, he was," said the queen. "The little openwork crown he always wore around the castle. I remember now."

"But when you saw His Majesty, Your Majesty, he had a boot on his head. Was the crown lying nearby?"

"No. In fact . . . I don't believe I've seen that crown since. I'm sure I haven't."

"As I suspected," Kedrigern murmured, nodding and stroking his chin. "Your Majesty, we must visit the countinghouse."

"You shall have free access, wizard."

"Both of us, Your Majesty."

Yulda's formidable jaw set firmly. Her nostrils dilated. After a pause, she said, "Very well. Both of you."

"All we require is access to the room where the wedding presents are kept. There is a list of items, with the names of the senders, is there not?"

"The Treasurer will provide it," said the queen. She turned to a servant and commanded, "Summon the Lord Treasurer!"

Once they were inside the room of gifts, with torches burning brightly in all the sockets on the wall, the Lord Treasurer dismissed the servants and excused himself. Word had somehow spread that the king's affliction was now definitely known to be the result of magic, and a degree of uneasiness was perceptible in everyone about the castle. Kedrigern and Princess were left to themselves: exactly the working conditions they preferred.

Kedrigern surveyed the jumble of ornate objects and said, "This could take some time."

"Why don't we just go down the list?" Princess suggested.

"No need, my dear. I know exactly what I'm looking for: a crown, coronet, or diadem, with a certain jewel set in a certain position."

"There's a crown! See it, right there, hanging from the trunk of the silver elephant with the emerald tusks?!" Princess cried excitedly, pointing to a figure standing on a chest before them.

Kedrigern took up the crown and examined it. He shook his head. "Wrong type. This is probably the one Tarpash was wearing when he entered. He took it off when he tried on the other."

"What other? Why the sudden interest in crowns?" Princess asked.

"Because Tarpash wasn't wearing one when he was found, and that's completely out of character for him. I haven't seen Tarpash for over thirty years, but even as a young king, he was a great believer in wearing a crown. He had summer and winter crowns, indoor and outdoor crowns, crowns for hunting, dancing, affairs of state, hawking, riding – anything and everything Tarpash did, he had a special crown to go with it. Even his nightcap was embroidered to resemble a crown."

"Kings do have their eccentricities," Princess said.

"Indeed they do. And his was well known. Anyone nursing an old grudge against Tarpash would know that crowns were his weakness. He couldn't see one without wanting to try it on."

"But wouldn't an enemy be more likely to employ a poisoned crown?"

Kedrigern shook his head. "Too obvious. Also easily traced. There'd be war in no time. No, we're dealing with a subtle enemy. A man might lose his wits for any number of reasons. Who would suspect a crown sent as a wedding present? And if the wedding has to be called off—"

"The present would be returned, and no one would ever know! That's absolutely brilliant!" Princess exclaimed.

"Thank you, my dear," Kedrigern said humbly.

"I meant the plot. But it was also a nice piece of deduction on your part."

"I like it myself. But unless we find the crown, it's all hot air."

"Let's get to work, then. I'll take the right side of the room; you take the left," said Princess, rolling back her sleeves.

Smiling placidly, Kedrigern reached into his tunic and drew out his medallion. "There's a much easier way," he said, raising it to his eye. He surveyed the chamber, moving his gaze slowly across the piles of gaudy, the heaps of ostentatious, the isolated beautiful, pausing now and then to lower the medallion and rub his eye. "A lot of interference in here," he explained. "Some of these objects were once enchanted, spelled, or cursed, and the residual magic fogs up my reception."

"Can I do anything to help?" Princess asked.

Kedrigern resumed his slow search, his gaze ascending a great mound of baubles in a corner of the room. "Ah," he said softly. "Yes, my dear, you can be a great help. At the top of that heap – flung there by Tarpash in his frenzy – is a golden crown with a cloudy stone on top. Would you mind . . .?"

Princess lifted off with a soft hum of wings. She hovered over the pile for a moment, searching, then snatched up the crown and flourished it overhead before returning to Kedrigern's side.

"Is this the fiendish device?" she asked.

"It is," he said, studying the milky stone through the Aperture of True Vision. "Subtle, indeed. Diabolically so."

"But lovely. That's a magnificent opal."

"Enchanted crystal," he corrected her.

"Oh, surely an opal," she protested. "Look at that vague, fuzzy, clouded interior."

"A perceptive description, my dear. You're looking at the king's wits."

The process of reversal was simple, but not without an element of risk. Kedrigern pried the cloudy crystal free, turned it upside down, and reinserted it in its setting. He then recited a long and complicated spell over it. This done, he held it out to Tarpash, shaking it gently to attract the king's attention.

The monarch, who had been roused from his nap, hurriedly dressed, and plopped down in his throne, was in a cranky state. But at the sight of the crown, his face lit up. He screamed, "I want! I want!", and made a grab for it. With Yulda assisting, and Middry close at hand, under Kedrigern's watchful eye – it would have been disastrous to put it on upside down – the king settled the crown on his head.

A wink of bright light flickered through the room, like lightning from nowhere. Tarpash twitched and blinked his eyes. He reached up to remove the crown, and studied the clear crystal stone at its centre. "A pretty thing, but uncomfortable," he said. "Where is my regular Wednesday crown?" Noticing Kedrigern, he cried, "Who are you? I know you, don't I? And who is that lovely lady with the wings? How did you get in here? Am I enchanted?"

"Not any more, Your Majesty," Kedrigern said.

"But I have been, haven't I? My head feels as if it's been squeezed," said the king, rubbing his temples.

"In a sense, that's exactly what happened. Your Majesty's

wits were stolen and locked in that crystal on the crown,"
Kedrigern explained.

"They were? For how long? What of my son's wedding?"
Middry, beaming, said, "It's still four days off, father.
Kedrigern hurried here and removed the spell."

"Kedrigern! Of course. I didn't recognize you at first. It's
been a long time. And this lovely lady – a fairy princess?"

"A very human princess, Your Majesty. This is my wife and
fellow wizard, Princess."

"My thanks to you both. All our thanks. You will be
generously rewarded," said the king, signalling to the Treasurer. "But would you mind telling me what happened? I
remember going to the countinghouse and looking over the
wedding gifts, and then . . ." Tarpash gestured in a manner
expressive of bewilderment.

"Your eye fell on that crown, a gift from Zilfric of the Long
Hand," said Kedrigern. "You liked it. You took off the crown
you were wearing, hung it on the trunk of the elephant figure
given by Inuri the Footloose, and put on the new crown. The
crystal, an object of great potency and heavily enchanted, drew
forth your wits in a single dazzling instant. In distraction, you
ran from the countinghouse and collapsed under the oak tree,
where you were found soon after with nothing to indicate the
cause of your affliction. You had the symptoms of a man struck
by lightning. In the purely magical sense, that's what happened. But there was no lightning from the sky that day. Your
condition was a profound mystery."

Tarpash smiled benignly on Kedrigern and Princess. "But
you solved it. And you will be rewarded. And Zilfric will be
punished, as soon as I can think of something nasty enough."

"If I may make a suggestion . . ." Kedrigern said.

"Please do."

"Hoist him with his own petard."

"We'll hoist him any way we can," snapped Yulda, her large
jaw jutting forward.

"Tell us your recommendation, Kedrigern, and if it likes us
well, we will leave the details in your hands," said Tarpash.

"It will take no more than a day to arrange – two at the most – if I may enlist the royal goldsmith."

"He is at your service," said the king with a wave of his hand. "Tell us your plan."

With a smile of anticipation, Kedrigern said, "First we will remove all traces of enchantment from the crystal and the crown."

"The crown is enchanted, too! Oh, villainy!" cried the queen.

"This was a very thorough piece of work, Your Majesties. It is the doing of one Gargumfius, an exceptionally malicious sorcerer known to be in the employ of Zilfric. The Gargumfius touch is unmistakable."

"Get the sorcerer, too!" said the king with a grim scowl.

"I plan to, Your Majesty. Once everything is completely disenchanted, I will have the goldsmith replace the stone in its original position. It will then be returned to Zilfric, accompanied by a letter."

"A letter? Is that all? I thought you were going to string the blackguard up!" said Tarpash angrily.

"I will, Your Majesty, but I will do it with subtlety," Kedrigern assured him. "Your Majesty will inform him that the entire royal family has worn the crown for lengthy periods of time, and has benefited in innumerable ways, mental and physical: deeper understanding of affairs of state, mastery of economic theories, improved memory, keener eyesight, better digestion, and greater sympathy for fellow rulers, which latter quality has moved you to return the crown, which you consider too precious to keep to yourselves. I leave it to Your Majesties to imagine the effect this communication will have on Zilfric, and his stratagems of revenge, and his dealings with Gargumfius."

Tarpash considered the proposal for a time, then laughed aloud and clapped his hands. "Capital! Much better than a punitive expedition. Those things are always such a bother. And so expensive, too."

"But will they suffer enough? We want them to suffer!"

Yulda said fiercely. "Why don't we just go after them and string them up?"

"Because I don't feel like going to war. Besides, this will keep Zilfric so busy, suspecting and accusing and fighting with his sorcerer, that he won't have time to bother us or anyone else. Get to it at once, Kedrigern. But first," said the king, summoning the Treasurer to his side, bearing a small carven ebony casket, "your reward."

Opening the casket, Tarpash withdrew a delicate necklace of gold-set rubies, which he placed around Princess's neck. To Kedrigern, he gave the black casket, saying, "Since we know of your dislike for personal adornment of any kind, we will reward you simply." The wizard smiled when he heard the clink of coins within, and felt the unmistakable weight of gold in his hands.

"And we invite you to be honoured guests at our son's wedding," Tarpash concluded, beaming.

"We accept with deep gratitude, Your Majesty," said Princess before Kedrigern could come up with a reason to duck out of the invitation and hurry home to Silent Thunder Mountain.

"We are honoured indeed," said Kedrigern, with a deep bow and a sigh of resignation.

The wedding of Belserena and Middry was a splendid spectacle. The feasting was elaborate, the tournament a great butchery, the entertainment elegant, the revelry ebullient. When the wizards set out for home after a ten days' stay, even Princess had to admit to satiety as far as her social needs were concerned. Kedrigern was desperate for peace, quiet, and solitude; so much so that he spoke scarcely a word until they had travelled half a day. Only when they stopped by a brook for a midday rest and a light snack did he relax a bit.

"It's wonderful to be going home at last," he said, sprawling on the cool grass.

"The past two weeks have been quite eventful," said Princess wistfully.

"Horribly so. All those people, and the noise . . . not a

minute to ourselves . . . always something going on." He shuddered at the memory.

"It was grand," she sighed.

"It was a vision of Hell," he murmured.

They reclined on the grass in silence for a time, until Kedrigern propped himself on his elbows, gazed up at the sky, and, apropos of nothing, observed, "The best part is that I solved the problem without using magic."

In an instant, Princess, too, was sitting up. "What about the reversing spell on the crystal?"

"That was an afterthought. The important things were achieved by sheer intelligence and reasoning," he said, tapping his forehead meaningfully.

"Isn't magic the reason people summon a wizard? Isn't it what they pay for?"

Irritably, Kedrigern said, "They pay me for what I *know*, not what I do. I'm not an entertainer; I'm a wizard."

"And wizards do magic," Princess said, as if that settled everything.

"When they must," Kedrigern added.

Princess moved closer and patted him on the hand. When he remained silent, she kissed him sweetly and said, "Never mind. It was a very impressive piece of reasoning. I don't believe there's another wizard who could have worked it out without resorting to magic."

Mollified, Kedrigern sought a way to respond to her gracious gesture. Taking her hand, he said, "It was truly regal of you, my dear, to treat Yulda so well. You were downright friendly. I know she's a difficult woman, but—"

"Difficult? I've known trolls with better manners! And that voice of hers . . ." Princess shook her head and made a little moue of distaste.

"All the more credit to you for treating her so nicely."

"I was thinking of Belserena. Sweet child. I didn't want to do anything to spoil her wedding."

"You were extremely generous to Belserena. That was a lovely pendant you gave her."

"Well, we were honoured guests. That sort of thing is expected of us."

"It is? I'm never sure about those things."

"I know," said Princess resignedly.

"It all seems so unnecessary. All this passing back and forth of gaudy baubles and trinkets. Like that necklace Tarpash gave you. It's a beautiful thing, and exquisitely made, but when will you actually wear it?"

"It's the thought that counts."

He cast a dubious glance at her. "Then why don't kings and princes and that lot just think well of each other, and stop exchanging plundered jewellery? It's all plunder, in one way or another, you know."

"It has its practical uses," Princess said with a sly, knowing smile.

"Oh?"

"You don't think I'd give that dear girl a mere trinket. Surely you know I placed a spell on it for her."

"My dear—"

"A simple spell for tenacity in disputation." Princess stood and made a gay and graceful pirouette on the grass, fairly glowing with the satisfaction of work well done. "Just what Belserena needs – and Yulda deserves."

THE BYRDS

Michael Coney

Coney is better known for his science fiction novels, which begin with Mirror Image *(1972) and have included* Syzygy *(1973),* Friends Come in Boxes *(1973) and* The Hero of Downways *(1973). In more recent years, however, he has turned to fantasy, and often humorous fantasy at that, such as* Fang the Gnome *(1988),* A Tomcat Called Sabrina *(1992) and* No Place for a Sealion *(1992), the last two at present published only in Canada, where Coney has lived since 1972. The following is a real off-the-wall item.*

Gran started it all.

Late one afternoon in the hottest summer in living memory, she took off all her clothes, carefully painted red around her eyes, cheeks, chin and throat, painted the rest of her body a contrasting black with the exception of her armpits and the inside of her wrists, which she painted white, strapped on her new antigravity belt, flapped her arms and rose into the nearest tree, a garry oak, where she perched.

She informed us that, as of now, she was Rufous-necked Hornbill, of India. And that was all she said, for the logical reason that Hornbills are not talking birds.

"Come down, Gran!" called Mother. "You'll catch your death of cold."

Gran remained silent. She stretched her neck and gazed at the horizon.

"She's crazy," said Father. "She's crazy. I always said she was. I'll call the asylum."

"You'll do no such thing!" Mother was always very sensitive about Gran's occasional peculiarities. "She'll be down soon. The evenings are drawing in. She'll get cold."

"What's an old fool her age doing with an antigravity unit anyway, that's what I want to know," said Father.

The Water Department was restricting supply and the weatherman was predicting floods. The Energy Department was warning of depleted stocks, the Department of Rest had announced that the population must fall by one-point-eight per cent by November or else, the Mailgift was spewing out a deluge of application forms, tax forms and final reminders, the Tidy Mice were malfunctioning so that the house stank . . .

And now this.

It was humiliating and embarrassing, Gran up a tree, naked and painted. She stayed there all evening, and I knew that my girlfriend Pandora would be dropping by soon and would be sure to ask questions.

Humanity was at that point in the morality cycle when nudity was considered indecent. Gran was probably thirty years before her time. There was something lonely and anachronistic about her, perched there, balancing unsteadily in a squatting position, occasionally grabbing at the trunk for support, then flapping her arms to re-establish the birdlike impression. She looked like some horrible mutation. Her resemblance to a Rufous-necked Hornbill was slight.

"Talk her down, Gramps," said Father.

"She'll come down when she's hungry."

He was wrong. Late in the evening Gran winged her way to a vacant lot where an ancient tree stood. She began to eat unsterilized apples, juice flowing down her chin. It was a grotesque sight. "She'll be poisoned!" cried Mother.

"So, she's made her choice at last," said Father.

He was referring to *Your Choice for Peace*, the brochure that

Gran and Gramps received monthly from the Department of Rest. Accompanying the brochure is a six-page form on which senior citizens describe all that is good about their life, and a few of the things that annoy them. At the end of the form are two boxes in which the oldster indicates his preference for Life or Peace. If he does not check the Life box, or if he fails to complete the form, it is assumed that he has chosen Peace, and they send the Wagon for him.

Now Gran was cutting a picturesque silhouette against the pale blue of the evening sky as she circled the rooftops, uttering harsh cries. She flew with arms outstretched, legs trailing, and we all had to admit to the beauty of the sight; that was, until a flock of starlings began to mob her.

Losing directional control she spiralled downward, recovered, levelled out and skimmed towards us, outpacing the starlings and regaining her perch in the garry oak. She made preening motions and settled down for the night. The family Pesterminator, zapping bugs with its tiny laser, considered her electronically for a second but held its fire.

We were indoors by the time Pandora arrived. She was nervous, complaining that there was a huge mutation in the tree outside, and it had cawed at her.

Mother said quickly, "It's only a Rufous-necked Hornbill."

"A rare visitor to these shores," added Father.

"Why couldn't she have been a sparrow?" asked Mother. "Or something else inconspicuous." Things were not going well for her. The little robot Tidy Mice still sulked behind the wainscoting and she'd had to clean the house by hand.

The garish Gran shone like a beacon in the morning sunlight. There was no concealing the family's degradation. A small crowd had gathered and people were trying to tempt her down with breadcrumbs. She looked none the worse for her night out, and was greeting the morning with shrill yells.

Gramps was strapping on an antigravity belt. "I'm going up to fetch her down. This has gone far enough."

I said, "Be careful. She may attack you."

"Don't be a damned fool." Nevertheless, Gramps went into the tool shed, later emerging nude and freshly painted. Mother uttered a small scream of distress, suspecting that Gramps, too, had become involved in the conspiracy to diminish the family's social standing.

I reassured her. "She's more likely to listen to one of her own kind."

"Has everyone gone totally insane?" asked Mother.

Gramps rose gracefully into the garry oak, hovered, then settled beside Gran. He spoke to her quietly for a moment and she listened, head cocked attentively. Then she made low gobbling noises and leaned against him. He called down, "This may take longer than I thought."

"Oh, my God," said Mother.

"That does it," said Father. "I'm calling the shrink."

Dr Pratt was tall and dignified, and he took in the situation at a glance. "Has your mother exhibited birdish tendencies before?"

Father answered for Mother. "No more than anyone else. Although, in many other ways, she was—"

"Gran has always been the soul of conformity," said Mother quickly, beginning to weep. "If our neighbours have been saying otherwise I'll remind them of the slander laws. No – she did it to shame us. She always said she hated the colours we painted the house – she said it looked like a strutting peacock."

"Rutting peacock," said Father. "She said rutting peacock. Those were her exact words."

"Peacock, eh?" Dr Pratt looked thoughtful. There was a definite avian thread running through this. "So you feel she may be acting in retaliation. She thinks you have made a public spectacle of the house in which she lives, so now she is going to make a public spectacle of you."

"Makes sense," said Father.

"Gran!" called Dr Pratt. She looked down at us, beady little eyes ringed with red. "I have the personal undertaking of your daughter and son-in-law that the house will be repainted in colours of your own choosing." He spoke on for a few minutes in soothing tones. "That should do it," he said to us finally, picking up his bag. "Put her to bed and keep her off berries, seeds, anything like that. And don't leave any antigravity belts lying around. They can arouse all kinds of prurient interests in older people."

"She still isn't coming down," said Father. "I don't think she understood."

"Then I advise you to fell the tree," said Dr Pratt coldly, his patience evaporated. "She's a disgusting old exhibitionist who needs to be taught a lesson. Just because she chooses to act out her fantasies in an unusual way doesn't make her any different from anyone else. And what's he doing up there, anyway? Does he resent the house paint as well?"

"He chose the paint. He's there to bring her down."

We watched them in perplexity. The pair huddled together on the branch, engaged in mutual grooming. The crowd outside the gate had swollen to over a hundred.

On the following morning Gran and Gramps greeted the dawn with a cacophony of gobbling and screeching.

I heard Father throw open his bedroom window and threaten to blast them right out of that bloody tree and into the hereafter if they didn't keep it down. I heard the metallic click as he cocked his twelve-bore. I heard Mother squeal with apprehension, and the muffled thumping of a physical struggle in the next room.

I was saddened by the strain it puts on marriages when parents live in the house – or, in our case, outside the window.

The crowds gathered early and it was quickly apparent that Gramps was through with trying to talk Gran down; in fact, he was through with talking altogether. He perched beside his mate in spry fashion, jerking his head this way and that as he scanned the sky for hawks, cocking an eye at the crowd, shuddering suddenly as though shaking feathers into position.

Dr Pratt arrived at noon, shortly before the media. "A classic case of regression to the childlike state," he told us.

"The signs are all there: the unashamed nakedness, the bright colours, the speechlessness, the favourite toy, in this case the antigravity belt. I have brought a surrogate toy that I think will solve our problem. Try luring them down with this."

He handed Mother a bright red plastic baby's rattle.

Gran fastened a beady eye on it, shuffled her arms, then launched herself from the tree in a swooping glide. As Mother ducked in alarm, Gran caught the rattle neatly in her bony old toes, wheeled and flapped back to her perch. Heads close, she and Gramps examined the toy.

We waited breathlessly.

Then Gran stomped it against the branch and the shattered remnants fell to the ground.

The crowd applauded. For the first time we noticed the Newspocket van, and the crew with cameras. The effect on Dr Pratt was instantaneous. He strode towards them and introduced himself to a red-haired woman with a microphone.

"Tell me, Dr Pratt, to what do you attribute this phenomenon?"

"The manifestation of birdishness in the elderly is a subject that has received very little study up to the present date. Indeed, I would say that it has been virtually ignored. Apart from my own paper – still in draft form – you could search the psychiatric archives in vain for mention of Pratt's Syndrome."

"And why is that, Dr Pratt?"

"Basically, fear. The fear in each and every one of us of admitting that something primitive and atavistic can lurk within our very genes. For what is more primitive than a bird, the only survivor of the age of dinosaurs?"

"What indeed, Dr Pratt?"

"You see in that tree two pathetic human creatures who have reverted to a state that existed long before Man took his first step on Earth, a state that can only have been passed on as a tiny coded message in their very flesh and the flesh of their ancestors, through a million years of Time."

"And how long do you expect their condition to last, Dr Pratt?"

"Until autumn. The winters in these parts are hard, and they'll be out of that tree come the first frost, if they've got any sense left at all."

"Well, thank you, Dr—"

A raucous screaming cut her short. A group of shapes appeared in the eastern sky, low over the rooftops. They were too big for birds, yet too small for aircraft, and there was a moment's shocked incomprehension before we recognized them for what they were. Then they wheeled over the News-pocket van with a bedlam of yells and revealed themselves as teenagers of both sexes, unclothed, but painted a simple black semi-matt exterior latex. There were nine of them.

In the weeks following, we came to know them as the Crows. They flew overhead, circled, then settled all over the garry oak and the roof of our house.

They made no attempt to harass Gran or Gramps. Indeed, they seemed almost reverential in their attitude towards the old people.

It seemed that Gran had unlocked some kind of floodgate in the human unconscious, and people took to the air in increasing numbers. The manufacturers of antigravity belts became millionaires overnight, and the skies became a bright tapestry of wheeling, screeching figures in rainbow colours and startling nakedness. The media named them the Byrds.

"I view it as a protest against today's moral code," said Dr Pratt, who spent most of his time on panels or giving interviews. "For more years than I care to remember, people have been repressed, their honest desires cloaked in conformity just as tightly as their bodies have been swathed in concealing garb. Now, suddenly, people are saying they've had enough. They're pleasing themselves. It shouldn't surprise us. It's healthy. It's good."

It was curious, the way the doctor had become pro-Byrd. These days he seemed to be acting in the capacity of press agent for Gran – who herself had become a cult figure. In addition, he was working on his learned paper, *The Origins and Spread of Avian Tendencies in Humans*.

Pandora and I reckoned he was in the pay of the belt people.

"But it's fun to be in the centre of things," she said one evening, as the Cros came in to roost, and the garry oak creaked under the weight of a flock of Glaucous Gulls, come to pay homage to Gran. "It's put the town on the map – and your family, too." She took my hand, smiling at me proudly.

There were the Pelicans, who specialized in high dives into the sea, deactivating their belts in mid-air, then reactivating them underwater to rocket Polaris-like from the depths. They rarely caught fish, though; and frequently had to be treated for an ailment known as Pelicans' Balloon, caused by travelling through water at speed with open mouth.

There were the Darwin's Tree Finches, a retiring sect whose existence went unsuspected for some weeks, because they spent so much time in the depths of forests with cactus spines held between their teeth, trying to extract bugs from holes in dead trees. They were a brooding and introspective group.

Virtually every species of bird was represented. And because every cult must have its lunatic fringe, there were the Pigeons. They flocked to the downtown city streets and mingled with the crowds hurrying to and fro. From the shoulders up they looked much like anyone else, only greyer, and with a curious habit of jerking their heads while walking. Bodily, though, they were like any other Byrd: proudly unclothed.

Their roosting habits triggered the first open clash between Byrds and Man. There were complaints that they kept people awake at night and fouled the rooftops. People began to string electrified wires around their ridges and guttering, and to put poison out.

The Pigeons' retaliation took place early one evening when the commuting crowds jammed the streets. It was simple and graphic, and well coordinated. Afterwards, people referred to it obliquely as the Great Deluge, because it was not the kind of event that is discussed openly in proper society.

There were other sects, many of them; and perhaps the

strangest was a group who eschewed the use of antigravity belts altogether. From time to time we would catch sight of them sitting on the concrete abutments of abandoned motorways, searching one another for parasites. Their bodies were painted a uniform brown except for their private parts: those were a luminous red. They called themselves Hamadryas Baboons.

People thought they had missed the point of the whole thing, somehow.

Inevitably when there are large numbers of people involved, there are tragedies. Sometimes an elderly Byrd would succumb to cardiac arrest in mid-air, and drift away on the winds. Others would suffer belt malfunctions and plummet to the ground. As the first chill nights began to grip the country, some of the older Byrds died of exposure and fell from their perches. Courageously they maintained their role until the end, and when daylight came they would be found in the ritualistic "Dead Byrd" posture, on their backs with legs in the air.

"All good things come to an end," said Dr Pratt one evening as the russet leaves drifted from the trees. It had been a busy day, dozens of groups having come to pay homage to Gran. There was a sense of wrapping up, of things coming to a climax. "We will stage a mass rally," said Dr Pratt to the Newspocket reporter. "There will be such a gathering of Byrds as the country has never known. Gran will address the multitude at the Great Coming Down."

Mother said, "So long as it's soon. I don't think Gran can take any more frosts."

I went to invite Pandora to the Great Coming Down, but she was not at home. I was about to return when I caught sight of a monstrous thing sitting on the backyard fence. It was bright green except around the eyes, which were grey, and the hair, which was a vivid yellow. It looked at me. It blinked in oddly reptilian fashion. It was Pandora.

She said, "Who's a pretty boy, then?"

*　　*　　*

The very next day Gran swooped down from the garry oak and seized Mother's scarf with her toes, and a grim tug-of-war ensued. "Let go, you crazy old fool!" shouted Mother.

Gran cranked her belt up to maximum lift and took a quick twist of the scarf around her ankles. The other end was wrapped snugly around Mother's neck and tucked into her heavy winter coat. Mother left the ground, feet kicking. Her shouts degenerated into strangled grunts. Father got a grip of her knees as she passed overhead and Gran, with a screech of frustration, found herself descending again; whereupon Gramps, having observed the scene with bright interest, came winging in and took hold of her, adding the power of his belt to hers.

Father's feet left the ground.

Mother by now had assumed the basic hanging attitude: arms dangling limply, head lolling, tongue protruding, face empurpled. I jumped and got hold of Father's ankles. There was a short, sharp rending sound and we fell back to earth in a heap, Mother on top. Gran and Gramps flew back to the garry oak with their half of the scarf, and began to pull it apart with their teeth. Father pried the other half away from Mother's neck. She was still breathing.

"Most fascinating," said Dr Pratt.

"My wife nearly strangled by those murderous brutes and he calls it fascinating?"

"No – look at the Hornbills."

"So, they're eating the scarf. They're crazy. What's new?"

"They're not eating it. If you will observe closely, you will see them shredding it. And see – the female is working the strands around that clump of twigs. It's crystal clear what they're doing, of course. This is a classic example of nest-building."

The effect on Father was instantaneous. He jumped up, seized Dr Pratt by the throat and, shaking him back and forth, shouted, "Any fool knows birds only nest in the spring!" He was overwrought, of course. He apologized the next day.

By that time the Byrds were nesting all over town. They

used a variety of materials and in many instances their craftsmanship was pretty to see. The local Newspocket station ran a competition for 'The Nest I Would Be Happiest To Join My Mate In', treating the matter as a great joke; although some of the inhabitants who had been forcibly undressed in the street thought otherwise. The Byrds wasted nothing. Their nests were intricately woven collections of whatever could be stolen from below: overcoats, shirts, pants, clothes lines, undergarments, hearing aids, wigs.

"The nesting phenomenon has a twofold significance," Dr Pratt informed the media. "On the one hand, we have the desire of the Byrds to emulate the instinctive behavioural patterns of their avian counterparts. On the other hand, there is undoubtedly a suggestion of – how can I say it? – aggression towards the earthbound folk. The Byrds are saying, in their own way: join us. Be natural. Take your clothes off. Otherwise we'll do it for you."

"You don't think they're, uh, sexually warped?" asked the reporter.

"Sexually liberated," insisted Dr Pratt.

The Byrds proved his point the next day, when they began to copulate all over the sky.

It was the biggest sensation since the Great Deluge. Writhing figures filled the heavens and parents locked their children indoors and drew the drapes. It was a fine day for love; the sun glinted on sweat-bedewed flesh, and in the unseasonable warmth the still air rang with cries of delight.

The Byrds looped and zoomed and chased one another, and when they met they coupled. Artificial barriers of species were cast aside and Eagle mated with Chaffinch, Robin with Albatross.

"Clearly a visual parable," said Dr Pratt. "The—"

"Shut up," said Mother. "Shut up, shut up, shut up!"

In the garry oak, Rufous-necked Hornbill mated with Rufous-necked Hornbill, then with Crow; then, rising joyously into the sky, with Skua, with Lark, and finally with

Hamadryas Baboon, who had at last realized what it was all about and strapped on a belt.

"She's eighty-six years old! What is she thinking of?"

"She's an Earth Mother to them," said Dr Pratt.

"Earth Mother my arse," said Father. "She's stark, staring mad, and it's about time we faced up to it."

"It's true, it's true!" wailed Mother, a broken woman. "She's crazy! She's been crazy for years! She's old and useless, and yet she keeps filling in all that stuff on her Peace form, instead of forgetting, like any normal old woman!"

"Winter is coming," said Dr Pratt, "and we are witnessing the symbolic Preservation of the Species. Look at that nice young Tern up there. Tomorrow they must come back to earth, but in the wombs of the females the memory of this glorious September will live on!"

"She's senile and filthy! I've seen her eating roots from out of the ground, and do you know what she did to the Ever-attentive Waiter? She cross-wired it with the Mailgift chute and filled the kitchen with self-adhesive cookies!"

"She did?"

And the first shadow of doubt crossed Dr Pratt's face. The leader of the Byrds crazy?

"And one day a game show called on the visiphone and asked her a skill-testing question that would have set us all up for life – and she did the most disgusting thing, and it went out live and the whole town saw it!"

"I'm sure she has sound psychological reasons for her behaviour," said Dr Pratt desperately.

"She doesn't! She's insane! She walks to town rather than fill out a Busquest form! She brews wine in a horrible jar under the bed! She was once sentenced to one week's community service for indecent exposure! She trespasses in the Department of Agriculture's fields! You want to know why the house stinks? She programmed the Pesterminator to zap the Tidy Mice!"

"But I thought . . . Why didn't you tell me before? My God, when I think of the things I've said on Newspocket! If this comes out, my reputation, all I've worked for, all . . ." He was becoming incoherent. "Why didn't you tell me?" he asked again.

"Well, good grief, it's obvious, isn't it?" snapped Father. "Look at her. She's up in the sky mating with a Hamadryas Baboon, or something very much like one. Now, that's what I call crazy."

"But it's a Movement . . . It's free and vibrant and so basic, so—"

"A nut cult," said Father. "Started by a loony and encouraged by a quack. Nothing more, nothing less. And the forecast for tonight is twenty below. It'll wipe out the whole lot of them. You'd better get them all down, Pratt, or you'll have a few thousand deaths on your conscience."

But the Byrds came down of their own accord, later that day. As though sensing the end of the Indian summer and the bitter nights to come, they drifted out of the sky in groups, heading for earth, heading for us. Gran alighted in the garry oak with whirling arms, followed by Gramps. They sat close together on their accustomed branch, gobbling quietly to each other. More Byrds came; the Crows, the Pelicans. They filled the tree, spread along the ridge of the roof and squatted on the guttering. They began to perch on fences and posts, even on the ground, all species intermingled. They were all around us, converging, covering the neighbouring roofs and trees, a great final gathering of humans who, just for a few weeks, had gone a little silly. They looked happy although tired, and a few were shivering as the afternoon shortened into evening. They made a great noise at first, a rustling and screeching and fluid piping, but after a while they quietened down. I saw Pandora amidst them, painted and pretty, but her gaze passed right through me. They were still Byrds, playing their role until the end. And they all faced Gran. They were awaiting the word to Come Down, but Gran remained silent, living every last moment.

It was like standing in the centre of a vast amphitheatre,

with all those heads turned towards us, all those beady eyes watching us. The Newspocket crew were nowhere to be seen; they probably couldn't get through the crowd.

Finally Dr Pratt strode forward. He was in the grip of a great despondency. He was going to come clean.

"Fools!" he shouted. A murmur of birdlike sounds arose, but soon died. "All through history there have been fools like you, and they've caused wars and disaster and misery. Fools without minds of their own, who follow their leader without thought, without stopping to ask if their leader knows what he is doing. Leaders like Genghis Khan, like Starbusch, like Hitler, leaders who manipulate their followers like puppets in pursuit of their own crazy ends. Crazy leaders drunk with power. Leaders like Gran here.

"Yes, Gran is crazy! I mean certifiably crazy, ready for Peace. Irrational and insane and a burden to the State and to herself. She had me fooled at first." He uttered a short, bitter laugh, not unlike the mating cry of Forster's Tern. "I thought I found logic in what she did. Such was the cunning nature of her madness. It was only recently, when I investigated Gran's past record, that I unmasked her for what she is: a mentally unbalanced old woman with marked antisocial tendencies. I could give you chapter and verse of Gran's past misdemeanours – and I can tell you right now, this isn't the first time she's taken her clothes off in public – but I will refrain, out of consideration for her family, who have suffered enough.

"It will suffice to say that I have recommended her committal and the Peace Wagon is on its way. The whole affair is best forgotten. Now, come down out of those trees and scrub off, and go home to your families, all of you."

He turned away, shoulders drooping. It was nothing like the Great Coming Down he'd pictured. It was a slinking thing, a creeping home, an abashed admission of stupidity.

Except that the Byrds weren't coming down.

They sat silently on their perches, awaiting the word from Gran. All through Dr Pratt's oration she'd been quiet, staring fixedly at the sky. Now, at last, she looked around. Her eyes were bright, but it was an almost-human brightness, a different thing from the beady stare of the past weeks. And she half-smiled through the paint, but she didn't utter a word.

She activated her belt and, flapping her arms, rose into the darkening sky.

And the Byrds rose after her.

They filled the sky, a vast multitude of rising figures, and Pandora was with them. Gran led, Gramps close behind, and then came Coot and Skua and Hawk, and the whole thousand-strong mob. They wheeled once over the town and filled the evening with a great and lonely cry. Then they headed off in V-formations, loose flocks, tight echelons, a pattern of dwindling black forms against the pale duck-egg blue of nightfall.

"Where the hell are they going?" shouted Dr Pratt as I emerged from the shed, naked and painted. It was cold, but I would soon get used to it.

"South," I said.

"Why the hell south? What's wrong with here, for God's sake?"

"It's warmer, south. We're migrating."

So I activated my belt and lifted into the air, and watched the house fall away below me, and the tiny bolts of light as the Pesterminator hunted things. The sky seemed empty now but there was still a fading pink of sunset to the west. Hurrying south, I saw something winking like a red star and, before long, I was homing in on the gleaming hindquarters of a Hamadryas Baboon.

POLLY PUT THE MOCKERS ON

Stan Nicholls

At one time Stan Nicholls was best known as a bookshop manager and for his magazine columns and reviews. More recently he has broken into the ranks of fantasy novelists with such series as The Nightshade Chronicles *and* Orcs: First Blood. *But none of this prepares you for the following story.*

The row about banks moving out of the countryside took a new twist yesterday when the countryside moved into a bank. Staff at the Ufton Paddesley branch of Clouts were taken aback when a customer wanted to cash a cheque. Nothing odd in that, you might think. Except this cheque was written on the side of a live pig.

Businessman Dirk Penhaligon proffered the pecuniary porker as his latest weapon in a long-standing dispute with the bank. "Clouts have caused me a lot of inconvenience," Mr Penhaligon, 41, insisted. "Now they know how it feels."

The entrepreneur, famed locally as a ballcock magnate, decided on his ploy after discovering that a cheque could be written on anything as long as it was signed and dated. "I know my rights," he said. "It's the law."

Clouts branch manager Sidney Doub, 59, commented,

"The rules clearly stipulate that we are obliged to honour a customer's request to withdraw their own money, whatever that request may be written on. For our purposes, this pig constitutes a cheque. Though we have yet to devise a humane way of stamping it."

Having pocketed his ten pounds, the amount the pig was made out to, Mr Penhaligon remained defiant. *"I believe I've struck a blow for many other dissatisfied bank customers all over this country,"* he declared. *"They too should make their voices heard."* But Sidney Doub ridiculed the threat. *"I'm sure I speak for the whole banking community in saying that our little difficulty with Mr Penhaligon is in no way reflected nationally. Bank customers are almost universally happy with our services, and have far too much good sense to involve themselves in these kind of antics. Believe me,"* he laughed, *"this is a one-off."*

The Qualmsley & Beagledale Chronicle

"Your mammals or your life!"

There was nobody else in the alley except the man blocking Eddie Markham's path. He was massively built, and when a flash of lightning briefly illuminated his face it proved weathered, mean and desperate. The gun he clutched had a muzzle like the mouth of a tunnel.

Sloshing through a puddle as he moved closer, the mugger repeated his demand with a hiss.

A chorus of muffled snorts and scufflings came from Markham's cart. Coolly, he stepped out of the reins. The would-be robber grinned, exposing broken teeth, savouring the prospect of enrichment.

"If you want it, you'll have to take it," Markham told him.

The mugger's face dropped. Confusion clouded his bovine eyes. He glanced down at his fist. "But I've got a gun," he remembered. "I'll use it."

"Go on, then."

"What?"

"Shoot."

"I *will*."

"So what you waiting for?"

"I'm not mucking about, you know." He raised the gun uncertainly, his hand shaking. "Give me your livestock or I'll pop yer."

"Go ahead."

"But—"

"You going to talk or shoot?"

"Well, I—"

"You're going to talk, aren't you?" He made a show of directing his gaze at the automatic. "Ah, I see why. Trying a bluff, eh?"

Incomprehension creased the big man's brow. "Eh?"

"Threatening me with a duff shooter."

"Duff?"

Markham gave him a knowing wink. "It is as long as the safety's on."

Ponderously, the brigand turned the gun side on and blinked stupidly at it. It gave Markham the chance he needed for a swift upward kick to the man's wrist. The gun went flying. Yelping, the mugger took a wild swing at him. Markham ducked and pummelled the thug's stomach. He doubled over, expelling a loud *Ooofff!* Markham landed a cracking blow to his attacker's jaw. Imitating a felled oak, he went down.

Markham picked up the gun. There was no time to do the good-citizen thing and get embroiled with cops. So he dropped the bullet clip through a drain grid. The gun he tossed into one of several large rubbish bins.

There was a rustling in the comatose mugger's grubby, voluminous overcoat. A couple of white mice shot out of it, followed by a small badger. Ill-gotten gains from some other poor devil, no doubt. The animals scooted off in different directions. Markham didn't bother chasing them, though he knew that if they weren't netted by somebody else they became treasure trove.

Ignoring the robber's groans, he went to the cart, lifted its

lid and spent a moment soothing his change. Then he climbed
back into the reins and continued his journey.

The rain was easing as he rejoined the teeming streets. Most
people were hauling carts. Some were so big that their owners
laboured to drag them, or else they were pulled by sweating
couples. Others were small enough to bounce along on tiny
wheels, drawn with a length of string. Markham's was somewhere in between, and about average.

As usual, the noises and smells were near-intolerable.
Slatted trucks nosed through the traffic, valuables bleating.
Horns were honked at a small herd of Friesians being shep-
herded by nervous security guards. Naively, someone in the
crowd pushed a battered supermarket trolley, their wealth on
open show.

Markham passed a shop with trays of hamsters, tortoises
and terrapins in the barred window. The standard offering for
a jeweller's. Next to it stood a block of luxury flats, his
destination. A doorman checked his appointment, then directed him to the visitors' holding pens. Markham deposited the
cart. Taking his ticket from a dour parking attendant, he
jabbed his finger at him and said, "Don't get any ideas. I
know what's nesting in there." He left the man suitably
affronted and made for a lift.

He stepped out of it into an opulent penthouse apartment.
There was no one about. He looked around at the sumptuous
furniture and expensive ornamentation. But what really impressed him were the more obvious signs of wealth. A big tank
of tropical fish, any one of which represented a month's
income for him. On the marble hearth, a pure white Persian
cat, eyeing them. And a gilded cage on a silver stand, housing a
pair of lovebirds.

He moved to a window occupying the far wall. Below was a
large back garden. It was surrounded by a high, electrified
fence and divided into corrals and wire-topped enclosures.
Some held cattle, mostly rare breeds. There was a flock of
flamingos, a group of antelope and a pack of baboons. He

spotted llamas and camels. Craning his head, he saw what might have been kangaroos. He was obviously in a moneyed burg.

"A gerbil for them, Mister Markham?"

He turned. The voice belonged to a fat man. But it was self-confident fat. He was in his middle years, though his chubby, babyish face seemed unmarked by time, as is the way with rich fat. A pencil moustache slashed his upper lip, his eyes were powder blue. He was immaculately tailored. By comparison, Markham was a scarecrow in a body bag.

"Lonnie Fairfax," the fat man explained, unnecessarily, "at your service." He oozed charm, but didn't offer his hand. "You were admiring my depository?" He nodded at the window.

"Like they say, money chirps. If you've got it, flaunt it."

"Good, we see eye to eye. How would you like something worth flaunting yourself?"

"I'd like it fine, Mister Fairfax. But I'm wondering why a guy who owns his own zoo needs a private investigator. You must have plenty of people on your payroll to do whatever it is you want doing."

"To the point. I like that." He indicated a table laden with food. "Take some refreshment while I explain."

It was an offer Markham would normally refuse, on the grounds of not mixing business with pleasure. But then he noticed meat, a rarity when only the rich could afford not to be vegetarians. He weakened.

"So how can I help you?" he asked, mouth full.

"It's a matter of some delicacy."

Markham took a swig of wine. "That's my speciality."

"A matter I wish kept confidential even if you turn down the commission. Though I don't think you will."

"Understood."

"I want you to locate something."

"Missing spouse? Stolen property? Runaway business part—"

"No, no. Nothing like that." Fairfax leaned closer. His voice dropped to an undertone. "Have you ever heard of . . . *the Macclesfield Macaw?*"

Whatever Markham expected the sealionaire to say, it wasn't that. "Sure," he replied casually. "Everybody has. What about it?"

"I want it."

"It's a myth. A story bankers tell their kids at bedtime."

"No, Mister Markham, it's not a myth." Fairfax's eyes burned with a messianic intensity. "The Macaw is very real."

"How do you know?"

"Believe me, it exists. It has narrowly eluded my grasp several times in the past. A bird of unusual size and markings. Quite a unique item."

"I would have thought a man like you had enough already."

"I have just about everything, true. But I don't have the bird. Ergo, I must acquire it."

"I bet you were a coin collector in the old days."

It was meant as a jibe, but Fairfax looked mildly surprised. "How did you guess?"

Markham figured that if a man wanted to throw his money away on a wild macaw chase he wasn't going to stop him, particularly if the money was crawling in his direction. "Okay, let's assume the bird does exist," he said. "How do I come into the picture?"

"I believe you may be able to obtain it for me. Based on information I'll supply."

"You haven't told me why you can't use somebody who works for you."

"You're not known to. That has its advantages."

"I won't do anything illegal."

Fairfax raised an eyebrow. "Of course not. As to your fee—"

"I've got a set rate."

That was waved aside. "For this task I expect to pay well. I'm offering a Thompson gazelle as a retainer. And shall we say a fully grown African crocodile on successful completion?"

Markham was awed. The most he'd ever pulled in for one

job before was a manky rhino. But he kept his face poker and pushed a bit. "Expenses?"

"You think I have Labradors to burn?"

Glancing around, Markham came back with, "Well . . . yes."

"How about a brace of woodcock a day?"

"Done." He raised his glass. "What's the information you have on this bird's whereabouts?"

"I'm told it's currently in the possession of Ray Blythe." Markham choked on his drink.

"I see you've heard the name," Fairfax reasoned.

"Who hasn't? He's one of the biggest crime bosses in town. Maybe *the* biggest. I can see why you're paying so well."

"All you have to do is establish contact and negotiate the bird's purchase."

"What if he ain't selling?"

"I'm prepared to go as high as a giraffe."

Markham let out an appreciative whistle. "You really want this bird, don't you?"

"Will you do it, Mister Markham? Will you achieve my ambition and bring me the Macclesfield Macaw?"

Draining his glass, Markham shrugged. "I'll give it a shot."

Outside, he was approached by a beggar who told him he hadn't got two shrews to rub together, and could he spare a marsupial for a cup of coffee? Feeling generous, Markham tossed him a budgie.

Back in his shabby office, Markham had hardly started telling his secretary all about it when she had to take a phone call.

"Markham Investigation Agency, Shirley Binch speaking. Oh, hello, Brenda." *My sister, Brenda*, she mouthed at him.

"I gathered," he mouthed back, and set to on a long thumb-twiddling session.

Eventually she hung up, and gushed, "It's her and Osbert's fourth wedding anniversary on Friday. I said I'd take care of the catering for their party. *And* I've been racking my brains for a suitable present. What's a fourth wedding anniversary?"

He was baffled; a not unfamiliar state in Shirley's presence. "What do you mean, what is it?"

"You know, diamond, gold, silver . . ."

"Oh, right. Er, bubblewrap, isn't it?"

She gave him one of her blistering looks and changed the subject. "What were you saying about this new job?"

"There's big bucks in it, Shirley."

"You haven't accepted those darn' pests for payment again, have you?"

"It was a figure of speech."

"Well, don't give me turns like that."

He sighed. "Just do something for me, will you? Turn up everything you can on Ray Blythe."

"*The* Ray Blythe? The crook? You're not getting into something deep, are you, Eddie?"

"That's why there's big . . . that's why the fee's high, if I earn it. But it's nothing dangerous."

She looked doubtful but held her tongue. "I'll get onto it."

His attention was caught by the TV set silently flickering in a corner. It showed a race meeting from Kempton Park. He increased the volume.

Shirley spun her swivel chair. "Do you have to have it so loud, Eddie?"

"*Sshhh.* It's the Jockey Handicap."

The jockeys were in line. Several pawed the turf, straining at their bits. The starting prices popped up, showing the number of horses wagered on each runner. If his bet came in he stood to win a very nice string.

Then they were off. Legs pumping, elbows jabbing, the runners vied for lead position.

"Who's yours?" Shirley whispered.

"Number five," he replied absently. "Calls himself the Twelfth Primate."

The jockeys were using their riding crops on themselves now. Their breeches were getting mud-splattered and here and there caps flew off.

"Come on, number five," he muttered, clutching the edge

of his desk, knuckles whitening. "Come on, Twelfth Primate."

His jockey was in the middle of the bunch, fighting to reach the front, jostling with the other competitors.

"Come *on*!" Markham yelled, waving a clenched fist. "You can do it, boy!"

They rounded a bend and went into the home stretch.

"Come on! Move it! *Come on, Twelfth Primate!*"

The finishing line was in sight.

"Come on . . . Twelfth . . . Pri . . . mate . . ."

It came in twelfth.

He turned his betting slip into confetti.

"Lose much?" Shirley asked, unable to keep a note of disapproval out of her voice.

"I had a pony on it," he told her glumly.

"I hope you're doing better with your more conventional investments."

He punched Teletext on the remote. The Stock and Fowl Market prices came up. "Hmm. Down a bit, actually." He flicked off the set and grumbled, "They should never have handed over the Exchange Rate Mechanism to the RSPCA."

"That reminds me," she said, "I'm running short on petty cash."

Markham went to the wire strongbox and fiddled with the combination. Scooping a handful of white mice, he deposited them on her desk as he made for the door, calling, "Back later."

He left her dropping the squeaking currency into a drawer.

The bar held the usual afternoon crowd of deadbeats and lounge lizards, although most of the latter were securely tethered.

Under his overcoat, Markham wore his best suit. Outside in the guarded parking lot his cart was crammed with wherewithal supplied by Lonnie Fairfax. The Dog and Ducat seemed like a good place to wait until Ray Blythe's casino opened.

Unfortunately, Markham hadn't reckoned on the attentions of a pub bore.

His name was George. For some strange reason he occupied the only table with a vacant seat. George started by complaining about the cost of a pint, and how it had gone up from a canary to a seagull in all the local boozers. He grumbled that you could pay as much as a greyhound for a decent bottled draught, and went on to bemoan not having the kind of rare fauna needed to buy spirits. Then he hit his stride.

"That bloody Penhaligon," he lamented, quickly adding, "Pardon my French. But, I ask you, they call him an 'ero. Bleedin' *menace*, I say." He sat back, arms folded across a swelling chest, and adopted the pose of public-house oracle. Markham fought an urge to strike him. "The banks were taking the mickey, granted," he continued portentously, "but can we really say we're any 'appier now?"

Markham shook his head in a vacant, noncommittal sort of way and daydreamed chainsaws.

"Anybody could 'ave told the banks other people would copy that twerp Penhaligon. So you had 'em taking in cheques written on cows, horses, sheep, all sorts." He began jabbing the air with an uncertain finger. "Where they went wrong, them banks, was in trying to discourage people by 'onouring 'em. Silly bleeders . . . 'scuse my—" He yawned cavernously. "Took the cheques and gave animals in exchange, didn't they? A livestock cheque for twenty pounds equalled . . ." His forehead creased. "What was it? A pair of goats, I think."

Markham wanted to tell him that he knew his history as well as anybody. Or else bottle him. While he dithered, he was lost.

"But it didn't put 'em off, did it?" George ploughed on. "Soon, everybody was cashing hedgehogs, tortoises and Highland terriers. Pop stars were having their royalty cheques written on zebras. The banks had to do away with their vaults and build pens. Next thing you knew the shops were taking animals for goods." He leaned in and confided indignantly, "My boss started paying me in chickens."

Markham wished he had a newspaper to hide behind.

But relief was at hand. Someone turned on the television above the bar. It carried a newsflash. There had been a daring robbery, caught on CCTV. They ran grainy black-and-white footage of hooded men rustling a herd of cows. A grim-looking announcer gave a telephone number and promised a reward that ran to fourteen hands. Then a financial wildlife programme came on and the sound was killed.

Fearing a further deluge of George, Markham avoided eye contact and reached for his glass. In the event, the pregnant silence was broken again when the jukebox started up. It belted out an old hit by the once fashionable Space Gals, a record that caught the spirit of the monetary revolution.

> *"Monkey can't buy everything, it's true*
> *But what it can't get*
> *I'll find at the zoo.*
> *Oh give me monkey,*
> *That's what I want . . ."*

Markham checked his watch. It was time to go. But something had been troubling him. He bent George's way and said, "What's a fourth wedding anniversary?" Responding to the blank look he got, he elaborated. "You know, twenty-five years or something is diamond and—"

"Oh, got yer. Me and me missus 'ad one of them. Let's see . . . fourth . . . fourth . . . Isn't that asbestos?"

Finishing his drink, Markham headed for the door.

At the bar, a young lad was paying for a round. Mindful of counterfeits, the landlord wouldn't accept the ferret he was offered without biting it first.

Ray Blythe's casino, Big Game, had the smell of affluence about it. Which is to say the smell of big game.

Having shown the doorman the colour of his magpies, Markham was ushered into the plush interior. After a cocktail at the bar, costing an arm and a claw, he sauntered into the playing hall. He stood for a moment to watch the action at a roulette table, where a suntanned punter was playing red continuously, slapping down guinea pigs and occasionally having a hedgehog slide back as winnings. Bigger rollers were leading away muzzled cheetahs.

Wandering off, he passed a row of obsessives feeding slot machines with sparrows, and arrived at the blackjack table. He began playing, to establish his credentials, and managed to lose two salamanders and a gecko in twenty minutes. Then he figured it was time to see Ray Blythe.

He approached one of the goons in ill-fitting dinner jackets who watched the hall. Employing one-syllable words and sign language, he conveyed that he wanted to see the boss, on a matter that could benefit him. The lout took it in without dribbling, then told him to wait. Markham leaned on the bar, watching the bustle and half-listening to the singer with the band.

"I'd like to get you on a slow goat to China . . ."

The goon returned, with a clone. They grunted for him to follow, and Markham wondered if they might be heading for a back alley. To his relief it proved to be a wood-panelled office big enough to have its own ecosystem, complete with the usual menagerie denoting conspicuous affluence.

Behind a desk fit for helicopter landings sat Ray Blythe.

That was a mistake; it only emphasized his titchy status. Three Blythes to one Fairfax, Markham estimated. And when he rose, his tiny frame was all the more apparent. Markham found himself bending his knees in an attempt not to appear to be looking down on him. It was a futile exercise. Blythe's head barely reached the PI's chest.

There were no pleasantries. "I'm a busy man," Blythe announced frostily. "State your business, Mister Markham."

"Fine by me. I only want a little . . . er, a few minutes of your time." Blythe glared at him, ready to take offence. Markham took another step into the linguistic minefield. "I mean, it's just a small . . . a *trifling* matter."

"Not too trifling, I hope," Blythe responded with a hint of menace, "or I might think you were wasting my time."

"The long and the short of it—"

Blythe's eyes narrowed.

Markham tried again. "The . . . *gist* is that I'm here to make you an offer for . . . an item I think you have."

"An item?"

"A certain avian asset," Markham replied, adopting a conspiratorial air.

"A *what?*"

"A bird."

"I've got flocks. What's special about this one?"

Markham suspected he was being toyed with, but carried on. "It's a one-off. Very unusual markings. In size it's said to dwarf—" Blythe winced. "—Uhm . . . it's big."

"And would this . . . bird come from a northern nest?"

"It would."

There was a tense moment while Blythe mulled things over. "Just suppose I did know this commodity's whereabouts. What of it?"

"I represent somebody who wants to trade."

"Who?"

"I'm supposed to keep that under wraps."

"It's Lonnie Fairfax, isn't it?"

"Couldn't say."

"You're a good bluffer, Markham, but it takes one to know one. It's Fairfax, isn't it?"

"Does it matter? The offer's genuine."

"It's Fairfax. He's got the hots for the damn' thing."

"Whatever. Point is, my client wants to buy and he'll pay top beast."

"If this bird's as rare as you say, why would anybody want to sell it?"

"It's unique, not easily passed."

"Except by its lawful owner."

Markham realized he'd implied Blythe wasn't. "True," he said slowly. "But how much better for its owner, whoever that might be, to exchange it for less conspicuous stock."

"There might be some benefit in that," Blythe conceded shiftily. "Leave your number and I'll see what I can do."

Markham nodded, flipped a business card onto the aircraft-carrier desk and made to leave. He stopped at the door. "One last thing."

"Yeah?"

"What's a fourth wedding anniversary? You know, gold, ivory . . ."

Blythe snapped his fingers at one of his aides.

"I think it's Latex, boss," the goon opined.

Markham closed the door quietly behind him.

It was raining again as he stood in a telephone box.

". . . And I *still* can't find a decent catering company," Shirley reported. "As for a present—"

She took a breath and he jumped in. "What did you find out about Blythe?"

"Oh. Er, more or less what you'd expect. Claims to be legit these days but nobody believes it. The police reckon he uses that casino of his as a sheep dip."

"Money laundering, eh? Figures."

"And he was recently suspected of involvement in a scam where polecats used to pay for costly shop items turned out to be low-denomination squirrels in zipped suits."

"Still up to his old tricks, then."

"You know what they say, Eddie: a leopard never changes his socks."

"Do they?"

"Well, cold hands, warm kippers. Something like that. Mind you, that client of yours, Fairfax, doesn't seem much better."

"Really?"

"Yeah, I checked. He was once charged with druggling smugs."

"You mean smuggling drugs."

"I know what I mean, Eddie. Smugs are small South American rodents. But you don't want to know what druggling is, take it from me."

"I believe you."

"Point is, both of them look like the sort of people who'd put ants in charity collection boxes."

He glanced at the display on the phone. "I've gotta go now, Shirley, my mice are running out."

"Why don't you get a mobile, skinflint?"

"'Cos I'm not made of wildebeest."

He was cut off.

Turning up his collar, he got into the reins and began the haul home with plenty to think about.

Next morning his way to a meeting was blocked by a commotion on the streets. Riot squads were out trying to keep dogs and cats apart as bewildered older folk struggled to herd their income support. He'd forgotten it was pension day.

Eventually Markham got to the café and found his contact waiting for him.

He used to be known as Harry the Ferret. Since events made that superfluous, he was more often addressed as Erstwhile Harry. Or simply, if controversially, Harry.

As far as Markham knew, Harry had never been a boxer. But he looked as though he had. His not-recently-shaven head was shaped like a roughly hewn granite block. He sported cauliflower ears and a nose badly reset after a break. His piglet eyes were never still, and there was always an air of furtive paranoia about him. He hunched.

Nodding at his informant, Markham ordered a late breakfast. When it arrived he couldn't help but wonder why he was eating it. Early in the new order, people cottoned on to the idea of breeding money, and speculators with large quantities of rabbits watched their investment multiply to a fortune. That was outlawed, and certain species excluded from the currency. A normal birth, of a calf or lamb, say, was regarded as honestly earned interest and tagged as such. Rabbits, having no trading value, filled another niche.

God, Markham was sick of Bunnyburgers.

After a bite he dropped it back on the plate and got down to business. "I want to know what the word is on the street about a certain bird," he whispered.

Harry's gaze darted nervously. "What bird might that be?" he replied guardedly.

"Some say it's mythical. And it's from the North."

"Would the thirteenth letter of the alphabet have some bearing on it?"

Frowning, Markham swiftly counted with his fingers, lips moving silently. "Er . . . yes. Twice."

Harry gave him a plotter's nod. "What about it?"

"I believe it's in the hands of . . . let's say a prominent member of the *alternative economy*."

"And would this wrong-side-of-the-tracks entrepreneur be associated with the second and eighteenth letters of the alphabet?"

"It's Ray Blythe, for goodness' sake!" Markham hissed.

"If you know that, why ask me?"

"I want to confirm that he really has it. And if he does, where."

"I might be able to help." Harry's eyes skimmed the café again. "For a consideration, of course."

"Of course." Markham glanced around the room too, then pushed a slumbering tawny owl across the plastic table top.

Harry quickly stuffed it inside his jacket. "The gentleman you're referring to has a small farm just outside town." He gave the location and added, "If you were looking for something, that's probably where it would be. But don't expect no chimpanzees' tea party. The place is gonna be well guarded."

"Thanks, Harry."

"You didn't hear it from me. Right?"

"Right." Markham stood, ready to leave. Then he paused. "There's another piece of information you might have."

Harry shrugged. "Sure. A man's got to earn a crustacean."

"You know how wedding anniversaries are associated with certain things? Coral, silver, that sort of stuff."

"Hmmm."

"What's a fourth?"

Harry creased his brow. "I'll put out the word," he promised.

"And you say you have a lead on the item's whereabouts?"
"Yes, Mister Fairfax."
"But you're not going to say where."
"Not on an open line. Sorry."
"Your next move?"
"A reconnaissance. To try and make sure the third party really has it."
"Very wise. Have a care, Mister Markham, and keep me informed."
The line went dead. Eddie hung up.
From the other side of her desk, Shirley had displeasure written all over her face. "Are you sure you know what you're doing? Ray Blythe's not the sort to tangle with lightly."
"I'm not going to tangle with him, just take a look."
"Your funeral."
He was only half listening. Her PC screen showed stock prices on the Internet. He thought they were looking a bit heated.
"Here." Shirley handed him a mobile phone.
"What's this? You know we can't afford—"
"It's pre-pay, and I've charged it with three stoats. After that you can fork out for it yourself."
Grumbling, he slipped it into a pocket.
"And keep it turned on," she commanded.
He left her making more calls to catering companies.

Markham took a devious route, in case he was being followed.
An hour later he parked in a lay-by off a country lane and proceeded on foot, alert for guards. There seemed to be nobody about, so he eased himself over the two-bar fence surrounding the farmhouse. Approaching furtively, he noted that the doors were firmly closed and all the windows were shuttered.
A lorry appeared on the road, horn tooting. Markham dived

behind a stone trough. Peeking over it, he watched as three men emerged from the farmhouse and opened the gates. Then they set to unloading a quantity of sacks bearing the logo of a birdseed company.

Once the cargo was dragged in and the truck had left, Markham crept from his hiding place. By the wall stood a row of dustbins. He went to them and began carefully lifting their lids. The first two were empty. But the third held several jumbo-size Frobisher's cuttlefish wrappers, and in the bottom of the bin he found a mass of millet husks, picked clean.

A distant, eerie noise froze him. Unless he was very much mistaken, it was a hearty squawk. Markham reckoned that clinched it.

He was halfway to the fence when shouts rang out. Looking back, he saw men spilling from the house. He ran, vaulting the fence, and made off down the lane. The cries followed, and he was fighting for breath when he reached the car and fumbled with his keys.

Pulling away as the first of his pursuers came into sight, waving their fists, he thanked goodness that dogs were too valuable to use these days.

Later, killing time while he waited for Blythe to get in touch, Markham took a walk and bought a sandwich. He went by a cinema showing the new spaghetti western everybody was talking about, *A Fistful of Dormice*, then came to a TV shop with a small crowd outside gaping at the screens. About to investigate, he stopped when he noticed that his trousers appeared to be ringing. Fishing out the forgotten mobile, he took a frantic call from Shirley.

No sooner had he taken it in – he was still reeling – than somebody laid a hand on his shoulder. He looked up at the expensively suited tough who had hold of him, then down a bit at the other two.

"You're coming with us," the giant announced.

Markham dropped his sandwich as they bundled him into a stretch limo with smoked windows.

They wouldn't tell him where they were going. Wouldn't speak at all, in fact. So he spent the time trying to listen to the car radio they'd left on low volume.

"Less than eighteen months after Penhaligon presented his historic cheque, the UK went over to the Bulldog standard. Before long, Bulls and Bears on the Stock Exchange were trading in bulls and bears." The goons weren't paying any attention. Markham strained to hear. *"The global implications were profound. Japan adopted the Goldfish standard, France the Snail and America the Eagle. Soon, every nation had based its currency on animal reserves. But now—"*

The driver snapped off the radio as the car swept into the underground garage of a swish tower block. Markham recognized it, and wasn't surprised.

Five minutes later he was hustled out of a private elevator for an audience with Lonnie Fairfax.

"You only had to call if you wanted a meet," Markham told him.

"I needed to be sure you'd come," Fairfax replied dryly.

"Now I wonder what you want to talk about. I don't think."

"I had a brilliant idea. I thought, why pay you to negotiate the purchase of the Macaw now that you've found out where it's being hidden? It should be a simple matter for me to arrange its . . . liberation and cut out the middleman."

"I'm sure that was never your plan from the outset," Markham returned sarcastically.

"So all that now remains is for you to reveal the location."

Markham started laughing.

"Bravado is very commendable, but it won't stop you telling." He nodded at his henchmen. "My colleagues can be very persuasive."

But Markham carried on guffawing. "You haven't been keeping in touch, have you, Fairfax?" he spluttered. "None of it matters now."

"What do you mean?"

Markham dabbed at his watering eyes and pointed to the TV. "See for yourself."

Scowling, Fairfax snatched up the remote. A news report flicked on.

"*. . . Events came to a head. The international money markets have nose-dived. United Aardvarks has crashed. Konsolidated Koalas went down sixty points in the last fifteen minutes. Investors have withdrawn support from the Australian Roo and the Transylvanian Bat, and the European Cuckoo is under extreme pressure.*" The newsreader was passed a sheet of paper. His expression grew sterner. "*There has been a run on the Swiss Poodle.*"

Ashen-faced, Fairfax punched through the channels. All showed scenes of financial chaos. Mobs stormed the banks, making off with herds of antelope and flocks of ewes. There was a brief *vox pop* of a man sporting the apron, peaked cap and shovel that marked him out as an accountant. People were pushing wheelbarrows full of white mice into baker's shops.

"You're wiped out, Fairfax," Markham smirked. "You, me, *everybody*."

Fairfax wasn't listening. Sweat-sheened, he had two phones to his head at the same time as barking orders to his goons. Frenzy prevailed.

Nobody noticed, or didn't care, when Markham slipped away.

He braved anarchy in the streets. It was a little easier without the cart. Shirley was in the office, but she wasn't alone. Ray Blythe and a cohort of heavies were waiting too, and they barred his exit.

The bantam-sized crime boss moved closer. A couple of goons backed him. Markham braced himself for a duffing-up, or worse.

Blythe loomed below him, his expression severe. "It seems we have some unfinished business," he intoned.

"Do we?" Markham responded in what he hoped was a casual manner but knew wasn't.

"Oh, yes." Blythe lifted a well-manicured hand and snapped his fingers.

Markham flinched. There was an intake of breath from Shirley.

But no onslaught ensued. Instead, another tough entered, bearing a large wicker basket draped with a blanket.

"Looks like we're all ruined now," Blythe said. "So I won't be needing this." The blanket was whipped away, revealing the head and neck of a massive, disputatious-looking bird with unusual markings. "Give that to your boss."

"I think Mister Fairfax has troubles of his own right now."

Blythe smiled sardonically. "Good." Then he beckoned his entourage. The bird was set down and they all trooped out.

Shirley and Markham vied for biggest sighs of relief.

"Well, you kind of cracked the case," she ventured, making the best of it. "Pity the thing's worthless."

"Bit of a drawback, isn't it? But we've got bigger fish to fry now. Probably literally."

"So what are we going to do?"

"Have a party. Brenda and Osbert's do is still on, isn't it?"

"Well, yes, I suppose so. I mean, we might as well. Though I never did find a catering company. Or a present, come to that."

"There's just one thing that's been bothering me."

"About the case?"

"No, about your sister's wedding anniversary. You found out what a fourth is, right? What represents it." A tone of desperation edged his voice. "*Tell* me!"

"What? Oh, that. No, I never did. Doesn't matter though, does it?"

He slumped, head in hands. A screech from the basket brought him out of it. He looked at the bird. The bird stared back, its beady, mean eye unwavering.

Markham hefted the basket and plonked it on Shirley's desk. The beast squawked belligerently. "There you go, for Brenda and Osbert."

"I hardly think devalued currency is appropriate as a present, Eddie," she sniffed.

"Who said anything about a present? This is the catering."

FERDIE

F. Anstey

F. Anstey was a well-known writer and humorist for over fifty years. His real name was Thomas Anstey Guthrie (1856–1934) and he intended to use the pen-name T. Anstey but the printer couldn't read his writing and he ended up as F. Anstey. In the end this was rather apt, since the name almost sounds like "fantasy" and Anstey was one of the pioneers of the genre. He wrote the still-popular Victorian novel Vice Versa *(1882) in which a father and son exchange identities. Amongst his other novels are* The Tinted Venus *(1885) and* The Brass Bottle *(1900). You can find a bumper offering of his works in the omnibus* Humour and Fantasy *(1931). The following story, however, seems to have been forgotten. So far as I can tell this is its first reprinting since it was collected in* The Last Load *(1925).*

I HAD better say at once that I don't set up to be literary. I get quite enough of pen and ink all day at the bank, and when I *am* free, I like to be out in the fresh air as long as I can.

So you will not expect "style" or "literary composition" or anything of that sort in this; it is just an account, as exact as I can make it, of a very unpleasant experience I had last Christmas, and you must let me tell it in my own way. If you think, as very likely you may, that I cut rather a poor figure in the course of it, all I ask is that you will kindly suspend your judgment of me till you come to the finish. Because you will see then – at least, I hope you will – that I couldn't very well have behaved any differently.

My name is Filleter – Lionel Alchin Filleter, if you want it in full – I am about twenty-four, and unmarried. My elder sister Louisa and I share a semi-detached villa in Woodlands Avenue, Cricklebury Park, within easy reach of the City by rail or motor-bus. Our house is called "Ullswater", and next door is "Buttermere"; why, I don't know, as neither boasts so much as a basin of gold-fish. But the name was painted on the gate when we came, and as we couldn't think of anything better, we stuck to it.

We have quite a decent back garden for the size of the house, and when there was nothing doing in the way of games, I spent most of my spare time in it. In fact, I got rather keen at last, and my bank being in the City, I used to look in as often as possible at Messrs. Protheroe and Morris's well-known auction rooms in Cheapside, on the off-chance of picking up a bargain. Sometimes I did; in March of last year, for instance, I happened to drop in while they were selling a consignment of late Dutch and Cape bulbs and roots, and secured a bag of a hundred miscellaneous anemone roots for half a crown. The lot was described in the catalogue as "*Mixed. All fine sorts, including St. Brigid, Fulgens, etc. Believed to contain some new varieties.*"

If you have ever seen any anemone roots you will know what black, dried-up-looking things they are, so queerly shaped that one can never be sure which end up to plant them. I planted mine the day after I got them home, along my S.E. border, where they would get plenty of sun, and make a good show in front of the phloxes the following June. Or rather I planted all but one there, that one being so much larger and more fantastically shaped than the rest that I thought it might possibly turn out to be a quite unique variety, like, as I told Louisa at the time, the celebrated "Narcissus Mackintoshi

Splendescens," which was bought in a mixed lot at an auction for a few shillings, and now fetches as much as five pounds a bulb!

So I put in this particular root by itself, just under the drawing-room window, with a labelled peg to mark the spot. Louisa rather jeered at my expectations: she has very little faith in me as a gardener, and besides, she takes no proper pride in the garden itself, or she would never have persisted as she did, in letting Togo out for a run in it the last thing at night. Togo is Louisa's black dachs, and, as I understand the breed was originally trained to hunt for truffles, you could hardly expect such things as bulbs and roots to get a fair chance if there is any truth in hereditary instinct. But Louisa objected to his running about in front, because of motor-cars.

Still, I'm bound to say that he did not seem to have interfered with any of the anemones, all of which came up well – except the root I had had such hopes of, which never came up at all. And, as I couldn't fairly blame Togo for that and Louisa seemed to have forgotten all about the subject, I didn't think it worth while to refer to it.

I soon forgot my disappointment myself, until I was clearing up my beds in November and came upon the peg. Then I decided to leave the root undisturbed, just in case it might be some variety that took a considerable time to flower. And then I forgot it once more.

Things went on as usual until it was Christmas Eve: Louisa. I remember, had been putting together our Christmas presents, among which were some toys for little Peggy and Joan Dudlow.

The Dudlows, I should mention, are far the most important and influential people in Cricklebury Park, where the local society is above the usual suburban level. They live at "Ingleholme", a handsome gabled house standing in its own grounds at the end of the Avenue. Dudlow is a well-to-do silk merchant, and his eldest daughter Violet is – but I simply can't trust myself to describe her – I know I should never get hold of just the right words. Well, Louisa had gone up to her room, leaving me alone in the drawing-room with an injunction not to sit up late.

It was getting late – very nearly twelve o'clock, indeed – and I was thinking of turning in as soon as I had read another page or two of a book I was dipping into. It was a rum old book which belonged to Anthony Casbird, our curate at St Philip's. To look at Casbird, you wouldn't believe he was bookish, being so ruddy in the face, but he has a regular library at his lodgings, and is always at me for only reading what he calls "modern trash". So, as I happened to let out that I had never heard of a writer called Sir Thomas Browne, he had insisted on lending me one of his books, with some notes of his own for a paper he was going to read at some Literary Society.

It had a jaw-breaking title: "Pseudodoxia Epidemica, or Enquiries into very many received Tenents and commonly presumed Truths," and had been published so long ago as 1646.

Now when I do take up a book, I must say I prefer something rather more up-to-date, and this was written in such an old-fashioned, long-winded way that I didn't get on with it.

But I had come to a chapter which seemed more promising, being headed, "Of sundry tenents concerning vegetables or plants, which examined, prove either false or dubious." I thought I might get a tip or two for the garden out of it.

However, it was not what I should call "practical." It began like this: "*Many mola's and false conceptions there are of Mandrakes, the first from great Antiquity, conceiveth the Roote thereof resembleth the shape of man*" . . . and, further on, "*a Catacresticall and farre derived similitude, it holds with man, that is, in a bifurcation or division of the roote into two parts, which some are contente to call thighes . . . The third assertion affirmeth the roots of Mandrakes doe make a noyse or give a shreeke upon eradication, which is indeed ridiculous, and false below confute! . . . The last concerneth the danger ensuing, that there followes an hazard of life to them that pull it up, that some evill fate pursues them,*" and so on.

I found a loose note of Casbird's to the effect that, to guard against this danger, a black dog was usually employed to pull up the root, which apparently was fatal to the dog: while its owners *"stopped their own eares for feare of the terreble shriek or cry of this Mandrack."*

Somehow all this vaguely suggested something, though for a while I could not remember what. Everyone knows how worrying that is, and I could not bring myself to get out of my chair and go to bed until I had found the missing clue. And at last I hit on it. The anemone root, of course! I recollected now that Louisa, who had had a low opinion of it from the first, had remarked that it was shaped "exactly like a horrid little man." Not that I saw much resemblance myself, though it certainly was forked, and even had excrescences on each side which, to a lively imagination, might pass for arms. But no doubt in old Sir Thomas's time a good many fairly intelligent people would have sworn it was a Mandrake, and been terrified out of their lives at it!

Now I came to think over it, I was rather hazy, even then, as to what kind of creature they supposed a Mandrake to be exactly – though I gathered that it must be some peculiarly malignant sort of little demon.

I was amusing myself by these speculations when I was startled for the moment by a succession of short sharp shrieks, ending in a prolonged and blood-curdling yell. Only for the moment, because I remembered at once that, though we are some distance from the railway line, you can hear the trains distinctly when the wind happens to be in the right quarter. At the same time I could not help fancying that the noise had seemed nearer than usual – that it sounded as if it might almost have come from my own garden.

I grew so uneasy at last that I threw up the window to see if anything had happened.

All was quiet again now: but, as my eyes because accustomed to the darkness. I thought I could make out a small black form lying motionless in the patch of light that was thrown on the grass-plot by the lamp behind me. It looked to me like Togo, Louisa must have turned him out as usual, and the servants have forgotten to let him in again, which was careless of them. He had had a fit, as had happened once before, and the screams I had heard had been his. Now I should have to go down and see after the poor brute . . .

But I never went. For, as I stood there at the window leaning out, I heard another sound below which drove all thought of Togo completely out of my head – a stealthy rustling and scrabbling, as if some large reptile – a chameleon for choice – were clambering up the ivy towards the window.

I knew I ought to shut it before the thing, whatever it was, could get in, but I couldn't. I felt paralysed somehow. I stepped back into the room and stood there, waiting.

I had not to wait long before a small black object sprawled over the sill and alighted with a flop on the Ottoman beneath. I cannot give any idea of its appearance except by saying that it was a wizened little imp of a thing, as black as your hat, and hideously ugly. As it recovered its balance and stood there, blinking its beady little eyes in the lamplight, I noticed that its expression was not so much malignant as obsequious, and even abject. Though I didn't like it any the better for that. And then it spoke.

"I hope you were not alarmed by the noise," it said, in a soft reedy pipe. "It was only me."

I can't say that I was exactly surprised at hearing it speak. I did not know enough about Mandrakes for that. But it was clear enough that old Sir Thomas Browne had been wrong for once in his life, for this thing couldn't possibly be anything else but a Mandrake. I did not answer it – what *can* you say to a Mandrake?

It jumped off the ottoman as I fell back into my chair; then it swarmed up the table leg with a horrible agility, hoisted itself over the edge, and sat down humbly on a wooden box of puzzle cubes.

"You see," it went on apologetically, "when that dog of yours dragged me out of bed so suddenly, I couldn't help calling out. I do not ask you to punish it – I wish to make no complaint – but it bit me severely in the back."

There was something so sneaky and cringing in its manner that I began to feel less afraid of it. "It's been punished enough already," I said shortly. "It's probably dead by this time."

"Oh, surely not!" it said, squirming. "It has merely fainted. Though I can't think why."

"You don't seem to be aware," I replied, without disguising the disgust I felt, "that your appearance is enough to upset anyone."

"I'm afraid," it admitted, as it began to brush the mould from its frightful little twiggy legs, "my person has indeed been a little neglected. But I shall be presentable enough, after I have been a few days under your kindly care."

I let it know pretty plainly that if it imagined I was going to take it in, it was considerably mistaken – which seemed to disappoint it.

"But why not?" it said, and blinked at me again. "*Why* can't you take me in?"

"Because," I said bluntly, "a house like this is not the place for creatures of your sort."

"Oh," it replied, "but I am accustomed to roughing it, and I would put up with any drawbacks for the pleasure of your society!"

The calm cheek of this was almost too much for me. "I dare say you would," I said, "but you're not going to get the chance. What I meant was, as a Mandrake – which you can't deny you are – you are not a fit person to be admitted into any respectable household."

It protested volubly that it couldn't answer for other Mandrakes, it could only assure me that its own character was beyond reproach. It added that it had felt strongly attracted to me from the moment it saw my face, and its instinct told it that I should reciprocate the feeling in time.

I made the obvious retort that if its instinct told it that, it lied; I said I had no wish to argue with it, but it had better understand that it must leave the house at once.

"Don't repulse me!" it whined. "I want you to treat me as a friend. Call me 'Ferdie'. Do call me 'Ferdie'!"

All I said to that was that, if it didn't clear out of its own accord, I should be obliged to take it by the scruff of its neck and chuck it out of the window, which, as I pointed out, was conveniently open. Though, to tell you the truth, this was only bluff, for I wouldn't have touched the thing for any money.

Then the plausible little beast tried to work on my pity; there had been no rain for days, it said, and it was feeling so parched and dry, and generally exhausted. "Well," I said, relenting a little, "I'll give you just one whisky and soda, and after that you must go." But it refused anything but plain soda, with which I filled a tumbler to the brim, and the Mandrake stooped down and drained it greedily with great gulps.

The soda water seemed to buck it up in a most extraordinary way. Its shrivelled little form began to fill out, and its extremities to look more like hands and feet, while its height actually increased by several inches. But in other respects I could see no improvement.

"I feel a different being," it informed me complacently. "It's just occurred to me," it went on, "that the prejudice which I can't help seeing you have against me may be due to my want of clothing. Underground that did not signify, but, in the world above, I quite recognize that the proprieties should be observed. Only I don't see – ah, the very things . . . *Will* you excuse me?"

It had suddenly caught sight of a large Golliwogg, which I had bought for Peggy, and which was lying on the table. Before I could interfere the Mandrake had deftly stripped the doll of its blue coat, white shirt, and red trousers, and arrayed itself in them. "Now," it remarked proudly, "you will have no need to blush for me!"

I think I never saw anything more outrageously grotesque than the spectacle that Mandrake presented in the Golliwogg's garments, which hung about its meagre body in loose folds. But it strutted about with immense satisfaction. "Quite a fair fit," it said, trying to twist its ugly head round and see its back. "Though I'm not sure there isn't a wrinkle between the shoulders. Do *you* notice it?"

I said I thought it need not distress itself about that, and again ordered it to get out.

"But where am I to *get* to?" it said; "I can't go back to the garden *now*. And it's *your* garden, which surely gives me some claim on your hospitality!"

I said it had no claims on me whatever; if anyone was responsible for it, Messrs Protheroe and Morris were the proper parties to apply to, and I gave it their address in Cheapside. Perhaps this was hardly fair on the firm, who, of course, would not have sold such a thing, knowingly, as an anemone root – but I had to get out of it somehow.

I did not pitch it out of the window; I showed it to the front door, like an ordinary caller. "Then you cast me from you," it sighed in the passage, as I undid the chain. "Are we to meet as strangers henceforth?"

"If we ever meet at all," I said, "which I see no necessity for. Good night." But it still lingered on the door-mat.

"Ah, well," it said, "it cannot be that I shall find all hearts as hard as yours. Did you say Cheapside?"

I said if it had any difficulty in finding the way it had better ask a constable. It thanked me profusely, begged me not to trouble to come to the gate with it, and left.

With all my instinctive repugnance, I could not help feeling slightly ashamed of myself; it did look such a forlorn and pitiable little wretch as it shambled down the path and slipped through the bars of the gate!

But what could I do? To keep it was out of the question; Louisa would never stand it – the thing would get on her nerves. And then there were the Dudlows. What would Violet, what would her father and mother, think of me if they discovered that I was harbouring such a beastly thing as a Mandrake?

I chained and barred the door, congratulating myself that, so far as I was concerned, the affair was done with. And then I went to bed, deciding that it would be better not to mention the matter to Louisa.

*   *   *

The next day, of course, was Christmas. I was sitting by the fire in the dining-room, which faces the road. Louisa was at church, and I ought to have been there, too. I didn't quite know why I hadn't gone, as I should certainly have met Violet there, and perhaps walked home with her afterwards – but I supposed I hadn't felt up to it.

Anyhow there I was, in an armchair with a pipe and a newspaper, when all at once I became aware of a low tapping at the bow window behind my back. I didn't look round, for I had a sort of presentiment of what it was. And then, in the bevelled plate-glass mirror of the sideboard opposite, I saw reflected a flash of scarlet and blue among the variegated laurels in one of the window-boxes, and I knew for certain that that infernal little Mandrake had turned up again. The tapping grew louder, but I took no notice, hoping that it would soon get tired of it and go away.

However, it persevered until I began to feel alarmed lest it should attract the attention of the people opposite, who are rather given to gossiping. So I got up and let the thing in, and asked it what the deuce it wanted now – for I was extremely annoyed. Without waiting for an invitation it took the armchair opposite mine, with a cough which was either deferential or due to the tobacco smoke. Then it explained that its intrusion, which it hoped I would overlook, had been prompted by an irresistible impulse to wish me the Compliments of the Season.

Of course I knew it had some deeper motive than that, and I made no answer, beyond grunting. It appeared that it had gone to Cheapside, but had found neither Mr Protheroe nor Mr Morris at home – which did not surprise me. It had been wandering about all night, though it had contrived – it did not mention how, and I asked no questions – to refresh itself with some cocoa and a slice of cake at a coffee-stall. And, its appetite having once been aroused, it had begun, it said, to feel hungry again. Might it trespass on me for a meal? It would be deeply grateful, even if I could do no more for it than a mince-pie.

I declined. Not from stinginess, but a conviction that it

would be the thin end of the wedge. I might have it staying on to lunch – and there were Louisa's feelings to be considered. It took the refusal meekly enough, and said it had another favour to ask of me. Perhaps I had not observed that it had been putting on flesh with a rapidity which it could only attribute to the currant cake?

I had already noticed a change. It was now at least two feet high; its blue jacket was reduced to a bolero, while its red breeches were hardly bigger than bathing-drawers. I forget if it still retained its shirt or not. The Mandrake represented that if this shrinkage were to continue, it would soon be ashamed to present itself in public, and asked if I could recommend it to a really good tailor – "not the one who made those things you have on," it explained. "I prefer a quieter style myself."

I knew there was no fault to be found with the clothes I was wearing, a neat suit in quite the right shade of green, and I might have shut the little beggar up pretty sharply if I had chosen. But after all, what *did* it matter what a Mandrake thought of my things?

"I feel sure I should be a success in society," it went on, wriggling with suppressed eagerness as it spoke, "if I were only decently dressed. I have many gifts, and even accomplishments. All my tastes are innocent and refined. You would find we had much in common, if you would only try to regard me as a friend. If," it entreated, with a smile which it evidently intended to be winning, but which came out on its gnarled wooden countenance as a revoltingly offensive leer, "If I could once hear you call me 'Ferdie'!"

It heard me call it several names – but "Ferdie" was not one of them. "Then do I gather," it said, "that, in your judgement, the mere fact of my extraction, if known, would be sufficient to exclude me from any social circle?"

I replied that that was distinctly my impression. "Then," it stipulated, "if I leave you now, will you give me your word of honour as a young English gentleman never to reveal to any living soul what I really am?"

What it really was must be so obvious to the most careless

observer that I felt I could safely promise, and besides, I was in such a hurry to get it out of the way before Louisa returned from church. Then it asked if there were not charitable persons called "clergy" who were in the habit of relieving deserving cases, and, with a sudden inspiration, I gave it Casbird's name and address, on condition that it did not mention who had sent it to him.

And at last, after having the unblushing impudence to inquire affectionately after Togo, it started. As I watched it slink across the road and round the corner in the direction of the curate's lodgings, I could not resist a grim chuckle. For I knew Tony Casbird not only as a fellow of strong common sense, but as a fair all-round cricketer and a first-rate half-back, and if this little beast was getting uppish, he could be safely trusted to put it in its proper place.

And anyhow, the job was more in his line than mine.

It must have been the same evening that Casbird came in. In fact, I know it was, because he said he couldn't stay long, as he was going on to "Ingleholme" to tell Miss Dudlow how pleased his vicar had been with the charming effect of the Christmas decorations, which she had taken a prominent part in arranging.

Casbird was a devoted admirer of Violet's – but I was not afraid of *him*, for I didn't think he stood a sporting chance. Just as he rose to go, he mentioned that on returning from service that morning he had found a most interesting visitor waiting to see him. I thought I could guess who it was, but I wasn't going to give myself away, so I merely said, "Oh, really?" or something of that sort.

"Yes," said Casbird, "I have seldom known a sadder, stranger case. He has come through so much, and with such splendid pluck and endurance."

Naturally Louisa wanted to know more about him. What was he like? Casbird said really he scarcely knew how to describe him. Handsome? Well, no, he should hardly call him *that* – in fact, at first sight, his appearance was somewhat against him. But such a bright, cheery little chap! So simple and fresh. "I assure you," the curate concluded, "that somehow he makes me feel quite worldly by comparison!"

I thought I *must* have been wrong – he couldn't possibly be referring to the Mandrake! "What do you call it – I mean *him?*" I asked.

"Well," said the curate, "I call him 'Ferdie' at present. It was his own wish, and he hasn't told me his other name yet. I am putting him up until I can find a suitable opening for him. He's a delightful companion, so touchingly grateful for the least kindness, so full of little delicate attentions! Why, when I came in to tea this afternoon, I found the little fellow had actually put my slippers inside the fender to warm, and was toasting a crumpet for me by the fire!"

I listened aghast. I knew Casbird rather went in for being broad-minded and tolerant and that – but I'd really no idea he would carry it so far as to chum up with a Mandrake! Well, it was his own affair. The thing was evidently an accomplished liar, and it would not surprise me in the least if when he got back he found that it had gone off with his spoons.

After Casbird had left, Louisa expressed a great curiosity to meet this new *protégé* of his, and was slightly annoyed with me for showing so little interest in the subject. I began to regret that promise of mine.

The Dudlows were having a children's party on the evening of Boxing Day, and I had been looking forward to it eagerly. For one thing, because I always do enjoy children's parties, and in Cricklebury Park there are some particularly nice kiddies. For another, because I had made up my mind that, if I had an opportunity, I would speak out to Violet before the evening was over. I wouldn't let myself feel too sure beforehand, because that is unlucky – but all the same, I had a kind of feeling that it would be all right.

And Dudlow was not likely to refuse his consent to an engagement, for I knew his wife would put in a word for me. Mrs Dudlow had approved of me from the first, when she saw what friends I had made with the younger children, Peggy and little Joan. Children, she always maintained, were "such infallible judges of character."

They had made me promise to come early, because, as Mrs Dudlow was kind enough to say, they depended on me to "set the ball rolling."

I got to "Ingleholme" as early as I could, but the moment Louisa and I had passed the "cathedral glass" portico, I was aware from the shouts of children's laughter that came from the drawing-room that the ball had begun to roll already without my assistance. And I must confess that it was rather a blow, on entering, to find that, instead of the welcome I had expected, my appearance passed almost unnoticed. But they were all much too absorbed in something that was going on in the inner room – even Violet's greeting was a little casual. "Such a wonderful conjurer," she whispered; "if you go nearer the arch, you will see him much better."

When I did, I must leave you to imagine my feelings on discovering that the performer who was holding his audience entranced with delight and amazement was nothing else than that miserable little beast of a Mandrake!

It had gone on growing, and was now the height of a middle-sized pygmy – but it was just as hideous as ever, and in spite of its being in correct evening clothes, I knew it at once. And what is more, I could see it knew *me*, and was trying to catch my eye and claim my admiration.

It was conjuring – or I should rather say, pretending to conjure – for while it kept on jabbering away with the utmost assurance, it never succeeded in bringing off a single trick. Now, I don't call myself a conjurer (though I can do a few simple things with eggs and half-crowns and so forth) – but I should have been sorry to make such an exhibition of myself as that incompetent little rotter was doing.

The odd thing was that nobody but myself seemed in the least to realize how poor the performance was; the Mandrake had got round them all, grown-ups and children alike, and deluded them into accepting its bungling efforts as a quite marvellous display of dexterity. Why, even when, after borrowing Dudlow's gold watch, it coolly handed it back smashed to fragments, he merely swept all the loose wheels and springs into his waist-coat pocket, and said that it was "Capital – uncommonly clever." And not out of politeness, mind you; I could see he really thought so!

After the conjuring there were games, which were entirely organized by the Mandrake. Nobody consulted *me*; if I hadn't joined in by way of asserting myself, I should have been completely out of it. I tried to behave as if I didn't know the Mandrake was in the room; but this was not easy, as the little brute made a point of barging into me and rumpling my hair and pommelling me all over, as if to induce me to take some notice of it.

People only remarked on its high spirits, but I couldn't help saying that there was a considerable difference between high spirits and downright horseplay; and really, to hear little Joy Hammond (a special pal of mine) coming up with flushed face and sparkling eyes when I was gasping on the carpet, trying to recover my wind and one or two of my enamel and mother-of-pearl waistcoat buttons, and asking me, "*Isn't* Ferdie a lovely toy-fellow?" was enough to put anyone a little out of temper!

The children all called it "Ferdie". Bobbie Clint, another intimate friend of mine, informed me proudly that it had "partickerily asked them to." It was simply maddening to see them all hanging about it, and making such a ridiculous fuss over that little horror, while Casbird looked on smiling, with all the airs of a public benefactor!

I felt it was almost too hard to bear when my beloved Violet reproved me privately for my stiffness, and added that, if there *was* one quality more than another she detested in a man, it was a sulky disposition!

I did not defend myself – my pride kept me silent; if she chose to misunderstand me, she must. But I was determined to have it out with the Mandrake privately at the very first opportunity – and I contrived to inveigle it out of the room on some pretext – "Dumb Crambo," I think it was.

It skipped into the hall with me readily enough; I fancy it flattered itself that I was coming round at last. But I very soon undeceived it: I told it that it knew as well as I did it had no business there, and I insisted on its leaving the house instantly, offering, if it did so, to save its face by explaining that it had been suddenly called away.

I can see it now as it sat perched on an oak chest, looking up at me with an assumption of injured innocence. It protested that it didn't want to go yet – why *should* it, when it was having the time of its life, and everybody, except me, was being so kind to it? It had the impertinence to add that it was sorry to see a character so fine in many respects as mine disfigured by so mean a passion as jealousy – which made me furious.

I replied that I was hardly likely to be jealous under the circumstances, and it could leave my character alone. All I had to say was that, if the Mandrake remained, I should be compelled to speak out.

"Oh no!" it said, "you will not do that, because, if you remember, you gave me your word of honour that you would never betray the secret of my birth!"

"When I gave that," I retorted, "I never imagined you would have the audacity to push yourself in here – and at a children's party too!"

It said it had always been its dream to be invited to a real children's party, and now it had come true and I must have seen how popular it was making itself. It was sure I would not be so cruel as to expose it – I was too honourable a gentleman to break my word.

It had found my weak point there and knew it – but I stood firm. "I don't consider myself bound by that any longer," I said. "It's my duty to say what I know – and, if you leave me no other alternative, I mean to do it."

"Listen to me," it said, with a soft but deadly earnestness, and I thought I could read in its little eyes, as they glittered in the rays of the hall lantern, a certain veiled and sinister menace. "I warn you, for your own sake, because I should like to spare you if possible. If you insist on denouncing me, you little know the consequences you will bring upon yourself! *You* will be the chief sufferer from your rashness."

I can't deny that this warning had some effect on me; so much so, in fact, that I am afraid I climbed down to some extent. I said that I was as anxious as itself to avoid a scandal, and that I should take no steps so long as it behaved itself. And then we went in and played "Dumb Crambo," or whatever it was, and I got mauled about by the Mandrake more severely than ever!

But I was beginning to have enough of it, and I took the curate aside and hinted that his friend struck me as a bit of a bounder, and that as he was already getting above himself, it would be as well to get him away before supper. Casbird was indignant; he said that "Ferdie" was the life and soul of the party, and he couldn't understand my attitude, especially when the dear little fellow had taken such a decided fancy to me! He had always thought, he said, that I was above these petty prejudices. So I didn't press it, and soon afterwards we went in to supper.

It made me feel positively ill to see all those nice kiddies almost fighting for the privilege of sitting next that little fraud, and then to watch it making an absolute hog of itself with sausage-rolls and lemon sponge! And the way they pulled crackers with it, too, and pressed the rings out of them on it as keepsakes, till its little claws were loaded with cheap jewellery. I sat between Violet and Peggy – but neither of them offered to pull a cracker with *me*!

Still, I bore it all without murmuring until towards the end, when Dudlow suddenly got up and asked us to charge our glasses and drink to the health of the new friend who had contributed so enormously to the general enjoyment that evening.

I knew what was coming, and so did the Mandrake, though it cast down its eyes with a self-conscious smirk, as if it could not think to whom its host was referring!

And then, all at once, I felt I could not stand any more. It was my duty to speak. Whatever it might cost me, I *must* prevent poor Dudlow – whom I liked and respected for his own sake as well as because he was Violet's father – from making such an irreparable mistake as proposing the health of a Mandrake at his own table!

So I rose, and implored him to sit down and leave the rest of his speech unspoken; I said I had reasons which I would explain privately later on.

He replied rather heatedly that he would have no hole-and-corner business under *his* roof; if I had anything to say, I had better say it then and there, or sit down and hold my tongue.

The Mandrake sat perfectly calm, with its beady eyes fixed warningly on me, but I saw its complexion slowly change from coal-black to an awful grey-green shade that made the blue-and-pink fool's cap it was wearing seem even more hideously incongruous.

But I had gone too far to stop now; I was no longer afraid of its vengeance. It might blast me to death where I stood – I didn't care. It would only reveal its true character – and then, perhaps, Violet would be sorry for having misjudged me so!

"If that – that *thing* over there," I said, pointing to it, "had not cast some cursed spell over you all, so far from drinking its unwholesome health, you would shrink from it in horror!"

There was a general outcry, amidst which Casbird sprang to his feet. "Let us have no more of these dastardly insinuations!" he shouted. "Tell us, if you can, what you accuse our Ferdie of having done!"

"It's not what it's *done*," I said, "it's what it *is*! Are you blind, that you cannot see that it's nothing more or less than a Mandrake?" I was going on to explain how I had bought it by mistake in a bag of mixed anemone roots, when Dudlow brought me up with a round turn that almost took my breath away.

"And if he *is* a Mandrake, sir," he said, "what *of* it?"

"What *of* it?" I could only gasp feebly. "I should have thought myself that that was quite enough to make him impossible – at a party like this!"

"And who are *you*," thundered the curate, "that you presume to sit in judgement on a fellow creature? Let me tell you that you might have some reason for this superciliousness if you were half as good a man as poor dear little Ferdie here is a Mandrake!" He patted it affectionately on the shoulder as he spoke, and I saw Violet's lovely eyes first shine on him in admiration of his chivalry, and then blaze on me with scorn and contempt.

Indeed, they all seemed to consider my conduct snobbish in the extreme, and the Mandrake was the object of universal sympathy as it endeavoured to squeeze out a crocodile tear or two.

"All *right*!" I said. "Pitch into me if you like! But you will see presently. It threatened me only half an hour ago with the most awful consequences if I dared to expose it. Now let it do its worst!"

But little did I foresee the fiendish revenge it was preparing. It got up on its chair and began to make a speech. *Such* a speech – every sentence of it reeking with the cheapest sentiment, the most maudlin claptrap! But clever – diabolically clever, even I could not help acknowledging *that*.

It began by saying how hurt it felt that I could imagine it would ever harm a hair of my head. Never, no, not even when I had driven it from my door last Christmas Eve, out into the bitter night and the falling snow (which was sheer melodrama, for Christmas Eve had been rather warmer and muggier than usual!), not even then had it had any sentiments towards me but the humblest devotion and affection! It did not blame me for resenting its intrusion among them that evening. Perhaps I could not be expected to understand what a temptation it had been to a lonely wanderer like itself to forget the inferiority of its position, and share for a few too fleeting hours in the innocent revelry of happy children, at a season, too, when it had fondly hoped that charity and goodwill might be shown to all alike. But I had made it realize its mistake – and now it could only implore our pardon and assure us that it would trouble us but a very little while longer.

At this its voice quavered, and it broke down, most artistically. There was not a dry eye – except mine – round the supper-table. As for Dudlow, he was blubbering quite openly, while Peggy, Joan, Joy Hammond, and all the other children entreated "darling Ferdie" not to leave them, and I heard myself described by Bobbie Clint as a "beastly beast," and Tommy Dickson passionately declared that I was a sneak!

All this was unpleasant enough – but nothing to what followed. That devilish little imp was keeping an even higher card up its sleeve for the climax. After mastering its emotion, it thanked all its dear young playmates for still desiring to keep it with them, but said that, alas, it was not to be! The sudden shock of learning that I, whose affection it had striven so hard to win, regarded it with such bitter antipathy had been too much for its high-strung, sensitive nature – it felt that its end was very near. One last request it had to make of me, and that was that I would accept the beautiful emerald ring it had on (off a cracker, if you please!), and wear it always as a remembrance, and in token that it forgave me, fully and freely!

And then, to my unspeakable horror, it collapsed in a heap on its chair, and shrivelled slowly away inside its dress-clothes until it was once more the wizened object it had been when I first saw it!

You may have seen those "dying roosters" they sell in the streets – well, it went down exactly like one of those. And up to the time its head fell over in a final droop, its evil little eyes were fixed on me with vindictive triumph.

It had scored off me thoroughly, and was jolly well aware of it.

I knew perfectly well that the little wretch wasn't really dead – but though I assured them all it was merely shamming, they only turned away in horror at what they called my "cold-blooded brutality."

It was like some horrible nightmare. I was in the right and they were all wrong – but I couldn't get anybody to see it. I would rather not dwell on the scene that followed: the wailing of those poor deluded little kiddies, Louisa's hysterical refusal to consider me any longer a brother of hers, Casbird's manly sorrow over the departed Ferdie, and Violet's gentle, loving

efforts to console him. I had no time to observe more, for just
then Dudlow ordered me out of the house and forbade me ever
again to cross his threshold . . .

I must have got back to "Ullswater" somehow, but I have
no recollection of doing so. Everything was a blank until I
found myself in our drawing room, lying groaning in an
armchair, with my head pressed against its side.

And then, as the incidents of that disastrous party came back
to me, one by one, I shivered in an agony of shame. I really do
not think I have ever felt so utterly miserable in all my life!

I had done for myself, hopelessly, irretrievably. I had lost
Violet for ever. Louisa would tell me, the moment she came
home, that we must arrange to live apart. Casbird would cut
me dead in future. Even the little kiddies would refuse to be
friends with me any longer! . . . And why had all this happened? Because I had not had the sense to hold my tongue!
What earthly business was it of mine if the Dudlows chose to
invite a Mandrake to "Ingleholme"? Why need I have been so
down on the poor little brute? At Christmas-time, too, when
any ordinarily decent fellow would have taken a more Dick-
ensy view of things! I couldn't understand my having behaved
so outrageously – it did not seem like *me* . . .

And yet, hang it all! I had only done the right thing. True, I
might have been more tactful over it. I could see now, when it
was too late, that to go and make a scene at supper like that was
scarcely good form. I might have thought more of the children's feelings.

Here a dreadful doubt took hold of me. Suppose I had been
mistaken all along in the Mandrake's character? I knew very
little about the creatures, after all – only what I had read in Sir
Thomas Browne, and even *he* seemed to hold that the stories to
their discredit were either exaggerations or vulgar or common
errors.

And, repulsive as I had found "Ferdie", I could not remember anything in his conduct that would seem very re-
prehensible, even in a choir-boy. And all his sentiments had
been exemplary. Had *I* been guilty of a "vulgar error"? Had I

really, as Casbird put it, "broken a loving little heart by my stupid cruelty"? Was I, as he had called me, a "moral murderer"? They might hold an inquest on the thing. I should be called on to give my evidence – the jury would add a rider to their verdict censuring me for my conduct, and the coroner would endorse their opinion with some severe remarks! It would get into all the papers; the fellows at the bank would send me to Coventry; I should be lucky if I did not get the sack! . . .

But stop – would they really make such a fuss as all that about a mere Mandrake? If they only made a few inquiries, when they calmed down, surely they would find out *something* shady about it. How did it get hold of those evening clothes, for instance, when all the shops were shut? It must have made a burglarious entry somewhere – I remembered how coolly it had appropriated the Golliwogg's . . . and at this point I shuddered and started, as, once again, that long shrill scream rang out into the night! Great heavens! Had Togo pulled up *another* of them? I felt I could *not* go through it all a second time. But this time the sound really was much more like a railway engine. What if, after all – I could settle it in a moment; I had only to turn my head – and, if I saw the Golliwogg lying there on the table with nothing on, I should *know!*

For some seconds I could not summon up courage enough to look.

And then, slowly, in deadly terror of finding my worst fears confirmed, I turned round . . .

What my feelings were on discovering that the Golliwogg was fully clothed I can't express – I could have sobbed with relief and joy on its blue shoulder.

I glanced at the old brown book which lay face downwards on the floor. It was still open at Chapter VI., "Of sundry tenents concerning vegetables or plants, which examined, prove either false or dubious." And then it occurred to me that, if I *must* dream any more about Mandrakes, it would on the whole be more comfortable to do so in bed.

*   *   *

The Dudlows' children's party was a very cheery affair, although there was no Mandrake to keep things going. And I *did* get an opportunity of speaking to Violet, and it *was* all right. At least, it will be, as soon as I get my next rise.

THE QUEEN'S TRIPLETS

Israel Zangwill

Here's another pretty-much-forgotten writer. If he's re-membered at all these days it's because of The Big Bow Mystery *(1895), the first great locked-room mystery. But in his day his reputation rested on his efforts for the recognition of the Jewish poor in east London, through the powerful novel* Children of the Ghetto *(1892), which earned him the nickname of "the Dickens of the Ghetto". What does seem forgotten is that Zang-will (1864–1926) was a noted humorist. He founded the comic paper* Ariel *in 1890 and he traded aphorisms and quips with Oscar Wilde (in fact, he looked a bit like Wilde) and Jerome K. Jerome (of* Three Men in a Boat *fame). The best of his early light fantasies were collected as* The King of the Schnorrers *(1894) from which the following story comes.*

ONCE upon a time there was a Queen who unexpectedly gave birth to three Princes. They were all so exactly alike that after a moment or two it was impossible to remember which was the eldest or which was the youngest. Any two of them, sort them how you pleased, were always twins. They all cried in the same key and with the same comic grimaces. In short, there was not a hair's-breadth of difference between them – not that they had a hair's-breadth between them, for, like most babies, they were prematurely bald.

The King was very much put out. He did not mind the expense of keeping three Heir Apparents, for that fell on the country, and was defrayed by an impost called "The Queen's Tax". But it was the consecrated custom of the kingdom that the crown should pass over to the eldest son, and the absence of accurate knowledge upon this point was perplexing. A triumvirate was out of the question; the multiplication of monarchs would be vexation to the people, and the rule of three would drive them mad.

The Queen was just as annoyed, though on different grounds. She felt it hard enough to be the one mother in the realm who could not get the Queen's bounty, without having to suffer the King's reproaches. Her heart was broken, and she died soon after of laryngitis.

To distinguish the triplets (when it was too late) they were always dressed one in green, one in blue, and one in black, the colours of the national standard, and naturally got to be popularly known by the sobriquets of the Green Prince, the Blue Prince, and the Black Prince. Every year they got older and older till at last they became young men. And every year the King got older and older till at last he became an old man, and the fear crept into his heart that he might be restored to his wife and leave the kingdom embroiled in civil feud unless he settled straightway who should be the heir. But, being human, notwithstanding his court laureates, he put off the disagreeable duty from day to day, and might have died without an heir, if the envoys from Paphlagonia had not aroused him to the necessity of a decision. For they announced that the Princess of Paphlagonia, being suddenly orphaned, would be sent to him in the twelfth moon that she might marry his eldest son as covenanted by ancient treaty. This was the last straw. "But I don't know who is my eldest son!" yelled the King, who had a vast respect for covenants and the Constitution.

In great perturbation he repaired to a famous Oracle, at that time worked by a priestess with her hair let down her back. The King asked her a plain question: "Which is my eldest son?"

After foaming at the mouth like an open champagne bottle, she replied:

"The eldest is he that the Princess shall wed."

The King said he knew that already, and was curtly told that if the replies did not give satisfaction he could go elsewhere. So he went to the wise men and the magicians, and held a levée of them, and they gave him such goodly counsel that the Chief Magician was henceforth honoured with the privilege of holding the Green, Black, and Blue Tricolour over the King's head at mealtimes. Soon after, it being the twelfth moon, the King set forward with a little retinue to meet the Princess of Paphlagonia, whose coming had got abroad; but returned two days later with the news that the Princess was confined to her room, and would not arrive in the city till next year.

On the last day of the year the King summoned the three Princes to the Presence Chamber. And they came, the Green Prince, and the Blue Prince, and the Black Prince, and made obeisance to the Monarch, who sat in moiré antique robes, on the old gold throne, with his courtiers all around him.

"My sons," he said, "ye are aware that, according to the immemorial laws of the realm, one of you is to be my heir, only I know not which of you he is; the difficulty is complicated by the fact that I have covenanted to espouse him to the Princess of Paphlagonia, of whose imminent arrival ye have heard. In this dilemma there are those who would set the sovereignty of the State upon the hazard of a die. But not by such undignified methods do I deem it prudent to extort the designs of the gods. There are ways alike more honourable to you and to me of ascertaining the intentions of the fates. And first, the wise men and the magicians recommend that ye be all three sent forth upon an arduous emprise. As all men know, somewhere in the great seas that engirdle our dominion, somewhere beyond the Ultimate Thule, there rangeth a vast monster, intolerable, not to be borne. Every ninth moon this creature approacheth our coasts, deluging the land with an inky vomit. This plaguy Serpent cannot be slain, for the soothsayers aver it beareth a charmed life, but it were a mighty achievement, if for only one year, the realm could be relieved of its oppression. Are ye willing to set forth separately upon this knightly quest?"

Then the three Princes made enthusiastic answer, entreating to be sped on the journey forthwith, and a great gladness ran through the Presence Chamber, for all had suffered much from the annual incursions of the monster. And the King's heart was fain of the gallant spirit of the Princes.

" 'Tis well," said he. "To-morrow, at the first dawn of the new year, shall ye fare forth together; when ye reach the river ye shall part, and for eight moons shall ye wander whither ye will; only, when the ninth moon rises, shall ye return and tell me how ye have fared. Hasten now, therefore, and equip yourselves as ye desire, and if there be aught that will help you in the task, ye have but to ask for it."

Then, answering quickly before his brothers could speak, the Black Prince cried: "Sire, I would crave the magic boat which saileth under the sea and destroyeth mighty armaments."

"It is thine," replied the King.

Then the Green Prince said: "Sire, grant me the magic car which saileth through the air over the great seas."

The Black Prince started and frowned, but the King answered, "It is granted." Then, turning to the Blue Prince, who seemed lost in meditation, the King said: "Why art thou silent, my son? Is there nothing I can give thee?"

"Thanks, I will take a little pigeon," answered the Blue Prince abstractedly.

The courtiers stared and giggled, and the Black Prince chuckled, but the Blue Prince was seemingly too proud to back out of his request.

So at sunrise on the morrow the three Princes set forth, journeying together till they came to the river where they had agreed to part company. Here the magic boat was floating at anchor, while the magic car was tied to the trunk of a plane-tree upon the bank, and the little pigeon, fastened by a thread, was fluttering among the branches.

Now, when the Green Prince saw the puny pigeon, he was like to die of laughing.

"Dost thou think to feed the Serpent with thy pigeon?" he sneered. "I fear me thou wilt not choke him off thus."

"And what hast thou to laugh at?" retorted the Black Prince, interposing. "Dost thou think to find the Serpent of the Sea in the air?"

"He is always in the air," murmured the Blue Prince, inaudibly.

"Nay," said the Green Prince, scratching his head dubiously. "But thou didst so hastily annex the magic boat, I had to take the next best thing."

"Dost thou accuse me of unfairness?" cried the Black Prince in a pained voice. "Sooner than thou shouldst say that, I would change with thee."

"Wouldst thou, indeed?" enquired the Green Prince eagerly.

"Ay, that would I," said the Black Prince indignantly. "Take the magic boat, and may the gods speed thee." So saying he jumped briskly into the magic car, cut the rope, and sailed aloft. Then, looking down contemptuously upon the Blue Prince, he shouted: "Come, mount thy pigeon, and be off in search of the monster."

But the Blue Prince replied, "I will await you here."

Then the Green Prince pushed off his boat, chuckling louder than ever. "Dost thou expect to keep the creature off our coasts by guarding the head of the river?" he scoffed.

But the Blue Prince replied, "I will await you both here till the ninth moon."

No sooner were his brothers gone than the Blue Prince set about building a hut. Here he lived happily, fishing his meals out of the river or snaring them out of the sky. The pigeon was never for a moment in danger of being eaten. It was employed more agreeably to itself and its master in operations which will appear anon. Most of the time the Blue Prince lay on his back among the wild flowers, watching the river rippling to the sea or counting the passing of the eight moons, that alternately swelled and dwindled, now showing like the orb of the Black Prince's car, now like the Green Prince's boat. Sometimes he read scraps of papyrus, and his face shone.

One lovely starry night, as the Blue Prince was watching the heavens, it seemed to him as if the eighth moon in dying had dropped out of the firmament and was falling upon him. But it was only the Black Prince come back. His garments were powdered with snow, his brows were knitted gloomily, he had a dejected, despondent aspect.

"Thou here!" he snapped.

"Of course," said the Blue Prince cheerfully, though he seemed a little embarrassed all the same. "Haven't I been here all the time? But go into my hut, I've kept supper hot for thee."

"Has the Green Prince had his?"

"No, I haven't seen anything of him. Hast thou scotched the Serpent?"

"No, I haven't seen anything of him," growled the Black Prince. "I've passed backwards and forwards over the entire face of the ocean, but nowhere have I caught the slightest glimpse of him. What a fool I was to give up the magic boat! He never seems to come to the surface."

All this while the Blue Prince was dragging his brother with suspicious solicitude towards the hut, where he sat him down to his own supper of ortolans and oysters. But the host had no sooner run outside again, on the pretext of seeing if the Green Prince was coming, than there was a disturbance and eddying in the stream as of a rally of water-rats, and the magic boat shot up like a catapult, and the Green Prince stepped on deck all dry and dusty, and with the air of a draggled dragon-fly.

"Good evening, hast thou er – scotched the Serpent?" stammered the Blue Prince, taken aback.

"No, I haven't even seen anything of him," growled the Green Prince. "I have skimmed along the entire surface of the ocean, and sailed every inch beneath it, but nowhere have I caught the slightest glimpse of him. What a fool I was to give up the magic car! From a height I could have commanded an ampler area of ocean. Perhaps he was up the river."

"No, I haven't seen anything of him," replied the Blue Prince hastily. "But go into my hut, thy supper must be getting quite cold." He hurried his verdant brother into the hut, and gave him some chestnuts out of the oven (it was the best he could do for him), and then rushed outside again, on the plea of seeing if the Serpent was coming. But he seemed to expect him to come from the sky, for, leaning against the trunk of the plane-tree by the river, he resumed his anxious scrutiny of the constellations. Presently there was a gentle whirring in the air, and a white bird became visible, flying rapidly downwards in his direction. Almost at the same instant he felt himself pinioned by a rope to the tree-trunk, and saw the legs of the alighting pigeon neatly prisoned in the Black Prince's fist.

"Aha!" croaked the Black Prince triumphantly. "Now we shall see through thy little schemes."

He detached the slip of papyrus which dangled from the pigeon's neck.

"How darest thou read my letters?" gasped the Blue Prince.

"If I dare to rob the mail, I shall certainly not hesitate to read the letters," answered the Black Prince coolly, and went on to enunciate slowly (for the light was bad) the following lines:

> "Heart-sick I watch the old moon's ling'ring death,
> And long upon my face to feel thy breath;
> I burn to see its final flicker die,
> And greet our moon of honey in the sky."

"What is all this moonshine?" he concluded in bewilderment.

Now the Blue Prince was the soul of candour, and seeing that nothing could now be lost by telling the truth, he answered:

"This is a letter from a damsel who resideth in the Tower of

Telifonia, on the outskirts of the capital; we are engaged. No doubt the language seemeth to thee a little overdone, but wait till thy turn cometh."

"And so thou hast employed this pigeon as a carrier between thee and this suburban young person?" cried the Black Prince, feeling vaguely boiling over with rage.

"Even so," answered his brother, "but guard thy tongue. The lady of whom thou speakest so disrespectfully is none other than the Princess of Paphlagonia."

"Eh? What?" gasped the Black Prince.

"She hath resided there since the twelfth moon of last year. The King received her the first time he set out to meet her."

"Dost thou dare say the King hath spoken untruth?"

"Nay, nay. The King is a wise man. Wise men never mean what they say. The King said she was confined to her room. It is true, for he had confined her in the Tower with her maidens for fear she should fall in love with the wrong Prince, or the reverse, before the rightful heir was discovered. The King said she would not arrive in the city till next year. This also is true. As thou didst rightly observe, the Tower of Telifonia is situated in the suburbs. The King did not bargain for my discovering that a beautiful woman lived in its topmost turret."

"Nay, how couldst thou discover that? The King did not lend thee the magic car, and thou certainly couldst not see her at that height without the magic glass!"

"I have not seen her. But through the embrasure I often saw the sunlight flashing and leaping like a thing of life, and I knew it was what the children call a 'Johnny Noddy.' Now a 'Johnny Noddy' argueth a mirror, and a mirror argueth a woman, and frequent use thereof argueth a beautiful woman. So, when in the Presence Chamber the King told us of his dilemma as to the hand of the Princess of Paphlagonia, it instantly dawned upon me who the beautiful woman was, and why the King was keeping her hidden away, and why he had hidden away his meaning also. Wherefore straightway I asked for a pigeon, knowing that the pigeons of the town roost on the Tower of

Telifonia, so that I had but to fly my bird at the end of a long string like a kite to establish communication between me and the fair captive. In time my little messenger grew so used to the journey to and fro that I could dispense with the string. Our courtship has been most satisfactory. We love each other ardently, and—"

"But you have never seen each other!" interrupted the Black Prince.

"Thou forgettest we are both royal personages," said the Blue Prince in astonished reproof.

"But this is gross treachery – what right hadst thou to make these underhand advances in our absence?"

"Thou forgettest I had to scotch the Serpent," said the Blue Prince in astonished reproof. "Thou forgettest also that she can only marry the heir to the throne."

"Ah, true!" said the Black Prince, considerably relieved. "And as thou hast chosen to fritter away the time in making love to her, thou hast taken the best way to lose her."

"Thou forgettest I shall have to marry her," said the Blue Prince in astonished reproof. "Not only because I have given my word to a lady, but because I have promised the King to do my best to scotch the Serpent of the Sea. Really thou seemest terribly dull to-day. Let me put the matter in a nutshell. If he who scotches the Sea Serpent is to marry the Princess, then would I scotch the Sea Serpent by marrying the Princess, and marry the Princess to scotch the Sea Serpent. Thou hast searched the face of the sea, and our brother has dragged its depths, and nowhere have ye seen the Sea Serpent. Yet in the ninth moon he will surely come, and the land will be covered with an inky vomit as in former years. But if I marry the Princess of Paphlagonia in the ninth moon, the Royal Wedding will ward off the Sea Serpent, and not a scribe will shed ink to tell of his advent. Therefore, instead of ranging through the earth, I stayed at home and paid my addresses to the—"

"Yes, yes, what a fool I was!" interrupted the Black Prince, smiting his brow with his palm, so that the pigeon escaped from between his fingers, and winged its way back to the Tower of Telifonia as if to carry his words to the Princess.

"Thou forgettest thou art a fool still," said the Blue Prince in astonished reproof. "Prithee, unbind me forthwith."

"Nay, I am a fool no longer, for it is I that shall wed the Princess of Paphlagonia and scotch the Sea Serpent, it is I that have sent the pigeon to and fro, and unless thou makest me thine oath to be silent on the matter I will slay thee and cast thy body into the river."

"Thou forgettest our brother, the Green Prince," said the Blue Prince in astonished reproof.

"Bah! he hath eyes for naught but the odd ortolans and oysters I sacrificed that he might gorge himself withal, while I spied out thy secret. He shall be told that I returned to exchange my car for thy pigeon even as I exchanged my boat for his car. Come, thine oath or thou diest." And a jewelled scimitar shimmered in the starlight.

The Blue Prince reflected that though life without love was hardly worth living, death was quite useless. So he swore and went in to supper. When he found that the Green Prince had not spared even a baked chestnut before he fell asleep, he swore again. And on the morrow when the Princes approached the Tower of Telifonia, with its flashing "Johnny Noddy," they met a courier from the King, who, having informed himself of the Black Prince's success, ran ahead with the rumour thereof. And Lo! when the Princes passed through the city gate they found the whole population abroad clad in all their bravery, and flags flying and bells ringing and roses showering from the balconies, and merry music swelling in all the streets for joy of the prospect of the Sea Serpent's absence. And when the new moon rose, the three Princes, escorted by flute-players, hied them to the Presence Chamber, and the King embraced his sons, and the Black Prince stood forward and explained that if a Prince were married in the ninth moon it would prevent the monster's annual visit. Then the King fell upon the Black Prince's neck and wept and said, "My son! my son! my pet! my baby! my tootsicums! my popsy-wopsy!"

And then, recovering himself, and addressing the courtiers, he said: "The gods have enabled me to discover my youngest son. If they will only now continue as propitious, so that I may discover the elder of the other two, I shall die not all unhappy."

But the Black Prince could repress his astonishment no longer. "Am I dreaming, sire?" he cried. "Surely I have proved myself the eldest, not the youngest!"

"Thou forgettest that thou hast come off successful," replied the King in astonished reproof. "Or art thou so ignorant of history or of the sacred narratives handed down to us by our ancestors that thou art unaware that when three brothers set out on the same quest, it is always the youngest brother that emerges triumphant? Such is the will of the gods. Cease, therefore, thy blasphemous talk, lest they overhear thee and be put out."

A low, ominous murmur from the courtiers emphasised the King's warning.

"But the Princess – she at least is mine," protested the unhappy Prince. "We love each other – we are engaged."

"Thou forgettest she can only marry the heir," replied the King in astonished reproof. "Wouldst thou have us repudiate our solemn treaty?"

"But I wasn't really the first to hit on the idea at all!" cried the Black Prince desperately. "Ask the Blue Prince! he never telleth untruth."

"Thou forgettest I have taken an oath of silence on the matter," replied the Blue Prince in astonished reproof. "The Black Prince it was that first hit on the idea," volunteered the Green Prince. "He exchanged his boat for the car and the car for the pigeon."

So the three Princes were dismissed, while the King took counsel with the magicians and the wise men who never mean what they say. And the Court Chamberlain, wearing the orchid of office in his buttonhole, was sent to interview the Princess, and returned saying that she refused to marry any one but the proprietor of the pigeon, and that she still had his letters as evidence in case of his marrying anyone else.

"Bah!" said the King, "she shall obey the treaty. Six feet of parchment are not to be put aside for the whim of a girl five foot eight. The only real difficulty remaining is to decide whether the Blue Prince or the Green Prince is the elder. Let me see – what was it the Oracle said? Perhaps it will be clearer now:

" 'The eldest is he that the Princess shall wed.'

No, it still seems merely to avoid stating anything new."

"Pardon me, sire," replied the Chief Magician; "it seems perfectly plain now. Obviously, thou art to let the Princess choose her husband, and the Oracle guarantees that, other things being equal, she shall select the eldest. If thou hadst let her have the pick from among the three, she would have selected the one with whom she was in love – the Black Prince to wit, and that would have interfered with the Oracle's arrangements. But now that we know with whom she is in love, we can remove that one, and then, there being no reason why she should choose the Green Prince rather than the Blue Prince, the deities of the realm undertake to inspire her to go by age only."

"Thou hast spoken well," said the King. "Let the Princess of Paphlagonia be brought, and let the two Princes return."

So after a space the beautiful Princess, preceded by trumpeters, was conducted to the Palace, blinking her eyes at the unaccustomed splendour of the lights. And the King and all the courtiers blinked their eyes, dazzled by her loveliness. She was clad in white samite, and on her shoulder was perched a pet pigeon. The King sat in his moiré robes on the old gold throne, and the Blue Prince stood on his right hand, and the Green Prince on his left, the Black Prince as the youngest having been sent to bed early. The Princess courtesied three times, the third time so low that the pigeon was flustered, and flew off her shoulder, and, after circling about, alighted on the head of the Blue Prince.

"It is the Crown," said the Chief Magician, in an awestruck

voice. Then the Princess's eyes looked around in search of the pigeon, and when they lighted on the Prince's head they kindled as the grey sea kindles at sunrise.

An answering radiance shone in the Blue Prince's eyes, as, taking the pigeon that nestled in his hair, he let it fly towards the Princess. But the Princess, her bosom heaving as if another pigeon fluttered beneath the white samite, caught it and set it free again, and again it made for the Blue Prince.

Three times the bird sped to and fro. Then the Princess raised her humid eyes heavenward, and from her sweet lips rippled like music the verse:

"Last night I watched its final flicker die."

And the Blue Prince answered:

"*Now* greet our moon of honey in the sky."

Half fainting with rapture the Princess fell into his arms, and from all sides of the great hall arose the cries, "The Heir! The Heir! Long live our future King! The eldest-born! The Oracle's fulfilled!"

Such was the origin of lawn tennis, which began with people tossing pigeons to each other in imitation of the Prince and Princess in the Palace Hall. And this is why love plays so great a part in the game, and that is how the match was arranged between the Blue Prince and the Princess of Paphlagoma.

CRISPIN THE TURNSPIT

Anthony Armstrong

I never tire of the clever wit of Anthony Armstrong. George Willis (1897–1976), to give him his real name, was a regular contributor to Punch *and other humour magazines and, in his day, was comparable with P.G. Wodehouse. The two of them often appeared in* The Strand Magazine *in the 1920s and 1930s. Armstrong wrote several satires dressed up as fairy tales, which are as fresh today as when first written. Some were collected as* The Prince Who Hiccupped *(1932) and* The Pack of Pieces *(1942), which are well worth tracking down.*

ONCE upon a time, a long while ago, there lived in the middle of a lonely wood a young man named Crispin, the son of a widow. He was a pretty good young man as young men went in those times, and did not hold with living a Gay Life – not that there *was* any Gay Life in the middle of the lonely wood. His mother, the widow, was extremely poor, except in conversational ability; and it was her son's ambition to make her rich before she died and to provide her with an elderly lady companion to talk to, at, with, and against, instead of himself. Preferably an elderly lady companion with "spazzums," for "the spazzums" was his mother's Subject.

Now Crispin had one peculiar gift. It may have been

bestowed on him by a fairy, for fairies were always performing little kindnesses in those days, such as granting you three wishes, or letting everything you touched turn to gold, and other well-meant civilities; or it may simply have come to him suddenly one day – like a legacy or the hay-fever. His gift was that he could understand what birds and animals said when they spoke in their own language. He first discovered this accomplishment through stepping on a solitary old wild boar one dark evening, and he was so surprised at his new power and so shocked at what the old boar said (which I cannot possibly repeat outside a club smoking-room, for you know what club boars are), that he went straight home and let his mother tell him about her "spazzums" for two hours without once interrupting.

After this he tested his newly-acquired faculty with other animals and found it quite durable and intensely interesting. He learnt from his mother's hens what they really said when they flew to the top of fences and talked about it for a quarter of an hour afterwards; and he learnt from the flies where they went in the winter time, and a lot of other things besides; and finally he decided that it offered opportunities of financial profit.

So he said to his mother one evening:

"I say, I'm going off tomorrow to the Royal Court to seek my fortune."

And his mother said:

"Bless my soul, that's a long way, well, you might ask people what they do for the spazzums there, and do you want any sandwiches to take with you?"

"Well," replied her son, "I'll do what I can for you while I'm there, and not if they're the stringy kind because I can't eat them tidily."

So that was settled.

A month later found him at the Court, where he had obtained a job as Deputy Assistant Turnspit in the Royal Kitchen and was only waiting for permission to show off his attainment in front of the King himself. He had applied to do this through the usual channel; that is to say, his formal application in duplicate had gone through the Assistant Turnspit and the Turnspit to the Head Turnspit, who had passed it to the Assistant Under Scullion, who handed it to the Lance Scullion, and so the application worked its way up through the Sergeant Scullion and Under Cooks to the Cooks, Chefs, Butlers' Major Domos (with a side excursion by error into the Mistress of the Robes' Department, who didn't see what it had to do with her and so marked it "Sez you!" in the bottom right hand corner), till at last it arrived in the "In" Tray of the Comptroller of the Royal Household. Here it stayed a month without being looked at at all, because the Comptroller had strong ideas on Organisation of Work, Efficiency of Comptrol, and Letting Things Take Their Turn.

At last it was observed and started again, and eventually reached the Vizier, who found it so covered with comments, blots, remarks, casual drawings, and portions of cookery, that after some trouble he came to the conclusion it was merely a complaint that either the spits weren't turning or the turns weren't spitting, he couldn't make out which. He was about to have the insolent complainant dismissed or beheaded or even fined, when, having scraped off a little more solidified gravy, he was able to decipher the original application, and said:

"Ha!"

Then he said: "I don't believe it! *I* can't do it."

Finally he showed it to the Court Magician, a nasty jealous old man with long finger-nails completely given over to alluvial deposits; and he was so emphatic about the thing being not worth looking into in the slightest that the Vizier thought there must be something in it after all. And anyway, he disliked the Court Magician – but of course not openly. Nobody dared to dislike Court Magicians openly, or survived in human form for long if they did.

So that night after dinner when the King had had his third glass of Marsala, the Vizier said airily:

"By the way, Your Majesty, there is one of Your Majesty's turnspits . . ."

"Turn what?" asked the King, suddenly looking up from his glass.

"Spit," said the Vizier.

"Tut, tut!" rebuked the King severely. "*Vietato sputare.* You ought to know that at your age. Penalty, forty shillings!" And he entered it up in a little blue notebook, while the Court Magician laughed sarcastically in his beard.

"There is one of Your Majesty's Scullions or what-not," repeated the Vizier patiently and somewhat sorrowfully, "who craves Your Majesty's permission to demonstrate in Your Majesty's presence in the hope of winning Your Majesty's approval . . ."

"Could you arrange to speak a little more clearly?" said the King. "I can hear nothing but 'Your Majesty', Now that the servants are out of the room it's hardly necessary."

The Vizier drew a breath and went at it again in words of one syllable, and to the Court Magician's annoyance the King appeared quite interested.

"We must have a look at him," said the King.

"Mere quackery, of course," remarked the Court Magician loftily, when a page had been summoned and despatched in search of young Crispin.

"Perhaps," said the King. "Perhaps not. But he might be useful as Court Magician in the future. We shall need one some time. Let's see, how old are you, Magus?"

Magus was understood to mumble huffily that he was younger than some people thought, and then, affecting complete unconcern, began to trace little designs with his finger on the table.

"Don't draw on the tablecloth!" said the King quite sharply. "That's five shillings." He was still writing hard in his little blue book when Crispin entered.

Crispin was very nervous. He had made himself look as nice as he could in the time, and one of the Under-Scullions had even given him some bacon fat that had been over from breakfast for his forelock, but even so a day's turnspitting does not make for personal tidiness.

"They tell me you can understand what animals say?" began the King pleasantly.

"So it please Your Majesty."

"It will, if you can do it," remarked the King. "I shall have a job for you . . ." He broke off and sniffed. "Peculiar smell of bacon there is about! We didn't have bacon at dinner, did we?"

"Not that I remember," replied the Vizier.

"Ah, well, never mind! Now tell me," he continued to Crispin, "what Bouncer here is saying." And he aimed a kick at a hound sleeping beside him, who woke with a sharp yelp.

"Please, sir, Your Majesty, he said: 'What the hell's up now?' "

The Vizier laughed and Magus scornfully muttered: "Very likely!" Bouncer sat up and whimpered.

"What now?" asked the King.

"Please, Your Majesty, sir, he's saying that that hurt!"

"Anyone could make up things like that," put in the Court Magician. The King looked very quickly at him, and Magus, somewhat confused, only just stopped himself from drawing on the tablecloth again.

Bouncer, now quite awake, began to whine eagerly.

"Well?" asked the King.

"Please, Your Sir, I mean . . ."

"Better make it 'Sir' all through," said the King in kindly fashion. "Don't mind me. I shan't consider it *Lèse Majesté*. I'm not at all a strait-laced Majesty. Ha! Ha!"

"Ha! Ha!" said the Vizier very quickly, just a few seconds ahead of the Court Magician. The King frowned at Magus and wrote again in his little blue book. Bouncer still whined hopefully.

"Please, Sir, he is now expressing a desire for a further chop-bone such as he was given by you earlier on in the meal."

"There!" said the Vizier, and looked triumphantly at the Court Magician.

"You have a future before you, my lad," added the King, and also looked at the Court Magician, who looked at the ceiling and murmured again that he was young for his age. "Would you like to take up magic as a profession?"

At this Magus got up abruptly and asked the Royal permission to fetch an animal of his own to try Crispin on. "I would like a further test to make certain he is not deceiving us," he concluded in tones which clearly showed what he thought about it himself.

"Certainly," said the King, who was busily waking up his other dogs and having their remarks translated. One of them, a lady dog, really ought never to have known such words, and Crispin felt a little embarrassed.

But just outside the door the Magician was talking earnestly to a frightened page whose collar he held in one gnarled hand.

"Now I'm going to change you into an animal," he was concluding, "and mind you say, in whatever language is used by – er – whatever sort of animal I change you into, exactly what I've just told you to say."

"But His Majesty will have me beaten," whimpered the boy, "if I say things like that."

"I don't mind," said the Magician. "Not in the least," he added. He paused thoughtfully. "I think I'll change you into a rabbit," he continued and waved his wand.

A large green and orange rabbit with four pairs of ears appeared before him.

The Magician seemed a little startled and looked closely at his wand.

"Tut, tut!" he murmured, "that's the second time that sort of thing has happened. I really must speak about this wand. The shoddy workmanship that one gets nowadays . . . However," – he surveyed the monstrosity – "you'll do for this job."

He opened the door and, followed by the metamorphosed page-boy treading awkwardly on some of his ears, strode again into the Royal presence. "And now," he said triumphantly to himself, "to finish off this upspit of a turnstart."

The King gave a sudden jump as they entered, and blinked rapidly. Then he looked very closely at the Marsala decanter, opened his mouth as if about to say something, thought better of it, and looked away, humming a careless little air.

"Ah, there you are, Magus!" he said at last, opening the conversation very carefully.

"Here I am!" said Magus in nasty tones.

"There you are, I see," continued the King, still looking everywhere but at the rabbit.

"I've brought my Animal," said Magus.

The King was for some reason overwhelmingly effusive at the simple remark.

"Ah, then it *is* . . . I mean, so you have. So you have. Just what I was going to say. I noticed it immediately. A fine – er – a fine – er – what is it?"

"A rare kind of rabbit," said Magus.

"Very rare," commented the Vizier.

"Well, let's hear it speak," commanded the King.

Magus stirred the Animal up with his toe – it was scratching itself rather comprehensively – and gave it a meaning look. It at once squeaked in a high falsetto like a badly handled slate pencil.

"What does it say?" asked the King interested.

"Yes, tell His Majesty what it said," purred Magus to Crispin.

Crispin, however, stood with his mouth open and kept a horrified silence. For he, and he alone, knew that the Animal had said:

"The King has an ugly red nose from drinking too much Marsala."

"Come, come," said the King, and added to the Vizier: "Have some Marsala!" He poured himself out a further glass, but was so busy sniffing it, he omitted to pass the decanter. It was obviously quite the wrong moment for literal translation of the Animal's remark.

Crispin stammered and said hesitatingly: "It says Your Majesty is a very handsome man."

The King stroked the back of his head and smirked at the ceiling.

"Oh, ah, does it?" he said, trying to look judicially un-biassed.

Magus only smiled grimly. He had known Crispin would not dare. Or if he did . . . Well, he had him either way. He again stirred up the wretched page, who had now got to work on the back of his neck with a hind foot.

The second remark was worse. It ran quite simply: "The King is a silly old buster!"

Crispin, more at his ease by then, translated that the King had the noblest heart in the Kingdom. The Vizier, who was beginning to suspect something, laughed and changed it hurriedly into a cough, as the King fixed him with a chilly eye.

"I see nothing to laugh at," observed the King coldly.

"I was coughing," apologised the Vizier.

"I see nothing to cough at," continued the King even more coldly. He produced his little blue book and made an entry, looking sternly at the Vizier as he did so.

Then with a sudden cry of triumph the Magician had burst into speech. "He is an impostor, Your Majesty. I knew it. He has not translated truly."

"How? Why?" asked the King, while the Vizier, who now knew that there was some funny business somewhere, merely nodded his head.

The Magician, talking excitedly, waved his wand over the Animal, which reverted to human shape.

"This is my animal, Your Majesty! Merely one of Your Majesty's pages masquerading as a – er – just masquerading. I was suspicious and so took the liberty of temporarily changing him." He observed that the page, though otherwise normal and still scratching the back of his neck, had four pairs of ears, said "Tut, tut!" and waved the wand again, abolishing the three superfluous sets. "I guessed he was an impostor. So *I* told the page something definite to say to see if this rogue could really translate."

"And didn't he?" asked the King.

"He did not."

"It seemed all right to me," said the King carelessly,

stroking the back of his head again. "Quite natural. I mean, it was what one might expect a rabbit of perception to say."

"Aha! Your Majesty. But it was not my test sentence. He has deceived you."

"Sir," began Crispin. "I . . ."

But here the Vizier interrupted. He leant forward and fixed the Magician with his eye.

"And what did you tell the page to say?" he asked slowly.

"I . . ." began Magus and then stopped. He perceived that, in his anxiety to ensure Crispin's not translating accurately, he had overlooked one contingency. "Er – something quite different," he explained, crestfallen. "Er – that is, just a trifle different," he added hastily.

The Vizier sat back with the air of a defending counsel who has caught out a witness. "Is the boy to be penalized because he makes a trifling mistake in translation?" he asked, with a reassuring wink at Crispin.

"Of course not," said the King. "Have some Marsala?"

"Shall we ask the page what he was told?" continued the Vizier, but the now frightened Court Magician, with a sudden wave of the wand, had caused the page to vanish. In his place there was only a tortoise – a tortoise still trying to scratch the back of its neck but without success, since, wonderful though Nature is, tortoises are not built that way.

"Ah!" said the Vizier.

"What on earth . . .?" began the King.

"A slight slip," said Magus, who had removed the incriminating evidence; for tortoises do not talk.

"Well, when you've quite finished with my page, I'd like him to refill this decanter," said the King in sarcastic tones.

"A slip, I assure you," stammered Magus.

"You're not quite yourself tonight," said the King sternly, who might have made this remark with more truth to his page. "You'd better go to bed. And," he added, producing his little book and writing in it, "don't make any more slips. You'll find them expensive."

The Court Magician went, casting a look at Crispin which

made that youth think furiously. The erstwhile page obediently followed after, but the door was banged in his face, a bare twenty minutes before he reached it.

"Now," said the King kindly. "Would you like to be Assistant Court Magician?"

Crispin, with memories of Magus' last glance, said hurriedly he didn't think he would, as his health wouldn't stand it.

"Well, what would you like? Come closer, my boy. . . . How strong that smell of bacon is! I really must speak to the butler . . . Well, what would you like? I promise you shall have it."

"Please, Sir," said Crispin in a tremble, "a house for my mother in the forest and money and some new treatment for the Spazzums but not too good a one, because she'll have nothing to talk about, and a lady companion if possible with Spazzums too! Oh, and a coach to take me back at once."

"Gobbless my soul!" gasped the King, and added a little later: "Why do you want to leave?"

"Perhaps," explained the Vizier with a meaning glance at the door by which Magus had so balefully left, "he thinks that if he stays he won't be – er – feeling quite himself by tomorrow."

"Ah!" said the King, seeing it at last. "Reasons of health!" he added and laughed as loudly as though he had made the joke himself. "Not feeling quite himself! Ha! Ha!"

"Ha! Ha!" said the Vizier very, very swiftly, and with a look of regret the King put away his little book which he was hopefully taking out.

"Well, it shall be granted," said the King. "But it seems a pity to waste your gift."

"It need not be wasted," said the Vizier.

"How?" asked the King.

"Appoint him to Your Majesty's Secret Service and let him send reports weekly from the forest of what the birds and animals say, so that Your Majesty may know what is going on all over the Kingdom."

"A good idea!" said the King.

"There are one or two people, even at Your Majesty's

Court, who are of a jealous disposition and may be inclined to plot. Well, the birds will hear of it and thus this young man, and so it will come to Your Majesty."

"A very good idea!" repeated the King. "I'm glad I thought of it." He looked sternly at the Vizier who had indignantly opened his mouth to speak. "A good idea of mine!" he repeated aggressively. The Vizier shut his mouth without speaking. He had great power of self-control – which was why he had become Vizier.

And so it was arranged. Crispin got for his mother all that she wanted, and lived in the forest and sent his weekly reports to the King. The King's omniscience became a marvel to everyone, though when people respectfully asked him how he did it, he used to reply: "Ah, a little bird told me!" which, as very few people know nowadays, is the real origin of that old saying.

TOUCHED BY A SALESMAN

Tom Holt

I can't imagine Tom Holt needs much introduction. Since he hit the comic-fantasy shelves with Expecting Someone Taller *(1987), he has produced a stream of ingenious and wickedly funny novels including* Who's Afraid of Beowulf? *(1988).* Flying Dutch *(1991),* Faust Among Equals *(1994),* Paint Your Dragon *(1996),* Snow White and the Seven Samurai *(1999) and* Valhalla *(2000). His work is remarkably diverse, as shown by the following story, totally different to either of the previous stories in this series.*

There are days that convince you that God is a game-show host, and that His hidden cameras are filming you while a studio audience laughs itself sick at your carefully staged misfortunes. At any moment you expect Him to walk out from behind a parked car or a burning bush and confirm that yes, you've been set up, none of it's really happening, and you're entitled to a free combination cafetiere/alarm clock as a reward for being such a good sport.

Yes, God, You definitely had me going there for a minute or two, Paul thought, as he walked out of the Swindalls building into the night. Still, it's all in fun, and you've got to laugh, haven't you? He paused for a moment and waited, but for some unaccountable reason God missed His cue and didn't appear, so Paul shrugged his shoulders and walked toward the bus stop.

And there are days that convince you that life is a tale told by an idiot, full of sound and fury, signifying nothing. Or, to be more precise, told by an idiot who earns his living writing storylines for an Australian soap, which would account for the lack of a decent interval between earth-shattering disasters. And there are days that lead you to believe that the soap God writes for is locked in a desperate *à l'outrance* ratings battle with a rival show, which has forced Him to pour a whole season's worth of unspeakable disasters into one half-hour episode. On such days it isn't even safe to stay in bed with the covers pulled up over your head; that's just inviting a freak tornado, flash floods or abduction by aliens. All you can do is spend the day in the company of those you like least, in the hope that some of your truly rotten luck will rub off on them.

A moderately large slice of his life limped by like an hourly paid glacier. No bus. Nothing unusual in that. The locals had long since come to terms with the fact that the 47 route passed through a pocket of non-relativistic space somewhere between Sainsbury's car park and Debenhams, with the result that what seemed like two minutes inside the bus actually lasted at least half an hour in real time, with the interesting concomitant effect that whereas (according to the schedules) the bus stopped outside Higson's Shoe Repairs at 19.37, if you arrived there at 19.35.15 precisely, you'd be just in time to watch its tail-lights disappearing round the back of Burger King. You could set your watch by the Number 47, the locals reckoned, provided your watch had been designed by Salvador Dali.

Paul sighed and glanced up at the sky, just in time to see something bright and quick whizz through a gap in the clouds: a shooting star, he assumed, or a bit of derelict TV satellite findings its way home. He followed the line and picked it up again on the other side of the cloud. To his amazement, it shot down to rooftop level and vanished with an audible thump.

After a moment's thought, he realized that it had passed in front of the council offices tower, which could only mean that it had pitched somewhere in the hoarded-off wasteland where C&W were clearing the site for a new DIY megastore.

If it hadn't been such a rotten day, he probably wouldn't have bothered. But . . . For some reason he'd always rather wanted to find a meteorite (and besides, he seemed to remember reading somewhere that they were worth good money). He hesitated for about ninety seconds, and crossed the street, heading for the gap in the hoarding where the kids had broken into the site two days ago.

As Paul slid aside the loosened rails and squeezed through the gap, he couldn't help feeling rather foolish. For one thing, how was he going to find a meteorite in a large building site in the dark without a torch? For another thing, what was he proposing to do with it even if he did find it? Sell it maybe, but who to? Putting a classified in *Exchange & Mart* wouldn't cut it, and he didn't know any geologists. Besides, didn't all meteorites found on British soil belong to the Queen, or was that sturgeons?

In the event, finding it wasn't a problem. Properly speaking, it found him; one moment he was walking cautiously past a parked cement mixer, the next his foot snagged on something and the ground came rushing up to meet him like a big, friendly puppy with its lead in its mouth.

"Oomph," said a voice in the dark.

Seen purely as a piece of hardware, the human brain is still way ahead of the competition. It's versatile. It's reliable. Its response times are excellent and it can multi-task effortlessly, as every schoolkid yelled at for daydreaming will confirm for you. Just as soon as someone comes up with a decent operating system to run it, in place of the weird lash-up of bugs and patches that comes installed as standard, we'll finally get to see its true potential. For example: even during the split second that elapsed between his foot getting caught and his nose pecking into the mud, Paul had already formed several hypotheses to explain what was going on. The most promising of these was that the person he'd just cannoned into must be a fellow treasure-hunter who'd managed to get there first. This thought was, of course, extremely annoying.

"You were quick," he huffed. "How long have you been here?"

There was a sound like a computer mulling over the strangeness of life and then a voice said: "Not sure. Not very long. Sorry if that sounds a bit vague, but I think I may have hit my head, because I'm feeling a little bit dizzy."

Maybe that was it, then; there was something about the voice that wasn't quite right. The accent, for example; it was a bit like a Scandinavian carefully imitating an American newsreader through a mouth full of sponge cake. The timing was odd, too – the words came out in bunches, two or three at a time, with the tiniest little pause between each batch. For some reason it reminded Paul of the synthetic voice you get when you call Directory Enquiries, or its even more irritating cousin who tells you to press One if you want the main menu. But, he supposed, a bang on the head might do that to somebody.

"Ah," he said. "You all right?"

"Give me a hand up, will you?"

"Sure," Paul said. He kneeled down and reached out. Something like a bad-tempered mole wrench fastened onto his wrist and dragged him sharply forward.

"Thanks," the voice said, as the grip relaxed. "This probably sounds like a dumb question, but where is this?"

"The building site, round the back of Tesco's," Paul replied. "How are you feeling now?"

Short pause. "My fault," said the voice, "didn't set the query parameters precisely enough. Let's start with the planet. Mercury?"

"Huh?"

"Which planet are we on? I'm guessing Mercury, but geography was never my strong suit."

Paul took a step backwards, just in case. "Sounds to me like you've definitely had a bump on the head. We'd better get you to a hospital."

"Hospital," the voice replied. "Right, that's helpful. Definitely a humanoid concept" (longer pause than usual before the word humanoid; definitely something odd about that voice), "so we're talking Earth or Proxima Centauri 7; and either I've got a bad cold or this isn't a nitrogen-based atmosphere, so I'm guessing Earth. Am I right?"

It took Paul a moment to get his voice back. "I really think you ought to see a doctor," he suggested.

"I'd rather not, if it's all the same to you," the voice replied. "If this is Earth, my guess is we're in the late twentieth century, possibly early twenty-first; and if our long-range scans are right about the state of your medical technology – well, no offence, but I think I'd rather take my chances with a fatal injury, if it's all the same to you. Actually, I think it's just a little bump on the head; can't have been all that bad, or the translator chip wouldn't still be working. Temperamental, you've only got to breathe on the damn' things – Hold on," the voice continued, "I hate talking to someone I can't see. Let's have some light, shall we?"

A sudden glare, brighter than arc welding or burning magnesium. Paul instinctively looked away. "What the bloody hell do you think you're . . .?"

"Sorry." The voice sounded hurt and bewildered; disappointed. "You don't like it?"

"No," Paul replied, trying to blink burning purple spots off his retina.

"Oh. Oh well. Maybe it's a bit dated. Went down a treat last time I was here, but that was, what, two thousand years ago? I guess fashions change."

A nutcase, Paul decided; worse, a nutcase with some industrial-grade pyrotechnics. That horrible blinding light wouldn't have gone unnoticed, he figured, as he remembered that he was trespassing on a building site. Security guards, big dogs (he was terrified of dogs), culminating in a ride to the police station. Strange to think that, a mere quarter of an hour ago, he was telling himself that the day couldn't really get worse.

"It's all right," the voice was saying. "I've turned it down."

Sure enough, the light was tolerable now, a mere ivory glimmer no brighter than the stairwell in a block of flats. He could see the man behind the voice.

"Anyway," the voice's owner went on, "this is all very well, but I suppose I'd better be making tracks. Which way is the spaceport?"

He'd seen pictures of them, back when he was a kid; in story books and *My First Scripture Reader* (in the latter, preceding generations of scholars had embellished the drawings with biroed-in beards, moustaches and other, more improbable physical attributes) and Christmas cards, of course. He knew exactly what he was looking at. Everything was just like it had been in the artwork (wings, halo, flowing nightgown; no harp, but harps were known to be optional). The only problem was that they didn't exist.

"You're an angel," he said accusingly.

A slight frown creased the angel's face. "Yes," it said. "The spaceport. Is it far?"

"But you can't be," Paul objected. "No such thing as angels."

The angel shrugged, giving Paul the impression that it had had this conversation before. "You're entitled to your opinion," it said. "Faith is an entirely personal matter, and freedom of belief is guaranteed by the Declaration of Sentient Rights. So; how about telling this figment of your imagination the quickest way to the spaceport?"

Paul started to back away.

"Oh, for . . ." The angel vanished. Paul was still trying to cope with that when it reappeared; only it wasn't an angel any more. It was a carbon copy of himself.

"Better?" asked the *faux* Paul.

"No."

"Oh. May I ask why?"

Paul did try to answer, but his voice didn't seem to want to work.

"No offence," said his double, "but I think you're being a

little bit unreasonable. All right, you don't like the bright light, it's probably something technical and species-specific that wasn't in the manual. You don't like the winged-messenger outfit; matter of taste, I guess, and like I said a moment ago, you're entitled to your opinion. But you can't seriously expect me to believe there's anything offensive about this; dammit, it's your own species."

Paul shook his head for quite some time. Eventually he managed to say, "Yes. It's me."

"What? Ah, I take your point. Well, I haven't met anyone else from your species in a long, long time." The doppelgänger sighed. "Clearly we've got off on the wrong foot here, and I have an awful feeling that whatever I do is going to make things worse, so why don't you just tell me how to get to the spaceport and you can forget the whole distasteful incident?"

"No spaceport," Paul stammered. "Not here."

"Drat." His mirror image clicked his (their?) tongue. "Now you're going to tell me it's on the other side of the island or something."

"No spaceport," Paul repeated. "No such thing."

Paul had the dubious privilege of seeing exactly what he looked like when he was forcing himself to be calm and patient when dealing with an idiot. "I must say, this belief system you've got going here is a new one on me. Some sort of hyperexistentialism, presumably. Let's see: you don't believe in the spaceport because right now you can't see it or smell it or touch it. All right, let's see what we can do. Supposing there was a spaceport—"

"You don't understand," Paul interrupted. "No spaceports. No such thing. Haven't been invented yet, except in *Star Trek* and stuff. Science fiction."

Now he had a valuable insight into what he looked like when he was thinking hard. Not a pretty sight.

"Ah," said the other. "I have an uneasy feeling that this is starting to make sense. Your culture hasn't yet developed interstellar flight. Yes?"

Paul nodded.

"Bother." This expression he knew well from his mirror. "Now that's a pity. No hyperspace radio communications? No heuristic self-updating simultaneous translation units? No contact with alien races?"

Paul shook his head.

"Oh boo." The other turned his head away, perhaps unwilling to betray emotion. "But just a moment," he said. "That's not right. When I was wearing the winged-messenger face, you recognized me. Said I was an angel."

"Well, you are," Paul replied. "Or, at least, you were."

"So you do know who we—Oh, wait, I'm forgetting. You don't believe in us."

Paul nodded again.

"Got you." There was a certain amount of relief in the voice. "Now I think I know what's going on here. It's a religious thing, right? Fine, now at least I know where we stand. You think I'm some sort of supernatural being; or at least you don't, because you don't believe. And quite right, too, because I'm not."

"Not what?"

The other smiled. "Not supernatural," he said. "Not in the slightest. In fact," he added with a slightly bashful grin, "I'm a rep."

"A what?"

"Rep. Sales representative. I go around selling things."

For some reason he couldn't quite fathom, Paul heard himself asking, "What sort of things?"

The other shrugged. "The generic name is novelty items," he replied. "Joke stuff, gifts, souvenirs. Junk," he added. "But all high quality, tasteful, high-class merchandise, nothing but the best . . . Junk," he repeated with a hint of sadness. "It's what my species is best at. Burning bushes, seas that part down the middle, giant fingers writing on walls, hitherto unnoticed stars that seem to follow you about. I'd give you a catalogue, only I left them all in my ship."

"Your ship."

"Yes, poor thing. My own silly fault. Wasn't paying attention to where I was going, slap bang into an asteroid, just enough time to eject. Incredibly lucky I was so close to this planet of yours; otherwise I'd be up there drifting about." He sighed. "Got to count your blessings, after all," he said. "However bad things may seem, they could always be a darned sight worse."

Strange . . . Twenty minutes ago, Paul had been standing at a bus stop believing that he'd reached the very bottom rung of the ladder of misery. Now he was talking (apparently) to a creature from another world, stranded on a distant planet with no hope of ever getting home, and the creature was being far more positive and upbeat about this terrible calamity than he'd been about his own trivial misfortunes. Quite unexpectedly, he felt ashamed.

"Uhm," he said. "If there's anything I can do to help . . ."

He hadn't intended to say that; it had just slipped out, like a cat squirming out of your arms to chase after a bird. Still, the words were out there now, and he couldn't very well take them back.

"That's extremely kind of you," replied the other him, his face brightening. "Right; we'll start with a hot bath, a change of clothes and a decent meal, and then we can get down to some serious engineering. Is it far to your house from here?"

"So this is where you live," said the Strange Visitor, looking around. His eyes glided over the empty pizza boxes and lit on the pile of unpaired socks wedged into the far corner of the sofa. "Interesting."

"It's a bit of a mess—" Paul began.

"Really? How's it different from the typical dwellings of your species? Those flat square containers, for example—"

"Sit down," Paul said. "I'll get you a cup of tea."

When the tea arrived, the alien looked at it for two, maybe three seconds. Then he plunged his fingers into it and started to rub his face.

"No," Paul said, "the bath is through there, in the bathroom. That's tea. For drinking."

"Oh." There was an unspoken *Are you sure?* tagged on the end. "Well, thank you very much. Oh, I see. You hold on to the curved bit and use it to manoeuvre the vessel toward your mouth. Your own invention?"

"No," Paul told him. "In fact, it's been around for quite some time."

"Remarkable," the stranger replied. "You people come up with something as clever as that, but you're still stranded on this one small planet. You know," he added, "I could make a fortune selling these back home."

"Really?"

"Oh yes." He took a sip of the tea, shuddered, and put the cup down on the coffee table, as far away from himself as he could get it. "My company would pay through its third nose for a brilliantly simple novelty idea like that. More than enough to cover outfitting a full-scale search-and-rescue mission, if only we could get in touch with them. Which reminds me—"

"Yes," Paul replied thoughtfully; then he said; "You mentioned something about serious engineering."

The other him nodded enthusiastically. "That's right," he said. "Basically, what I had in mind was, build a simple hyperspatial beacon. Nothing fancy, you understand; just enough to send a simple repeating distress call. The next ship to pass through this space picks it up, marks the coordinates and informs the authorities; they send a ship to pick me up. It'd be different if this was some sort of Bronze Age planet, where everybody lived in mud huts and kept pigs, and reckoned portable communications modules were the cutting edge. But a race that can come up with integral beverage-container handles—" He shook his head in apparent wonder. "And there I was, beginning to lose hope."

"Quite," Paul said. "What sort of things do you think you'll need?"

"Oh, nothing fancy," the stranger replied. "Zebulon crystals, barconium chips, hyperconductor wire, some antimatter, a bit of hardboard and a screwdriver. You've probably got most of that right here on the premises."

Paul pursed his lips. He had a screwdriver; at least, there was a screwdriver attachment on his Chinese copy of a Swiss Army Knife, but he'd bent it trying to pierce the foil on a milk bottle. "It may be a bit harder than that," he said.

"Oh. You mean we may have to buy some things? Well, of course, as soon as I get home, obviously I can send you a cheque."

"It's not that," Paul said, as tactfully as he could. "Truth is, I've never heard of zeb-whatsit and the other stuff you mentioned – which isn't to say we haven't got it, because you could write what I don't know about science on the back of North America, assuming you've got very small writing. But you mentioned antimatter—"

The stranger nodded. "Just the regular commercial grade," he said. "Unleaded."

"Right," Paul replied. "Well, I know for a fact that we haven't got any of that, because I saw something on the telly about scientists trying to invent it, and the bottom line was—"

"Telly?"

"Television. Sound and pictures broadcast through the air. Every house has a receiving device. It's very popular here."

"Really." The alien nodded twice, slowly, deliberately keeping any trace of expression off its face. "So," he said, "no antimatter. Nuisance."

"Of course," Paul said, "if you know how to make the stuff—"

"Piece of cake," the alien replied.

"Hey!" A grin burst out all over Paul's face. "I could make an absolute – I mean, I'm sure that given time we could get some big company interested in, um, helping you out. On humanitarian grounds."

The alien shook his head. "Piece of cake," he repeated, "provided you've got a quadriphasic particle scoop hooked up to a megatherium dolly slaved to a tritoberyllium ram. And maybe I'm slandering your people rotten, but something tells me—"

Paul nodded. "Fair enough," he said. "Look, is there

anything else you could use instead? Like putting honey in coffee when you're out of sugar?"

The expression on the stranger's face gave Paul the impression that the simile wasn't particularly helpful. "Not really," the stranger replied. "Antimatter is antimatter, there's not much you can do without it. And I wish I could tell you how to build a quadriphasic particle scoop, but I can't. Like I said, my company's more into novelty items. Toys. Gadgets. Fridge magnets."

That seemed to be that. The stranger hunched forward a little, possibly facing up to the true ghastliness of his situation for the first time. Once again, Paul felt the unfamiliar itch of compassion on the inside of his mind, where he couldn't reach to scratch.

"What's your name?" he asked.

The stranger looked up. "Name," he repeated. "Oh, you mean my ID code? 6340097/227/3."

"Ah. I'm Paul."

"Paul," 6340097/227/3 repeated. "Pleased to meet you."

"Likewise."

Silence again; and Paul's thoughts began to drift slightly. So, he thought, this is really an angel; angels actually do exist, and this is one of them. Except that they aren't divine heralds or celestial social workers who get their wings every time a child claps its hands (or whatever); they're salesmen, the alien equivalent of the scumbags who overtake you on the inside lane, with their jackets hanging from little hooks . . . Somehow, that made rather more sense than the orthodox version. A shame, nevertheless; right now he'd be glad of the intervention of a guardian angel, someone who could straighten out his life and make everything all right again.

As if. He could (apparently) bring himself to believe in angels, and whooppee-cushion vendors from distant galaxies, but even he wasn't that stupid.

Nevertheless; "Sounds like you've had a pretty rotten day," he said.

6340097/227/3 nodded. "You could say that."

"Me too," Paul said. "First, my car breaks down and I'm late for work. Then my girlfriend calls me and says she's dumping me. Finally, I get the sack from my job. I'd call that a pretty rotten day, myself. What do you think?"

6340097/227/3 looked up at him. "Let's see," he said. "I'm not sure I've understood all the culture-specific terminology, but I think I get the drift. You own a malfunctioning piece of technology. Your intended mate has deselected you in favour of another. Your work group has released you from your non-genetic-clan labour obligations, in the process terminating your rations entitlement. Is that about the size of it?"

Paul nodded. "There or thereabouts," he said. "Sounds like the same sort of thing happens where you come from."

"Indeed," 6340097/227/3 replied. "But I thought you said it'd been a bad day."

"Too bloody right it's been a bad day. Didn't I just . . .?"

6340097/227/3 shrugged. "Sorry," he said, "I must've misunderstood. Or things are different here. For example, where I come from, discovering that you own a piece of technology that doesn't work is generally a cause for celebration, since it means you can sue the manufacturers for punitive damages equal to twenty times their average annual turnover. On the other hand, our service obligations to our non-genetic clan structure are fairly strict. Basically, you work for them 88 hours a day, 769 days a year until you die in return for the basic minimum calorific value required to sustain life. Rather a bind, really, considering that most of us live to be at least, let's see, in your terms well over seventy thousand. That, I ought to point out, is why employment is a punishment reserved for criminals whose offences are too serious for the death penalty – whereas our social security system is extremely generous, and accounts for 69.2% of our population dying of cholesterol poisoning before they reach the age of twelve. As for being rejected by your destined sexual partner . . ." He pursed his lips and shuddered just a little. "Unless it's completely different here, and your females don't devour their males two hours after mating . . ."

"I see what you mean," Paul said. "Actually, things *are* rather different here."

"Really?" 6340097/227/3 looked rather wistful. "Sounds like this is quite a nice place to live, then."

"I suppose so," Paul replied thoughtfully (and he was thinking, two hours later; *eeww!*) "All depends how you look at things, really."

6340097/227/3 nodded. "Well," he said, "let's do something to cheer ourselves up, shall we? I know," he added, with a grin Paul couldn't quite fathom. "Let's have a look at this television of yours."

Nothing else to do, Paul thought; and while he's staring at the goggle-box, maybe I can find some tactful way of telling him that, much as I feel for his plight and the desperate situation he finds himself in, he can't stay here indefinitely . . . Though exactly what the marooned alien was supposed to do next, he really couldn't imagine. Maybe the day would come when someone would finally invent the multiphasic whatever-it-was and start pumping out antimatter in handy family-sized packs, and he could finally go home; he'd dropped hints that his species had rather more staying power than the measly human threescore-and-ten. Until then, presumably, he was going to have to settle down and get a job. (And that's curious too, Paul reflected. In his case, that seems like an awful tragedy, a worst-nightmare scenario – living on Earth, going to work every day, paying off a mortgage, coping as best he can with blocked drains and the Single European Currency and tennis elbow – whereas I've never seriously contemplated life not being like that. If I'm lucky.)

"What's that?" 6340097/227/3 asked suddenly.

It was one of those cosy-detective series, where people get horribly murdered in the heart of the idyllic English countryside.

"What's that?" Paul replied, squinting at the screen in case he'd missed something. "That's a church."

6340097/227/3 was staring, his mouth open; then, quite suddenly, he kicked both his heels up in the air, yelled

"Woo-hoo!" and started prancing round the room. Nervously, Paul reached for the remote and changed channels. Ah, the snooker. That ought to calm him down.

"That thing," 6340097/227/3 panted, pausing to catch his breath. "Where is it?"

Paul frowned. "I don't know," he replied. "Looked like any other church to me."

"You mean there's others?"

"Hundreds. Maybe thousands."

6340097/227/3 sank to his knees and smiled. For a split second, Paul was jealous. That was an exact copy of his face, and he was sure he'd never in his life looked so beatific. "What's so wonderful about a church?" he asked.

6340097/227/3 shook his head. "Is there one near here?" he asked.

"I suppose so. Can't say I've ever really noticed. I mean, they're so common you just take them for granted . . . Did I say something funny?"

"No, really." 6340097/227/3 had his hand clamped to his mouth. "Listen, I'm really sorry to impose on you like this, but it's vitally important that we find one of these – what did you call them?"

"Churches."

". . . One of these churches, as quickly as possible. Please?" the alien added, with a lost-puppy look in his eyes that Paul couldn't have figured out how to do in a million years.

"Sure," he replied. "Now this minute?"

"Yes."

Embarrassingly, there was a church not three minutes' walk from Paul's front door, and he'd forgotten all about it until he saw the steeple against the skyline. He wasn't sure of the rules about going into churches after dark; but the door wasn't locked, so he guessed it was probably all right. "Is this the sort of thing—?" he started to say; then he realized that 6340097/227/3 wasn't next to him any more. He'd vanished.

"Hey," the alien's voice bounced off the vaulted roof. "This is quite old, yes?"

"Could be," Paul replied. "Lots of churches go back hundreds of years, but I really don't know . . ."

"Yes! Oh, this is . . . Get up here, quick. I'll need your help with a few things."

He found 6340097/227/3 kneeling before the altar; a reasonable thing to do, Paul figured, in a church. But the alien seemed to be looking for something. Weirder still, it wasn't long before he found it.

"Marvellous," 6340097/227/3 muttered, pulling away an access panel. "Of course it's been a while, but I did my basic training on these babies. Now then, which of these is the circadium feed?"

Paul stared. Behind the panel was a dense chow mein of glowing fibre-optics and glinting metallic conduits, with a keyboard of some kind fixed to the back wall, its keys marked with bizarre symbols. 6340097/227/3 was grabbing handfuls of cables and swapping them over, plugging them in or splicing them together. "Got it," he said, and slammed the panel shut. "Now then, let's get this beauty warmed up, and then I can lay in a course out of here. No disrespect," he added, "but I don't think I'd have liked it here. The thing with your females is tempting, but your night's the wrong colour and the sky's a bit low for my taste. Besides, there's no place like home, is there?"

Paul took three steps back. "You're telling me," he said slowly, "that this church is really a spaceship?" 6340097/227/3 laughed. "A late model ZZ885 Starglider," he replied over his shoulder. "Must've been left behind by some of my people at some stage. Either a colonizing party landed and never went home, or we were planning to build a base here and the project got abandoned. These things happen. Did you say there's a lot of these?"

"Lots and lots," Paul replied. "God knows how many, all over the world. You're saying they're all spaceships?"

6340097/227/3 shrugged. "Don't know," he replied. "What do you use them for?"

Paul wasn't quite sure how to answer that. "Religion," he said.

"Ah," 6340097/227/3 replied. "Figures. Wouldn't be the first time. Probably some of them are copies you people made, thinking they were just, you know, buildings. Not to worry, though, this is definitely the real thing." He was inside the organ now, fiddling with pipes and stops. "Plasma level's a bit down," he said, "but the main reactor's in pretty good shape, considering. Just as well nobody's been fooling about with it, really. There's enough fuel in there to blow your island off the map if it cooks off."

Paul visualized thousands of middle-aged ladies playing church organs all over the country, twice every Sunday, and shuddered down to his socks.

"Now, then." 6340097/227/3 had emerged from inside the organ and was clambering up the pulpit steps. "All I've got to do now is lay in a course, and she's ready to roll." He leaned out of the pulpit, reached for the little board headed "Hymns" and slotted in 134, 96, 308; ditto for "Psalms", 42, 90. "Well," he called out, wiping his forehead, "I guess this is goodbye. Thanks for all your help."

Paul looked at him. If he'd been waiting for something along the lines of *Unless, that is, you fancy coming too*, he'd have been disappointed. But of course, he'd have refused.

Of course . . .

"Safe journey," he said, rather lamely, and added, "Um, Godspeed."

6340097/227/3 nodded. "At least till I'm out of your atmosphere; then I can throttle back and save on fuel." He frowned, as if worried about something. "It's all turned out pretty well for me," he said, "assuming this crate actually makes it off the surface, but I'm fairly sure it will. Hope things work out as far as you're concerned."

"So do I," Paul replied; and smiled, because you don't meet an angel and help him get back home and walk away empty-handed, it says so in the rules. No: you go home, and when you get there, everything's been sorted out. Your girlfriend's waiting by the door with tears rolling down her cheeks, and as soon as you're inside your boss rings to apologize, and then the garage calls to say it doesn't need a new cylinder head after all, and everything is happy ever after. "Well, cheers," he said; and he turned away and walked out, closing the door firmly behind him.

Just in case, he retired what he felt would be a safe distance; outside the churchyard (presumably it had originally been the designated danger zone) and a hundred yards further down the street, for luck. Nothing happened for what seemed like a very long time; and then, quite suddenly, there was a blinding flash of pure white light – He couldn't help looking away. By the time he turned his head back, the church was already way up in the sky, white fire roaring from all four flying buttresses, the steeple piercing the darkness like – well, like the nose of a skyrocket. Knowing it was a pointless gesture, he waved, until the black dot was folded back into the night, and there was nothing left to see except the faint glow of smouldering grass beyond the churchyard gates.

Right, he said to himself, turning homewards. Now for the fun part.

He didn't run back to his flat, he had enough self-restraint for that. But there was nobody waiting for him, no messages on the answering machine, no notes slipped under the door. He stayed awake as long as he could, but nobody came. He woke up at four a.m. on the sofa, still fully dressed, wondering if it had all been a dream; then he caught sight of the teacup, pushed halfway across the table where the angel—correction, where the travelling salesman had left it.

Next day there was a bit on the local news about a fine old church having been torched by vandals, but no repentant girlfriends or apologetic employers, and the garage rang to say that the rear shocks were pretty well knackered as well.

Angels, he thought. Yeah, right.

Three months later Paul was sitting on his sofa, watching the afternoon soaps, wondering if he could be bothered to shave and nibbling last night's cold pizza, when something crashed through his window, nearly lacerating him with broken glass. It was a meteorite – a meteorite with a button on the side. He pressed it, and two slips of thin plastic film fell out.

On one of them was written, "Dear Paul, Got home safe. Sold the cups-with-handles idea to our biggest corporation for an obscenely vast amount of money. Fifty-fifty, do you agree? Regards, 6340097/227/3."

The other slip of plastic was a cheque, bilingual in English and bizarre squiggles, for 90,000,000,000,000,000, 000,000,000,000,000,000 czxyskd, drawn on the Bank of Gamma Orionis Four.

Eventually, Paul had it framed and hung it on the wall. It cost him twenty quid to get the broken window mended.

MATH TAKES A HOLIDAY

Paul Di Filippo

Paul Di Filippo is one of the best of the modern generation of
humorists. Cleverly observed quips and remarks shimmer
from his computer like a dog shaking itself after a swim.
Although he sold his first story in 1977 he didn't really hit
his stride till the mid-eighties, since when there has been a
regular flow of ingenious and unusual stories, observations
and commentaries on this weird world and others. My
favourite amongst his works so far is The Steampunk
Trilogy *(1995), a grotesque and fascinating creation of*
an alternate Victorian world. There are more anarchic
stories in Ribofunk *(1996),* Fractal Paisleys *(1997),* Lost
Pages *(1998) plus a new novel,* Spondulix *(2001). The*
following story, completed with the approval of Rudy
Rucker (in case you wonder!), is pure Di Filippo.

Lucas Latulippe pitied the religious physicists and mystical
biologists, the prayerful chemists and godly geologists of his
acquaintance. As a mathematician who chanced also by a
fervent and unexpected mid-life conversion to be a practising
Catholic, Lucas felt extreme sadness when he contemplated
the plight of his fellows in the scientific community who
sought to reconcile their spiritual beliefs with the tenets of
their secular professions. The Creation versus the Big Bang,

the Garden of Eden versus Darwinism, the Flood versus plate tectonics. What a mind-wrenching clash of diametrically opposed values, images, priorities and forces these valiant men and women faced every day! To embrace the rigorous cosmos of Einstein, Hawking and Wilson without letting go of the numinous plenum of Augustine, Mohammed or Krishna – an impossible task on which one could waste much valuable mental energy better spent formulating theorems.

Lucas owed his unique peace of mind and consequent productivity entirely to his youthful choice of discipline. When his epiphanical conversion had ineluctably struck him – one cool autumn day while daydreamily crossing the campus and witnessing a dove alight on the chapel steeple – Lucas had faced no interior conflicts. His newfound faith offered no impediments to his practice of theoretical mathematics, nor did his academic pursuits interfere with his worship.

That was the beauty of the kind of rarefied math Lucas practiced. It was completely divorced from practical implications, had no bearing on the workings of the universe, and thus held no potential for conflict with the received wisdom of the Church. Oh, certainly the other, less refined sciences used math to embody and clarify their own findings, contaminating the glorious legacy of Pythagoras and Euclid to a certain degree. Lucas would not deny, for instance, the famous observation that a simple little equation underlay the hard-edged reality of the atomic bomb. But admitting this much was like saying that a few of the same glorious words employed by C. S. Lewis could be utilized in the instruction sheet for assembling a playground swingset.

Blessed with such an ethereal conception of his discipline, Lucas enjoyed an ease of worship that he was certain scientists of any other ilk could not experience. He attended Mass daily with a clean conscience and an undisturbed soul. In the parish church not far from his office (attended mostly by Hispanic immigrants with whom Lucas exchanged few words), he was able to feel an unconstrained and untainted relationship with

God, Whom Lucas actually dared to think of as the Supreme Mathematician.

Lucas Latulippe pitied his peers. He prayed daily they could all some day experience the raw glory of mathematics.

"Dear God, please allow my mocking colleagues to witness the transcendental glory of Thy sovereign mathematical Holy Spirit—"

But despite his deep faith he never really expected that one day his prayers would be answered.

For some unfathomable reason of His Own, at this exact non-instant of the eternal, unbegun Now that filled Heaven from one infinite end to the other, God had chosen to manifest Himself as a Sequoia Tree, albeit the largest Sequoia ever to exist. The crown of this enormous redwood standing in for the ineffable Face of the Creator soared into the Heavenly clouds – galaxies? – far out of sight of the two human figures standing at its gnarly base rooted not in soil but in the very stuff of celestial hyperexistence.

Despite the immeasurable distance separating the two auditors and the invisible foliage of the God Tree – from which Crown as from a Burning Bush one might reasonably assume any Voice ought to issue – the Words of God resounded quite plainly in the ears of the man and woman standing tensely at the Tree's base.

"Do I have to send both of you to your Mansions, or will you cease this bickering instantly?"

The dark-eyed woman continued to glare at the man, who glared just as fixedly back with gaze of piercing blue. Their enmity seemed implacable, until an ominous quaking of the numinous stratum beneath their bare feet conveyed to them the actual measure of God's rising displeasure. The tension and anger dissolved then from their postures, and they turned partially away from each other, pretending to adjust their identical white robes or study the unvarying quilt of uncreated Ur-stuff on which they stood.

"That's much better," God commended. "Now you're both acting like real Saints."

The young woman shook her black wavy hair and smiled, an expression that lent her rather coarse and Mediterranean features an alarming rather than reassuring cast. Her long flowing samite robe failed to conceal a not unattractive figure. "Some of us never forgot the humility we exhibited in life. But those who lorded it over peasants back on Earth seem to have become even more haughty once beatified."

Beneath furry brows, the eyes of the older male Saint threatened to combust. His magnificent, almost Assyrian beard seemed to writhe as if alive. "You wilful daughter of Eve! Disobedient toward your mortal father in life, you continue to disrespect your Eternal Father after death!"

"Dioscorus, my earthly father – just in case you've forgotten, Hubert – was a disreputable pagan who had his pious Christian daughter beheaded. Should I have honoured such a parent?"

"You are deliberately obscuring my point, Barbara. I am merely arguing for a proper chain of command and obedience—"

"Because you're descended from the kings of Toulouse! And because you were once a bishop!"

"What of it? I'm proud to have been Bishop of Maestricht and Liege!"

"Certainly, certainly, a wonderful item on your CV. But you were once married as well, don't forget!"

Saint Hubert coughed nervously. "The Church had different policies back in my time—"

Saint Barbara crossed her arms triumphantly across her chest. "On the other hand, I am still a virgin. A virgin *and* a martyr!"

Stiffening his pride, Saint Hubert countered, "I was tutored by Saint Lambert himself!"

Barbara snorted. "I learned my precepts at Origen's knee!"

"I was vouchsafed a vision – a cross appeared between the horns of the stag I hunted!"

"I experienced a miraculous transport from my tower prison to a mountaintop!"

"As Bishop, I converted almost the whole of Belgium!"

"I was one of the Fourteen Holy Helpers! You probably prayed to me!"

"You – you insolent young pup!"

"Young pup? I was born four centuries before you!"

"Where's your historicity, though? Not a single documented proof of your actual existence. Why, you're positively mythical!"

"Mythical! You dirty old huntsman, I'll show you what a sock from a mythical Saint feels like—"

"ENOUGH!" God's thundering command froze the Saints just at the point of coming to blows. Chastised, they separated and attended circumspectly to God's further speech, His Utterances tinged with a rustling of Sequoia foliage.

"Now, pay attention. I summoned you before Me, Hubert, because I had a new assignment for you. Conversely, Barbara, you intruded yourself. What claim do you make upon My Audience?"

Barbara sniffed like a frustrated teenager. "It's not fair. We're both Patron Saints of Mathematicians, but You're always giving Hubert the best missions. Pardon me, Lord, but it strikes me that Heaven might have a, shall we say, glass ceiling?"

The Sequoia shivered nervously. "Please, Saint Barbara, do not raise this touchy issue. I have spent the past mortal century trying to remedy this perceived imbalance between the sexes in My Church, and I don't need to have My Works undone by hasty accusations. Why, how many appearances of the Virgin have I authorized this year alone—? But why am I humouring you thus? I do not have to justify My Ways. This is one of My favourite Privileges. Now, tell Me what objections you have to your recent assignment."

Saint Barbara placed her hands on her hips. "I've been watching over the same fellow for several years now, and I'm sick of his face. I need a change."

God paused in that endearing fake way He had, as if consulting a file. "Hmmm, one Rudy Rucker. Yes, you've done an admirable job of reforming him. He's truly treading the path of righteousness now. But wouldn't you like to hang in there until he wins the Nobel Prize in 2012?"

"No, I wouldn't. The last time I visited this Rucker character he pinched my arse so hard I was black and blue for days!"

Saint Hubert muttered, "Virgin – ha!"

"Well," God continued, "I suppose I could transfer his care to Saint Francis de Sales, under Francis's remit for writers, since that's what Rucker's Nobel Prize will be awarded for . . . Consider it done! Now, are you arguing that you should take over Hubert's new task?"

Saint Barbara seemed a trifle discomposed at her easy victory, and disinclined to ask for too much. "Not take it over, exactly. Perhaps we could share?"

Saint Hubert nearly shouted. "Share my mission! With this little chit? How she ever got to be patron of mathematics anyway, I'll never know."

"I have as much mathematical ability as you, Hubert."

"You commissioned one measly tower window as a mortal patroness of architecture, and that qualifies you? In my day—"

"QUIET!" God ordered. "My Mind is made up. Both of you will answer the prayers of My faithful servant by name of – ah, I have it right here – Lucas Latulippe. Go now, and manifest My inscrutable Being."

The Sequoia popped out of existence without apprehendable transition, leaving the two Saints face to face.

Hubert sighed wearily. "Thy Will be done. Shall we take a chariot pulled by some cherubim?"

"If you're too tired. But on such a beautiful day, I prefer to walk."

Saint Barbara set off across the pastures of Heaven, and Hubert gamely followed.

"Why I didn't pot that cursed holy stag with an arrow when I had a chance—"

*　　*　　*

Pisky Wispaway weighed a muffin short of three hundred pounds. Old family photographs (from idyllic days in Piscataway, New Jersey) testified to her early existence as an indubitably trim child of elfin features who must have evoked many a smile from adoring adults when queried as to her name. Unfortunately, the whimsical legal name bestowed on her by her parents sat less endearingly on the fatty shoulders of the dean of the Astronomy Department at Lucas Latulippe's university. Yet so good-hearted was Pisky – so relatively reconciled to her sad status as campus butt of all sniggering fat jokes was she – that she never winced when called upon to introduce herself, even insisting to just-met acquaintances, "Call me Pisky, please." With bouncing curly auburn hair of which she was inordinately proud, clad in one of her many billowing, colourful tent dresses and several yards of costume-jewellery necklaces, Pisky could often be seen sailing across the quad like some massive galleon pregnant with cargo from the Far East.

Today Pisky sailed into Lucas's office, catching him behind his desk. A big smile bisected her round face, causing her eyes nearly to disappear within the crinkled flesh surrounding them.

"You're coming to our party this afternoon, aren't you, Lucas? For our new professor, remember? Doctor Garnett."

Lucas liked Pisky well enough as a distant colleague. She was an intelligent and affable individual. But he had come to intensely dislike her increasingly frequent visits to his office, often on the slightest of pretexts. He suspected that certain romantic inclinations underlay these pop-ins, feelings he did not now feel capable of reciprocating. Moreover, she so filled Lucas's small quarters that he invariably felt suffocated, especially when trapped behind his desk, away from the window. Not a sizeable fellow himself, Lucas simply could not compete for spatial domination with the oversized woman.

Anxious now to empty his office of Pisky's bulk, Lucas nonetheless felt compelled to prolong the conversation by asking, "Will Hulme be there?"

"Why, of course Owen will be there. He's our senior professor."

"I don't know if I will attend then. You realize of course that we don't get along—"

Pisky brushed Lucas's objections aside with a wave of one hammy be-ringed hand. "You just have to ignore Owen when he tries to get a rise out of you. That's what all the rest of us do. He's prickly with everyone, you know. 'Brilliant but prickly,' that's just how *New Scientist* characterized him."

Lucas squirmed in his chair, finding it hard to breathe. Was Pisky actually using up all the air in the room? "I comprehend those personality defects, Pisky, and I would be perfectly willing to overlook Hulme's barbs if they didn't always concern my faith. That's one topic where I cannot let his insults slide off me. He's not just demeaning me, you know, but two millennia of holy men and women."

Pisky decided to rest one oxen-like haunch on Lucas's desktop, overlooking his instinctive shrinking-back. The castors of Lucas's chair hit the wall, and he was forced to end his retreat. Pisky leaned forward to convey the intimacy of her request.

"We need your stimulating presence at this party, Lucas. I promise you that I'll intervene personally if Owen steps over the bounds of good manners. Please, won't you promise to come?"

"Yes, yes, certainly, I'll be there!"

Pisky regained her feet with surprising grace and ease considering her tonnage and moved toward the door. "I'll see you this afternoon in Crowther Lounge, then."

After Pisky had left, Lucas directed his eyes to the crucifix hanging across the room. He tried to compose a small prayer of thanks for his restored solitude, but his mind was diverted by the sight of the agonized Christ's distended ribcage. When was the last time Pisky had seen her own ribs? Lucas found himself helplessly wondering.

★   ★   ★

Crowther Lounge sported the usual mix of unappealing chairs and couches marked by threadbare armrests and stained stuffingless cushions resembling in shape the defective haemoglobin of sickle-cell sufferers. On a formica-topped folding table an assortment of novelty crackers and unnatural cheeses occupied plastic silver trays. Jug wine in assorted surreal shades begged to be decanted into plastic cups, tasted once, then surreptitiously poured into the sickly potted plants scattered around the room on the traffic-grooved carpet.

When Lucas arrived, the soiree was already in full swing. The faculty of the Astronomy Department, supplemented by volunteers from allied divisions, busily besieged both the refreshments and the famous Doctor Ferron Grainger Garnett, the university's latest star hire. Garnett had achieved a measure of media prominence with his television special, broadcast on both the BBC and PBS: *When Bad Universes Happen to Good Sapients*. Mixing pop psychology with cosmology, shallow philosophy with the many-worlds school of physics, the series had appalled Lucas. Naturally, it had been a smash.

As soon as Lucas entered the lounge Pisky spotted him and began to wave. Sighing helplessly, Lucas moved through the crowd to within a tolerable distance of his large friend.

"Oh, Lucas, you must meet Doctor Garnett! Here, let me introduce you."

Pisky gripped his elbow and forcibly manoeuvred herself and Lucas through the crush around the superstar astronomer. Once within the inner circle, Lucas was horrifed to realize that his nemesis, Owen Hulme, stood directly at Garnett's right hand. Moreover, Hulme's aggressively sparkling wife, Britta, flanked Garnett much too familiarly on the newcomer's left.

For a brief moment before anyone registered Pisky and her victim, Lucas sized up the trio. Stocky and bulldoggish, Owen Hulme had chosen to offset his monkishly bald pate with a fierce dark beard. Lean and whippet-like, his wife Britta overtopped him by a good six inches, half of her advantage inherent in a magnificent teased crown of blonde hair. Lucas could not help but think of the couple as minor caricatures from a *Tintin* comic. (Lucas had confessed this sin of uncharitableness more than once, but kept sinning helplessly every time he saw the pair.) Ferron Grainger Garnett, on the other hand, possessing the rugged virility of a Burt Lancaster or Spencer Tracy, had seemingly been ordered up from Central Casting to fill the role of manly astronomer.

"Doctor Garnett," enthused Pisky, "meet my dear colleague, Lucas Latulippe. Lucas holds the Ashley Chair in the Mathematics Department. He's the university's prime candidate for a Fields Medal, if ever we had one."

Embarrassed by the praise, Lucas extended his hand too precipitously, nearly jostling Garnett's drink. Managing to connect after some fumbling, Lucas sought to deprecate his accomplishments. "Hardly, hardly. Just a few minor papers concerning n-dimensional manifolds, appearing in the odd journal here and there."

"I think I've seen your work footnoted," said Garnett, pleasantly enough. "In a paper by Tipler, perhaps?"

This conventional scientific compliment on Lucas's quotability index failed to please the mathematician. The last thing he desired was to have his pristine work find practical application in the far-out theories of some cosmic snake-oil salesman. Nevertheless, Lucas bit his tongue and offered a demure acknowledgement of the supposed honour.

A red-faced Owen Hulme had been glaring at Lucas throughout the exchange. Now the brusque compact fellow slugged back his wine, thrust his face forward and said, "Lucas is our resident mystic. A regular saint, in fact. Claims numbers come direct from God, or some such bosh. Or is it the Pope who delivers your axioms?"

A smouldering rage, kindled at the mere sight of Hulme, now threatened to flame up within Lucas's bosom. He battled to control himself. "Professor Hulme's words conceal, as usual, a seed of truth within a husk of hyperbole. My private faith, centred in the earthly representative of God known as the Bishop of Rome, does increase my reverence toward my vocation. And I plead guilty to having claimed that mathematics offers proof of a divine basis for creation. I think perhaps that in the best of all possible worlds we would all feel this synergy between our work and our devotional impulses."

Britta Hulme contributed her thoughts now. "My hairdresser, Simon, has started practising Santeria. He claims that the goddess of the sea, Yomama or some such silly name, guides him when he gives shampoos."

Garnett tried to smooth over the nearly visible tension with a chuckle and a platitude. "Well, all religions have their share of wisdom now, don't they?"

Lucas's disgust expanded exponentially, and he blurted out his true feelings. "That is the kind of spineless guff that leads to indulgence in the worst sort of pagan nonsense. Witches, astrology, druids!"

Hulme said, "You should talk, Latulippe! Your beliefs verge on the Kaballah!"

"The Kaballah! Why, I never—"

Pisky intervened. "Lucas, I'm sure Owen meant nothing critical against your beliefs or against the Jewish religion either. Why, look – you don't even have a drink! Come with me and I'll get you a glass of vino."

Lucas allowed himself to be steered away. Hulme could not resist a parting shot. "Has your Pope burned any astronomers lately, Flowerboy?"

Turning back to offer an indignant reply – something along the lines of John Paul's graceful millennial *mea culpa* – Lucas found himself yanked so violently by Pisky that he lost the opportunity.

At the refreshment display Pisky apologized profusely, but in whispers. Calming down somewhat, Lucas accepted her apology but insisted on making an immediate departure.

Outside, Lucas unchained his Vespa from a bike-rack and donned his safety helmet. Unable to afford both a car and the accompanying monthly garage fees, Lucas had hit upon this type of motor scooter as the ideal mode of transportation for his daily short-range needs, having witnessed the utility of the little motorbike on Roman streets during a pilgrimage to the Vatican.

Halfway to his apartment, Lucas pulled up outside his church. Father Miguel Obispo, refilling the fount with holy water, greeted Lucas kindly. Distracted, Lucas nodded rather too curtly and proceeded to the Communion rail nearby the altar. He kneeled and began fervently to reiterate his daily prayer for the chastisement of unbelievers.

Midway down the sunbeam road between Heaven and Earth, Saint Hubert turned to Saint Barbara and said, "Persistent fellow, isn't he? Doesn't he know we're already on our way?"

"Did you ask the Bird to announce us?"

"Why, no, I thought you did."

"Saint Barbara huffed. "Forgetful old coot!"

"You juvenile hussy!"

The rest of the trip passed in frosty silence.

Lucas Latulippe woke up to his burring alarm the morning after the disastrous Astronomy Department party feeling positively sanctified. That spontaneous detour for prayer had settled his soul. He couldn't recall ever feeling so hale and hearty, in both mind and body, this early in the morning. Why, he felt almost as if the Rapture had occurred while he slept. Still lying in bed with his gaze fixed on the familiar stippled ceiling, he patted himself tentatively through the coverlets. His bodily sensations seemed within the normal range for mortal existence, and no Last Trump sounded from outside, so he reluctantly concluded that he had better get up and start his normal routine.

After a visit to the bathroom, Lucas, belting his dressing gown about him, headed to the kitchen. Oddly enough, he could smell fresh coffee. Had he left the coffee machine on overnight? And what was that radiance spilling out of the room? Had he forgotten to turn off the overhead light as well? Usually he was meticulous about such things—

An elderly bearded man, somewhat grouchy-looking, and a youngish woman of definite vivacity, both strangers to Lucas, occupied two seats at his small kitchen table. Each wore a flowing silken ivory robe terminating just above their bare feet. Each cupped hands around a mug of steaming coffee, gratefully and even a trifle greedily inhaling the aroma. And each sported a floating halo dispensing several thousand candlepower.

"Won't you join us, Lucas?" the woman said agreeably.

"Pull up a chair, son," advised the man

Like an obedient zombie, Lucas did as he was bade. The man poured him a cup of coffee, and the woman asked, "Sugar? Cream?"

"Nuh – neither," stammered Lucas.

The woman lifted her cup and drank eagerly. After setting it down, she said, "Ah, that was blessed! It's a shame there's no coffee in Heaven."

The gowned man had duplicated his partner's actions and now agreed with her sentiments. "A beverage reserved for Earth and Hell, unfortunately."

"Who – who are you two?"

"Oh, I'm so sorry," apologized the woman. "Allow me to make the proper introductions. I'm Saint Barbara, and my friend is Saint Hubert. We've come in answer to your prayers. We're the two patron saints of mathematicians. But I suspect an intelligent worshipper such as yourself knew that already."

The awe and reverence Lucas had been experiencing now began to be subsumed by a natural suspicion and paranoia tinged with anger. "Saints, are you?" Lucas half arose and swished his hand between the unsupported halos and the tops of the intruders' heads. "A nice effect, but I'm not taken in so easily by a simple hologram. Who sent you to play such a mean-spirited trick? Was it Owen Hulme? Of course, who else would stoop to such an irreligious prank?"

The man who had been introduced as Saint Hubert showed

some irritation. "We know nothing of this Hulme fellow. We're obeying God's direct instructions. You requested, as I recall, that your mocking colleagues be allowed 'to witness the transcendental glory of Thy sovereign mathematical Holy Spirit'."

Lucas grew deeply confused. "How could you know the contents of my prayers?"

Saint Barbara expressed some impatience of her own. "Hubert *explained* it quite sufficiently to you. God heard your prayers and sent us down to satisfy them."

Lucas cradled his head in his hands. "I don't know what to believe. Could you at least turn those halos or holograms or whatever they are down a trifle? They're giving me a splitting headache."

"Oh, sorry." "Certainly, no problem."

Once the halos had dimmed, Lucas looked up again. "Hubert, Hubert – I don't ever remember reading about a Saint Hubert. Barbara, now, though, I recall your story. Quite dramatic. Your father had your head chopped off, didn't he?"

Saint Barbara smirked at her partner. "Yes, he did. And then he held it up for everyone to see, just like this."

Saint Barbara grabbed a handful of her own thick hair at the crest of her skull and lifted her entire grinning head off the sudden stump of her neck, separating the two at an indiscernible wound. An enormous quantity of blood gouted out, splattering across the table into Lucas's lap.

Lucas's own head, still attached to his body, shot backward in horror and hit the wall. He slumped unconscious to the floor.

"If there's one type of person I detest most heartily," Hubert said peevishly, "it's a showy martyr."

Barbara's head, speaking in gory isolation, was a disconcerting sight even to Hubert. "Showy, maybe. Convincing, definitely."

When Lucas awoke for the second time that morning, he felt more damned than exalted. His head ached, and he was disinclined to open his eyes. Perhaps his earlier nightmare would prove consequenceless if he just lay here—

"You'll feel much better if you sit up and drink your coffee," Saint Barbara said.

Lucas groaned and opened his eyes. He had been carried to his parlour couch. No trace of blood remained on his pristine clothing. The visiting Saints flanked him solicitously. As if reading his thoughts, Hubert volunteered, "I apologize for my partner's shock tactics. Your kitchen is spotless again. I even emptied the filter basket on the coffeemaker."

Lucas sat up with a groan and accepted the mug of coffee. "If I acknowledge your Sainthood, could you please make my headache go away?"

"Only with some aspirin," Barbara said. "We can't really perform healing miracles, you see. That's not our provenance. We have to stick to mathematical miracles. Each saint has his or her own area of expertise."

"No healing of lepers," affirmed Hubert. "No raising the dead." He paused thoughtfully. "Multiplying fishes. We can do that, since it involves math. Wouldn't that qualify as something of a biological miracle? I wonder if we'd be trespassing on anyone's territory there?"

Barbara waved off this quibble. "There's overlap, certainly. But I don't think He would mind."

"I appreciate hagiology as much as the next person, but if one of you could get me those aspirin now, please—"

After two cups of coffee and the aspirin, Lucas felt considerably better. Growing accustomed to the reality of his celestial visitors, Lucas found his curiosity and interest growing. "Mathematical miracles, you say? Exactly what would those be like?"

Hubert answered, "Oh, basically the practical realization of any abstruse mathematical proof or theorem or concept. For instance, why don't you get up and try walking into the kitchen?"

Lucas stood, took a single step—

—And found himself instantly two rooms distant. He turned to confront the gleeful Saints in the doorway.

"How did you do that?"

Hubert answered smugly. "I simply gave you momentary access to a few of the higher dimensions you're always speculating so blithely about. Hardly broke a sweat."

An enormous sense of the possibilities inherent in having two mathematical Saints apparently ready to do his bidding in the campaign to enlighten his pagan enemies suddenly burst over Lucas, and he smiled broadly. He suddenly felt like he imagined the unburned Joan of Arc must have.

"Am I the only one who can see you two?"

"We will manifest to whomever you please," Barbara said.

Lucas chafed his hands together like a silent-film miser ready to foreclose on a mortgage. "Excellent. Let me get dressed, and then I'll ride into the university. You can meet me in my office."

"We can transport you there instantly," offered Hubert.

"No, no, I can't waste God's gifts on trivialities. Save your sacred powers for the reformation of the unbelievers."

Lucas departed to shower (despite being clean, he couldn't quite shake the memory of his earlier bloodbath) and to dress in street clothes. When he had closed the bathroom door behind him, Barbara said to Hubert, "What a charming fellow. Really sweet and cute, too. And he's so much more considerate than my last client. I don't know how many times I had to transport *him* to campus when he was running late."

Rather than utilize his favoured bike rack, Lucas parked his Vespa outside the Blackwood Building that housed the Astronomy Department, dropping the kick-stand but not chaining the bike. He looked over his shoulder at the empty air and asked in a low voice, "Hubert, Barbara — are you there?"

His skin pringled as if with a wash of holy radiation and Hubert's voice issued from a fluctuating crack in space. "We're right behind you, lad. Consider yourself shielded in Godly armour."

Reassured by his invisible choir, Lucas strode boldly into

the building and straight for the office of Owen Hulme. Fluorescent light shone through the frosted glass inset into the designated door, and Lucas heard muted voices from inside. He knocked boldly on the door and was answered with a gruff, "Come in!"

Bracing his shoulders, Lucas entered the lion's den like angel-guarded Daniel.

Hulme occupied his desk chair while Doctor Garnett sat in the single visitor's seat. The two men evinced differing reactions to Lucas's appearance. Garnett expressed mute embarrassment, as if recollecting Lucas's humiliation at the reception, tinged with a general air of uninterest, while Hulme actually let loose with an involuntary bestial growl.

"What brings you here today, Latulippe? Unless you intend to make a full apology for your disgraceful behaviour yesterday, you might as well turn straight around and hie yourself back to your private miniature Vatican."

Feeling his cheeks redden, Lucas nonetheless spoke boldly. "Far from intending to apologize, I have come here today to throw your impious folly back into your hairy face, Hulme! Prepare to meet the messengers of an angry God. Barbara! Hubert! Reveal yourselves!"

The two barefoot Saints popped into existence at floor level, flanking Lucas.

"Yes, God was indeed angry the last time we saw Him," Hubert volunteered, reaching up to adjust his canted quasar-bright halo. "But we two were the focus of His wrath, not these gentlemen."

Barbara rudely admonished her partner. "Shush, you old fool!" The astronomers had started slightly at the miraculous visitation, but soon regained their coolly rational, dismissive attitudes. Hulme in fact seemed more irritated than stunned. "Very impressive, Latulippe. Just like a third-rate Mystery Play. But unless you get these two shabby conjurors and yourself out of my office immediately, I will have to call Campus Security."

Lucas trembled with indignation. "You dare to mock God's

chosen representatives? What will it take to convince you that your whole materialistic life is founded on a lie?"

Hulme did not deign to answer, but instead punched buttons on his phone, receiver already held to his ear. "Hello, Security? This is Professor Hulme. Please send over a squad car to deal with some intruders—"

Lucas felt the situation spiralling out of his control. What had gone wrong? No one was following his plan. These unbelievers appeared unfazed by Saintly auras. Earlier, Lucas had imagined this moment as his invincible triumph. But nobody seemed to know their lines in the script he had mentally written. Desperate to regain the upper hand, Lucas shouted a command:

"Barbara, stop him!"

The phone receiver clattered to the desktop, although Hulme's hand still remained closed. And although the man's mouth continued to move beneath his beard, no sounds issued from it. Something seemed wrong about Hulme's whole appearance, in fact. He seemed flattened, subject to ripples racing across a body rendered insubstantial. And when Hulme turned sideways to look imploringly at Doctor Garnett, he disappeared completely.

Lucas realized instantly what Saint Barbara had done. "You've reduced him to two dimensions!"

Barbara exhibited an immodest pride. "Euclidean, my dear Watson. The quickest and neatest solution to your request."

The thinner-than-paper Hulme was vapouring about the office in a dither, appearing and disappearing randomly as he alternately displayed his remaining visible dimensions or accidentally angled them away from the observers. Meanwhile Garnett had shot to his feet in alarm.

"I don't know what you've done to Owen, you popish madman! But I won't let you get away!"

Garnett lunged at Lucas, who darted one side in a narrow escape. "Hubert, help!"

The newest addition to the Astronomy faculty suddenly flopped to the rug, unable to stand. His limbs had been replaced with smaller complete copies of his entire body. Where his hands and feet should have been, Garnett now boasted scaled-down versions of his own head. And the limbs of these bizarre appendages consisted of even smaller bodies, and so on and so on till Lucas's eyes glazed over.

A chittering noise of the infinite heads all complaining at once overlaid the macro-assaults coming from the original Garnett mouth. Lucas sagged down into Hulme's chair. Hulme would certainly not be needing it, for the flat professor had accidentally slipped into a closed desk drawer through a slit.

"You've fractalized him?" asked Lucas wearily. "Rendered him self-similar?"

Hubert grinned. "Precisely. A little something I picked up while peering over Mandelbrot's shoulder one day."

Lucas heard a siren then. Hopelessly, he opened the drawer into which Hulme had vanished. The papery savant shot out like a jack-in-the-box, causing Lucas to surge wildly to his feet.

At that moment Britta Hulme strode gaily into her husband's office, spotting her transformed husband in a moment of deceptive substantiality.

"Ready for an early lunch, dear? We need to hurry if I'm not to keep Simon waiting—"

The filmy ghost of her husband silently beseeched his wife for help. His weird anxiety finally registered on the dense woman.

"Are you feeling all right, dear?"

The sight of Owen shaking his head was not something Lucas would have chosen to view or to retain in memory. The professor's head seemed to snap in and out of existence as it rotated through one plane after another. For nausea-inducing properties, the display rivalled Saint Barbara's earlier demonstration of her past misfortunes with an executioner's axe.

Britta screamed with operatic violence. Lucas opened his mouth to reassure her, but she screamed again. And again. And again—

Her fourth scream possessed less volume. The next even less.

Britta was shrinking. Dwindling while retaining her perfect proportions, her voice dopplering to insignificance, she passed the size of a child, a cat, a mouse, a bee, a midge, then vanished utterly.

"I assumed you'd want her silenced," Saint Barbara explained matter-of-factly. "So I recalled some interesting corrollaries in a paper by Stephen Smale from the *Journal of Nonlinear Dynamics* about strange attractors with a flowline sink leading down to the Planck level—"

Before the loquacious Saint could finish her explanation, various exclamations from the gathering crowd of horrified people at the office door interrupted her.

Lucas was covered in a stinking sweat. His mind roiled like the surface of a fractal sea. "We have to get out of here," he husked.

Pleasant sunshine fell upon Lucas and the two Saints, and a mild breeze played with Lucas's damp hair and ruffled the Saintly robes. Higher-dimensional transit had its definite advantages during emergencies.

However, they were not out of the woods yet. Having parked alongside his Vespa, the Campus Security squad car was just disgorging its officers.

The lead cop resembled the cult film director, John Waters, except possessed of a mean scowl. "Where's the trouble, sir?"

"Up – upstairs."

The other rent-a-cops studied the two Saints suspiciously for a moment, until Lucas mastered himself enough to offer a pretext for their uncouth looks. "My, ah, my visiting friends are old hippies, officer. They teach at, um, Berkeley. West Coast, Mother Earth, nature worship, all that bosh. Those halos? You know the lightsticks kids use at raves? Of course. You understand, I'm sure."

The cops grunted and raced off toward the growing noisy disturbance inside Blackwood. At the outer entrance of the building they met the immovable bulk of Pisky Wispaway, clad in a hideously checkered tentlike shift. A brief, Robin-Hood-meets-Little-John-on-the-log-bridge struggle for passage occurred, from which Pisky emerged victorious. She waddled as fast as she could toward Lucas, her costume jewellery rattling like a bead curtain in a hurricane.

Before his large lady friend could arrive, Lucas turned to the saints.

"Can you undo what you did to those three people?"

"Of course," said Barbara.

"I really don't know if we should obey his orders any more," quibbled Hubert. "After that awful lie he told the police. Old hippies indeed!"

Lucas fought not to yell. "It was only a venial sin! I'll confess it as soon as I can and do whatever penance the priest assigns!"

"Well, in that case then—"

Barbara sounded a practical note. "You realize that as soon as your opponents are restored to normality, they'll accuse you of all sorts of horrid things. It'll be just like the nasty scene when my father heard about my conversion."

"I know, I know, but I'll deal with that somehow. Just put them right."

The Saints nodded to each other, blinked once, then chorused, "Done."

Pisky joined the trio now. Her flushed face showed nothing but sympathy and concern for Lucas, mingled with some natural curiosity directed toward his strange companions.

"Oh, Lucas, whatever is the matter? Did you and Owen get into a fight?"

"Yes, I fear we did, Pisky. I simply showed up on his doorstep with proof of the certainty of his eternal damnation unless he repented, and he reacted badly. I confess that I was forced to defend myself."

"How dreadful! Lucas, I was so worried about you! I've been thinking over all my deep feelings for you all night long, and I just want you to know how much I admire your principles. You can do no wrong in my eyes. I'm so proud of you for standing up to Owen!"

Pisky gripped Lucas's arm and leaned her bulk against him. He experienced a claustrophobic sensation akin to what the Princess's pea beneath a thousand mattresses might have felt. Grateful enough for Pisky's declaration of alliance, he nonetheless sought gently to extricate himself.

"Ah, well, yes, thank you, Pisky. I did not emerge victorious alone, of course. I had the help of these two Saints. Allow me to introduce Saint Barbara and Saint Hubert, Heaven's mathematical experts."

Hubert took Pisky's hand and kissed it genteelly like the courtier he once had been. "Charmed, madame. Your voice reminds me of Empress Theodora's."

Barbara returned no handshake, but only a somewhat frosty verbal greeting, smoothing her robes across her trim waist rather ostentatiously. Lucas thought to detect a certain flattering jealousy in his female protector, but could not concentrate now on what otherwise might be a stimulating opportunity.

Such pleasantries, however strained, instantly terminated the next moment, as the Hulmes and Professor Garnett appeared on the steps of the Blackwood Building, backed by a force of concerned bystanders.

"There they are, officer! Arrest them!"

Lucas hopped upon his Vespa and cranked its motor into sputtering life. "Pisky, we'll continue our interesting discussion later. I have to flee immediately, until I can figure out how to clear myself of these ridiculous charges."

"I'll come with you, Lucas!"

Before the mathematician could protest, Pisky hoisted her skirts and swung her leg over the passenger seat of the tiny machine, engulfing it. The Vespa sank down upon its rear tyre so far the front wheel almost rose from the ground, in partial mimicry of the Lone Ranger's steed.

"Pisky, please—"

"Go, Lucas, go – they're running toward us!"

Lucas goosed the throttle and the protesting, overburdened bike moved off at a pace barely faster than a jog. The Saints, in fact, easily kept abreast on foot, without supernatural exertions.

"This is no good!" wailed Lucas. "Hubert, Barbara – can't you get us away any faster?"

"Where would you like to go?"

"I don't know! I just want us to fly off!"

The Saints fell back and put their heads together to whisper as they ambled. Lucas caught snatches of their dialogue:

"– cosmological constants –" "– numerical in nature –" "– don't believe we'd be contravening –"

Their pursuers had almost caught up when the Saints finished their intense discussion. Hubert began to lecture. "You are aware, perhaps, of the universal force designated "Lambda'—"

Lucas could actually hear Owen Hulme's angry growls amidst the crowd noise. "Whatever you're going to do, for God's sake just do it!"

Why was the ground falling swiftly away from beneath the Vespa? Had the Saints opened up a crevasse in the earth? Had Lucas been gulled all along? Were Barbara and Hubert actually demons, perhaps, finally taking their tormented victims down to Hell? Lucas felt no sensation of falling, though, smelled no brimstone. Instead, he realized that he was ascending, rising into the air. The ground remained fixed.

The Vespa was flying, its front wheel pointed toward the sun.

Pisky was squeezing Lucas so hard around his midriff that he could barely breathe. "I didn't believe, I didn't believe! But now I do, now I do!"

Lucas turned to look downward over his shoulder. The agitated mob had come to a dead stop, their upturned faces fixed in slack-jawed amazement on the bouyant bike and its incredulous riders sailing off into the sky, the levitating Saints alongside like pilot fish.

Before they got much higher, Lucas heard a guy on the

ground say, "Hey, I can see right up the broad's robe! She's
buck naked underneath it!"

Barbara's face darkened. "Why, you ill-mannered spawn of
a toad! Let's see how you like your guts twisted into a Möbius
strip—"

"No, don't!" ordered Lucas, and Barbara obeyed, although
she continued to grumble.

As the bike soared higher and farther away without mishap,
Lucas gradually relaxed, as did Pisky. His natural scientific
curiosity reasserted itself enough to have him ask, "How does
this flight qualify as a mathematical miracle?"

Hubert appeared proud of their accomplishment. "Our first
step consisted of suspending the commutative and associative
laws for tensor operators. Once quantum inertias failed to
group, we next altered the numerical value of Lambda – the
force that controls the expansion of the universe – in a small
pocket around you, resulting in directed antigravity. The
whole cosmos is based on just six numbers, you know. N,
E, Omega, Lambda, D, and Q. Now, take Q for instance—"

"I appreciate the beauty of the theory, Hubert. But where
are we headed?"

"That is entirely up to you, sir. I suppose we could perch
out of sight atop a cloud. It's what we Saints are commonly
thought to do, after all."

Now Pisky spoke. "Oh, Lucas, they really *are* Saints! I
thought you were just joking. How wonderful! And to sit on a
cloud and look down on the Earth – I've dreamed of such a
romantic thing since I was just a little girl back in Piscataway."

Lucas sighed, and gave his consent. The Vespa speeded up,
and before too long pierced the lowermost cloud layer. On the
far side, the bike halted above the fluffy sunglazed and
shadowed terrain, a pasture of purple and gold.

"Step off," said Barbara.

Lucas regarded the feisty Saint warily. Would she play a
deadly trick on him for thwarting her revenge on the Peeping
Tom? Yet what choice did he have but to trust her?

Pisky settled his doubts by dismounting first. She sunk into the clouds up to her ankles, but no further.

"A slight local alteration in the values of N and E—" began Hubert.

Now standing on the cloudstuff, Lucas walked to the nearest edge, accompanied by Pisky. They looked over tentatively at the patchwork Earth, a quilt of browns and greens stitched by roads.

"It's so beautiful," cooed Pisky.

Saint Barbara snorted. "Anything gets old after a millennia or two. Even love, I suspect – though I couldn't say for sure," the female Saint wistfully concluded.

Pisky grabbed Lucas's hand fervently. "Oh, I don't know about that. I'd like enough time to find out, though."

Lucas gently disengaged himself. Such idle talk would be pleasant enough, if all else were well. But his current troubles filled Lucas's mind to such a degree that he could spare no attention for Pisky's romantic babble. And yet some subtle hook in her speech lured his thoughts along possible lines of salvation.

Inspiration struck Lucas. "Time! Of course! Can you two somehow—"

Hubert sighed. "Here it comes again. Reverse time? Naturally. Strictly a mathematical phenomenon. Actually, that old dodge is the way we get out of most fixes."

"I can't tell you how bored I am with that tiresome tactic," complained Saint Barbara. "If only mortals had a little more imagination. Now what if we altered the Sun's radiational output—"

"No! I don't care about imaginative solutions! I just want my old life back. But I need to keep my memories of all this, so that I never let my pride and piety get the better of me again."

"Easy enough. Okay, get ready—"

Pisky surprised everyone by intervening. "Stop! I don't care if I have to lose all memories of this glorious moment in order to help Lucas. But could I ask one favour of you?" The big woman looked down bashfully and kicked a divot of cloud.

"Could you make me skinny? Even if only for a minute? Please?"

The Saints conferred again: "– reverse Banach-Tarski –" "– conformal mapping into the lemniscate–"

Saint Barbara turned to address the other woman with a certain condescending sympathy. "All right, dearie, just close your eyes."

The transformation of Pisky Wispaway pulled an involuntary grunt from Lucas. Her figure seemed to implode in an organized fashion, while the checkerboard pattern of her dress morphed to a horseshoe-crab-shaped pattern out of a Saupe and Pietgen textbook. Stripped mathemagically of nearly two hundred pounds, she also lost her oversized altered dress and undergarments, which slipped off to pool around her feet, leaving her clad only in strings of beads. A most attractive daughter of Eve, the newly svelte naked Pisky hurled herself into Lucas's arms. He surprised himself by clutching her eagerly.

The Saints regarded the pair of mortals affectionately.

"Get ready for time-reversal," said Hubert.

Barbara leaned in to kiss Lucas's cheek. "You were one of my nicest clients."

"Speak kindly of us to God in your prayers," said Hubert. "We can always use another letter of recommendation to our Employer."

In a blink, the mortals disappeared.

Hubert turned to Barbara. "Well, another assignment satisfactorily completed."

"I thought this one turned out much better than that botch you made of Fermat's Last Theorem. 'No room in the margin', indeed."

Hubert sniffed. "And what of your little cold-fusion debacle?"

Barbara winced. "I've improved over time." She offered her arm for an escort back to Heaven, and the linked Saints walked away over the cloud-tops.

"That, I believe," offered Hubert, "is God's plan."

★   ★   ★

Lucas Latulippe envied his conflicted peers. The war in their bosoms between faith and scepticism allowed them to pursue their scientific careers with a certain useful level of doubt in both arenas. Unlike Lucas, they were not always looking over their shoulders warily, nervous about the possibility of inconveniently real miracles.

But after several years of freedom from Saintly intervention, Lucas had learned to tamp down his unease. Frequent prayers beseeching God to provide an uneventful daily existence helped. And of course, having a beautiful, slim, loving wife like Pisky would make any man's life quite happy.

And, after all, they were the only couple they knew whose marriage had literally been made in Heaven.

BROADWAY BARBARIAN

Cherith Baldry

A former teacher and librarian, Cherith Baldry first became known for her series of children's books, Saga of the Six Worlds, *but she has since established herself as a writer of intensely human fantasy stories, many with Arthurian settings. Her latest novel is also Arthurian,* Exiled from Camelot *(2000). This story takes us into the wonderful world of Damon Runyon*

One evening along about seven o'clock, I am seated in Mindy's restaurant wrapping myself around a portion of beef stew, and thinking of this and that, and especially where I will find the scratch to bet on a hot prospect tomorrow, when who should bob up but three characters as follows: Harry the Horse, Spanish John and Little Isadore.

Of course I am giving them the big hello, although naturally these characters are not such as I will wish to be associated with, in any way, whatsoever, as they are very hard characters, indeed. But I do not let on to Harry the Horse, Spanish John and Little Isadore that I am not glad to see them, as they may take offence, and if they take offence they may take me for an airing, and such guys as Harry the Horse takes for an airing do not come back.

Well, Harry the Horse slaps me on the back, and he says to me like this:

"We are looking for a guy called Eugene Edmonton," he says. "Do you see Eugene Edmonton around and about lately?"

Now I do not hear of Eugene Edmonton before this, and I am thinking that even if I do know this guy, the chances are I will not be telling Harry the Horse his whereabouts, or Eugene Edmonton might be turning up very seriously dead.

"We are looking for Eugene Edmonton," says Harry the Horse, "because we have a proposition to put to him," and he tells me as follows.

Last Thursday along about four bells in the morning, we are meeting Eugene Edmonton in Good Time Charley Bernstein's little joint on Forty-eighth Street. He is sitting at the next table crying into his drink, which is maybe the best thing to do with Good Time Charley's drinks, at that.

He is a little guy with a small moustache and gold-rimmed cheaters, and all dressed up in a good tuxedo, and I am thinking that such a guy should be stepping out around the nightclubs, instead of sitting in Good Time Charley's crying into his drink.

After a while he says to us as follows:

"Friends," he says, "I am the unhappiest guy in the world. I am in love with Miss Paulette Patrick, but she plays plenty of chill for me. I do not wish to live if Miss Paulette Patrick will not love me. In fact," he says, "I am thinking of scragging myself."

We commence to think that he is more than somewhat daffy, to consider scragging himself because some doll will not love him, especially such a doll as Miss Paulette Patrick, who is no more than a dancer at Miss Missouri Martin's Sixteen Hundred Club. Furthermore, we do not wish him to scrag himself while we are in the neighbourhood, as we figure the cops will think that we are the parties who do the scragging, and will be asking some very awkward questions, indeed.

But we do not say this to him, and pretty soon he comes to

sit at our table and buys us drinks, although of course we do not drink them.

"I send Miss Paulette Patrick diamond bracelets and fur wraps," he says, "and she sends them back to me. She says she does not wish diamond bracelets and fur wraps. She says to me, 'I will never love a guy who does nothing but hang around the nightclubs. The man I marry will have to do heroic deeds. I wish a knight in shining armour,' she says."

Now this makes us think that Miss Paulette Patrick must also be more than somewhat daffy, since knights in shining armour are few and far between in this man's town, while Eugene Edmonton looks like a guy who has plenty, and if Miss Paulette Patrick becomes his ever-loving wife the chances are she will have more diamond bracelets than she has room on her arms.

Well, Eugene Edmonton is just ordering some more drinks, when suddenly the door of Good Time Charley's joint flies open, and standing in the doorway is such a guy as I never see before in all my life, and (says Harry the Horse) I see a few.

This guy is about seven feet tall and about five feet wide, and his muscles look like melons in a sack. He is wearing nothing but a sort of fur apron, about as much as will make a cover for a niblick, if it is a small niblick, hairy boots, and a leather belt with a sword.

At first I think this is nothing but an advertising stunt, but I cannot see where the guy is selling anything, and if he is selling anything he is not the sort of guy that respectable citizens will give their potatoes, or have any truck with whatsoever, in any way.

This guy marches over to the bar, and he says to Good Time Charley: "Me Thurg."

Now Good Time Charley is looking somewhat disorganized, and he does not say anything, until the big guy slams a hand down on the bar and says, "Give Thurg drink."

"Coming right up, Mr Thurg," says Good Time Charley, and he reaches for the bottle of Scotch to pour Thurg a shot.

Thurg grabs the bottle, bites off the neck and spits the glass on the floor, and pours the Scotch down his throat. This surprises us all more than somewhat, since I know for a fact that this Scotch is made by Moonshine Joe Brady in a basement on Eleventh Avenue, and Moonshine Joe gets very critical of citizens who ask him what he puts in it.

Before this I never see any guy stay on his feet after drinking a couple of shots of Moonshine Joe's Scotch, leave alone the whole bottle, but Thurg just tosses the empty over his shoulder and says, "More drink."

So Good Time Charley gives Thurg another bottle, and I consider it very bad taste on Thurg's part to spit glass on the floor, especially as it is Good Time Charley Bernstein's floor. We can all see that Thurg is one dead tough mug, indeed.

When Thurg finishes this new bottle, he slaps himself on the chest a couple of times, and says, "Thurg seek Eye of God."

Now when Little Isadore hears this he begins sniggering more than somewhat, because if a guy is seeking any part of God he will not be finding it around and about on Broadway, except maybe at the Save-a-Soul mission.

And when Thurg hears Little Isadore sniggering he seems very much excited, and steps up to our table and grabs Little Isadore by the neck and holds him off the floor like a bag of wet washing, and says like this:

"Thurg great warrior. Not laugh at Thurg."

Now naturally when I see this I go for the old equalizer, but I fail to find it, as on this particular night I am not rodded up, because Good Time Charley does not approve of guys shooting other guys in his joint, or at least not much.

Little Isadore is turning blue in the face when Thurg drops him, and he lies on the floor and takes no more interest in the proceedings.

Thurg says, "Eye of God is ruby, from temple statue. Where Thurg find?"

Well, when Thurg mentions a ruby, I begin to find his proposition very attractive, indeed, but I say nothing, because I do not know where he will find the Eye of God, and if I do know, the chances are I will not be telling Thurg.

Now all this time Eugene Edmonton is sitting at our table, looking very sad indeed, but when Thurg says this he jumps to his feet.

"Mr Thurg, I do not know where you can find the Eye of God, but I will help you look for it," he says. "It will be a heroic deed, and then maybe Miss Paulette Patrick will love me!"

Thurg looks all pleasured up when Eugene Edmonton says this, and he slaps Eugene Edmonton on the back, so that Eugene Edmonton's gold-rimmed cheaters fly off.

"You brave warrior!" he says. "You Thurg friend."

Then he strides over to the door and on out, and Eugene Edmonton finds his cheaters and goes after him, and I go after him too, because where there is a ruby there is a percentage, and I am such a guy as is always looking for a percentage, in any way I can. And Spanish John picks Little Isadore off of the floor, and we all go out onto Forty-eighth Street, and Eugene Edmonton calls a cab.

Now it so happens that this cab is one of those old-time horse-drawn victorias, and Eugene Edmonton tells the hackie to drive to the Sixteen Hundred Club. I do not know why Eugene Edmonton expects to find the Eye of God there, but I figure that if he is to do a heroic deed, he wishes Miss Paulette Patrick to be there to see it. And the dolls at the Sixteen Hundred club will be wearing diamonds and rubies and emeralds and other such items, so maybe it is not such a bad idea, at that.

At first as we drive off Thurg is still looking all pleasured up, and says, "This good chariot. Thurg like," but soon he starts peering around and about on the street, and there is a scowl on his map.

He says to us, "You know wizard? Great wizard Alphazor?"

Now I do not hear of this character before, or any wizard of any kind, except maybe Three Card Clancy, who is a wiz at the Three Card Trick, and Find the Lady, and other such entertainments, with which Three Card Clancy earns many potatoes from citizens who do not meet him before.

"No," says Eugene Edmonton. "We do not know Alphazor."

"Alphazor evil wizard," says Thurg, and he scowls blacker than ever. "Alphazor seek Eye of God also. But Thurg will find!"

Now I wonder what happens if the evil wizard Alphazor catches up with Thurg, because it is clear to me that if there is one guy Thurg does not care for, it is the evil wizard Alphazor. But it is also clear to me that Thurg is not right bright, and maybe he is wrong that the evil wizard Alphazor is looking for the Eye of God. And so I dismiss him from my mind.

Well, when we get to the Sixteen Hundred Club, Eugene Edmonton tells the hackie to wait, and we go in, and Eugene Edmonton gives Moosh the doorman a pound note not to ask questions about Thurg, though when Moosh sets eyes on Thurg the chances are he will not be asking questions of any kind, whatsoever.

Inside the Sixteen Hundred Club, Miss Missouri Martin's jazz band, the Hi Hi Boys, are playing, and Miss Paulette Patrick is out on the floor doing her dance. She is a tall doll with black hair, and I can see that nothing about her is phoney, for all she is wearing is a couple of pink feathers and a fan, and it is a small fan, at that.

So Eugene gets us a table at the edge of the dance floor, and we sit there watching Miss Paulette Patrick, and I can see that to Eugene Edmonton she is a very pleasant sight, indeed.

Thurg does not sit with us at the table, but instead he goes around and about among the customers at the Sixteen Hundred Club, looking at the dolls' necklets and bracelets, but nowhere does he find the Eye of God. Furthermore, the prominent citizens who are with the dolls get very much excited and wish to do something harmful to Thurg's health, although some of the dolls do not seem to mind, at that, and this causes Thurg to slug several of these prominent citizens kerbowie on the bean.

Miss Missouri Martin commences to look seriously annoyed and she comes over to our table and says like this to Eugene Edmonton:

"Mr Edmonton, I must ask you to take your friend out of here as quick as you can say scat, and maybe quicker. He is not refined," she says, "and the Sixteen Hundred Club is such a club that is refined at all times."

Now Miss Missouri Martin is an old doll who loves nothing better than to stick her nose into other people's business, but she is a nice old skate, at that, and I figure that if Eugene Edmonton tells her all about the whole cat-hop she will help him to do a heroic deed so that Miss Paulette Patrick will love him.

But before Eugene Edmonton can explain anything, Miss Paulette Patrick finishes her dance, and Thurg also finishes lamping the rubies in the Sixteen Hundred Club, and commences lamping Miss Paulette Patrick instead, and it is clear to one and all that what he sees impresses him no little.

So Thurg steps up to Miss Paulette Patrick, and he says like this: "Thurg like. You Thurg woman now."

Well, Miss Paulette Patrick hauls off and gives Thurg a right hook to the jaw, but of course this is no more than a flea bite to Thurg. He picks Miss Paulette Patrick up and tosses her over his shoulder like a sack of corn, and heads for the door.

Naturally, Miss Paulette Patrick commences shrieking more than somewhat, and Miss Missouri Martin is yowling like a whole barrel-full of cats, and when Miss Paulette Patrick sees Eugene Edmonton sitting there she yells, "Eugene! Save me! Save me!"

So Eugene Edmonton grabs a bottle of champagne and biffs Thurg over the noggin with it, so that the bottle breaks and champagne showers all over the customers at the Sixteen Hundred Club, which arouses their indignation, but Thurg is not inconvenienced at all, and goes on out to where the cab is waiting.

Now when Thurg gets outside he slings Miss Paulette Patrick across the cab horse, draws his sword and cuts the harness, jumps up behind her and digs his heels in, so Thurg and the horse and Miss Paulette Patrick commence tearing down the street and out of sight.

Eugene Edmonton calls another cab, and yells to the hackie, "Follow that horse!" and we all get in, but I am betting plenty of six to five that we do not catch Thurg, because our horse has to pull the cab with Eugene Edmonton and me, and Spanish John and Little Isadore, while Thurg's horse has only to carry Thurg and Miss Paulette Patrick.

But if I have a bet down I will lose, for we are not going more than a few blocks when we see Thurg's horse standing by the sidewalk, and Thurg has Miss Paulette Patrick over his shoulder again, and is staring into the window of Rosenberg the jeweller's, where there are always very nice rings and bracelets and items such as rich guys love to give their dolls.

And when we come up to Thurg he points into the window and says, "Eye of God."

And I see in the middle of the window a ruby all by itself on a velvet cushion, and this is such a ruby as I never see before. If a doll wears such a ruby she will have a hard time lifting her neck off of the floor.

So when Thurg sees Eugene Edmonton he hands Miss Paulette Patrick over to him and says, "Hold Thurg woman."

Then he takes a run at the window and smashes the glass with his head, and all hell breaks loose.

Miss Paulette Patrick is still screeching up a storm, and Rosenberg's burglar alarm starts blasting out, and citizens start running from every which way to see what is going on.

Thurg steps in and grabs the Eye of God and hides it away in a little pouch hanging from his belt. I am thinking that I might remove some of the rings and bracelets from among the smashed glass in the window, when I see a couple of cops tearing down the street, so I stay where I am and have nothing to do with the rings and bracelets whatsoever, as I do not wish the cops to put the old sleeve on me.

Then Thurg turns to Eugene Edmonton and says, "Now I go. Give Thurg woman."

Now all this time Miss Paulette Patrick has her arms tight

round Eugene Edmonton's neck, and she is shrieking, "No! No!" and other similar expressions, and it is clear to one and all that she is not in favour of going anywhere with Thurg.

So Eugene Edmonton stands between Miss Paulette Patrick and Thurg, and I am thinking that I would not like to be in his place, for such a guy as stands in Thurg's way is likely to find himself flattened into the sidewalk.

Then Eugene Edmonton says to Thurg like this: "This my woman. Me Thurg friend. Thurg not take his friend's woman."

Thurg stands there and thinks about this, and from his face I can see that thinking is not something he does very much, or maybe not at all.

Then Thurg shakes his head and says, "No. This Thurg woman," and gives Eugene Edmonton a punch in the snoot with a fist the size of a piledriver.

The punch drops Eugene Edmonton, and Miss Paulette Patrick kneels on the sidewalk beside him and takes his head in her lap. She is sobbing plenty, and she says to Thurg like this: "You have killed him, you big trambo!"

Thurg is looking much displeased when Miss Paulette Patrick calls him a big trambo. He draws his sword, and lets out a roar like a lion calling for its mate.

But before he can grab Miss Paulette Patrick, there is a light like twinkly blue stars in Rosenberg's window, and suddenly a guy is standing there, among the broken glass and the diamonds.

He is an old geezer with long white hair and beard, and he wears a blue robe with stars on it, and a long pointy hat, and he carries a staff in one hand.

He strides out of the window onto the sidewalk, and he points the long staff at Thurg, and he says, "Thurg! Sheathe thy sword! Can I not take mine eyes off thee for two minutes without thou quittest thy proper dimension and troublest these good folk?"

Now these words are highly impolite, and I am expecting that Thurg will give the old geezer a good poke in the stomach with his sword. Instead his mouth drops open and his eyes bug out, and he looks like nothing more than a Bismarck herring.

He waves the sword about, but it is a feeble wave, at that, and he says, "Alphazor! Let Thurg alone. Thurg find Eye of God."

Well, then I realize that the old geezer is nobody but the evil wizard Alphazor, but I wish to say that he does not look evil to me, or anyway, not much. He bows to us all, and he says like this:

"Good people, forgive my servant his discourtesy. I will remove him immediately. Thurg, follow me!"

This statement is surprising to one and all, as nobody ever calls us "good people" before. But Thurg, instead of obeying the evil wizard Alphazor, jumps onto the cab horse, whacks it over the rump with the flat of his sword, and skedaddles lickety-split down the street and away.

The evil wizard Alphazor raises his staff, and a bolt of lightning flashes out of the end, but Thurg is going so fast that the evil wizard Alphazor misses him and only fuses a fire hydrant.

"Excuse me," says the evil wizard Alphazor, and he takes off after Thurg, with sparks spitting out of the end of his staff, and I am quite astonished to see that his feet are six inches off the ground, and all around him are little twinkly blue stars.

And he vanishes down the street, and we do not see him or Thurg again.

Now Eugene Edmonton is by no means killed, and as Thurg and the evil wizard Alphazor disappear, he sits up and says to Miss Paulette Patrick as follows:

"I am sorry," says Eugene Edmonton, "that I do not do a heroic deed for you."

"Oh, Eugene!" says Miss Paulette Patrick. "I do not like heroic deeds, for I see now they are nothing but the phonus bolonus. A girl can be greatly inconvenienced by taking part in such events. I do not wish a knight in shining armour any more. I wish for such a guy as will take me dancing, and maybe buy me a diamond bracelet now and then."

And then she hauls off and gives Eugene Edmonton a big kiss ker-splat right in the smush.

Now this kiss revives Eugene Edmonton more than somewhat, so he gets up and helps Miss Paulette Patrick into the cab for a little private guzzling.

Meanwhile all the citizens around and about are deciding that since wizards do not appear and disappear in twinkly blue lights, or at least not in this man's town, then they do not see it, and they have pressing business to attend to elsewhere. So the cops have little to do, though one of them would like to put the arm on me, and Spanish John and Little Isadore. But there are many citizens who swear that we do not go anywhere near Rosenberg's window, and so they have to let us go.

"So that is all the story," says Harry the Horse, "and that is why I am looking for Eugene Edmonton. For what Eugene Edmonton does not know is that just before Thurg takes it on the lam, I borrow his pouch with the Eye of God. And since I am somewhat short of scratch at present, I wish to ask Eugene Edmonton if he will buy the Eye of God for Miss Paulette Patrick, for a wedding present."

THE WINDS OF FATE

Tony Rath

When I read this story I kept thinking of The Goon Show. *It has all the feeling of the irreverent and surrealistic humour that works so well on radio and in our imagination. There is no way this story could work on television. It has to be in our minds. Although Tony Rath has sold several stories in collaboration with his wife Tina, this is his first solo appearance. For many years Tony has performed as an opera singer – so he knows all about wind!*

December is not a good month to go sailing off the French coast, particularly in a tubby old two-decker affectionately known by her crew as the Pissyant. HMS *Puissant* was an old ship and was, in the view of their Lordships, the most expendable of His Britannic Majesty's ships of the line. In the officers' wardroom the three male passengers were not comfortable. Indeed, they were grimly clinging to various parts of furniture as the plunging vessel battled through the winter seas.

The captain had company in his command. Four wild dervish-like figures, chanting and spitting onto the deck, were coaxing, cajoling and cooing to the winds to smooth out the sea in front of the bowsprit and create an envelope of gentle, purposeful breezes to propel the ship to France. They were expensive, temperamental and extremely smelly but HM's Wind Wizards were plying their trade for King and country.

The largest of the male passengers, Sir Danvers Roke, fourth of that name, was wondering again what had made him answer that midnight summons from the Admiralty. The ship's bell sounded to denote some change in the orders and he dozed fitfully.

It was the best of chimes, it was the worst of chimes. Sir Danvers had been restless after an eventful night involving a family dinner party presided over by the delightful Lucy, his lively bride of six months. The dinner was part of a series of events to celebrate the coronation of Charles the Tenth, the latest in a long line of Charlies who had risen to the Stuart throne. Sir Danvers was engaged in a serious internal discussion with some buttered lobster, which refused to lie down and digest, when the church clock struck midnight.

As the noise of the church bells subsided, there could be heard the sound of the front door being assaulted by someone demented. Baskerville, Sir Danvers's trusty manservant, hastily went to the door and unlocked it cautiously, keeping one hand free for a loaded pistol.

"Who are you, sir, and what do you want at this hour of the night?" he demanded of the tall but rather skeletal old man who was trying to raise his hand to assault the knocker again.

"I, sir, am from the government," announced the elderly visitor.

"Well, we don't require any at this hour of the night. May I take a message for you, sir?"

"I require to speak to Sir Danvers most urgently. I am Withering."

"I am sorry to hear that, sir. Who shall I say is calling?"

"Dammit, man, I am Lord Withering from the Admiralty. I have a message that must be delivered to Sir Danvers most urgently NOW!"

Sir Danvers strode downstairs and Baskerville stood to one

side. As the two men faced each there was an instant drop in the temperature.

"I am Lord Withering from the Admiralty, sir. The First Sea Lord would like a word with you most urgently. A carriage awaits."

Sir Danvers suddenly belched lobster. Annoyed at this disturbance, he smiled sweetly at the visitor and said, "Tell me, Lord Withering, what is your first name?"

"Jasper, sir, but what is that to you, pray?" said the old man who was ageing visibly before their eyes.

"Because I always like to know the first names of those whom I am about to fling down the steps of my house. You have two seconds, sir, to remove yourself or your coach will be carrying your bones back in a startlingly new formation!" Sir Danvers advanced and Lord Withering was forced to retreat. A man more suited to hiding behind hatstands was no match for seventeen stone of very angry beef, beef enhanced with lobster at that – a most unhealthy combination.

"But, sir, I must protest," Withering dithered. "At another time I should know how to answer your insults, but I am on government business and it is a most urgent matter."

"What matter, sir, can justify you intruding on my privacy at midnight when I have already retired?"

"One of our agents, LeBroque by name, is in France. He is injured and we have to extract him and you seem to be the only person he trusts. Will you come with me, sir?"

Sir Danvers harumphed in his own inimitable way, and then signalled to Baskerville, who disappeared and returned with his master's cape and new beaver hat. Danvers was about to depart when a small, furious female appeared at the top of the stairs.

"An' just where the friggin' 'ell do you fink you're goin' at this time of the night, and oo's this long streak of piss and misery coming disturbing us?"

"This, my love, is Lord Withering. He is from the Admiralty. They require to speak to me concerning our old friend LeBroque who has got himself into a scrape in France. Apparently he is injured."

"Picked up galloping knob-rot from some poxy whore, more like," sniffed her ladyship, retreating upstairs.

Sir Danvers coughed and Lord Withering, who had witnessed all this, remembered to close his jaw. He turned to Sir Danvers and said, "Your wife has a remarkable turn of phrase, sir, for such a young, uhm, lady."

"Remarkable," agreed Sir Danvers, following him outside to the coach.

Upon their arrival at the Admiralty they were quickly ushered in to the First Sea Lord who jumped up, greeted Sir Danvers effusively and poured him some wine. After some general conversation he said briskly, "To business sir. Our agent in Brittany is a man you know as LeBroque. He was sending us reports until some time ago about Bony's invasion fleet, also making contact with those who would like to see the French King back on his throne. He kept asking for money to pay people off until the clerks decided that they needed some form of proof to show where the money was going. He took this very badly, said we obviously didn't trust him, which, to be honest, is true. Everything went quiet for a while and we thought that he had been captured or done away with until we received a message by, uhm, certain channels, to the effect that he was injured and could we send someone to get him out as he cannot move very easily. He also mentioned some very disturbing news about the recruitment of Wind Wizards."

"Wind Wizards! Pray what is my involvement in this matter? Surely you have other agents who could help him!"

"Trouble is, he don't trust anyone from government service. Very stubborn, these Channel Islanders. Says he don't like you but he knows you are a man of honour; says he will only deal with you. Thing is we have had trouble recruiting Wind Wizards – need 'em to control winds for large fleets and ships of the line, but the supply seems to have dried up, so the clerks tell me. It appears that Bony has invited them to a series of routs and revelries in France. Most worrying, you know. They are all freelance, so we have no hold over them."

Sir Danvers nodded. He knew that Wind Wizards were a malodorous group of gentlemen, recruited from the far north in Lapland, who had the ability to control the winds and were essential on large ships. He also knew that they were in extremely short supply and noted for their temperament and rapacity in negotiating favourable financial terms for themselves. He said, "I am flattered, I am sure, by Mr LeBroque's regard for my honour, but what is it you require of me?"

"There is a ship waiting to slip across to France. You can be aboard by tomorrow evening and go and talk to this man and see what his situation is. He must be got out of France. Fella knows an awful lot about Bony's fleet and the, uhm, wizard situation."

"Pray, what if I meet this man and he refuses to leave, because of some no doubt imagined injury suffered at the hands of the government?"

The admiral met his gaze unflinchingly and said simply, "I repeat, sir, he is not to remain in France alive. Dead he does not matter to us."

Danvers stood up, outraged, and made to leave. "Good day, sir. I am not a paid assassin. Get someone else to carry out your dirty work."

The admiral, moving quickly for such an elderly man, ushered his guest back to his seat, tutting, "Sir, you misunderstand me. I am sure that no such action is necessary but it will not be up to you."

The odour of raw meat came into the room wrapped round a tall cadaverous figure swathed in a dull grey cloak.

The little admiral pointed at this and said to Sir Danvers, "This is agent Kokki from the Finnish Board of Interrogation. He will accompany you and take certain steps if necessary."

It is indeed difficult to speak with any authority while pinching one's nostrils.

"You mean, he is to kill LeBroque if he is not pliable to your wishes," said Sir Danvers bleakly.

The little admiral merely bowed and said, "Come sir, time is passing. Will ye go?"

"I may regret this decision, but yes, I will go."

"Good, we shall convey you by one of the new steam coaches. Most interestin' experience. Use it meself regularly. Mind you, first time I was sick, second time me hat blew off."

Two hours later, trying to sleep in a rattling, bouncing contraption on the Portsmouth road, Danvers wondered whether he had made a rash decision. They had been met at Blenheim Station and conveyed to the bowels of the earth by a series of steam-powered moving staircases, there to be greeted by the stationmaster, who had received them most graciously and explained that a special coach had been prepared for them and that the tunnels had been cleared. The coach was a large carriage set on rails with a separate engine mounted on wheels, which required, as they explained, two men to stoke it and a driver. The experience of going through darkened tunnels had left all of them shaken; at one point they could hear the river above them. They had emerged at Greenwich and the relief among them had been manifest. The engine men, as they insisted on being called, had carried on with that cheerful smugness that comes with special knowledge.

Agent Kokki was concerned with nibbling on a large raw pork chop, which he offered to Danvers, saying it was the custom in his country to share a joint.

Baskerville sat seething, having received a tongue-lashing from her Ladyship when he went to collect additional clothing, pistols and Danvers's huge sword. She had burst into tears and somehow blamed him for everything, calling him a great lobcock (whatever that meant) and other sundry terms. Her parting shot had been to warn him not to bring Danvers back "wiv any bits chopped orf".

They reached Portsmouth by mid-morning, after several stops for refuelling. Kokki seemed to know the way and, in between bites of calves' liver ("Offally good," he said, with a ghastly smile), had directed the driver to the inn which was their destination.

Their arrival was punctuated by the curses of other vehicle

owners. Steam coaches running on the road were new and the average horse did not appreciate them. Neither did the average horse owner.

Upon arrival they were met by a tall thin man in his late twenties clad in neat but shabby naval uniform with the single epaulette of a post captain on his shoulder.

"Good morning. I am Captain Bruce Partington. Here is the plan. I have been charged with arranging passage for you to the coast of France this evening. There you will be met by representatives of the monarchists who will convey you to your destination."

"How is our passage to be achieved, Captain?"

"I have discussed this with the local admiral who has directed me to convey you part of the way to the coast in my own command and proceed in small boats for the final trip to the beach. I presume this gentlemen will be going with you." He gazed distastefully at Kokki, who had produced some sheeps' eyes from a large bloodstained bag, which, he explained with a droll smile, would see him through the evening.

"I will see you at nine this evening," said the captain, backing out hastily to the sounds of crunching.

Promptly at nine o'clock in the evening there was a gentle tap on the door and the naval gentleman appeared. They proceeded down to the harbour to be picked up by the captain's pinnace. Sir Danvers and his company, not being proficient in matters nautical, stepped gingerly down into the vigorously bobbing craft. The water had a light chop but the oarsman soon had them to the side of the ship. The wardroom proved to be very long and low and quite unsuited to one of Sir Danvers's dimensions. As he explained to Baskerville: "Feels like a coffin with sails."

The rank odour of uncooked flesh and unwashed clothes suddenly permeated the atmosphere and they could hear the rhythmic chanting and exhortations as his Majesty's loyal Windmaster pounded up and down on the deck above them and screamed incantations in an increasing frenzy. There was a lurch and a puff of breeze and the ship was under way. Danvers asked Kokki what the words meant, but he shrugged and said, "Buggered if I know, master, I dink they make it oop mineself."

"Your command of English is very unusual, I must say. Pray which school did you go to?"

"I spent two years on an English merchantman out of Liverpool, under Captain Richard Starkey. He drummed it into me."

Sir Danvers concluded silently that Captain Starkey had introduced Kokki to the *Joe Miller Jest Book* as part of his tuition.

The journey was uneventful and they were only roused by the captain announcing they were ready to land. Danvers noticed that all the boat crew were carrying pistols and cutlasses or boarding axes and wearing nondescript dark clothing and that both the boats had been fitted with a light cannon, which, on enquiry, he was told was loaded with grapeshot. Evidently some trouble might be expected. The captain and a warrant officer each took charge of one of the boats.

There was no incident until the boats reached the shore. Sir Danvers and his companions were stepping out onto the wet pebbles when there was a volley of shots and one of the seamen clapped his hand to his thigh and yelled in outrage. He was dragged on board and the craft took off into the just-discernible dawn.

"Oh hell, here's trouble," said Danvers as he saw a French guard boat appear and pursue their friendly vessels. They could hear a fusillade of shots and muffled crack from the light cannon, followed by curses and yells in French.

The three men ran for a stand of trees at the top of the beach and took stock of the situation. They had the clothes they stood up in, some ammunition and shot, enough food and water for one day's sustenance and no sign of the official welcoming party.

Sir Danvers braced his back against a stout tree and checked the priming of his pistols. He glanced surreptitiously at Kokki, who seemed entirely unconcerned by their situation. After a two-hour wait by Danvers's watch they drank some of their water. Then they heard the jingle of harness. It was Baskerville's turn to be suspicious and he shot a hard look at the agent's back, but he, too, was now looking tense and nervous, gnawing at a sausage, which looked like the very rude part of a large male horse.

The three men instinctively dropped to kneel on the ground. Baskerville wordlessly passed a pistol to Sir Danvers, who eased the long barrel round the thick trunk of the tree, ready to take aim. He saw three riders leading saddled horses and a huge dog. The riders' costume was of a faded grandeur that bespoke nobility and wealth fallen on hard times. Sir Danvers looked towards his companions and handed the pistol back to Baskerville. He took a deep breath, tugged his sword hilt straight and stepped out from the trees, holding his hands up in the air. It was a tense moment. There was a muted shout as he was seen. The leading rider spurred his horse up to Danvers and spoke.

"You are ze Englees milord?"

Sir Danvers bowed slightly.

"I am Armand de la Tocque. Zese are my brothers, Pierre and Henri and . . . uhm . . . Alois. We are the Three Cavaliers."

"But there are four of you," Danvers observed.

"Alois doesn't count," Armand responded.

"He doesn't read or write, either," added Pierre.

Much bowing and scraping followed and Sir Danvers signalled to Baskerville and Kokki to join them on the pebbly beach. It was getting light and although the brothers were no doubt charming companions he did not want to attract the attention of any more guard boats. He was also somewhat nervous of Alois, who was a rather wolflike creature with deep-set hazel eyes and a nose that would have been a great boon in the national cheese-rolling contest. Agent Kokki seemed delighted to meet him and dropped to all fours to engage in a protracted bout of bottom-sniffing. Alois was rewarded with some giblets and bounded off to scout ahead.

The journey took some hours and several times they were forced to conceal themselves as troops of French cavalry passed by. They were provided with advance warning by Alois, who seemed able to communicate with his brothers by a series of meaningful yelps and short barks.

Eventually they reached a small converted manor house with a dry moat and clattered across the stone bridge into the courtyard. They were welcomed, if so it can be described, by LeBroque who was standing with his arm round a pretty, plump girl who seemed most attached to him in every sense.

Sir Danvers dismounted. He looked closely at Mr LeBroque and said accusingly, "I was told, sir, that you were injured, yet you appear to me to be in excellent health. Pray, what is the meaning of this?"

Mr LeBroque glared icily at him and bowed stiffly.

"I see you have not lost your charm sir. It was this gentleman," he added, nodding at Kokki, "I wished to see most particularly. Enter, please."

He turned and went inside. Danvers noticed that although he tried to conceal it, LeBroque moved slowly, as if in some discomfort. LeBroque's comments about Kokki had set his nerve ends quivering.

The Three Cavaliers disappeared to stable the horses and joined them later as they ate a leisurely breakfast. The frosty atmosphere had eased slightly as Sir Danvers had explained the circumstances of their meeting.

LeBroque said, "Today is the 22nd of December. I have reliable information that as soon as 1803 strikes on midnight of the 31st, all non-Frenchmen will be interned, with their goods and property. This will include all the Wind Wizards who are currently visiting on an extended stay. It was Bony's intention to lure them in and hold them hostage until they could be employed by him on a special excursion. Bony never intended to keep the truce any longer than he had to."

Agent Kokki cleared his throat and said, "Dis excrusion – vot is it, wack?" Sir Danvers noticed that a decidedly Liverpool tone crept into his voice as he grew more serious.

"The excrusion, uhm, excursion is this. Bony has acquired a number of things from his Egyptian campaign, including a lot of useless old oil lamps, and a large number of flying carpets. These come with a manual, of course, written in old Aramaic. Unfortunately there are no Old Aramaics around to translate, and as there are very few who know this language the flying carpets are somewhat erratic. An experiment was carried out with a Bohemian officer, one Dudcek, who tried to fly one of these devices and fell off as it suddenly turned over. He was impaled on a flagpole. The locals thought he was a wind-vane at first. They are now making experiments on how to control the carpets and have worked out a stratagem that involves a large number of Wind Wizards. Hence the projected internment."

Kokki snorted and said, "Hey pal, dere's no chance of that, like. Me mates is gonna tell dis scally to go and fook himself. Dese carpets, how many 'as he got, like?"

LeBroque said, "He had about four hundred but some of his flyers became expert very quickly and flew away. Some joined us and are now, of course, Allied Carpets. Approximately three hundred and eighty are left. He has joined some of them together to cover an area sufficient to hold a large number of troops. The plan is to mount sails on them and fly troops across to England with a Wind Wizard who can direct the elements so that they land in the right places. The French know how to raise and lower the carpets but cannot direct them. They will use Wind Wizards to do that. Needless to say, the Wizards will be under close surveillance. They will be shot if any treachery is attempted."

There was a silence for a while, broken only by Kokki crunching on a beef-bone that he had produced from his bag. Bonaparte had tried to defeat the British Navy before, but his ships could not clear the Channel. This plan, although fraught with peril, could work. Danvers cleared his throat and said, "I refer to my earlier comments regarding your injuries. An explanation is, I am sure, readily available."

Danvers had already heard rumours that LeBroque had had an accident whilst fleeing from some dalliance in which Alois was somehow involved. It appeared to involve a leap over a wall at which Alois was more adept than LeBroque. The strapping and bandages subsequently required had made it impossible for LeBroque to move all parts of himself in unison. But Danvers had dismissed this as malicious gossip.

For several moments Sir Danvers and LeBroque held each other in a steely gaze. LeBroque stiffened, then relaxed and said reluctantly, "I am indeed injured, although recovering. I had an argument with swords with a local gentleman who insulted not only my companion, but our Royal Family. He is of the Jacobite tendency and no friend of the current government, or of his Britannic Majesty."

Sir Danvers was not convinced but let it pass. He sighed and said, "Do they still cling to their ridiculous claim? James of Monmouth was lucky to escape after Sedgemoor, his son got hopelessly lost at Gravelly Hill and his son, when he landed at East Bourne, totally failed to arouse its inhabitants."

LeBroque shrugged and continued, "It is worse than this. Jacobites will lead the troops on the carpets. They have sworn to overthrow the King and set up the current Duke, Andrew, as the new monarch. Now to my own concerns. I have been feeding reports concerning fleet movements, which seem either not to be believed, or to be ignored. My demands for legitimate expenses have only been half-met. My pockets are to let, all my money is spent and I need to report to London directly, gentlemen."

They were digesting this information when Kokki suddenly stiffened, arched his back and let off a truly thunderous eructation of wind. The sound seemed to go on for ever and on the final rasp his head jerked and he broke into a rapid stream of explosive phrases and grunts, his head shaking from side to side. Eventually his head slumped, he coughed, grinned and said, "Sorry about dat, folks, der vind joost slipped out, like. Me head was full of wirds from me mates, who are being held not too far away. Dey joost let me know dat tings is bad."

Baskerville went and quietly opened windows and the acrid stench eventually dispersed.

Danvers coughed and said, "How do you communicate with your friends? By spirit messages or some such? I have heard of such things but I had never believed them. And is the, uhm, digestive attack part of the process?"

Kokki beamed and said, "Well, de voices coom because de others unite dere minds, like, and send me messages. It just works, nobody knows how like, we call it mindspeak. But my body's allergic to it, like, but instead of sneezing I just let rip. I've been known to rise from de floor when a particularly volatile message comes through."

"What's this latest message about?"

"Dey say that de Frogs have threatened them like, dat dey will be shot unless dey guide de carpets across to England on New Year's Day. Dey reckon everybody will be off-guard and dey can make a successful invasion, like."

Danvers drew in a deep breath, immediately regretted it and said, "Why have they not communicated with us earlier?"

"Free drink, unlimited women and horsemeat for days, wack, and dey wasn't sayin anythin' to anyone except, more horsemeat with a side order of chips."

Danvers cringed and tried not to think of Wind Wizards indulging carnal appetites, or, indeed, of what staunch females would engage in such practices with them. He said, "Can you speak to them now?"

"Yeah, dey is woke up and sober now, but you'd all have to leave de room. It could get noisy and a bit overwhelming in here. Vot shall I say?"

"Tell them that we shall endeavour to escape ourselves. They must not risk their lives, but carry out their orders. We will think of a way to receive them without risk to their personal safety. By the way, do the Admiralty know of the special power of mindspeak?"

"Ve haff mentioned it to dem, but some lughead named Captain Branson said it vos not possible, so ve don't charge for it."

"Do you have any other special gifts, apart from waking the dead with your arse?"

"Vell, dis is big secret like but . . ." and he leaned closer to Danvers who made a private resolution to have all he stood up in, including the boots, burned to ashes and to bathe four times a day for the rest of his life. Danvers felt his spirits lift and his nose contract as his nostrils tried to hide, to leave his face, to do anything to escape the horrible stench.

He left the room taking deep gasping breaths and signalled to LeBroque and the brothers that he wished to have a word. It took twenty minutes' hard talking to sketch out a plan and to draft the basic tactics. All the while a noise like an elephant's tea party came from the room in which Kokki strained to make contact.

After a fierce argument over details concerning the planned reception of the carpet squadrons, Danvers looked at LeBroque and said, "It all depends, of course, on our extricating ourselves. I assume you have some reliable means of escaping our situation as I also assume we cannot simply present ourselves at a port and leave."

"It would be found that our papers were not in order, we would be forced to delay our departure and then of course it would be too late. I fear also that the house is being watched. Alois tells me that there are agents in the grounds."

"I would be interested to know how Alois can communicate with you so eloquently. His, uhm, body is not adapted for long conversation, I think."

"Alois is only a wolf sometimes and anyway, as brothers, we have a special bond."

"I see. And do you have the ability to change your appearance in such a way as Alois? I would see you as a Jack Russell myself."

"I can, but choose not to. Raw meat does not suit me and I always end up with a bad attack of the mange."

"How dogmatic. I am going to risk life and limb by going into that room again to ask Kokki to see if he can send a message to any of his colleagues in London. If I do not emerge within thirty seconds, tell my wife that it was for England." And with those words Danvers strode towards the source of the noise.

Kokki was eating again and nodded as Danvers, standing as far away as possible, asked him if he could mindspeak to London. Kokki said nothing for a while, then nodded and said, "Yiss, it is possible. I joost spoke to me brooder, Juha, who is junior assistant vind vizard (3rd Grade). Joost giff him warming, joost a minute, please." Danvers only just made it out the door before eruptions started.

He returned with a candle. This was not a good idea, as the resulting explosion removed half his eyebrows and singed a seriously ugly ancestral wall-mounted portrait. Danvers wrote hurriedly in his pocketbook and, tearing out the sheets, handed them to Kokki, who grinned and rose three feet off the ground as internal gases propelled him into the air.

After some more buttock music Kokki shouted that they would be picked up at the beach at two the following morning, and could he have some sparkling wine to settle his stomach.

The hours passed slowly, their tedium only enlivened by the appearance of the young lady, Arlette, in a very fetching boy's costume. The resulting comments from all sides had brought a blush to her cheek and a dangerous sparkle to the eyes of Mr LeBroque. However, their gallantries were quelled by Alois, who growled very softly deep in his chest, and disappeared. Soon afterwards they were joined by an extremely hirsute young man with deep-set grey eyes. Danvers was fascinated to hear his voice, which was light and breathy. He told them that the agents had been alarmed by the numerous noisy interludes and had left to report to their local supervisor.

Danvers and the others took advantage of this and departed for the beach. Danvers looked at his watch and winced as a little breeze sent searching nasty cold fingers into his body. Two hours to go. He glanced at the others. Arlette was huddling close to LeBroque; the de la Toques were muttering together and Kokki and Baskerville were debating whether to look for driftwood and light a small fire. Suddenly the sound of French voices could be heard. Either they had been followed or the servants had been induced to talk. Kokki grinned and, turning his back, produced a rapid volley of musket-like sounds. There were shouts and screams because, as Danvers noticed with interest, the noise was accompanied by the flamelike effects of a number of firearms being discharged. Kokki was a veritable arsenal. The French voices retreated and there was silence. Kokki grinned and took Baskerville to look for firewood.

The French brothers, after many whispered speeches, clattered away, and the rest of Danvers's group shivered in the dark until the sound of oars slowly splashing through the water alerted them. The boat stopped some distance away out to sea and a smaller shape got out and splashed through the shallow waters to reveal itself as a soaking midshipman.

"Captain's compliments and could you make your way to the boats, please. Can't come in any further for fear of guard boats." He turned and splashed back the way he had come.

Sir Danvers gritted his teeth and plunged into the freezing water. He swore and slipped his way until he came to the side of a very large rowing boat with mounted swivel-guns. He climbed aboard, to be joined by the others. Arlette's boyish appearance produced some excited murmurs, which were stifled by a few sharp words and a blow to the back of the head of one rather forward seaman who took a little too much trouble assisting her aboard. Kokki was not so welcome and quickly found a space for himself. Courtesy had miraculously appeared among the crew.

They had hardly got under way when there was a *swoosh* and a huge splash nearby which caused the boat to plunge wildly so that the oarsmen missed their stroke and the craft slowed. The commander let out an oath as another explosion set the vessel tipping crazily again and the men clung to the sides and stopped rowing or dropped their oars. Danvers pulled one of the smaller men out of his place, grabbed the flailing end of his oar and started pulling with all his might. Kokki and Baskerville followed suit and the three civilians puffed and strained. A bosun started smacking the seamen and screaming in their faces above the din of falling shot. Gradually the boat picked up speed and the flickering lights of the chasing enemy craft diminished. But still they were too close for comfort.

Suddenly, from above, a volley of fire came out of the faint dawn and raked the pursuing boats, sinking several and causing panic among the survivors. The boat crew started shouting and gesturing upwards until forcibly restrained by the warrant officer who screamed at them to row like buggery. The captain had stood up to wave his thanks when he fell forward howling and clutching his thigh. A small French craft had crept up unseen and fired on them, causing several casualties.

Danvers glanced up cautiously and froze. There appeared to be four elongated craft suspended above them. They were painted black and he could see slung underneath them a cabin with large portholes. A barrel protruded from one of these portholes and hellish fire rained down on the enemy who circled and fruitlessly shot musket balls into the air.

Danvers looked round and saw with dismay that some of the enemy boats' lights were gaining on them. He redoubled his efforts and resumed pulling and the men followed. They began to move slowly away as a patter of musket shot skittered across the murky water. They reached the side of the ship drenched in sweat, their hands bleeding and sore, and were helped aboard. The second-in-command, after seeing his superior go below for a painful session with the surgeon, bellowed out orders and the old ship started to move slowly. The airships loomed menacingly over the remaining pursuers and poured deadly fire upon them in streamers and lances of flame. The pursuers replied with a final defiant, if ragged, volley of shots, some of which crashed into the vessel's side.

Before he went below Sir Danvers asked one of the younger officers, a serious young gentleman who gave his name as

O'Brian, about the airships. He shrugged and said, "They are one of our very special squadrons. They are kept aloft by a very powerful gas newly discovered and they are propelled and controlled by junior Wind Wizards. The men who crew them are commanded by Captain Lucas and they are known as Skywalkers. Only the most intrepid will take on the duty – it is a very hazardous section of the navy. Those who operate by night are called the Stealth Squadron."

The civilians were ushered into the officers' wardroom, which was being used by the surgeon, just in time to see the semi-conscious and pale figure of the captain being carried to his cabin. Their hands were soothed with grease and their insides with grog and they recovered their breath.

LeBroque had taken no part in the foregoing festivities as he had been covering his lady friend's body with his own. This had no doubt been very noble and brave of him, but Danvers reckoned he would have preferred him to take a turn on the oars. He escorted her to the wardroom where the surgeon, summing up the situation, had offered her brandy and water and a not too clean blanket to cover herself. Alois, who had also taken no part, confined his activities to shaking himself thoroughly and soaking everyone around him. Kokki, who had fired off numerous shots from his arsenal as he acted as rear gunner, was nibbling on some rather rancid pork procured from the officers' servant.

A series of crashes and screams came from outside and Danvers and Baskerville grasped their weapons and rushed on deck. A large number of Frenchmen, led by a big man waving a cutlass, were coming over the side. They'd flown there on huge wings, which they shed on landing.

Danvers unsheathed his sword, tied the cord attached to the hilt to his wrist and plunged forward towards the large Frenchman who, seeing him, across the main deck ran to meet him. He hurled himself at Danvers, who skipped to one side and made a short stabbing movement with his sword into his opponent's groin. The Frenchman parried the stroke and they locked their arms and swayed but Danvers sensed that sheer weight of numbers was pushing the Englishmen back to defeat.

Suddenly there was a patter of feet behind the main body of French and they were assailed from the rear by men descending on rope ladders from the airships that had lowered themselves to allow their crew to assist the ship's fighting men. On seeing this and also getting the full odour of the young Wind Wizards who headed the crew, the remaining Frenchmen promptly surrendered.

The mopping-up took another half an hour and then HMS *Puissant* hoisted sail and took to the open sea. After they had landed, Danvers took LeBroque to one side and asked him if he still had their proposal to foil the invasion. LeBroque tapped his coat and after profuse handshakes all round with the ship's crew they stepped into the coach and headed swiftly for London.

On hearing the coach stop Lucy raced downstairs and wordlessly flung herself into the arms of the huge figure. The servants all stood around, waiting for instructions. Sir Danvers raised his head and with a slight nod indicated that they should withdraw.

His wife, taking her opportunity to speak, said somewhat breathlessly, "And just where the flamin' 'ell have you been? Nearly missed Christmas, cully. I've got something hot in the oven for you, mate, which I've been cooking for a few days."

The next day at breakfast, after a suitably edited version of events had been given to her, Lucy said, "Where's this LeBroque, then?"

"We parted on the Admiralty steps, my love. I believe he wished to pursue certain – hem – activities."

Danvers recounted matters. The meeting with the little Admiral had been most interesting. LeBroque had produced his reports and accounts, and Arlette and Alois had provided corroboration for some of the events. Kokki had been interrogated by an equally odorous senior agent and confirmed the internment of the Wind Wizards. The plan formulated by

Danvers and the others to rescue the Wind Wizards and to foil the invasion was discussed with much head-shaking until Kokki threatened to start using mindspeak with rectal flourishes there and then.

Shortly afterwards the plan was agreed and Kokki was left alone in a room not used by anybody, not likely to be used in the foreseeable future (say for fifty years or so), to communicate the final details to his colleagues in France. It took four hours and two pounds of finest beef to send the message successfully.

Christmas had come and gone and New Year's Eve was upon them. Sir Danvers stared up at the sky from his vantage point and decided that, say what you liked, you would never get him up in one of those things. The carpets looked most flimsy. Troops were sitting on them, some holding ropes to which were attached sails, the Wind Wizards were chanting and exhorting and the whole aerial armada was just sailing serenely over the waves at five hundred feet or so, when it happened.

As one, the Wizards simply stepped off the carpets and stood motionless in the air, chanting. The chant changed note, and they levitated higher and higher until they were over a thousand feet in the air, suspended, motionless.

Suddenly the sky was full of cries in French and English, as carpets went up, carpets went down, carpets went sideways, in fact went anywhere except towards the English coast. Voices could be heard squealing in surprise and fright as bodies plummeted into the icy Channel. There were fruitless volleys of shots into the air to bring down the Wind Wizards, but they simply moved higher, hummed deeper and broke wind in a grand finale of anal eruption.

There is a golden rule with flying carpets. DO NOT MOVE ABOUT. This had not registered with the troops and the Jacobites, who began shouting at each other and letting go of the sails and the rigging and the large aerial rudders that gave the craft direction. Some of the troops jumped carpet and splashed into the chilly Channel where they were picked up, shivering, by small boats and submersibles.

The Wizards climbed even higher, and then the note of their humming changed to a menacing roar, the wind changed direction, and with a mighty *whoosh* it swept most of the carpets helplessly back towards the French coast. The sky lit up as bright as day.

The carpets with stitching started to come apart and many a poor soul disappeared shrieking as they were stranded in mid-air with their legs straddling separating carpets. It was a case of jump or split, and some jumped and some did the splits as they hit the water. Very hard.

Sir Danvers observed all this as a guest aboard the submersible HMS *Enterprise* under Captain James Church. On seeing the fliers disperse, *Enterprise* and the other six submersibles in the squadron rose to the surface and, ignoring the pleas for mercy from the remaining carpeteers, opened their conning towers. The Wind Wizards waited patiently as the craft positioned themselves and one by one they lowered themselves into safety.

The English onlookers marvelled at the power and precision of the Wind Wizards as on a cold winter's night they hung suspended, bathed in light, waiting to enter the submersibles.

Danvers's final image of them before they finally descended was of a few black shapes floating in the winter dark.

"Pity we could not use the Stealth Squadron, Captain."

"Well, Sir Danvers, they would have been blown away with all the turbulence. Only junior Wizards in those things and they couldn't cope. Just a minute, sir, a message for the Jacobite lads up there. HAPPY NEW YEAR, CULLIES. HOME, JAMES, AND DON'T SPARE THE SHAG-PILE!" This last was delivered in a loud bellow.

Several days later, while reading the newspaper at breakfast, Lucy pointed out the paragraph that outlined some details of the battle to Danvers, who shook his head, and said that but for the action and talents of Kokki and his fellow countrymen, England would now be invaded.

He looked at his wife and asked if she were still hungry. She nodded and, holding her hands out, said, "I fancies a bit o' meat about this long."

He blushed. "You exaggerate, my dear!"

"Not by much, mate," said her ladyship.

NOT OURS TO SEE

David Langford

As I said when introducing David Langford's story in the previous volume, the range of his wit and wisdom is awesome. He is, by profession, a nuclear physicist, and his "wisdom" surfaces in a number of serious tomes such as War in 2080 *(1979) and* The Third Millennium *(1985). But he's best known for his "wit", often in the science-fiction fan magazines. He has received umpteen Hugo Awards for his fan writings, some of which have been collected as* The Dragonhiker's Guide to Battlefield at Dune's Edge: Odyssey Two *(1988),* Let's Hear it for the Deaf Man *(1992) and* The Silence of the Langford *(1996). Langford enjoys spoofs. His first book,* An Account of a Meeting with Denizens of Another World, 1871 *(1979) was taken seriously by UFO devotees. He has also parodied nuclear research in* The Leaky Establishment *(1984), and the disaster novel in* Earthdoom! *(1987), written with John Grant (whom you'll find elsewhere in this anthology). Come to think of it, I said all that last time. But at least the following story is different.*

The usual group of old acquaintances was gathered in the lounge bar of the King's Head pub, huddled over pints of traditionally insipid beer and speculating upon the infinite.

"If . . ." said crusty old Major Godalming to me, "if only it were possible! To pierce the veil of futurity, to glimpse the ineffable radiance of days to come, and to make an absolute killing in the National Lottery!"

Carruthers snorted. "Speaking mathematically, I can inform you that if it were possible to predict next week's winning numbers, half the country would very soon be doing it and the payout per one-pound ticket would slump to approximately 13.7 pence." Like all the best statistics, this had the compelling air of having been freshly made up on the spot.

Among our circle that evening was the well-known psychic investigator Dagon Smythe, who preserved his silence but now shuddered theatrically. I recognized the symptoms and took rapid action, crying: "Beastly weather this week, chaps! Would you call it seasonal for the time of year?"

But it was too late. Before the razor-sharp wits around the table could pounce upon this always fruitful topic, Smythe interrupted in his peculiarly penetrating tones. "Speaking of prediction . . . I once dabbled a little in the divinatory arts."

"And you have a tale to tell," said old Hyphen-Jones with a trace of resignation.

"Of a terrible and frightening experience," Smythe continued unstoppably. "But I anticipate. Let us begin from first principles. Methods of prediction are quite numerous. Palmistry, for example, has its adherents . . ." I am of the opinion that our friend had learned his anecdotal persistence from the Ancient Mariner. He seized my hand and announced that the Line of Life indicated a small but imminent financial upset, such as might be caused by buying a round of drinks. As I pointed out with some bitterness, the loud and eager assent of the others made this a regrettably self-fulfilling prophecy.

When I returned from the bar with my slopping burden, Smythe had completed a brief demonstration of cartomancy using only a handful of beer mats, and was well launched into his narration. "The problem with all the well-known modes of divination is, if I might put it paradoxically, that they are too well known."

"Incredible," grunted old Hyphen-Jones.

"I have formulated what might usefully be known as Smythe's Law: that too many prophets spoil the broth. That is, predictions by cartomancy or crystallomancy suffer aetheric interference from all the thousands of other enthusiasts with their Tarot decks and crystal balls. Those faint shadows cast back through time by future events might be likened to frail and shy creatures of the night, suddenly confronted by the psychic equivalent of a horde of press photographers with flashguns. The sheer pressure of attention dispels any possible message. I will not mention Heisenberg's Uncertainty Principle . . ."

"Thank God," I muttered. I have always admired Smythe's genius for selecting awesomely bad analogies.

"Sounds like you've just shot down the whole idea of successful divination," said the acute Carruthers.

"Not at all. To vary the metaphor a little, the trick is to listen on a less crowded waveband. For example: haruspication, the art of prediction through the study of fresh animal entrails, is rarely practised – and please, Major, please don't make your usual joke about the contents of the hamburgers they serve here."

Major Godalming projected sulkiness into his mug of beer.

"So when I set about the series of predictive experiments that had such ultimately unsettling results, I sifted the more obscure divinatory modes. Have you ever heard of spodomancy, the finding of portents in ashes? Or ophiomancy, all done by study of serpents? (You just can't get the serpents these days.) Or rhabdomancy, the use of divining rods? That's supposed to be good for locating water and oil, but one doesn't see where to point the rod to take aim at the future. Sideromancy involves watching the movement of straws placed on red-hot irons, but it turned into spodomancy too quickly for me – or capnomancy, which is divination by smoke, if I hadn't been too busy coughing. Ceromancy uses melting wax, which gets all over everything. Myomancy depends on the actions of mice; all my mice seemed to do was eat and pee a lot (but let's not talk about uromancy). Cromyomancy is prediction by cutting up and studying onions . . . I tried that diligently, but it all ended in tears.

"Once I even came to this very public house and attempted both oenomancy – using libations of wine – and gyromancy, being divination performed by walking in a circle until dizziness supervenes. And I want you to know that the conclusions which you lot all loudly drew were both distracting and unfair."

Meanwhile Carruthers appeared to be demonstrating divination by utter apathy and torpor, or – as it is technically known – dormancy. I suggested gently, "Perhaps we could skip the failures and hear about the experiment that worked?"

"Er, yes. Actually it is a trifle embarrassing. In addition to the need, according to Smythe's Law, to use a rare and obscure divinatory focus, you have to find something that specifically works for you. Someone who can achieve nothing at all through stichomancy (using random literary extracts . . . I thought you'd never ask) might find his hotline to the future lay in lampadomancy (which is divination through the use of a torch flame). In the end, ah, I came across my own personal "mancy" when I was, um, feeding the cat."

"Divination through observation of cats!" marvelled Hyphen-Jones. "That would be, let me think . . . *ailuromancy*."

"Not quite," Smythe mumbled. "I appear to have been the first prophetic investigator to stumble upon *ailurotrophemancy*, or divination through the study of cat food."

We sat aghast.

"Not just *any* cat food, mind you. It was a rather expensive brand called Vitamog, to which my little tom-cat Pyewacket was unreasonably addicted. The effect was remarkable! As I spooned out those glistening, glutinous lumps of what purported to be gourmet-cooked liver . . . by the way, divination by inspecting the livers of animals is known as hepatoscopy . . . where was I? Oh yes: I saw . . . visionary things in the Vitamog. You may well snigger, gentlemen, but I saw it: glinting fragments of the future. There was one flash of a newspaper headline – ROYAL SEX SCANDAL: MONARCHY DOOMED? – and sure enough, it appeared on the front page of *The Times* on the very next day."

"As indeed it does in most weeks," said Carruthers the die-hard sceptic.

"There were other confirmations, though rarely anything truly useful. A vision, accurate to the penny, of the total amount of my next grocery bill. A glimpse of a blazing car that, within the week, I saw again in a James Bond movie on TV. And for natural reasons of sympathetic magic, I often saw the future doings of cats in my back garden. Disappointing, really, once the first amazement had worn off. We psychic investigators are above mere sordid matters of finance, but –" here a note of sadness entered Smythe's voice "– one good stock-market tip or set of winning lottery numbers would have been useful objective confirmation."

"Hear, hear," said the Major, with feeling.

"One point of minor interest was that, although I experimented with other brands of feline food, only Vitamog ever glistened with numinous visions. Even Powermog, from the same manufacturers, was of no divinatory use at all. One wonders what the closely guarded secret formula for Vitamog might be . . . But at the time this seemed a trivial issue compared to my growing sense that there were good reasons for my seeing only these tantalizing glimpses beyond the present day. Something else, something greater and darker, overshadowed everything I scried in the oracle of the Vitamog. Day after day, as tin after tin of the miraculous cat food passed through Pyewacket and into history, I saw that my view of the future was being obscured by a monstrous, formless fore-telling that – if I may lapse for one moment into the technical jargon of the occult – was heavily *doom-laden* and exuded a pungent *reek of wrongness*."

"*My* cat keeps herself perfectly clean," said Hyphen-Jones.

"*Psychic* wrongness, my friend. Day by day the sense of doom grew: a terrible blank, as though something were coming irrevocably to an end. By reference to the few glimpses to which I was able to assign future dates, I gleaned that absolutely no forthcoming events after a certain date – the sixteenth of June this year – could be seen. It was as though the world were fated to be swallowed up by one of those nameless but inconceivably deadly astral entities from the Outer Spheres. A fearful burden of knowledge, as you might imagine. And then I was seized with a more personal fear."

"This would be the old one about not being able to see beyond the end of your own life?" suggested Carruthers, who like the rest of us had heard scores of Smythe's psychic anecdotes and developed a certain uncanny skill at divination through literary familiarity. (Would that be called romancy?) "Yet here we are in the month of November and there you sit, which does rather lessen the suspense."

"It is a distinct problem of this narrative form," Smythe agreed with a sigh. "But there was a tragedy, nonetheless. If only I had been able properly to interpret the meaning of that awful blankness!"

Hyphen-Jones said, "Obviously it was the cat who snuffed it. Poor old Pyewacket."

"Hush," said Smythe. "I took careful occult precautions as 16 June approached and time – all of time, everywhere – seemed to be running out. The utter emptiness of the revealed future was deeply unnerving. On the evening of 15 June I constructed a pentacle and multiple layers of psychic wards to defend against whatever threatened. I was resolved to stay within these supernatural defences for the whole of the fatal day, plus a few extra hours for luck. As midnight approached, I opened the last tin of Vitamog remaining in the house, and stared into a final scrying-bowl of the catalytic cat food – to see only one blurred and tantalizing glimpse of a daily newspaper, before all of futurity was swallowed in that frightful blank. Then I entered the pentacle to await destiny. You can imagine the psychic turmoil that racked me through the twenty-four hours that followed . . ."

"We can," I said. "Effortlessly."

"Well, it was a strain. Pyewacket mewed a great deal and

refused to remain within the wards; at one stage he departed through the back-door cat flap and returned with a present in the form of one of the neighbours' goldfish . . . which I decided not to use for ichthyomancy. Otherwise, events were few."

"And when the fateful day was over?"

"Ah, now comes the interesting part of the story. At dawn on 17 June, I cautiously emerged from my pentacle and found the world unchanged . . . except that, as usual, the previous day's newspaper had been delivered and lay on the doormat. With a thrill of recognition, I saw that the layout of the front page corresponded to the last fading vision that I had obtained through ailurotrophemancy!" Smythe fumbled in his wallet. "I have the relevant clipping here. It was the smallest story on the front page, but not without a certain piquant intellectual interest. See!"

CAT-ASTROPHIC. Following a scare about poisonous contaminants in some tins, MoggiMunch Ltd have today completely withdrawn their Vitamog brand of tinned cat food from the market. The sister brands Powermog and MoggiGorge are unaffected.

A somewhat protracted silence followed.

"Now," said Smythe with a rhetorical wave of his hand, "which of you mentioned 'the old one about not being able to see beyond the end of your own life'? The psychic implications are so very fascinating, the more you consider them . . ."

We looked at him. It was hard to know what to say, but eventually I found appropriate words to honour his raconteur skills. "Smythe," I said, "it's your turn to buy the drinks."

There was general applause.

THE CALIBER OF THE SWORD

Larry Lawrence

Larry Lawrence has spent most of his life in a small town in Indiana. He's been writing since the seventh grade, but has only begun seriously submitting stories for publication since 1998. He has written in a variety of genres, but prefers fantasy and horror. He's sold seven short stories to Internet publications with one appearing in an Australian small press "Best of the Web" anthology for Antipodean SF. *Larry has a degree in computers and repairs them, self-employed. He is a voracious reader but collects fantasy and horror objects and figurines which are displayed around his writing area. Which reminds me of a quip by Robert Bloch who used to say that he had the heart of a little boy – he kept it in a jar on his desk!*

The old god of all blacksmiths had just finished his finest creation when a messenger arrived. The messenger looked at Vulcan's forge and said "Longer."

"What?!" roared Vulcan. "Why?!"

"The Lady in the Lake wants it longer. Something about an 'extension of manhood'. Add a couple of inches to it."

"You've got to be kidding! I just spent two hundred years

on this and *now* she wants it longer?" Vulcan turned the exquisite sword. It dazzled in an unknown light source.

"One day, this sword will create a king and she wants it longer."

"Short, long, what difference does it make? It's only going to be a symbol, for Zeus' sakes. She's going to keep it under water until it is needed, then it's going to be put in stone for a few years, and after the King's reign it goes back to the bottom of the lake. I don't know why it matters how long it is for that."

"Well, don't stab me; I'm just a messenger," he said as he left.

Vulcan placed the sword upon his windowsill to cool, grumbling, "Brings me back out of retirement, she does. Brings me all the way from Olympus. Asks me to make something for her. 'Create a sword for me,' she says. Bah!"

Vulcan took another, longer piece of steel from the forge and pounded it with his hammer, shaking everything in his workshop. The newly made sword rattled off the windowsill and fell to the land of England far below where it rested unnoticed for many years.

(Fast-forward those many years . . .)

Brison rode out of the forest into a pasture. He stopped his horse and looked around the English countryside. "I think we're lost, Swayback. I knew I should have turned left at that last fork. So much for trying to take a short cut."

The mangy brown horse snorted in contempt.

"Well, *you* wanted to follow that white rabbit. Who knows where *that* would have taken us?"

The horse snorted again. He shook his head.

"Come on, let's go this way," said Brison.

The rider led his horse across a green meadow sprinkled with red flowers to the far end where it joined another forest. Once at the far end, the horse stopped abruptly. Brison absently kicked the horse to make it go again, gaining a dirty look from the steed. The rider looked at the ground in front of them.

"Well, well, what do we have here?"

The horse looked at the object in question and snorted once more.

"Is that all you can ever do?" asked the rider.

The horse snorted.

The rider nimbly slid off his mount and walked over to the obstacle. From a big pile of manure, he pulled a sword that had been buried to the hilt.

Finally

Startled, the rider dropped the sword back into the manure point first.

Mphff Ungmph Hmmp Hmff!

Brison looked at the sword and withdrew it again.

Please don't drop me again

"So it was you I heard in my head. You can communicate."

Yes, it was me. I can communicate my thoughts to anyone within a reasonable range at my whim. Would you be so kind as to clean me off? I've been in there a long time

"Certainly." The rider took the sword and rubbed it against the grass, then took a cloth from his pouch and polished the blade.

Ahhhh. That's better. Much better than being in a pile of—

"Uh, I didn't quite get that last word."

Confound it, I can't even swear properly! All comes with being made a good sword, I guess. Many times, though, I wish I could have sent a string of curses into the air

"Do you have a name?"

Of course. All swords have a name. Mine is Calibre

"Calibre? But isn't that King Ar—"

*Hah! I am the original. I was supposed to be the fabled sword. Why do you think they call his *Ex*-calibur?*

"Never thought about it before. Anyway, my name is Brison."

Pleased to meet you

"So how did you end up here?"

*Long story. Actually, long fall, boring story. Needless to

say, I am here and you have pulled me from – from – my resting place*

"Does that make me a king?"

Afraid not. I wasn't given the final instructions on how to do that

"Oh."

Cheer up, there still may be something I can do for you in exchange for freeing me from my fertilized state

"Okay. Shall we go?"

Let's

Brison walked over to his horse and dropped the sword into a saddlebag.

No, don't put me in there!

He quickly pulled the sword back out, "What's the matter?"

Uh, sorry, guess I got a little claustrophobic over the years, being buried like that

"Okay, I understand. Hang on a sec." The rider took some leather binding and made a sling across his back, slipping the sword into it. "Better?"

Much better. Thank you

Brison got back upon his horse and trotted into the forest, Calibre bouncing lightly against his back. They came to a small clearing just as it was getting dark. Brison decided to camp for the night. He tethered the horse and unfurled his bedroll. He ate a few bits of dry bread and then lay down after bidding the horse and sword good night.

The morning dawned bright and clear upon the trio. The horse grazed while Brison and the sword talked during Brison's breakfast.

Sh–,shi–,shoot! I just can't do it

"Sure you can. How about this? Try holding your tongue and saying 'I was found in a pirate ship'."

. . .

"Well?"

Swords do not have tongues

"Oh yeah, sorry."

Thanks for trying to help me, though

"Any time. I'm just not sure that I can teach you anything. I'm no priest, but I haven't done anything particularly bad, either."

Any help I get would be greatly appreciated

"I'll try. Are you sure you want to stop being a good sword?"

I'm sure. Spending those years stuck like that has left me bitter. I think just one major act of unkindness would help push me to the other side

"Okay. As long as you're sure."

So what's next?

"I – I don't know." Brison mused to himself for a moment then said, "Betraying someone is always bad. That might help you. Uh—" Brison stopped as he realized that the sword knew only one person.

Despite me wanting to change my nature, I cannot betray the one who found me. That cannot change. I still have some rules I need to follow

"Whew." Brison relaxed.

Any other ideas?

"I suppose if I stole something and used you to help me, then that might help you tarnish yourself."

Yes, I think that would be a very good start

"Okay, sounds good to me, then. I'm sure an opportunity will present itself." Brison broke camp and did a few exercises to keep himself agile. He climbed a nearby pear tree for some fruit to eat later and swung back down to the ground. Brison then mounted his horse and continued his journey. The sword bounced against his back as the horse trotted along the forest path.

So, where are we headed?

"Camelot. For the annual tournament. I go every year."

How long will it take to get there?

"Well, I think I know where we are now, so we have should have six days of riding and camping ahead of us yet."

Good. It will give us time for more lessons. I will also start thinking of a plan

For the next few days, Brison taught the sword what he could and spoke of his life. Brison's parents had been killed in a freak ox-cart accident when he was only five. His grandmother had raised the boy ever since. She had also taken Brison to see the tournament that year to help the boy overcome his grief. They had gone together every year since. Until this year anyway, his twentieth year. His grandmother was sick, and Brison planned to ask King Arthur for help.

★The sick grandmother story, uh-huh★

"How come everyone says that when I tell my story?"

★Never mind, please continue★

Brison had sold and spent everything he could to get his grandmother the best care. Finally, he had asked a neighbour woman to watch over his grandmother. Borrowing a horse from another neighbour, Brison came to the tournament this year specifically to see King Arthur. He was hoping Merlin would have a remedy for his grandmother.

★Sounds very noble★

Brison shrugged, " 'Tis nothing for my grand-mater. She's done a lot for me."

They rode out of the forest on the seventh day and Camelot spread before them across a flat, brown plain. Many different-coloured banners flapped in the breeze and a crowd of serfs, priests, knights, and nobles were mingling among the brightly hued tents and pavilions, waiting for the jousting tournament to start. The castle guards walked casually through the mob, but each kept a sharp eye out for pickpockets.

"There's quite a crowd this year," said Brison.

★Quite★

"There should be ample opportunity for us here."

★Actually, I do have a plan in mind I've worked on while we've travelled★

"Really? Let's hear it."

★Well, you need to get King Arthur's attention so you can tell him your story. Plus we need to do something dishonest so I can change my nature. So I thought maybe we could steal Excalibur★

"What? I seriously doubt if we could pull *that* off."

Now hear me out. From what you have told me about the tournaments, Excalibur is one of the trophies on display for the tournament. All of the King's knights vie for the right to wear it for one week. You will go look at it. I will create a diversion. When everyone's attention has been shifted away, you will switch me with Excalibur. We were made similar in appearance and the switch will not be noticed right away. I know you are quick and agile enough to make the switch. When it is discovered, you can later say you found Excalibur. King Arthur might even offer a reward for its return. Wouldn't that it be worth it to help your grandmother?

"It might work," Brison mused.

*It *will* work*

"Okay. I'll do it."

Brison rode Swayback across the plain to the edge of the crowd. He dismounted and tethered Swayback next to the other horses. A few of the nobles snickered and poked each other in the ribs at the sight of Swayback. Brison sauntered through the crowd, nodding here and there out of common courtesy. He edged through the people toward the huge royal pavilion set up lengthwise along the east side of the jousting field. The King and Queen had not made their appearance yet, but Excalibur was displayed for all to see and admire. Brison did indeed see that the two swords were similar and felt more confident that he could pull the switch.

Okay. Now be ready. I'll tell you when to switch me with Excalibur

Brison looked over the people, wondering what the Sword had planned.

Hey, move, you old cow!

"What?" A rather large lady in the crowd stopped and looked behind her at another gentleman. "How dare you!"

"What?" the gentleman behind her said, genuinely puzzled.

"Edgar," the woman said to her husband who was walking beside her. "This scallywag just called me an old cow."

"Huh!? Hey, no, I never said any such thing!"

Edgar glared at the man, then swung at him. The man retaliated.

On the other side of Brison, another fight was breaking out in the crowd.

"What do you mean, 'my father must've mated with an ox'?" An ogre of a man had grabbed two fistfuls of another's tunic. The helpless one's companion swung a board at the ogre's head. Others joined in the free-for-all. The guards and knights hammered through the crowd, anxious to stop the riot before Royalty arrived.

Now, Brison!

With a start, Brison realized what he needed to do and pulled the switch quite deftly. Trying not to look guilty, he inched his way through the riot and as far away as possible. Some of the more violent men decided to charge a few of the guards and the crowd swayed back and forth with the ebb and flow of the fighting. A sudden surge toward the platform of Excalibur sent it crashing down. This stunned the crowd into submission, and the horrified guards stumbled over themselves to clean up the mess and fix it before King Arthur saw. One of the more observant guards picked up the red velvet pillow and noticed the sword was not quite as long as the indentation Excalibur left in the material.

"Whoa! Wait a minute. This isn't Excalibur!"

"What?!" the crowd gasped as one.

Brison stopped for a moment, paralysed with shock that the switch had been discovered so quickly. He shook off his catatonic state and tried to slink away. The same guard noticed him.

"Hey, you! Grab that man!" He pointed to Brison.

Instantly, the people swarmed over Brison; he never stood a chance. The guards came, arrested him, and led him away inside the castle after retrieving Excalibur. The people followed, eager for some early entertainment. Calibre, the original sword, lay forgotten upon the ground. Swayback chewed through his tether. He walked over and gently picked up Calibre with his teeth.

Brison was sitting in a cell when he heard a familiar voice in his head.

Ho, Brison. Which cell are you in?

"I'm in here," Brison stood upon his hard narrow bed and was just able to see out the cell's only window. The window sat at ground level, and Brison saw Swayback walk over to him with Calibre in his mouth.

"What went wrong?" he asked the sword.

Nothing

"I don't understand."

My dear Brison. This was all according to plan. Either you would be successful or you would be caught. Whichever way it happened, it would help me change my nature. If you had stolen Excalibur and had gotten away, I would have committed a crime by taking the place of the rightful sword if only for a little while. This was my main intention, of course. I still feel I should be the one at King Arthur's side. But you got caught, so my sin is a little worse. Committing a crime and putting the blame upon someone else

"But — but you said you couldn't betray me!"

*Wrong. I said I could not betray the one who found me, and it was really Swayback who found me first. While you slept at night, Swayback taught me *real* lessons on being evil. Plus a few other things*

Brison looked at the horse, "How could you? You know I have a sick grandmother to look after. How can I do that from in here?"

The horse snorted with contempt.

Hey, shit happens

"What — what did you say?" asked Brison.

Swayback walked away with Calibre. Brison sat down upon his hard cell bench while Calibre's deep rich singing voice filled Brison's head with some of the dirtiest limericks Swayback had taught the sword.

GUNSEL AND GRETEL

Esther Friesner

This is Esther's second story in this anthology and it's a brand new one. Need I say any more?

It was a hot, humid, LA afternoon, a day when the ceiling fan just stirs the air around slow, like a witch's brew, the kind of day that makes me ask myself why I ever left the cool shade of the German forests for this city, this office, this job. Lucky for me, all I had to do to find the answer was open the paper and see Hitler's smiling face. There are worse things in this world than muggy weather, hard-nosed cops, and overdue dentist bills.

I was about to meet another one.

I knew she was trouble the minute she ankled into my office. They always are, if they're coming to see me. Somehow I never seem to attract the sweet young things trying to get their own back from some kiss-and-tell toad or the frumpy *hausfraus* out to nail Prince Charming for getting horizontal in someone else's glass coffin; just the dames.

This dame I knew. I watched her baby-blues go wide when she recognized me. I kind of enjoyed it. Yeah, we had a past, and if they ever wrote it up in the history books it'd make Waterloo, Pearl Harbor, and Custer's Last Stand read like *The House at Pooh Corner*.

"Hello, gorgeous," I said, taking my feet off the desk. I accidentally stepped on the cat's tail. He screeched, but things are tough all over. "It's been a long time. What's a nice kid like you doing in a dump like this?"

She had the class to lower her eyes. You come face to face with the person you think you bumped off years ago and a little embarrassment's only good manners. That's what I always say.

"I'm – I'm sorry," she mumbled. "When I saw the name on the door, I never thought—"

"—That it was me? Why should you? Give your mind the five-cent tour down Memory Lane, sweets. Aside from shacking up with me, leading me on, running out on me and leaving me for dead, you didn't once think to ask my name. Never formally introduced, and us nearly a lifetime item. Tsk-tsk, what would Emily Post say?" I grinned until I could feel the tip of my nose touch the tip of my chin.

She gave me a hard stare. "Like *that* would make a difference." She always was feisty, more snap to her than a box of rubber bands. That's okay: I like them feisty. "That's a *man's* name on your door."

"It's a man's world, sugar."

"You're operating under false pretences."

"You should feel right at home." The cat jumped into my lap. I petted him until he started shedding, then I dropped him to the floor. I don't give a damn what they say: Black fur *does* show on a black dress. "So, now you know it's me, I guess you'll be going. Drink before you leave? For old times' sake?" I opened the bottom drawer and took out the bottle and a pair of glasses.

She shook her head.

"Mind if I indulge?" I didn't wait for an answer: I poured a tall one and knocked it back fast and smooth.

She gave me the fish-eye. "How can you drink that stuff?"

"In case you haven't noticed, cupcake, I'm sitting down. You can do the same, or you can leave. The door works both ways."

She sat down on the only other chair in my office, looking about as comfortable as a beautiful princess at a wicked stepmothers' convention. Her hands closed tight over the clasp of a cheap red plastic pocketbook balanced on her nyloned knees. Her whole outfit screamed two-bit canary with a sideline in grifting. I gave her the once-over, saw how she'd changed. The years had been pretty good to her. Last time I saw her, she was a skinny little piece of cheesecake; *too* skinny for my taste.

Tastes change; so had she. She'd filled out nice, real nice. She was still trying to play the innocent, though. That was a laugh. If there was ever a tough cookie, she was it, and believe me, I know tough cookies.

She finally found her tongue. It was right there in her own mouth. For a change.

"I'm not going to lie to you," she said. I managed not to laugh. "Even if you are . . . who you are, I still want you to take my case. I came here because a friend of mine – one of the other girls down at the La Zazz Club – gave me your name. The one on your door, I mean."

"The La Zazz Club," I repeated. The name rang a bell – it was a notorious jive joint – but that was all. I tried to think if I ever had a client who worked there.

I get quiet when I'm thinking. My visitor didn't like things quiet. She started yakking to fill up the silence: "My friend said you helped her out of a tough bind. She said you got the job done and you didn't ask the wrong kind of questions to do it. She said she'd trust you with her life, that you're the best in the business."

"Flatterer."

"I mean it!" She slammed a fist down on my desktop so hard it made my glass clink against the bottle. I took this as a sign to fill it up so it wouldn't make too much noise and upset the neighbours. "I've got a real problem. I need help."

This time I sipped my drink slow. "Keep talking."

"It's my brother. He's disappeared."

I thumbed back the brim of my hat and set down the empty glass. "Some reason the cops can't handle this?"

She didn't say anything. That said it all.

"In case it's slipped your pretty little mind, sweets, my past association with your family hasn't exactly been a romp in the forest. I wasn't looking for you to show up on my doorstep, but Destiny's a funny dame. She's got a way of giving you the brass ring with one hand and ripping your heart out with the other. You want me to go out there, pound shoe leather and get my Sunday-go-to-meeting broom all dusty looking for your brother? *Trying* to find him? I'm about as interested in finding that scrawny little bastard as Japan is in giving back Mongolia. Find yourself another sucker."

That was when she turned on the faucets. I watched her smear her mascara into skid marks for a while, and when I saw she was crying real tears I reached up my sleeve and tossed her a handkerchief.

"Please, don't turn me down," she begged, dabbing at her eyes. "You can't; you're my last hope."

"That so?" I thumbed my hat back again, only this time I pushed it too far. It fell off my head and rolled around on its point until the cat jumped on it and crushed the brim. I lost my patience and turned him into a toad. He gave me this ominous croak that as good as told me he was going to accidentally-on-purpose use my shoes for a litter box as soon as I turned him back. I've lived with worse threats.

"Your last hope, well, well," I repeated as I grabbed my hat off the floor and put it back on. The toad hopped away to sulk in a corner. "And here you were just now, saying I was your first choice. Either the honeymoon's over already, or you're not playing it square with me, sugar. I wouldn't recommend that."

"I'm sorry." She took a deep breath. It did things. "I lied."

"I'd like to say I'm surprised, cupcake, but since it's you . . ." I shrugged. "Tell you what, you give me the facts in the case, I listen, and maybe I take it. Maybe not. No promises. Okay, one: You lie to me again, you're out of here on your cute little bustle. Got it?"

"Got it." She sniffled one last time, but the fire was back in her eyes. She got out her compact and started repairing the damage while she told me the whole story:

"It's been two weeks since I heard from Hansel. That's not normal; we're close. Usually he calls me every other day, or I call him. We get together on the weekends, catch a movie, maybe take a drive up the coast."

"With the war on?" I gave her a warning look. "What's your car run on, Coca-Cola? Even I can't make gasoline out of thin air."

She shrugged, but she didn't back-pedal. "It's his car. I guess I never thought to ask him where he got the fuel for it. It's a fancy ride, powder-blue Packard sedan, white leather seats."

I snorted. "The Easter Bunny bring it? No one makes cars that look like that!"

"You got enough money, you can always find someone to make you anything you want," she said. She talked like a woman who knew.

"So your little brother did all right for himself, and pretty fast, too. The pair of you couldn't have been in this country much longer than me."

"We came over in '38."

I whistled, low and long. "That *is* fast for someone to make good; especially for a johnny-come-lately punk like your brother. I'm impressed. What's his racket?"

"I don't know. He never told me."

I got up and went for the office door. I threw it open and told her: "Get out."

She didn't move a muscle. "It's the truth. The one time I asked, he gave me the brush-off. Said something about being in public relations."

"The kind the cops run you in for when they catch you trying it in Griffith Park?" I would've laughed, but I sort of forgot how.

She stood up. "You said you'd listen. I said I'd tell the truth. So far I'm keeping up my end of the deal."

If she was waiting for an apology, she was going to be twice as grey and wrinkled as me before she got it. Still, I closed the office door. "All right, sweets, you made your point. I'll listen."

She gave me a look like ex-wives give their husbands when the bastards swear the cheque is in the mail. "Like I said, my brother and I have always been very close, but that doesn't mean we're all over each other's business. Ever since our mother died, we looked out for one another. Daddy never had time for us; he had to earn a living, put food in our mouths. Being a woodchopper's no ball."

"Can the sob story and cut to the chase," I told her.

"I'm not looking for sympathy. I'm a big girl. I can take care of myself."

She had me there. Last time our paths crossed, she almost took care of *me*. Permanently. I went back to my desk and motioned for her to go on.

"Like I said, he calls me a lot, so when I didn't hear from him for two weeks straight, I got worried. I went over to his place, the Chez Moderne apartments."

The Chez Moderne . . . Ritzy name for what was basically a run-down old hotel so far downtown that the cockroaches had to take the streetcar. Not the address I'd expect of the man who owns his own powder-blue Packard. I shot her a searching look but it bounced right off. If she'd ever wondered about why her brother drove *that* but lived *there*, she didn't let on.

"I had the extra key, so when no one answered my knock, I let myself in." She shuddered, remembering. "The place looked like an earthquake hit it. Someone had been there before me and they tore it up, top to bottom."

"You sure? Maybe your brother just wasn't a very good housekeeper." Her eyes poured me a double dose of arsenic, straight up, so I stopped trying to pass for one of the Marx Brothers.

"Everything was ruined. Whoever'd done it even sliced up the mattress and ripped the lining out of the drapes. The bathroom floor was wall-to-wall pills, all the empty bottles smashed in the bathtub."

I didn't like to bring up what could be a pretty ugly possibility, but I had to ask: "Any blood?"

She shook her head. "I was thankful for that much. My first instinct was to go to the cops, but when I got home, there was a letter waiting for me. It was from my brother."

I held out my hand, waiting for her to cough it up. I kept on waiting.

"I burned it," she explained.

"How convenient."

"You don't understand: I had to!"

"Why?"

"Because he told me to. He didn't want me getting involved. It was too dangerous. If they got their hands on that letter—"

"Not so fast. Who's 'they'?"

"He didn't name names. The same creeps who wrecked his place, I suppose."

"Tough call. What else did the letter say?"

"It said that he was going away for a few weeks, maybe a few months, on business. He didn't come right out and say so, but he hinted that this was it, the big score, something that was going to put the two of us on Easy Street for the rest of our lives. He said he'd be in touch, and for me to sit tight until I heard from him again."

"Did he say how he'd contact you?"

She shook her head.

"So tell me this, cupcake: If you're such a *good* little girl – keeping your nose out of your brother's business, not asking questions, burning that letter strictly on his say-so – then why are you here? Why aren't you back in your own place, sitting tight like he told you?"

There were tears starting up in her eyes again. "Because he's not the one who wrote that letter."

"Not his handwriting?"

"Nothing that amateurish. But I could tell. Someone dictated every word he wrote; it didn't sound like him at all. That was when I decided to get help. That was when I came to you. Will you help me? Please?"

I wrinkled my nose. Her story smelled worse than Fisherman's Wharf, up Frisco way. This dame was spinning a yarn with more loose ends than Rapunzel's marcel wave and expecting me to buy it. She had brass, but all the nerve in the world can't make up for being stupid. Trying to play me for a fool is *real* stupid.

She'd done that once before, in the Old Country, her and her rotten little brother. I didn't see so good back then – try to find a decent eye-doc in the sticks – but so what? There's not much worth looking at in the heart of the Black Forest. You seen one squirrel, you seen 'em all. That was how those brats managed to give me the runaround. Every time I told the punk to stick his finger through the bars of the cage where I had him locked away to fatten up, he'd stick out a chicken bone. The gristle should've tipped me off. Too soon old, too late smart, like they say.

As for her, I had hopes: She was a sweet little thing and I was lonely. If they ever made a movie of my life, the screenwriters'd have to call me an old maid or a career gal or just not the marrying kind because the truth would bring the Hays Office down on their necks faster than a well-oiled guillotine. And before you get all hot under the collar, thinking she was just a kid and I was some kind of monster, let me clue you in on something not everyone knows: She and her brother were no babes in the woods, no matter how they twisted the story later. They might've *looked* like kids, small and scrawny on account of growing up at the Hard Knocks Hotel, but they were both safely past the age of consent when they came nibble-nibbling at my door. And believe me, she let on like she *would* consent any day, if I didn't pull a Betty Crocker on her. So that's why he was in the cage but she had the run of the place. Oh yeah, she played innocent-but-willing-to-learn, and she played it good.

That's why I believed her when she said she didn't know how to tell if the oven was hot enough. That's why I stuck my head in first, to show her how it's done. My head was full of stardust, dreams of her and me in that kitschy little woodland cottage, me with my feet up on the pile of kiddie bones, her by the oven, baking gingerbread, everything strictly *Ladies' Home Journal*.

Next thing I knew, my face was full of live coals. She'd shoved me into the oven, locked the door, freed her brother, and beat it.

I'd be a pretty poor witch if I didn't keep an escape spell on the tip of my tongue at all times. But she didn't know that. By the time I got myself out of the oven and under the pump, drenched but extinguished, those two were long gone. Them and my life's savings in gold.

Like I said, we had a past.

That's why I didn't have any second thoughts about nailing her with the same toad spell I used on the cat. It was sweet: One minute she was standing there trying to work the bunco, the next she was squatting on the floor, brown and lumpy as a bowl of boarding-house oatmeal.

I picked her up easy and dropped her on the desk, then poured myself another drink. This time I got out some cookies to go with all that milk. One chopper left in my head and wouldn't you know it's a sweet tooth? In between sips and swallows, I told her the score:

"Next time you want to work the old shell game, sister, make sure you've got a real chump on the line. That, or get your story straight. First you act all surprised to see a woman gumshoe, then you say your friend gave you the lowdown on me. And she didn't mention *that* little detail? Next we've got the little matter of your brother's fancy car and his invisible means of support. A smart cookie like you wouldn't grill him for some answers there? I'm not buying. As for that letter you say he sent you, the one you knew he didn't write . . . Why'd you act like it was the real McCoy when it came to doing what he said, burning it, only the next words out of that pretty little mouth of yours were 'I knew it wasn't really his'? Your story's got more holes in it than Dillinger. I think you need a little time to think over what a bad girl you've been. You sit right there while I do some digging on my own. Okay, cupcake?"

I wasn't dumb enough to expect an answer. Toads talk less than Charlie McCarthy when Bergen's in the can. I left her with the empty milk bottle and nabbed her purse from the floor. When I dumped it out on the desk, she jumped off and flopped around my ankles, croaking like crazy, but she couldn't do a damn' thing to stop me.

I found what I was looking for inside a little plaid change purse. It was a piece of onionskin paper, folded up small. *Dear Gretel*, it said. *You were right, Mr LeGras doesn't really care about me, no matter what he says. I'm just another one of the hired help to him, and now he's come back from San Francisco – one of his "business" trips – with that so-called English valet, Carlisle. English! The closest that dog biscuit's been to England is the seat of Mr LeGras's tweed pants.*

When I told Mr LeGras how I felt, he gave me the brush-off, said it was all my imagination, threw me some extra scratch and told me to go out and buy myself a good time. No one treats me like that and gets away with it. I'm getting the hell out of here, but before I go, I'm going to leave Mr LeGras something to remember me by. Or should I say I'm going to take something?

The black bird.

Yes, that black bird. The one I told you about, the one you say can't possibly be real. But it is real. Real enough to be the source of Mr LeGras's fortune. Real enough to do the same for us.

Think of it, my dearest sister! No more warbling your heart out in cheap dives like the La Zazz for you, and for me, no more faking that a pig like Mr LeGras is my maiden dream of love.

I looked up from the letter. "The black bird," I said aloud. "That's a step up from stealing gingerbread."

The brown toad gave an inquiring croak from the floor.

"Don't tell me you never heard of the black bird, sugarplum," I told her. "Every two-bit hustler and small-time hoodlum in this town knows about the black bird. You want I should draw you a map or just write you a screenplay? Get your hands on the black bird and you're set for life, and I'm not talking ration books, I'm talking gold; solid gold."

I went back to the letter: *I'm going to make the big touch soon, this week. If I don't, I might wind up plugging Carlisle first, making the snatch second. It's easier for me to hide a bird than a body, ha, ha. Soon as I knock over the bird, I'll get word to you. When that happens, meet me up at the place on Lake Arrowhead and we'll blow this popstand. I'll be waiting. Love, Hansel.*

I folded the letter and put it back in her purse. "I love the way he keeps calling him *Mister* LeGras," I told her. "Even when he's talking about playing him for a sucker. That's class." I crossed my arms and stared down at her. "So you did like he told you: You waited for word, but the week went by and all you came up with was a goose egg. You went over to his place, maybe thinking he lost his nerve and hadn't done it, maybe scared he *had*, and then decided not to cut you in on the score after all. When you found his place wrecked like that, you must've figured that he *did* pull off the heist, only sloppy. LeGras caught wise before Brother Dear could make his getaway, but *not* before the goof managed to hide the swag. So LeGras hired some muscle to get back his property, probably told them that if they wanted to practise their tap-dancing on the little creampuff's face, he wouldn't mind."

The toad launched a rapid-fire burst of angry croaking, slapping its feet on the linoleum floor. I clucked my tongue.

"Hey, I'll talk about your brother any way I want, angelcake. You think he walks on water? He's still a weasel, a slimy little gunsel who got in too deep and who might be getting in deeper as we speak, courtesy of a pair of cement overshoes. Hard to walk on water then."

The toad made a mournful sound and turned its back to me. Its lumpy little shoulders were working like an oil rig in a dry hole. I didn't know toads could sob. Against my better judgement, I felt like a heel.

"Can the waterworks, sweets," I said, squatting down in front of her. "I'll help you, only not the way you asked. We don't need to find your brother. We need to find the bird."

The toad anted up a croak that was as good as a question. I got her drift. "Because if his place was torn up as bad as you say, I'm willing to bet they were after a clue to where he stashed the bird,'' I explained. "Maybe they found one, maybe not. If they did, well, it's lights out for Hansel; nothing I can do. But if they didn't—" The toad looked hopeful. "—Then he's still alive. LeGras wants his precious tweetie back; he won't let his goons kill the rat until it squeals. If *we* can find the bird before before Junior cracks, we've got a bargaining chip that just *might* save the little reptile's bacon.''

The toad croaked at me indignantly. I snorted. "Yeah, yeah, so reptiles don't have bacon. You want to play egghead games or you want to save your brother before they send him back to you in a box?'' The toad looked sorry for having brought up the whole subject. I patted her on the head and said, "Never mind, honey. Let's hit the bricks. Our next step is back to Junior's place so I can—''

I never got to finish saying what I had in mind. A galaxy of stars exploded inside my head and my next step was sprawled flat on my face on the office floor. That's life: Sometimes it hands you a gingerbread house, sometimes it shoves you head first into an oven, and sometimes it's happy to have some gorilla sneak up from behind and bean you with a blackjack.

When I came to, I got a first-hand idea of what Junior's ravaged apartment must've looked like. Someone had torn through my office like a two-headed ogre with a migraine. I pulled myself to my feet using what was left of my desk and surveyed the damage.

There were papers everywhere, not a drawer left in place. My file cabinet was stretched out like a coffin, my chairs were kindling, and something very important was missing from the room:

My client.

I didn't need a crystal ball to tell me what had happened, though I could've used the entrails of a black he-goat to fill in the details. The same goon-or-goons-unknown who had ripped up Junior's digs had come a-calling at my door. They'd probably been tailing Gretel, looking to put the snatch on her. I guess some whizz-kid figured that if Junior wouldn't sing to save his own skin, maybe he'd twitter through a scale or two to save his sister's. When she came to see me, all nice and private, they got their chance.

I touched the egg growing out of the back of my skull and winced. "That's no way to treat a lady," I muttered. I crossed to the coat closet, avoiding shards of glass and piles of chocolate-chip crumbs. They'd busted my cookies. Nobody busts my cookies.

Lucky for me my uninvited guests had left my broomstick alone. Probably thought it belonged to the cleaning lady. I appreciate opponents with no imagination; it's no loss to the world when I put them away for good. My head was still spinning, but I'd flown with hangovers that were a damn' sight worse. Now I needed just one more thing before I could hit the wild blue yonder . . .

"Here, kitty," I called. "Here, kitty, kitty, kitty! Here, Bogey, come to Mama."

The first thing they teach you in my line of work, even before you get within spitting distance of a magic wand or a cauldron or that plug-ugly black pointy hat, is that you don't go up without a co-pilot. You can't. Cats and witches don't hang out together just for the conversation: We need the beasts to power our brooms. Witches know that every living thing's a source of potential energy. You ever spend a whole day watching a cat? Most of the time he's curled up asleep in the sun, when he's not feeding his face. All intake, no output; the perfect storage battery. Get enough cats together and you could launch a flock of B-29s.

"Bogey-boy, come on, I need you. Puss, puss, puss. Bogey, I'm *calling* you, you mangy fleabag! Get *over* here, Bogey, I mean it!"

Nothing. That wasn't unusual. You show me the cat who comes when he's called and I'll show you an enchanted prince waiting to be kissed. That, or a sick cat. But I was doing more than just beating my gums: I was using his name as the focus for an attraction-spell. If Bogey was anywhere within the sound of my voice, he'd be dragged in and set down at my feet in two minutes. "Bogey, come *here*!"

Two and a half minutes later, I was worried. Nothing could keep Bogey from responding to my attraction-spell if he were alive. "If anything's happened to him . . ." I gritted my teeth. He was more than just a cat to me: He was my partner. No one takes out my partner and gets away with it.

Suddenly, I heard a weak sound coming from the corner behind my toppled file cabinet. "Bogey, is that you?" If I was the church-going type, I would've wasted time saying a little thanksgiving prayer. Instead, I got right to work, moving the cabinet so he could get out. "Hold on, kitty, Mama's coming."

It wasn't a kitty; it was a toad. I forgot that I'd pulled the old shape-change on him before, when he got on my nerves. I was forgetting a lot of things, mostly thanks to that lump on my head.

"Hold still, kid; this won't take a second." I made with the mystic bushwas to restore him to his original shape. There was a hokey puff of smoke as the spell hit him.

"It's about time!" Gretel snapped at me. Her eyes flashed all around my wrecked office. "Thorough bastards, aren't they? Serves you right. Now, where's my purse? I'm getting out of here." She started pawing through the rubble.

I grabbed her arm and pulled her back. "Not so fast, sugar. Aren't you forgetting a little something?"

"You mean my brother?" she shot back, jerking out of my grasp. "Hardly. He's all I'm gonna be thinking about the whole way to New York City, which is exactly where I'm headed as soon as I find my purse." She went back to digging up the ruins, a regular Schliemann in shantung.

I hauled her back to face me a second time. "Cool your heels, sweetie-pie. What's all this about New York?"

"It's the farthest away from here I can get, that's what," she said. "By bus, anyway. Maybe you didn't see the pair of thugs that were just in here—"

"They gave me the bum's rush to Slumberland before they bothered to introduce themselves," I replied, with a twisty little smile. It hurt. "So there were two of them, you say?"

She nodded. "Big ones. Ugly, too. A couple of reject heavy-weights from palookaville."

"Names?"

"I heard one call the other Max; that's all I know. Max was the one who slugged you."

"Max, huh?" I made a mental note to give Max a tour of the La Brea tar pits from the bottom up when our paths crossed again.

"Anyway, it turned out they'd been spying on us for a while, probably standing out in the hall, eavesdropping, so they knew what you'd done to me. As soon as you were down, Max's partner said, 'Okay, grab the toad and let's blow!'"

"How did you manage to get away?" I asked.

"As soon as I knew they'd come for me, I hid. That's how come they tore up the place, looking for me. They just happened to find the other toad first." She shrugged. "I guess I'm a lucky girl."

"Sure you are." I pretended like I believed her, but I had a feeling it hadn't gone exactly the way she told it. More likely she'd done something to draw those two goons' attention to where Bogey was hiding, then hopped away fast while they bagged the wrong batrachian. "So, they say anything else?"

"Only that Mr LeGras would be real glad to get his hands on me. That's when I figured it all out: LeGras was going to use me to make Hansel tell where he hid the black bird."

"I'm surprised you didn't go along quietly," I said. "Why pass up a chance to help your darling little brother? You the same girl who was just telling me how close the two of you are?"

She looked away. "Not close enough for me to want to share the same grave. Even if they'd managed to grab me, bring me to LeGras's place, do . . . things to me, Hansel wouldn't talk. I know him, and he knows LeGras. He used to say that once LeGras squeezes the last drop of juice from a lemon, he throws the peel away."

"Can't say I know a lot of people who save it, sugar," I said.

"You know what I mean! Once Hansel tells LeGras where the bird is, LeGras's got no reason left to keep Hansel alive!"

"So he'll clam up? Even if it means buying a few more hours at the cost of your life?"

"Even if it buys him a few more *minutes*," she replied. "Why the hell you think I'm heading for New York?"

"That would not be advisable."

Both of us turned at the sound of an unfamiliar voice from the doorway.

"Mr LeGras, I presume?" I said.

"The same. May I come in?"

He asked, but he didn't wait for an answer. He barged into my office like he owned the place. For all I knew, he did. He was a big man, but he moved silently and gracefully. So had the *Hindenberg*. Our Mr LeGras would have to watch himself. Offhand, I could name five, six practising fairy godmothers in the downtown area who'd get one eyeful of that pumpkin-shaped body and try turning him into a coach-and-four. He was impeccably dressed in a dapper white suit and Panama hat, a fresh red carnation in his buttonhole. He balanced his enormous bulk on a pair of obscenely tiny feet in glittering black Oxfords, real Italian leatherwork. A silver-headed mahogany walking stick in his left hand took some of the load off. A pearl-handled revolver in his right put some of the heat on.

He was alone. That did surprise me. I'd expected him to show up backed by the two apes who'd wrecked my office, at least. He was a confident s.o.b., our Mr LeGras. Maybe he'd make a confident toad. I smiled.

"Pray, put any thoughts of thaumaturgy from your mind at once, *gnädige Hexe*," he said. His voice was deep, with a raspy wheeze that made me want to start smoking cigarettes just so I could quit the habit. "Oh yes, I know you for what you are. A man in my position is not without his sources of, aha, reliable information. Knowledge is power. So too are certain, hrrrumph, connections. They permit one to take the appropriate precautions proper to the immediate circumstance."

He held out his hand. At first I thought that maybe he was cuckoo and wanted me to kiss it, like he was the Pope or something. Then I saw the little jade-and-pearl ring crammed onto his pinky. It gave off a protective aura strong enough to fade the letters in a locked grimoire at fifty paces. Any witch stupid enough to try casting a spell at that boy would have it bounce back in her face and do triple damage.

I forced myself to keep smiling. "I guess you want me to be impressed," I said.

"Your reactions are of startlingly minuscule importance to me, my dear," he replied. "I have done you a kindness by allowing you to perceive the ring's power. In ordinary circumstances, it remains hidden until aroused. You should thank me for sparing you a very nasty – and perhaps fatal – surprise."

"Thanks," I said, deadpan. "I'd offer you a seat and ask you to stay to tea, but your boys took care of my chairs."

He laughed. Everything shook except the gun. "You have a sense of humour. Good, good. I find it much easier to deal with people who see the inherent absurdity of life. They are far less likely to take a foolishly heroic stand on matters that do not, in essence, involve them."

"Oh, I'm no hero, dumpling," I replied. "I'm just a poor old lady who wants to get her pussycat back. Your boys picked him up by mistake."

"So we discovered in short order. The same, hrrm, person who supplied me with this ring perceived our mistake without even bothering to remove the unhappy creature's toad-form."

I wondered which of my colleagues was down-and-out enough to take LeGras's money and be his *sorciére de joie*. Then I decided that I was happier not knowing anyone *that* desperate.

"No surprise there," I said. "Bogey's more than my cat, he's my familiar. All us girls in the life can tell another witch's familiar on sight, no matter what shape it's wearing. Bring him back to me and you can have the girl. Hell, you can have her now. Take her. She was just telling me how much she misses her little brother. It'd be cruel to keep them apart."

LeGras laughed again. "Ah! An excellent jape. The Algonquin Round Table is the poorer for your absence. Rest assured, it is my intention to reunite brother and sister with due celerity, to the ultimate benefit of, ahem, all parties concerned."

"How sweet. Well, don't let me keep you."

He didn't take the hint. "I am afraid, my dear, that I have not made myself clear: I have come for the young lady, but prudence dictates that you accompany us as well." He made a discreet but unmistakable motion with his gun.

I don't believe in wasting time on useless arguments, especially when my respected opponent has six hot lead arguments at his disposal. "Mind if I get my hat?" I asked.

LeGras made me a dancing-school bow. "Not at all, dear lady. Fetch your gloves as well, if you so desire. How I deplore the growing disregard for the proprieties of personal appearance in today's society! The numbers of young women I have seen traipsing about with neither *chapeau* nor chaperone would break your heart."

"You're assuming I've got one." I breezed past him to the closet. I could feel him tracking me with the muzzle of his revolver the whole time, feel his fat little trigger finger itching to punch me a one-way ticket to hell if I tried anything funny.

I'm a witch, not a comedian. I got my hat off the top shelf of the closet and dropped the old butterball a curtsy. "Ready when you are, sweets."

LeGras herded us out of my office, down the hall, and into the wheezy old rattletrap of an elevator. There were four passengers in it plus Steve the shaft-monkey. None of them seemed to notice that the two lovely ladies accompanying the personable fat man were doing so under pearl-handled protest. LeGras's pet witch probably slapped a no-see-'um charm on his gun.

His car was waiting for us right outside my office building, a Cadillac the colour of fresh cream. There was a big goon uglying up the space behind the wheel. I wondered if it was my buddy Max, but the circumstances weren't social so I couldn't ask. LeGras jerked his head, silently ordering us into the back seat. He climbed in after, shut the door, and gave the order: "Home."

I wondered where "home" was. I was betting it was somewhere up in the Hollywood hills, a popular nesting spot for the cash, flash, and trash crowd. I had the window seat, with Gretel wedged in between me and LeGras. I guess I could've tried something smart, like pulling a Houdini when the car stopped for a traffic light, but I didn't. I knew that if I skipped, Gretel'd be stuck paying the full bill.

Yeah, tell me I'm a sucker. Then tell me something I don't already know.

I like riding in cars. You get places faster when you fly a broomstick, but in cars you don't get bugs in your teeth. I leaned back against the upholstery and closed my eyes. For all I knew this was going to be my last ride; might as well enjoy it. If I was going to die, at least I was wearing a nice hat for the occasion. LeGras didn't know it, but there was a reason I'd grabbed this little beauty out of the closet instead of rummaging through the office wreckage for the hat I'd been wearing earlier. *This* hat was special. *This* hat stood up straight and proud, and not just because I'd asked for extra starch at Ling Po's Genuine Chinese Hand Laundry.

This hat was packing a rod.

I had it all planned: We'd get to LeGras's place and he'd bring us face to face with Hansel – unless he handed us over to his goons for some preliminary softening-up first. He'd try to make the little gunsel sing, but he'd come up against the biggest case of laryngitis known to man. Then he'd start putting the screws to Gretel. The most he'd get out of that would be some cheap entertainment for the hired help. I had LeGras and his gang of creeps pegged for the type who got their kicks watching a woman get hurt. He'd keep his gun on me the whole time, but not his eyes. He'd have more . . . *amusing* things to look at.

That was when I'd ask if I could take off my hat and stay awhile.

Maybe I couldn't use the wand to hurt *him* while he wore

that stupid ring, but I *could* use it to create a distraction, like setting the place on fire, or breaking the water mains, or making Max's head explode like a party balloon full of brains and blood. You know, little things. And in the confusion, I could get Gretel and me the hell out of there, easy as—

"We're here." LeGras's wheezy voice busted up my pretty dreams.

I opened my eyes in time to see the car pull up in front of one of those bijou hideaway hacienda-style mansions. It had a tapestry brick driveway, brutally neat flower beds, and an ornamental pond where a quartet of swans paddled around looking bored. Silent film stars used to buy up places like this by the bagful, like penny candy, only to toss them back on the market at a dead loss when the talkies showed no signs of going away. It was tucked into the armpit of a mountain with the nearest neighbour located a body-drop below.

A butler answered the door. He looked like a refugee from a Karloff flick. He bowed slightly to Gretel and me and asked if he could take my hat.

"No thanks, Spooky; it's carrying my personality," I told him.

"It is also carrying a concealed weapon," he replied, slick as a lounge lizard's manicure. "I regret to inform you that all such artefacts are powerless within these walls."

I goggled at him like a sea bass with goitre. LeGras escorted me over the threshhold, chortling. "Do not be surprised, madam," he said. "I have long been a collector of esoteric souvenirs. The black bird is merely the, hrrm, most profitable in a series of the same. I am sure you would agree that any malefactors interested in thieving such items must of necessity be versed in the Darker Arts. With that in mind, it would be unwise not to place certain, ah, protective wards upon my property. Just as your ordinary homeowner might have the double security of a high fence to keep housebreakers out and a vicious dog to deal with any who do get in, I too have diversified my defences. Some, like Stanton here, detect the presence of uninvited magic or magical appurtenances.

Others, like this ring that you have already noted—" he flashed his pinky at me "—repel outright sorcerous attacks. Now be a good little witch and hand over the hat."

Nobody ever called me a good little witch. Nobody still in need of oxygen. I glared daggers at Stanton, but I gave the big stiff my hat. What choice did I have? He pulled out the hidden rod and held it out for his boss's inspection like a cat proudly puking up mouse-guts on the doormat.

"A magic wand," LeGras said, tapping it aside with the nose of his revolver. "How quaint. Thank you, Stanton, you may dispose of it."

"Very good, sir." The butler's hand closed on my rod. There was a grinding sound and the whole thing broke into a million splinters. This Stanton wasn't your everyday butler.

I turned to LeGras. "Zombie or golem?" I asked.

"Golem," he replied. "Zombies do not afford quite so much upper-body strength, and one does need to feed them on occasion. Shall we proceed?"

Stanton led the way into the depths of LeGras's house, down a hall and up to a pair of heavy double doors. At a touch of his hands, they rolled into their wall pockets silently, revealing a parlour big enough to host a ball game. It'd have to be for the girlie league, though. Everywhere I looked, I saw chintz, gilding, and frou-frou. It was like being trapped inside the brain of a wedding cake designer gone ga-ga.

In the centre of the floor was a plain wood kitchen chair. A man was tied to it. It was Hansel. Big surprise. The thick velvet drapes were drawn tight and there was only a single lamp lit, but I could see him good enough. He'd changed about as much as his sister. The grubby-faced kid who'd been too scrawny to pop into my bake-oven had grown up into a man with the body of a has-been athlete and the face of a cherub.

That cherub should've been more careful about where he flew. He'd obviously glided into the bad part of town where some punk grabbed him by the wing and used his face for a punching bag. I wondered whether Hansel's lips were always that pouty or if they'd just swollen up from the beating. One eye was battered shut, the other squinted sullenly in our direction. If he recognized me, he didn't let on. Then again, seeing as how he was flanked by a couple of burly chaperones, maybe he didn't want to get spanked for talking to strangers.

"How goes it, dear boy?" LeGras exclaimed, sidling up to Hansel. He passed his walking stick and gun to one of the two guard-goons. "Have you taken advantage of my absence to repent the error of your ways?"

"He ain't spilled nothin', Boss," the second ape said.

"Ah." LeGras turned to me and shrugged apologetically. "Dear lady, you must forgive Max. He lacks the benefits of a course in proper English."

Max, huh? Hel-looo, nurse. I did my best to keep a poker face. "I don't know, sweets," I said. "That's pretty bad grammar. Someone ought to teach him a lesson."

"Perhaps. In the meantime, I would prefer to limit my attempts at, ha, pedagogy to this young man." He approached Hansel and stooped over – not without a whole lot of effort – just so he could be at eye level when he wheezed: "Was this the face that launched a thousand ships? No longer, alas. Such a needless waste of beauty when beauty is ethereal at best. You disappoint me deeply, my boy. You might have spared yourself this."

"Save it," Hansel growled. "I didn't talk for these creeps and I'm not talking for you. Think I can't see who *that* is?" He nodded in our direction. I gave Gretel a sidelong look. She was staring at her brother, tears streaming down her cheeks, but unless you were close enough to see them in the dim light, you'd never have known they were there. She didn't make a sound. A pair of granite bookends, those two. "You wasted your time, bringing her here," he went on. "I know I'm a dead man, no matter what. Say I *did* tell you where the black bird's stashed, you want me to believe you'd let me go – me *or* her – like nothing ever happened? Fat chance."

LeGras took that last remark personally. "You would choose to perish, knowing your innocent sister must share your fate?"

Hansel grinned, showing off some recently administered gaps in his pearly whites. "Yeah. So? I'd die knowing that you'll never see the black bird again in this lifetime. Who says you can't take it with you?"

LeGras waved one fat hand languidly. "Edgar, my things," he said. The goon who wasn't my pal Max fetched a green tin box from the shadows and set it down on the table holding the lamp. LeGras opened it and took out a pair of black rubber gloves and a neatly folded white cloth. While LeGras pulled the gloves on, Edgar spread the cloth over the tabletop, then reached into the tin box and started laying out the tools.

"Stanton, see to the lady," LeGras directed. The golem butler grabbed Gretel and hauled her forward. Max got another kitchen chair and more rope from somewhere behind the Louis-the-Whatever settee and tied her up like the Sunday roast.

"Never send a boy to do a man's job," LeGras murmured, an ugly little smile on his blobby lips. "You see, lad, the question is no longer *if* you will die but how long you will be about it. You are about to have a demonstration of what awaits you, performed with the kind assistance of your own dear sister." He picked up one of the tools from the white-shrouded table. Lamplight glittered along the edge of the blade like a string of fresh-dipped rock candy.

Hansel went pale. He opened his mouth – nothing came out – then closed it and tightened his jaw. I knew that look. Tough guy.

I've got no use for tough guys. I had to leave my home in the Old Country when the tough guys took over. I know their kind: They're real brave as long as they outnumber you, or when it's someone else's neck on the chopping block. Dig the brown-shirted bastards out of their burrows one by one and they stop barking and start whining, no teeth and all tail.

That's why I spoke up when I did:

"Hey, LeGras, do you *like* to waste time?"

He stopped making goo-goo eyes at the blade and gave me a slow, contemptuous look. "I assure, you madam, I shall proceed with all requisite alacrity." He snapped his fingers. Max made a move for Gretel. She screamed like she was auditioning to play an air-raid siren

I laughed. LeGras raised one stubbly eyebrow. "You take pleasure in the impending misfortunes of others? How . . . unsuitable a character trait in a woman. I can't say I approve."

"I'm not laughing at her," I told him. "I'm laughing at you. You're a fool, LeGras, a fat fool." Legras's driver made a grab for me, but I held up one hand and talked fast: "Call him off, LeGras, or kiss the black bird goodbye."

"Hold, Geoffrey." LeGras's trained gorilla stopped dead in his tracks at the sound of his master's voice. LeGras himself set down his sharp, shiny toy and came over to me. "What are you saying, my good woman? That you have some arcane knowledge that may facilitate our search? That you would be willing to place your sorcerous powers in my service to the end of recovering the bird?"

"Right you are, cupcake."

"And I suppose your price will be their lives?" He didn't even bother looking back at his prisoners, he just shook his head and said, "I am afraid that would be out of the question."

I blew his words away like they were smoke rings. "What do you take me for, a sucker? *Me* bargain for *their* lives? What's the matter, gumdrop, your mama never read you any fairy tales at bedtime? Do you even know who I *am*?"

It was a beautiful thing, watching the little light bulb go on over LeGras's head. "You mean to say that you are *that* witch? My word, this *is* an honour." He grabbed my hand between both of his and shook it briskly. The rubber gloves squeaked and left my palm all sweaty. Beaming, LeGras babbled on: "How fortuitous. Of course you would never ask for *their* lives in fee. Not after what they put you through, eh? Pardon my previous ignorance, but it is understandable. Anyone who has ever heard your story assumes that you perished in the oven where that graceless *cocotte* left you. Well! This puts quite a different complexion on things."

"I'll say." I got my hand out of his clutches and wiped it dry on my skirt. "You want my powers at your service, you got 'em. Pay me what you paid the gal who conjured up that gangbusters ring of yours. Say, not to cut my own throat or anything—" I gave Max a *Wouldn't you like to try?* leer "—but if you need magic to trace the bird, how come you don't give your bought-and-paid-for witch a call?"

LeGras made an irritated noise deep in his jowly throat. "The unmannerly hag left my employ some months ago, complaining that I did not show her the respect her art deserved. She is of no further consequence, thanks to you. Sorcerous aid will make the search for my treasure far less tedious. *Can* you locate the black bird for me, my good woman?"

"Depends," I said. "Can you locate my cat?"

"Your . . . cat? Ah! Your cat, of course." LeGras smiled. "More than reasonable. Restore the black bird to me and I promise you that not only shall you have your beloved familiar back, but that you shall also remain on permanent retainer in my employ. You shall find me to be, er, decidedly generous."

"So I hear." I stared at Hansel and made sure to do it so that LeGras got my meaning. "Okay, LeGras, bring me my cat and we'll get started."

"Madam, I beg your pardon but you will only receive your cat after I am again in possession of the black bird. Those are my terms and I promise you, they are not negotiable."

"In that case, I hope you packed a lunch because this job's not going any further without Bogey. I told you, he's my familiar. Do you even know what that *means*? He's the supernatural servant I hired at the price of my soul the minute I got into the life. I give the orders, he carries them out; we're a team."

LeGras curled his lip. "So you are powerless without him?"

"Applesauce!" I snapped my fingers under his nose. "He didn't turn *himself* into a toad, did he? I've got plenty of Moxie on my own, but he boosts my capabilities. It comes in handy for the big jobs. You want someone to dig you a grave, do you give him a spoon or a steam-shovel? Bogey's my steam-shovel."

"I see." LeGras barked a few commands to his boys. Edgar scuttled out of the parlour quick and came back quicker. He was holding a toad. He would've handed it over to me when his boss stopped him. "Before I allow this charming reunion, *fräulein Hexe*, permit me to remind you that I am still protected." Again with the pinky ring. I was sick of the sight of it. It made that pudgy white finger of his look like a grub wearing a garter belt.

"Think I was going to pull a fast one?" I smirked. "Nothing could be farther from my mind."

"Is that why you came into my home carrying a concealed weapon?"

"Which your butler destroyed. I'll send you a bill for the replacement as soon as I'm on your payroll. Look, LeGras, I admit I was thinking about using that rod, but that was before I realized we're playing on the same team. I don't bite the hand that feeds me. Heck, until I get me a decent set of dentures, I'm not biting anything tougher than a slab of gingerbread. All I'm gonna do is restore Bogey to his true form. That okay by you, Boss?"

Boss. LeGras liked the sound of that, I could tell. "By all means." He waved his hand at me like he was the sultan of Turkey ordering a harem girl to dance.

I'd give him a dance.

The spell for the restoration of an enchanted being's true form is short and sweet. I got through it faster than a chorus girl with a playboy's bankroll. Edgar was still holding Bogey when the change hit. One second he had his hands wrapped around a toad, the next he was holding eight-foot-six of bright green demon by the tail. Bogey's head turned slowly, his eyes a trio of pits filled with the fires of Hell, his jaws dribbling sulphurous foam, razor-sharp fangs set in a permanent come-to-Papa leer. He snapped off Edgar's head with a crunch like a little kid biting a lollipop.

Cat shape or true shape, Bogey never did like anyone to pull his tail.

Max was next on Bogey's disassembly line, followed by Geoffrey the driver, followed by Stanton. It took Bogey a couple of tries to swallow the golem, but he managed. I'd probably be up all night, nursing him through the bellyache. I was sorry that I couldn't give my old pal Max a personal thank-you for what he'd done to my office and my noggin, but *you* go bother a demon at dinner time.

LeGras was the last to go. The fat man fell to his knees, waggling his pinky ring at Bogey. "You can't touch me!" he squealed. "I am proof against all magical attacks! It will go ill with you if—"

Bogey made four neat bites out of him, then spat out the ring like it was a watermelon seed. He always was a show-off.

I pocketed the ring and rattled through the spell to return Bogey to feline shape. A demonic familiar has his uses, but a cat takes up less room at the foot of your bed. While Bogey sat there washing up after his feed, I untied Gretel's bonds.

"How – how did you do that?" she gasped, rubbing some circulation back into her hands. "Doesn't that ring—?"

"—Work?" I finished for her. "Yeah, it works. But it only repels magical attacks. Nothing magical about a demon turning mortals into chop suey; it's what they do, if you give them half a chance. I gave Bogey a whole one."

"How kind of you," said a prim voice behind me. "That is more than I shall give you."

When you've been in my line of work long enough, you can tell a lot from a voice. I didn't even have to turn around to know that this one belonged to someone young, healthy, British, and armed. The last part was a gimmee: He had a gun jabbed into my shortribs hard enough for me to know what calibre.

"Mr Carlisle, I presume?" I said. I played it cool, but mentally I was kicking my own tail seven ways from Sunday. How could I have forgotten about Carlisle, LeGras's some-time valet and full-time prettyboy? The first rule of a good gumshoe is to keep count of your enemies, their weapons, and how many rounds they've already squeezed off. If you screw up the first one, don't bother about the other two; you'll be too dead to care.

"Correct, madam." I felt the gun ease off some and heard the creak of shoe leather on parquet as he took a step away from me. "Please face me. I dislike shooting anyone in the back unless absolutely necessary."

"Not cricket, huh?" I did what he said, turning around and sizing him up. He was easy on the eyes, I'll give him that, one of those tall, thin, English blonds so pale-skinned that a good blush would probably make his cheeks explode. He had a pickpocket's long, delicate fingers. At the moment one of them was wrapped around the trigger of a .45.

"One must play by the rules, mustn't one?" He waved me aside with the heater, then fixed his eyes on Gretel. They were blue and steely, like his gun. "Free him." He nodded at Hansel.

"That's *it*?" I asked while Gretel attacked her brother's bonds. " 'Free him'? You don't want to get in line to slap him around until he tells you where the black bird's stashed?"

Carlisle's laugh was about as warm and human as plate glass shattering. "Do you mean to say you haven't guessed the truth even now? A fine detective you are! I should stick to baking gingerbread if I were you."

"Don't be too hard on the old broad," Hansel said. He was on his feet, one arm around his sister. "She's sharp enough, when love's not making her stupid."

"Besides," Gretel chimed in, smiling like a fallen angel, "it's not like we wanted a *smart* cookie for this job."

The truth dropped on me like a grand piano, and the song it played when it hit was *Variations on a Theme for Suckers*. "You were all in this together from the start," I said. "You knew that if you snatched the bird, LeGras and his goons would hunt you down no matter how far you ran or how long it took. You had to get them out of the way, permanently, so you could lie back and enjoy your loot in peace."

"Precisely," Carlisle said. "But given the fact that Mr LeGras was so well protected – by physical as well as arcane resources – we stood in need of someone of your particular talents. We knew that if we drew you in, you'd find the way to dispose of him for us. We were right."

I watched as Hansel slipped his other arm around Carlisle's slender waist and gave him a kiss on the cheek, so as not to distract his aim. So all that talk about the two of them being rivals was just a lot of jive cooked up to make me dance to their tune. If I had any more egg on my face I'd be an omelette.

Bogey gave me a worried look and meowed. Carlisle laughed again. "Poor pussy. You'd like to destroy us as well, wouldn't you? But I'm afraid you'll remain a cat for the duration. If your mistress so much as begins to utter her demon-freeing spell, I'll kill her by the third syllable." Bogey's tail dropped. I felt the same way.

"Game, set, and match, Carlisle," I conceded. "Since you've got me licked, do an old lady a favour? Before you rub me out, I mean."

"How can I refuse so elegant a plea? What do you want?"

"The black bird," I said. "I want to know how you managed to hide something that size from LeGras and his goons."

"She really *isn't* a very good detective, is she?" Hansel giggled. "The hell with her and her last requests, she's too stupid to live. Shoot her and let's blow."

"Not so fast." Carlisle could've been the love-child of Vincent Price and Lesley Howard, a good-looking bad guy who liked to watch his victims squirm. "It's a not unreasonable request. Let us show her, by all means."

They took me out of the house and down the front walk to the pond. As soon as I locked eyeballs with the swans, I knew. Swans are nasty, evil-tempered creatures with vicious streaks a yard wide. Three of the birds sailing across the water looked like they'd wreck their own nests just to throw an eggnog party, but the fourth . . .

"You bastard," I breathed. "You sharp little bastard."

Carlisle was loving it. " 'The Purloined Letter' never does go out of style. Care for a closer look before you die?"

"Don't bother on my account."

"No bother, my dear," he replied, like we were all sitting down to cucumber sandwiches and Earl Grey tea. "None at all. Hansel, if you would—?"

"*I*'m not wading in there." Hansel pouted like a hell-spawned Shirley Temple. "Bad enough I had to let LeGras's apes work me over and *now* you want me to get my pants wet?"

"Would it be the first time?" I muttered.

Carlisle made an impatient sound. "Very well. Gretel, *you* do it."

"Me?" she squealed. She eyed the birds nervously. The three genuine swans gave her the glad-eye, a trio of feathered sharks. "Why do *I* have to? I'm with Hansel: Shoot her now."

Carlisle sighed. "Whether I shoot her now or later, we must retrieve the bird *sometime*. Get it."

Gretel began to whimper. "But I'm scaaaaared! Those swans *bite*. Can I at least go into the house and get a golf club or something to—?"

Carlisle shifted the gun. "If you don't do as I say, I'll be pleased to teach you the meaning of the word *expendable*, my dear."

Grousing and whining, Gretel kicked off her shoes, stripped off her stockings, hiked up her skirt, and stepped into the pond. "Here, goosey," she called timidly, holding out one hand to the ringer swan. "Here, nice goose-goose-goosey. Come to Mama." The way all four of the birds kept their distance, she might as well have been waving a hatchet. Hansel and Carlisle observed her fruitless efforts at poultry-herding with rising amusement, laughing until the tears ran down their faces.

"Good Lord!" Carlisle exclaimed, gasping for breath. "That girl couldn't get a goose at a stag smoker."

"Let the old doll do it," Hansel suggested. "She wanted to see the black bird so bad, make her work for it."

"A capital notion," Carlisle said. He gestured meaningly with his gun.

As a disgruntled Gretel waded out of the pond, I sloshed in past my ankles. It took me all of twenty seconds to cut the right swan from the flock and herd it onto the grass, much to the astonished whispers of Carlisle and his cronies. I'll tell you a little secret from my long-gone childhood: Before Hansel and Gretel, before the gingerbread cottage, even before I first heard the Black Arts whispering my name, I was a snot-nosed German peasant brat like ten thousand others. And when you're a dirt-poor farmer's daughter, you know the first job they hand you, almost as soon as you can toddle? Goose-girl.

The three of them gazed at the phony swan like it was the answer to the fifty-dollar question on *Beat the Band*. Carlisle said a few words over the critter's head: Its neck shortened and its webbed feet went from black to red while its plumage went switcheroo from white to black like a cheating woman's heart. The bird looked around stupidly, honked once, settled down on the grass and laid an egg.

A golden egg.

Gretel pounced on it like a studio head on a starlet, but Hansel got there first and strong-armed her away. "What's the big idea?" she shrilled. "I *earned* this!"

"The hell you did," he countered, shoving her away a second time. "I guess it was *your* face got treated like a tough steak? If anyone earned anything, it's me!" The over-confident little creep bent over to seize the egg. He learned the error of his ways when his adoring sister kicked him in the pants, sending him head first into the pond. He got up dripping duckweed and grabbed her by the ankle, dragging her into the water with him. The swans took off, flapping their wings and making enough racket to wake the dead.

"Children, please." Carlisle rolled his eyes like a woman who's wondering whether retroactive birth control isn't such a bad idea after all. "The bird will lay more eggs; there will be enough for all of us, in time."

The pair of them paused in mid-shindy. Hansel glowered at the English prettyboy: "This is between me and my sister."

"Yeah!" Gretel hauled herself out of the muck bottoming the pond and tucked a dripping lock of hair behind one ear. "Don't tell us what to do. You wouldn't even be in on this caper if not for Hansel. He was the one who made sure LeGras got an eyeful of you up in Frisco, but he could've picked any other two-bit swish for the job. We were the brains, you were just the bait. You think you're the only pebble on the beach?"

"No," the limey admitted. he raised the .45. "But I *am* the only one with a gun. And now that I come to think about it, I don't believe I want to share at all."

He sent a bullet whizzing past Gretel's ear. Any closer and you could call the story "Hansel and". Brother and sister exchanged a look, then took to their heels like they had a flock of Zeros on their tail. Carlisle squeezed off a few more shots to speed them on their way. The black bird honked like crazy at the sound of gunfire but stayed put surer than if someone had driven a railroad spike through its foot. Carlisle laughed like a crazy man.

He was anything but.

"Now that's what I call sporting," I remarked. "Aren't you afraid they'll come after you . . . *sister*?"

He quit laughing and flashed me a look like a shiv, sharp and ugly. "How did you know?" His features started to blur at the edges, then to run like cheese on a griddle, but his grip on the 45 was rock solid.

"Maybe I'm not such a bad shamus after all. *You* were the one who lifted the disguise spell off the black bird. That means *you* had to be the one who slapped it on in the first place." I looked over to where the goose was still trying to take it on the lam, in spite of the invisible tether holding her down. "Pretty impressive sorcery from a sugarpuss-for-hire. That little holding spell you've got on the goose confirms it: You're one of us, sister."

Carlisle's prettyboy looks were all gone by the time I finished. His slender body filled out, his short blond hair went long and grey, and his gigolo get-up flashed into a heap of gypsy-bright glad rags. Me, I prefer to work in traditional black, but it's not like we're unionized.

A witch can wear what she wants.

"You *dare* include me in your pathetic, penny-grubbing witcheries?" my newly unmasked colleague countered. "You are a petty hireling, I am a mastermind! I used those stupid mortals as my tools: They did the dirty work, I reap the prize. And it was so easy!" She threw back her head and laughed. "Like you, I was a refugee, a despised foreigner in this so-called 'Land of the Free'. *Free!* All things here have a price, all costly. I lived hand to mouth on *their* sufferance, accepting the pittance they deemed a 'fair' wage for my services. Bah. I spit on their 'fair' wages."

She did, too. Bogey jumped out of the way. It was all he could do. She'd sold her soul to his Head Office, same as me, so he was powerless to attack her, with or without my say-so: Professional courtesy.

I didn't like her spitting on my cat, but there was something I liked even less: She was riding the Red broomstick. If she was so in love with Comrade Stalin's way of doing things, why did she bother coming here when she left the Old Country? Maybe because back then, Iron Joe was in Hitler's pocket deep enough to call him sweetheart? I got a bad feeling in my gut. If they ever got up another witch-hunt in this country, I'd know who to blame.

"There was a better way, I knew it," she went on. "A road to the big score, a clean shot at Easy Street. No more dabbling in love potions and impotence tonics, no."

"Six of one—" I began. She ignored me. She was tuned in to *Life Can Be Bitterful* and she couldn't hear anything else.

"My chance came when LeGras hired me. While in his employ, I discovered he possessed the black bird. I resolved to make it mine, to use it to obtain luxury beyond my wildest dreams."

"Sweet dreams," I remarked. "That must've been when it hit you: You couldn't use your magic to pull off the heist because you set up most of the spell-shielding tools in this dump before you found out about the bird. *That* must've stuck a burr under your saddle."

She ground her teeth together, remembering. "A galling

situation, but temporary. It was only a matter of finding the proper cat's-paw for the job."

"Namely Hansel? I'll bet he jumped at the chance to get rich quick. Greedy little bastard."

Her lip curled. "Will it surprise you to learn that the lure of gold was secondary in persuading him? Who would expect a common gunsel who sold his favours to be a romantic at heart? It was simple to disguise myself as Carlisle and seduce him, then open his eyes to the possibility of obtaining a fortune at his former master's expense. I even made him think it was his own idea. Oh, I am brilliant!"

"And still you chased him off like that? After all the two of you meant to each other?" I clicked my tongue. "Flirt."

The look on her face would have given Beelzebub a case of frostbite. "He is lucky I let him escape alive, him and his floozy sister. Do you think I ever intended to share *anything* with them?"

"That goose can lay enough gold eggs to satisfy everyone in LA, if you don't count the boys down at City Hall. What's the matter, Einstein? You can't divide by three?"

"*You* would ask me to retain them as my partners? To *trust* them? *You*?" She sneered. "How long do you think it would be before they decided there was one too many hands in the egg basket and shoved *me* into a bake-oven, hmmm? Perhaps you did not learn from your previous experience with those brats, but I am no such fool. Farewell." She was done with the .45, so she turned it into a hankie and waved bye-bye with it before picking up the goose and starting to go.

"Hold it, sister!" I called after her. "You think you can just walk away from this?"

I'd been dealing with mortals too long; I'd forgotten what it was like to confront one of my own people. I just got my last word out when she turned on me faster than milk on a hot summer day and slammed me with the same lousy immobilization charm she'd used on the black bird. I felt my feet root themselves so firmly to the ground that I knew my ordinary escape spell was useless. A team of hopped-up gophers couldn't dig me free. Unless she ended it or something ended her, I was planted for the duration.

Maybe I couldn't move, but I could still fight. I struck back with my own incantation. It left my fingertips like a bolt of lightning, but it hit her like a splash of cheap cologne.

"My specialty is shielding spells," she said, coolly wiping my splattered sorcery off her face. "Or have you forgotten all I did for LeGras? None of your puny magics can touch me. *Now* will you let me leave in peace, or do I make you regret it?" She didn't bother waiting for an answer. I was beneath her contempt. When she showed me her back, she might as well have slapped my face.

"Aloha," I growled, and whispered the rest of what I had to say.

The black bird exploded in her arms like a honking cherry bomb. Feathers flew everywhere, blood drenched her carnival-coloured skirts, and one webbed foot landed smack on top of her head like the latest word in Paris millinery fashion. She whirled on me, shrieking: "*What have you done?! What in seven hells have you done?!*"

It was my turn to gloat and I did it pretty. "Just a little something for the war effort, sugar. *My* war. How long you think it'll be before the cops show up and find me stuck here? Bogey's a sloppy eater. With all the blood he spilled inside that house, they're gonna be asking a lot of questions, like about what happened to LeGras and his buddies. If my neck's got to pay the final bill for your shell game, I'm making sure that you don't get anything out of it except a couple slices of white meat and a bellyful of might-have-beens." I slipped my hands into my pockets, casual, and added: "Don't you listen to *The Shadow*, sister? *Crime does not pay.*" I tried to ape Lamont Cranston's creepy laugh; it came out a cackle.

"And fools do not live!" she screeched, her empty hands filling with the biggest damn' fireball I'd ever seen in all my years of witchcraft.

That was when I knew I'd bought me some serious trouble. You don't use a fireball unless you mean business,

and a witch only means that kind of business when she steps
into a no-holds-barred duel-to-the-death of sorcery. Fireball
spells contain the power of five hundred thousand sticks of
dynamite. Casting one takes so much out of you that you're
useless for a week after. On the other hand, one is usually all
it takes.

A fireball spell is so much destruction tucked into one little
package that it's a good thing only a few witches know how do
it. Too bad I'm not one of them.

When she saw me standing there, not even trying to conjure
up a fireball of my own, she smiled. For a second I knew how
Poland must've felt when the Wehrmacht swept over the
border. My last thoughts, just before she pulled back her
arm, took aim, and let fly, were: *Thank the Powers there's
nothing like this in mortal hands, and I hope there never will be or
we can kiss our broomsticks goodbye.*

Then the flames hit me.

I put back the glue brush and smoothed down the edges on the
latest newspaper clipping in my scrapbook. The accident was
still fresh enough for the dailies to use type so big I could read
it without my glasses. The gas company kept yapping about
how gas was safe, blaming the whole thing on customer
negligence, saying that Mr LeGras or one of his servants
must've done *something* wrong with the pipeline to call up
the biggest explosion in the history of the greater LA area.
They were partly right. LeGras *did* do something wrong, sure
enough, but the only pipeline with his name on it was the one
that went straight to Hell.

Bogey jumped up on my desk and sat on the open scrapbook, forcing me to pay attention to him. He was born a
demon, but he's all cat at heart. I'd be peeling gluey newsprint
off his tail for hours.

"Want your toy?" I asked. I took the silver chain off my
neck and let him swat at the little jade-and-pearl pinky ring
dangling from it. While Bogey played ping-pong solitaire, I
marvelled how something so small had contained power en-

ough to save my skin. Bogey's too. He'd ducked under my skirts just as the fireball hit.

Hit and bounced straight back onto the one who'd launched it. Thanks to the shielding spell on that little ring – a spell she'd set in place herself – the rogue witch got everything she'd been aiming at me, only tripled. Her own shielding spells couldn't stand up to that. There wasn't enough of her left to grease the wheels of a kiddie car.

"That was a close one," I told the cat. "Too close. When I couldn't take her down with my magic, I knew I'd have to turn her own against her. Too bad I had to blow up the bird, but I had to make her mad enough to want me dead. Lucky I managed to slip this baby on my finger in time or she'd've got her wish."

Bogey caught the ring with a left hook, yanking the chain out of my hand. I let him chew on it awhile. "I'm getting too old for this job," I sighed. "Even a cat can play me for a sucker. Gretel did it too, easy; *too* easy. I *knew* better than to trust her, but still I let her reel me in like a prize marlin. Suckers make lousy detectives. Pretty good corpses, but lousy detectives. Maybe it's time I retired, found a cosy cottage up the coast, got back into the bakery business, a little baby-sitting, six of one—"

My office door flew open with a bang. She was five-foot-six of danger, half of it legs, the other half fireworks. "I need your help," she said. She had one of those breathy voices that leave you gasping for air like you've just been kissed, long, hard, and professionally. "It's my stepmother. I – I think she wants me dead."

I nodded her into a chair. When she crossed those gams, my little dream house on the coast went up in a fireball bigger than anything LeGras's pet witch ever threw at me. Oh sure, I knew the odds were stacked against her giving me a tumble, but I do my best work when I've got more stars in my eyes than Graumann's Chinese Theater's got in their cement.

That was when I knew that this was how my life was going to stay, until the day they chucked my broom into the janitor's closet at the LA morgue: One case after another, rubbing elbows with the dolls and the deadbeats, the chumps and the chisellers, the gophers, gorillas and goons, with maybe a princess or two thrown in to keep the game interesting. A whole lot of fairy tales and not enough happily-ever-afters.

But hey. That's the way the cookie crumbles. Or the ginger-bread.

FROG

Tina Rath

*You've met Tony Rath, now here's his other half, Tina.
Tina has been selling stories for nearly thirty years, including a poem that was published on a bus in Hackney! Please
don't ask why. She is noted for her knowledge of vampires in
fact and fiction, though the following story has shapechan-
ging of another kind. When I started this anthology I made
up my mind I wasn't going to have any more stories on the
theme of the Frog Prince. Not one. Not even half of one.
Well, maybe a bit. But this is different.*

"This is going to be a very difficult letter. You see, I don't
really know where to start, or even who to address. Dear
everyone, I suppose. Well, then – Dear everyone – I'm really
sorry. No, truly I am. I know you did your best for me, and
don't think that I'm not grateful. You stood by me when the
tabloids mounted that campaign suggesting that I'd left eight
hundred fatherless tadpoles in the Well at the World's End,
and you said that DNA tests wouldn't be necessary to disprove
the allegations, although I was perfectly willing to—"

The prince sat back for a moment, staring down at the thick,
marbled paper. And was that because they really did trust me,
he wondered, or because they were afraid the tests might show
that those tadpoles were my offspring? After all, I was in that

well for a hundred years, and a frog can get pretty lonely – am I sure even now that those tests would have put me in the clear? He sighed, and started to write again.

"And when that cable channel wheeled out Sir Mortimer Groaning, the pop-genealogist, who said that in spite of my having clearly undergone a successful transformation there was always a chance that I would introduce frog genes into the royal bloodline, you came right out there, fighting for me—"

Although perhaps it might have been done with more, well, sensitivity. He remembered his then future father-in-law shouting at his fainting then future mother-in-law, who'd had a preview of the tapes.

"For Heaven's sake, woman! Look at your own family, I mean look at them with an unprejudiced eye, and tell me that most of them wouldn't be improved by the addition of a few frog genes. I mean to say, frog genes aren't the worst thing in your blood-line, if you'll allow me to remind you of it. Look at your aunt Ethelburga. I know your family always told everyone that she was rescued by young Siegefried from that dragon just in the nick of time, but I'm not so sure of that. Oh, I know, they arranged a quick marriage, because of course it was love at first sight, they said, and then a good long honeymoon to allow them both to recover from their ordeal, and lo and behold they come back from a year in the wilds of Ruritania with those triplets. Well, they could be Siegefried's, I suppose, he was no oil painting, but I do have to say that Franz and Ernst are the only young men of my acquaintance who have never needed to borrow a cigar lighter. And that girl, Ethelinda, she's got scales! Iridescent green scales! – Not unattractive, in an odd sort of way," he added thoughtfully.

His then future mother-in-law muttered something into her sodden handkerchief.

"Yes, madam, I do know that your mutual great-grandmother was a mermaid, but it seems very odd to me that scales haven't come out in any other part of the family. And you are not going to tell me, I hope, that she was also a fire-breathing mermaid!"

The prince smiled wryly. His now never-to-be father-in-law had not really liked him any more than the rest of the family had. But he loved his daughter and the circumstances of his transformation had been, well, even in this day and age, just a tad unfortunate. The old man might even have been grateful that he was so anxious to go through with the wedding. There can be few fathers who react with delight when they discover that their only daughter's pet frog has turned into a young man overnight, especially when she has chosen to keep him in her bedroom . . . Not that the princess had seemed to mind at the time . . . but he mustn't think about her. He went back to his letter:

"In fact, you all did your best to make me welcome and I know that it's my fault that I just didn't fit in. I did my best too, but I'm afraid that a hundred years in the well at the World's End hasn't really fitted me for a life in the spotlight. There always seems to be so much to do here—"

Always, he thought, an abattoir to open, or some provincial mayor to engage in stilted conversation, or some deadly dull state function to attend. But he might have been able to put up with it all, even the mayors and the abattoirs if – but when he'd seen her stricken face tonight – it was tonight's banquet that had finally finished him, of course.

"—And I've come to believe that I'm just not the right person to do it. It wasn't really the incident tonight. That was no one's fault, and I'm sure—"

Well, it *was* someone's fault, actually. He'd seen Franz and Ernst, sniggering in those long moustaches they wore to conceal their ever-so-slightly non-human dentition, just before the man-servant had lifted the lid on the dish he was presenting to him to reveal – frog's legs! He couldn't help it. He'd rushed from the table, and later sent a message that he was too ill to join the rest of the family at the grand ball. And then he'd locked his bedroom door, and, in fear and hope, he'd sat on his bed and dialled a certain number. Would she be in? Would she, after all this time, still be alive? And if in and alive, would she be willing to help?

He tried to remember the exact circumstances of his trans-frogmification. Everyone – even the tabloids and the satellite channels – had assumed that it was a christening curse: some bad-tempered old bat whose invitation had gone astray in the post had turned up at the ceremony anyway and given the baby webbed feet. It happened every day. Well, every hundred years, and mostly in royal circles but it *did* happen. The trouble was, he didn't think it had been quite like that. A hundred years is a long time, but he had a feeling that it had been more – personal. And that she hadn't been an old hag at all . . . the phone was still ringing. She wasn't going to be there . . . and then someone picked up the receiver at the other end of the line.

"Had enough, have you, then?" she had asked in that achingly familiar voice, even before he told her who was speaking. "Thought you might. Well, I can transform you into a frog again, but that'll be it. A frog you'll be and a frog you'll stay. No more disenchantments for you, my lad."

"That's just what I want," he said.

"Quite sure?"

"Quite sure," he echoed desolately.

"All right, then. Here's what you do—"

He looked at his letter. It already said too much, and at the same time not nearly enough. Abruptly he picked up his pen and scrawled:

"Sorry again. Love you all. Don't try to find me. Goodbye."

Then he went out onto his balcony. It was an easy jump to the garden, particularly for him. He was very good at jumping. Following the witch's instructions, he moved quietly over the dew-wet lawn. The Well moved about a bit, and just now he had been promised it would be at the end of the gardens. He thought, as he had found himself doing so often recently, of his years in the well. It was astonishing how much time you could spend watching cloud shadows on water. And leaves. It was true, that old saying that no two leaves are alike. And of course there were more exciting times: fierce crystal days of frost when the edges of the Well crisped into ice, and, almost best of all, those long still evenings at the end of a hot day, when the upper part of the Well water was almost the same temperature as the cooling air, and you could lie on a lily leaf, not sure if you were in water or sky . . . For a moment he hesitated, gazing back at the darkened palace – thinking how much he had wished he could show his princess just how wonderful his Well had been – and then a rustle in the bushes jerked him back to the present. He rather hoped it was Franz or Ernst. No one was going to stop him now, and he would much prefer to clobber either or both of those gentlemen than an innocent palace guard.

But then a bright head emerged from the undergrowth, followed by a pair of pale shoulders and a white satin dress.

"Where are you going?" hissed his betrothed.

"I'm going back to the Well," he said desperately. "I must. It would never have worked—"

"It won't work here," she agreed. "That's why I'm coming with you."

"What!"

"You want to be a frog, I'll be a frog. That's what marriage is about, after all."

"But the kingdom—"

"Let Franz and Ernst fight over it if they want it. If anyone will let them, after the scandal."

"What scandal?" he asked.

"The scandal that is going to break in tomorrow's papers. You see, Aunt Ethelburga's dragon had a mate. She was brooding her eggs at the time, which perhaps accounted for the thing with Aunt Ethelburga, and in spite of the trauma she managed to hatch them all. Two boys and a girl. Apparently this is what dragons usually produce. The boys don't want to talk, they're willing to let bygones be etc, typical male, but the girl will. She is, she claims, Franz and Ernst's half-sister. And she'll take a blood test to prove it. And she'll do topless pix if the price is right."

"Topless?" he said blankly.

"Dragons," she said, "are rather unusual. They hatch their

young out of eggs, but they also suckle them. And this young
female is quite – sinuous. I understand that she has six out-
standing reasons for appearing on page three in one of our
most popular tabloids."

"Six?"

"Six. Dragons have six."

"Does Ethelinda—?"

"No one knows – but she's never appeared in public wearing
a bikini – of course, that could be because of the scales."

"How did you find out about – all this?"

"We've always known, but until tonight I was ready to go
along with the family cover-up. Until I saw your face when he
took the cover off that dish."

"But – I thought when I looked at you that you'd given up
on me."

"No. I'd given up on *them*."

He whistled softly. "Are you sure you want to be a frog? I
mean, the Well at the World's End can be very quiet—"

"Yes," she said firmly. "I've burned my boats, really. I
want to spend a hundred years watching cloud shadows."

"I never thought you were listening when I told you about
them."

"I was listening, all right. What do we have to do?"

"The witch said: Follow the Silver Road across the lawn."

"Silver Road?"

"Snail trails," he said prosaically. "They'll lead us to the
Well, and by the time we get there—"

"We'll have changed." She hauled up her satin skirts and
led the way, peering at the grass for snail tracks. He followed
her, completely taken aback by this turn of events. As they
walked towards the Well the sky began to lighten. The tiny
trails of snail slime glowed, glittered and expanded. They
really were following a Silver Road. And as the witch had
promised, the Change began to happen. His horrible dry skin
became cool and delicious, another whole organ of sensation:
he could feel the freshening morning air, and the sweetness of
the dewy grass in every exquisite inch of it; his clumsy feet and

hands became delicate webbed paws – he hopped free of his banqueting clothes and glanced nervously towards his betrothed. Her dress lay on the grass, and the most beautiful lady frog he had ever seen was negligently disengaging herself from a pearl necklace.

"Do I look all right?" she asked shyly.

"You look – wonderful." He kissed her emerald snout, and paw in webby paw they scurried towards the Well, reaching the kerb just as the sun rose. They dived into its wonderful, cool mysterious depths – and vanished for ever from mortal sight.

To live, happy for ever ever after.

THE SWORDS
AND THE STONES

E.K. Grant

E.K. Grant is a very private and paranoid person. It is not that he is really mentally ill; he says he just hates answering telephones and doorbells while he's trying to write, and adds that They are always out to get him anyway. He has, at various times, been an Eagle Scout, a newspaper journalist, a professional photographer, a police reservist, a private pilot, a salvage diver, a ski patrolman, a small-arms instructor, a wilderness search-and-rescue specialist, a movie and TV scriptwriter, and a semi-professional couch potato specializing in short-lived but unrewarding TV series. Oh, and he occasionally teaches college courses in Electrical & Electronic Engineering, Computer Science, and English Lit. Anyway, that's what he tells me. But otherwise I don't know who the hell he is.

This wasn't the way it was supposed to be. He was supposed to be a mighty-thewed warrior with a massive, majicked, two-handed sword slung over his back. He was supposed to be huge, and strong, and gifted in the arts of war. He wasn't supposed to be famished, dehydrated, bleeding through a dozen clumsily bandaged minor wounds, and having trouble breathing.

Worse, the Singing Sword hadn't ceased its pained cater-wauling since it had been broken. The half-blade in his pack tended to moan at a slightly higher pitch, an elfin whining counterpoint to the soft wailing of the half-sword in his belt scabbard, that set his teeth on edge. No one had ever warned him a magic Singing Sword would switch to an agonizing duet if it got broken.

Thol leaned against a cairn of stones, pursing his lips and blowing hard. He'd found it helped the dizziness. Below, far below, and leagues to the west, he could see the Rapid River snaking its way across the Valley of Ild, the breadbasket of the Gilded Kingdom. The very thought was torture; it was late enough in the season that there was no snow left, and at these higher elevations, there were no freshets of snow-melt handy for drinking. For two days he'd had no water left in his gourd. The springs were dried up and the trees turned to desiccated dead wood, stark in the high-altitude winds that tore the moisture from his lips and left him croaking through a tor-tured throat. If he didn't find water soon, he wouldn't be able to make it back down into the valley. But this was where the Sword wanted to go, and it was a case of go where the Sword wanted to go, or listen to it howl even louder.

He'd tried burying it, but it caught up to him the first time he stopped to sleep; so he buried it under the biggest rocks he could move, and it caught up to him the first time he stopped to sleep. Hanegral the Mage had made that sword for the Royal Family of Ild, and it was bound and determined to stay with the last surviving member of the family.

He shifted his weight a bit, trying to move into the cairn's shadow, and the hilt of the half-sword at his belt banged into the rock with a metallic clinking noise. The Sword emitted an ugly sound, a sort of musical snarl. A mountain marmot poked its head out of the rocks on the uphill side of the trail, looked him over, and said, "Beat it, guy. You're on my land, and the wife and kids want to come out and sun themselves."

Thol shook his head. He'd heard about mountain visions caused by thin air and exposure, but wouldn't have believed it could happen to him. He tried to spit at the marmot, but his mouth was dry as desert stone. "You're not real," he said. "Get lost." His throat was so dry that his voice barely sounded, and it hurt from the attempt.

The marmot looked at him quizzically, braced its forepaws against a large rock, and rocked it out of the loose pile. It fell and rolled, gathering speed, and bounced across the path to smack against Thol's ankles, knocking his feet from beneath him. He started sliding, and barely managed to jam a clenched fist into a gap in the rock when his lower body was already over the edge. As he levered himself back up to the path, another big rock came bouncing at him, and he moved his head aside barely in time to avoid being bashed a good one right between the eyes.

"Hold still, will you?" complained the marmot.

"Not a chance," said Thol. "I didn't climb all the way up here to get killed by an overgrown rat." He moved frantically, making it over the edge and back onto the pathway in time to leap aside when the next big rock came tumbling past.

"Curse you!" said the marmot. It squirrelled its way through the loose rock-fall stacked against the uphill side of the pathway and took up a position directly above Thol. "Now just hold still a second while I get this one moving, that's a nice human." It set its forepaws against a rock twice the size of Thol's head, and strained at it. It teetered slightly.

Thol drew his half-sword, ragged-tipped and about a forearm long, and moved closer. Marmot blood would be a great thirst-quencher, and he could worry about talking marmots after he found out if uncooked marmot meat was palatable. Great Golth knew he'd eaten worse things in recent days.

"Help! Murder!" screamed the marmot, and darted into the depths of the rock slide, chittering snottily.

Thol moved closer cautiously, and realized there was some sort of chiselled sign in the rock-wall behind the big rock the marmot had been pushing. Keeping a wary eye out for further attacks, he moved it aside, and found two deeply incised runes that must date from ages ago, since the rock in the cuts had weathered to the same shade as the surface. Danger? Beware?

"BEWARE (the) < something >" they said. He didn't know the second sign. It looked like an animal symbol rather than a name symbol, more of an ideograph than a letter-rune. It had four wide flat legs, a long neck, and there seemed to be large teeth, but perhaps that was just the way the rock had chipped.

He realized there was more below, and shoved loose rocks aside to read much newer, shallower runes someone had added. "AND THE MARMOTS."

The marmot popped out again, close above, and another head-sized rock bounced down, grazing his shoulder. Reflexively, he swung the broken sword, turning it at the last moment to smack the marmot with the flat side, dazing it. He grabbed the thing by its head and yanked it out of the rocks, amazed to find that it had six legs, the front two ending in tiny hands. He tossed it on the ground belly up, put a foot firmly on its chest, and threatened it with his sword while it recovered.

"What goes here? Six-legged talking marmots? Not to mention attacking instead of hiding. Where's the wizard?" He looked around, keeping an eye on the marmot under his boot.

The marmot squeaked, making gasping noises. He moved the broken sword-edge against its throat and eased up a bit.

It gasped for air and said, "Get off, you oaf! I'm suffocating!"

Thol pressed down again. "Nothing doing. I'm dying of thirst, and I figure marmot blood should do about as well as water."

There was a sudden wail of panicked squealing to his right, and he looked over to see another large marmot, and a half-dozen small marmot faces, sticking out of gaps in the rockfall. "Noooooo!" they chorused.

"The wife and kids?" he asked.

"Do your worst," said the marmot. "Just leave them alone."

It angled its head up to provide easier access to the side of its neck.

Thol took his foot off the marmot and sheathed his half-sword. "Hmm. Ten points for the value system, even if you are a snotty roadside murderer. No more rocks, and we call it even, okay?"

The marmot thought for a second, nodded, got its feet under itself, and staggered back into the rocks.

There were scrabbling noises, and then its head poked out between a couple of rocks. "There's water further up the slope behind us. Look for the cave. Be real polite to the old man. He doesn't like company either." The marmot heads all disappeared into the rocks, as though attached to the same puppeteer's string.

Thol scrambled up the heap of rocks and realized that the rockfall covered an old side-trail, winding up the mountainside out of view. There was crumbled scree all over it, with no footmarks apparent in the loose surface.

Intriguingly, his sword was crying in a less agonized tone; this must be the direction it wanted to go. It took him a palm-width of sun movement to reach the top, since he had to keep stopping to breathe. He passed a series of rune-signs, variations on the ancient warning by the rock-slide, all containing the odd-animal symbol. Moving warily, he peered around a large rock and saw the opening of a cave, with potted plants all around it and a small pool of water in front, and forgot his fatigue.

He approached carefully, stepping around crudely chiselled steles covered with rune-signs he did not recognize although the odd-animal symbol was a recurrent motif. He went straight to the pool, kneeling warily, trying to look in all directions at once as he filled his gourd. Being this close to water and not being able to leap into it was agonizing, but this was unknown territory.

"Good," said the old man who hadn't been there a split second before. "You're not one of these undisciplined louts who goes face down in the first puddle, presenting an easy target."

The half-sword at his belt chimed a happy, bell-like tone, and Thol suspected he'd found his man. He asked, "Your name wouldn't be Hanegral, would it?"

The old man whipped a full-length staff out of thin air and twirled it menacingly. "Who wants to know?"

The wariness was a good sign. Hanegral was known for having been hounded out of a neighbouring kingdom a few years back, something about a payment dispute, a Shrinking Curse, and a king's favorite organ. Wizards tended to live highly peripatetic lives, especially when they refused to forgive contracted debts.

Thol stood, carefully holding his gourd in his left hand. He knew he couldn't stand up to a skilled staff-wielder with half a sword, and if he had to run for it the water was going with him.

"I'm Thol, Prince-Designate of Ild. Our capital was overrun by Krollok's forces six days ago, and my father killed in battle. I bear the Singing Sword of Ild, which was crafted by the Mage Hanegral, and I need to find him to get it fixed."

The old man's face darkened, and he grounded his staff with a thump. "Krollok, you say? You have your father's look about you, that's for sure. And that looks like one of mine." The staff vanished into thin air. He gestured to the sword. "Let's see it."

Thol drew the sword gently, and handed it over hilt first. It warbled like an injured bird as the old man took it, and the old man winced.

Hefting the half-sword, the man said, "Yes, definitely one of mine. But how the Flames could it have been broken? We guarantee this model unbreakable." He looked at Thol and added, "For Sun's sake, man, drink. You're in no danger."

Thol gratefully lifted the gourd and sipped about half of it as slowly as he could. The old man nodded approval and said, "Good. Hold off for a time, let yourself adjust. Then you can slug down a proper drink without losing it."

He held the sword up to the sun and sighted along the blade. "No bend, no warp. I don't suppose you have the rest?"

Thol opened his pack and handed over the other half.

While the old man held that part to the sun and looked along its edges, shaking his head, Thol took the opportunity to kneel and refill the gourd to its top, cork it, and sling it at his belt. The sword-halves were warbling a muted, happy, off-key duet.

"No bend or distortion here, either," said the old man. "I don't understand it. Well, come on inside and we'll check it over."

Carrying a part of the Singing Sword in each hand, he led the way into the cave mouth, and Thol followed closely. His relationship with the Sword was, at best, highly adversarial, but he wasn't about to lose track of it after all this trouble.

The cave mouth was only a couple of man-heights wide, and perhaps one and a half tall, but just inside it widened greatly. Thol could see some sort of illumination farther inside, and make out dim walls slanting up and away.

"Here," said the Mage. "A bit of light so you can see the digs." He transferred the parts of the Sword into one hand, and the staff reappeared in the other, its upper tip now a blaze of white fire. The old man bowed formally to the wall and said, "By your leave, may we please pass?"

Thol looked around at a forest of glittering stalactites and stalagmites, and caught his breath as he looked at the wall stretching up to the side. It was roughly flat, and there were bones set into it, something huge, squashed, embedded for ever in the living stone. The body was long and oval, perhaps three man-lengths, and it had four legs, not set like a walking animal's, but wide and paddle-shaped. The neck was a long, looping curve rising to a small head many feet above.

The Mage smiled softly. "It's a swimming lizard that lived here long, long ago. It was old and tired, and sank in the mud at the bottom of the sea, buried for so many years that its very bones turned to stone. But while it was dying, it dined on passing creatures. See?" He indicated a heap of strange petrified bones in the rock before the creature, a tumble of fragments that indicated more than one meal.

Thol was amazed. "I've never seen anything like that.

Sometimes diggers find bones made of rock, but the philosophers tell us they're the bones of rock giants who died and were buried."

The Mage shook his head. "No. I was intrigued, and spent a lot of time working spells to let me see and talk with the creature as it died. It was so long ago that we can't even number the years exactly, and the world had no men, nor any giants, in it then." He turned away to move farther into the cave. "A good exercise; I learned a great deal about talking to creatures, and earning their aid. We often reach through time to talk to each other, although its interests are somewhat limited. I always try to address it politely, since even though it's not terribly bright, it appreciates formal courtesy. Politeness is very important to it. Did you see the elegant curve of the neck? I think of it as a 'Please-and-thank-you sea Saurian'."

They entered a brightly lit room, and the Mage's staff dimmed and disappeared again. The Mage walked over to a wide stone workbench next to a dully glowing forge, and set the pieces of the Singing Sword down, juxtaposed as they would have been were it whole.

He picked up a huge pane of mica set in a circular bronze frame, tapped it with a wand that appeared in one hand, and looked through it at the blade.

"Incredible," he said. "Here, take a look."

Thol moved forward to see through the circle. The Singing Sword was a bar of glowing, pulsing, purple light; there were flaring red areas in it, and at the jagged break the ends of both pieces were an ugly bloody colour.

"You see?" asked the Mage. "At these points—" he indicated the red spots "—something has acted to destroy the spell that makes it a whole, the magical temper that makes its steel unbreakable."

Thol's memory flashed back to the apocalyptic duel of champions, his father against Krollok. There had been a huge flash of sparks every time the swords clashed. He said, "I think those spots are where Krollok's sword hit it."

The Mage looked off into the distance for a moment.

"Interesting," he said. He looked around, spotted a couple of bits of metal on a nearby table, and brought them over to the bench. A few moments of experimentation established that the spots that showed bright red under the viewing circle were highly magnetized.

The old man nodded and turned to face Thol. "Krollok. I wondered when I heard the name, and now I know; this kind of thing is exactly his style. Lazy ex-student of mine, not one I'm proud of. Ran off when he failed his first Journeyman's tests, couldn't be bothered to keep at his studies. He can't make a Singing Sword himself, but he knows enough about them to attack their strengths. Looks like he magicked his blade to create intense jolts of magnetism at points of contact – the harder the blow, the more intense the magnetism. Sufficiently intense magnetism destroys the spell-temper of the special steel I use in Singing Swords, not to mention just shattering your basic run-of-the-mill sword."

"So there's nothing I can fight him with."

"Of course there is. I've been working with a new alloy, and magnetism won't touch it. It won't be a Singing Sword, but it'll do the job."

Thol pointed to the blade on the bench. "The Singing Sword is an – emblem – of the Kingdom of Ild. My father carried it for decades, and it never failed him. When it was broken, the heart went out of our people."

"Understandable," said the old man. "That model had an exceptional repertoire, especially when in its own scabbard. I'll do my best to mend it for you, but we need to set you up with something you can use to fight Krollok. Bad for business, having my customers get hurt." He stuck a couple of fingers into his mouth and whistled an ear-piercing shriek.

A couple of small fuzzy creatures gallumphed into sight, craning up to peer at the Sword. They were grey, the colour of granite, and they'd come right out of the stone walls. Rock gnomes.

The old man gabbled at them in their weird language, and they gabbled back. The discussion ended, and one of them walked over to the forge and began pumping it up to a white heat.

"Come on," said the old man. "They'll do the repair weld, and a basic reforge, and it won't be fun to be here. Your average Singing Sword gets really noisy when you heat it up white-hot and start whacking on it with hammers. And the way they scream during the magical tempering process, it's horrible." He shuddered.

Thol winced sympathetically; his imagination was good.

In another chamber, the old man dug out a new sword with a strange golden colour and handed it to him. "Here, give this one a try."

It was thicker and broader than an average fighting sword, but seemed lighter. Puzzled, Thol tapped it and listened to the ring. It had an eerie chiming tone.

The old man grinned. "That's god-metal, left in the earth by the Titans. Cursed hard to separate out; easy to find, hard to smelt and work, strong as steel, but a third lighter. I usually alloy it with bronze to make it more workable, since it's almost impossible to forge. Have to use special spells to get the heat up high enough to soften it."

He pointed over to a workbench. "Need special tongs, too; at those temperatures, regular tongs just melt." He pointed to a practice pell set in a hole in the floor. "Give that a few whacks and see how it balances for you."

A few sweaty minutes later, the pell was matchwood and Thol was admiring the sword, running through practice phrases with it. "Amazing," he said. "The way you've got it balanced to compensate for the oversize tip."

The Mage just grinned. "Look at the edges very closely." There were tiny wavy lines in the edges, different-coloured ripples. Thol looked up at the Mage, curiously.

"It's a trick they use in the east," said the Mage. "You use two metals, one very hard but brittle, and one softer and elastic. You work them in layers, folding them over again and again, and get a sword that's the best of both, very hard and very elastic. That piece is made of my two best alloys of Titanmetal and bronze. Cuts through standard sword-metal pretty easily."

"And it's proof against the spell that destroyed the Singing Sword?"

The old man grinned evilly. "Should be very educational for Krollok. There's no magic in that sword to attack. We used magic to make it, but magic isn't part of what it is, if you get my drift."

Thol looked down at the golden sword in his hand. "You understand, I can't pay you for this. Krollok and his troops have complete control over the central valley, and I'm penniless."

The old man passed it off with a wave. "I charged high for the Singing Sword, and guaranteed it unbreakable. Think of it as a loaner while we do warranty repairs on your father's sword. I owe your family, anyway; I should have followed through on that rotten apprentice when he ran off. If I had, your Singing Sword would still be in good working order. I'd have killed him like a shot if I'd suspected he was going to use magic to go into real-estate acquisition. Complete violation of Guild rules."

"Still, I feel that I owe you a debt."

"Very well," said the Mage. "If you live, bring me back that sword—" he pointed to the golden blade "—and bring me back Krollok's sword, so I can figure out how he made it, and perhaps find a way to proof against the damage it can do. Can't have my whole product line's reputation compromised because someone's built a sword specifically designed to destroy mine."

"Done," said Thol.

There was a strange, sourceless chittering in the air around them and the Mage cocked his head, listening intently. "Umm. My marmots report a group of men have gotten past them. Well, they're only the first line of defence, anyway. Let's go see what we have to deal with. Anyone following you?"

Thol nodded unhappily. "I don't know how. I've tried not

to leave any trail, I've walked in rivers for miles, travelled over hard stone whenever I could. I thought I was a good woodsman."

"You probably are," said the Mage. He pointed a thumb back over his shoulder. "But tracking a Singing Sword is something any journeyman can do, especially if he's got the scabbard. Any of the gold mountings from the scabbard will resonate to the Sword. That's how we generate the major chords. Let's go see who's following you."

They walked back toward the entrance, passing the chamber where the rock gnomes were working at reforging the Singing Sword. The air was tortured with its screams, and Thol noticed the rock gnomes had tufts of waxed cotton stuffed in their ears to reduce the noise. He winced a bit at every shriek. The Mage said, "Don't let it bother you too much. Singing Swords aren't really alive, they just like to put on airs. Prima donnas."

They passed the wall with the bones of the "Please-and-thank-you" water lizard, the Mage doing a quick bow and whispering a polite greeting, and Thol saw a moving shadow outside. He reflexively pushed the old man behind him, drawing the golden sword. There were crashing noises and splashes.

"Damn," whispered the old man. "I hate when this sort of thing happens."

Thol muttered an imprecation and added, "Really sorry about this. I'll hold them off while you get away."

The Mage shook his head, and his staff appeared in his hand. He gestured toward the opening, inviting Thol to accompany him. They edged out warily, and found a half-dozen of Krollok's men kicking the potted plants around and roistering in the pool. One of them had a big six-legged marmot and a couple of little ones hanging from his belt, their necks circled by tight loops of gut. He was engaged in pushing over one of the rune-steles while the rest cheered him on.

Thol walked to a clear area, ignored by the intruders, and

yelled, "STOP THAT." To his side, he was peripherally aware of a humming staff twirling through the air, and a hollow wooden clonking sound. One of the men took a header into the pool he'd been climbing out of, limp as a boiled mackerel.

The man just in front of Thol rushed at him, his sword cutting down in a straight blow, and Thol got the golden sword around and into a rising block just in time. It sheared the man's sword, leaving him with a short stub in his hand, and Thol was able to take off his head with a neat backstroke. He turned instantly to face two more coming at him, one with a staff and one with another sword. It took a bit more finesse, but not much, since the golden sword cut through their weapons like a knife through hot butter. He'd launched a crude horizontal cut, intending to take out one and go after the other on recovery, and was surprised when the golden sword cut through both on the same swing. He turned again to check on the Mage, and saw him standing over two bodies, one still face down in the pool. That left one. He pivoted madly, just in time to see a huge glowering face with a great ugly gold tooth, as a club took him in the side of the head.

He managed to whip the golden sword around as he fell, cutting the club off just above its wielder's hand, but he knew he'd taken a good whack, since he was hallucinating. He could have sworn the big marmot hanging at the man's belt winked at him as he was falling to his hands and knees. There was a sound of running footsteps, and the Mage's voice yelling "NO! DON'T GO IN THERE!" and the world went black.

He came to slowly, realizing that his head was ringing like a gong, in slow agonizing throbs. He forced his eyes open, and saw the Mage's face looking down at him, concerned.

"I was afraid we were going to lose you there."

Thol tried to talk, and all that came out was a croak. The Mage slipped him a bit of water from a cup and helped him sit up. The pain in his head was receding rapidly, and he dared to feel the area where he'd been struck. Odd; there was no tenderness or swelling. He looked down beside him and saw a bloody poultice and some phials of potions marked with mage-runes.

The Mage nodded. "Yes. You've made it this far, you'll be good as new in a few more minutes."

"The last man," Thol said. "He was running into your cave. We have to catch him!"

"No. He's no longer a problem."

Thol struggled to his feet. "He had a gold tooth. Does that mean anything?"

"Probably," said the Mage. "Krollok could have magicked him a new tooth using one of the golden bosses from the Sword's scabbard. Instead of being led around by the nose, he's been following his tooth to the Sword."

Thol picked up the golden sword and sheathed it, and the Mage extended a supporting arm to help him walk to the cave entrance. The staff appeared, illuminating the gloom, and Thol saw strands of shredded gut that had held the murdered marmots, a chopped-up heap of rent fibres. There were chitterings and rustlings in the dark among the stalagmites.

"I don't understand. Where did he go?"

The Mage pointed to the wall, where the huge water-lizard's bones loomed. The head and neck appeared to be in a slightly different position than Thol remembered, and when he looked at the heap of fossilized bones before it, the topmost set looked almost human. There was a tiny glint of corroded gold among the teeth in the crushed skull. He nodded slowly, remembering the Mage's comment about "first line of defence".

Hanegarl explained. "When I worked my spells to reach him, they also allowed him to reach anywhen through the eons. He's been guarding those who live in this cave and attract impolite predators since the cave itself formed. Didn't you notice all the warning runes?

"Should we get started digging graves for the other five?"

The Mage shrugged. "Not necessary. My rock gnomes love

fresh meat, and they can use the two live ones for slave labour as long as they behave themselves."

Thol looked at the glints of sparkling little marmot-eyes watching him from the gloomy shadows among the bases of the stalagmites.

The Mage noticed his gaze and commented, "The cheeky little buggers are great at playing dead until they get a chance to rip your jewels off. They picked their time and held him up just long enough so the water lizard would wake up and reach through to now for a snack. Always nice to have them on your side, even when they're being lazy and playing dead."

A sarcastic chitter came out of the darkness, and a flying pebble bounced off the Mage's forehead. "Of course, there are still moments when I think that giving them hands was a considerable error."

Thol placed his left hand on the pommel of the golden sword and said, "With this, I'll have a chance against Krollok. But it occurs to me that if I lose, I should arrange for him to stop by and meet your friends. I'll set up some good bait, just in case. Perhaps a letter directing my loyalists to come here for more of these god-metal swords, without mentioning your name."

Hanegral smiled. "I doubt you'll lose in a fair fight. Krollok never had the discipline to be much of a swordsman. But if it happens, I'll do my best to introduce him to my pet water-lizard for you. After all, to a very polite water-lizard, Krollok will just be one more uncouth snack."

A CASE OF
FOUR FINGERS

John Grant

*John Grant (or Paul Barnett to give him his real name) has
published over fifty books under one name or another,
including about twenty novels and children's books. His
best-known non-fiction books are probably* The Encyclopedia of Walt Disney's Animated Characters *(third edition, 1998) and (with John Clute)* The Encyclopedia of
Fantasy *(1997). His fiction includes* Albion *(1991),* The
World *(1992), the Leonie Strider space opera series and the
twelve novels in the* Legends of Lone Wolf *series. Paul has
received the Hugo Award, the World Fantasy Award, the
Mythopoeic Society Scholarship Award, the Locus Award,
the J. Lloyd Eaton Award and a British Science Fiction
Association Special Award (all as John Grant). No wonder
he had to move to America with all those awards. We can't
have such talented people living in Britain!*

They'd engraved the tombstone of Pretty Polly McTavish
with the parrot's tragic last words: "Hello Sailaaargh."

It was a touching gesture, and I don't think there was
anyone among the small huddle of mourners at the pet
cemetery who didn't have a tear in their eye as the Reverend

Jeremy Harcourt-Fruitcake plummily read out the last rites. Pretty Polly had sacrificed her life so that Miss Grimthorpe, the so-called Pantry Detective, could solve her forty-seventh and best-selling case so far, the grisly *Who Slew the Cockatoos?*

The grim service over, I headed off alone down Curling Lane to my home and workplace at the edge of the village.

Birds sang.

Bees buzzed.

Trees rustled.

Clouds did whatever it is that clouds do.

It was Indian Summer, always a busy time in the village.

Always a busy time for me.

Today I was going to have to process Pretty Polly McTavish and, if memory served aright, half a dozen other carcasses. Human ones.

But first I needed a cup of tea.

Strong tea.

Later I sat on my porch, savouring the Broken Orange Pekoe, looking at the sky, wondering if it was time for me to start searching, just out of interest, you understand, through the *Sits Vac* columns in the newspaper. Ten years – ten years I'd been doing this job, and that's a long time out of anyone's life. Especially since, if you looked at it another way, I'd been doing the job for something like a century. And despite the fact that even a long time doesn't take much of a chunk out of eternity.

But the century felt like an eternity in itself, is what I'm getting at.

The village always looked good in Indian Summer, which lasts about half the year in these parts. Christmas takes up a good part of the rest. Hallowe'en lasts a week and a half.

Maybe I'd better explain.

Maybe I'd better not.

Not yet.

I drained the last of the tea and flicked the cup so that the damp leaves at the bottom flew to land among the oleanders. God alone knows how they flourish so well, all year round, since I hate gardening. It's the digging. Makes me feel creepy.

Superstitious.

But that's the way I am.

The cup washed and put away in the cupboard, I sauntered from the house across to my workshed. It was tatty, corrugated-iron-roofed, wooden-walled, brown and greasy, just like it had been yesterday. Along one side of it were the heavy green plastic hoppers where the remains of the deceased were regularly dumped by the Authorities. One hopper per corpse. In Indian Summer it can get so busy that I need a dozen hoppers, but today, according to my accounts book – more accurate than my memory – there were only eight corpses to deal with. Still quite a number, but not as bad as it sometimes is.

Hopper number one. Accounts book and pencil out of pocket. Tick off Pretty Polly McTavish in the RECEIVED column. The brute had dispatched her with a baseball bat, so she wasn't a pretty sight. She'd require stitching before she was ready to be seen out and about again.

Hopper number two. The first body of a set of five, I knew. This one and the other four had been exotic dancers, all stripped naked except for skimpy red underwear, all slashed and mutilated in inventive ways. Dave Knuckle had been in town for the Case of the Parboiled Detective, soon to be published as *Smack My Butt, Babe*. Which of the mangled bimbos had been actual victims and which were merely his discarded girlfriends was always a tough one. Best left to the Authorities.

Hopper number seven. *Tick* went the pencil. The by-product of an ongoing case for Sir John. An Ashmolean sub-curator smothered by having a rolled-up paperback copy of *Piers Plowman* rammed down his throat. The acne scars were as livid as vintage port.

Hopper number eight.

Empty.

I coughed into it to listen to the little echoes confirm the evidence of my eyes. I stared at my accounts book in histrionic disbelief – these things should be done properly or not at all.

In my own neat, crabbed writing the entry was there, just as I'd written it down the night before when the Clerk of the Authorities had dictated it to me over the telephone.

"One corpse, male, with severed hand. Identity: Gerald G. Dukes, a.k.a. The Even Mightier Spongini. Profession: Stage magician. Age: 28."

There followed a few further personal attributes. The Clerk would have been bound to mention it had invisibility been one of them.

No, the hopper was definitely empty.

There'd never been an error before – not in the whole long ten-years-that-was-really-a-century-that-felt-like-eternity. Never *could* be.

But I ran to the house and the telephone to call the Clerk anyway.

Just in case.

And now maybe I better *had* explain. About the village of Cadaver-in-the-Offing, and about the way things are around here, and perhaps a bit about myself as well – even though I don't like the, you know, limelight.

Nestled among the rolling hills of Barsetshire, one of the lesser-known Home Counties, Cadaver-in-the-Offing is a sleepy little place – two shops and a pub and a scattering of houses, not to mention the church and the vicarage – but behind this veneer of tranquillity lurk seething passions and unfettered violence. More passions, more violence than in the rest of the country put together.

Because Cadaver-in-the-Offing is the place where detective stories happen.

The village has a population of about two hundred, if you look at it one way, and about two hundred thousand, if you look at it another. There have to be enough people so that the lesser characters in detective stories – the victims, the witnesses, the murderers, the romantic leads, the local colour – are always different. But economies can be made, and usually are, by recycling those characters.

Endlessly.

Who can honestly recall the countless lusty young men who've accompanied Dr Gideon Fell or Sir Henry Merrivale, and who've waltzed off with the pretty, young but feistily independent ingenue at the end of the case? Who can recall those ingenues either, come to that? The victims in Perry Mason's cases form a long train of utter anonymity, as do the various gorgeously pneumatic soubrettes who clutter up the proceedings. Who *didn't* commit the murder or solve the case in *The Nine Tailors* or *The Sign of Four* or *Inspector Queen's Own Case* or *The Mysterious Affair at Styles* or . . .

I could go on.

Once upon a time all these forgettable individuals actually had an independent existence, even if you couldn't tell them apart from each other any more than I'd been able to distinguish Dave Knuckle's discards in my hoppers.

It was wasteful.

Decades ago the Authorities, during one of their periodic spurts of cost-cutting, realized this. Downsizing was the zeal of the day. Why expend effort hiring individuals for the bit parts, why have to put out the cash for the undertaker's bills, when people could be found on the unemployment queues who'd be only too eager to accept zero wages in exchange for board, lodging . . . and immortality? Oh, sure, they'd have to accept being murdered every once in a while, but they wouldn't be dead long before being revived, given a different name, maybe a fresh wig, a new home to live in, a new role and probably a new spouse or lover.

Acting in conjunction with the Anti-Blood Sports League, the Authorities founded Cadaver-in-the-Offing.

And hired me.

Yes, I suppose you're probably still wondering about me. Frankly, the less said about me the better. I had my own reasons for coming to work in Cadaver-in-the-Offing, but presumably the law-enforcement agencies of various obscure Middle European countries have forgotten all about me by now – which was one of the reasons why I was contemplating resigning my post, that day in the midst of the overlong Indian Summer.

Or maybe they haven't. That's one of the reasons I won't resign quite yet.

The other? All will become clear, Tonstant Weader.

So let's just say no more than that it's my job to take the . . . the *secondary products* of the detectives' industry and . . . and *mend* them.

That's all you need to know.

Other than that, let my past be an obscurity and my present something only dimly perceived; let me be a faceless and nameless cypher.

"Hello, Victor," said the Clerk wearily when finally he answered the telephone. He packed decades' worth of disdain into those two words: just because Cadaver-in-the-Offing couldn't continue to function without my services – or those of another like me – doesn't mean that people are courteous to me. Oh, no: far from it. Most of them avoid me like the plague, and, whenever they're forced to deal with me, look at me like they've just trodden in something the cat's done.

Tell you the truth, I prefer it that way.

I explained my problem. For once I knew that I had his attention. I could hear the click of his keyboard in the background as he checked up on what I'd been telling him.

"Yes," he said at last. "I have the entry here on screen in front of me . . . Dukes . . . Even Mightier . . . inscrutable . . . magician. Hum. Ho. He is – *was* – part of a case for Inspector Romford."

"The one with the pipe, the puppies, the paunch and the passion for peppermints?"

"The very same. Big in the library market. Would be even bigger if it weren't for the difficulties he had kicking his crack habit. Hmm . . . he was supposed to have solved this case by now – it's just a short story. It was one of his stage rivals did it

– The Mighty Thrombosis – on account of the wife, Zelda. The Mighty Thrombosis's wife, that is. Usually the wife in a Romford case."

Even though the Clerk couldn't see me I held up a hand to stem the flow of words. "That's all as might be," I said, "but the fact of the matter is that I'm still a body short of my quota."

"Don't suppose you've got even the, harrumph, severed hand?"

"Not so much as a bleeding fingernail. I told you, I checked the hopper proper."

"Well, it's not my responsibility – I don't deal with the detailed stuff, as you know."

"I know."

In other words, the Clerk thought this was likely to be a knotty problem, and the quicker he got his rear covered the better.

"Delegate, boy, delegate," he said. "That's my motto. Eh?"

"I know."

He was going to dump me in it and leave me to sink or swim.

"Tell you one thing, though," he added, then paused. "This sounds like—" and I could almost hear the drums roll"—a Case For Inspector Romford!"

The phone went dead.

Quite how Inspector Romford's inability to solve a Case For Inspector Romford could be a Case For Inspector Romford was a logical tangle that part of me was trying to unravel as I ambled up Curving Lane towards the centre, if the village could be said to have such a thing, of Cadaver-in-the-Offing. It was about lunchtime, and so Romford would certainly be in the Heart & Sickle, drinking brown ale and keeping an ear open for clues. It's an old technique and can be effective. The sole disadvantage is that the brown ale tends to mean the clues, though gathered, get lost again.

I found him at a table in the corner, nursing a pint. Beside it was a whisky chaser. I raised my eyebrows.

"Needed a drop of the hard stuff," he said, seeing the direction of my gaze. "Don't mind telling you, whossname, that I'm bamboozled."

With the accent on the middle syllable, I thought, but I said nothing.

"Right there in front of my eyes it was done," he continued, "bold as brass and twice as natural. I thought I had it all sewn up within minutes, but it wasn't to be. Mark my words, there's more to this case than meets the hand."

I must have looked puzzled, because he added, leaning forwards confidentially towards me, "I would have said 'eye' but the hand's quicker, see?"

I said I saw.

"Bleeding conjurors, prestidigitators, stage magicians, illusionists, call them what you will," he mumbled through the froth on the top of his beer.

Pulling the wooden chair scrapingly back over the slate floor of the Heart & Sickle's snug, I asked him what he meant.

And he explained.

The previous night had seen a grand gala at St Boniface's Church Hall, beside Dead Man's Crossroads in the middle of Cadaver-in-the-Offing. The *Barchester Bugle* had been full of it for weeks. It was a rare honour for a conjuror so internationally prominent as The Mighty Thrombosis to treat a place as small as Cadaver-in-the-Offing to one of his performances, but his mother came from hereabouts and he wanted to try out a few new tricks in front of an unimportant audience, so to here he'd come.

ONE NIGHT ONLY
An Informal Evening with
THE MIGHTY THROMBOSIS

– the advertisements and handbills had said. And under that there was further news:

ably supported by
Helsinki's Most Dazzling Acrobatic Troupe
The Family Brød
"The Seven Deadly Finns"

Mrs Romford had booked tickets at once for herself and the Inspector, telling him that he'd just have to juggle his duty hours to accommodate her wishes. He'd made a song and dance about the difficulties of disrupting his schedule, but in fact he'd been glad enough to go: ever since he'd first dropped a hidden pack of cards as a child he'd been fascinated by the whole charisma of stage magic – the greasepaint, the aethereally beautiful assistants, the mystery, the spectacle, and the whole participatory *game* whereby the audience *knew* it was being hoodwinked yet believed in magic all the same.

So when his day's labours were over he changed into his second-best tweed suit, checked his mobile phone was working in case of emergencies ("There'd better *be* no emergencies," he'd growled at fresh-faced Sergeant Mutton), made sure he'd got plenty of tobacco and peppermints in his pocket for the walk home, and set off with his wife for the Church Hall.

They were among the first to arrive. The Reverend Jeremy Harcourt-Fruitcake had laid out the hard wooden chairs in neat rows from the front of the hall to the back, but so far only a handful of people were there to sit in them. Ignoring each other's protestations, the Romfords strode determinedly down the central aisle to settle themselves firmly as near to the middle of the front row as possible.

This was their big night out, and they wanted to miss nothing.

They weren't to be disappointed, although the magic they would see would not be quite of the kind they expected.

Romford chewed steadfastly on the stem of his dead pipe for what seemed like hours as the Hall slowly filled up. He recognized most of the people there, of course: Mrs Dora Griggs of Griggs House, still in mourning for the death of young Clarence, murdered during a performance of *Julius Caesar*; Dr Smithies, the bluffly reliable GP who had played such a hand in that case; Donald Glover, who ran the garage – all the noteworthies of Cadaver-in-the-Offing, in short, each of them looking as eagerly anticipatory as he himself . . .

At last it was time for the lights to dim.

A hissy recording of a fanfare split the air.

The silence throbbed.

Mrs Romford opened a packet of peanuts.

Someone sneezed.

Breath was bated.

And the curtain jerked open to reveal the Seven Deadly Finns standing in a triangle atop each other, poised on tiptoe – particularly difficult, Romford thought, for the three load-bearers on the bottom, but they showed no signs of strain – and with their arms outstretched, fingers pointing towards the wings. They were dressed in silver lamé suits, and the even teeth in their uniformly broad smiles glistened and gleamed every bit as much as the suits.

The recording lurched into something by Strauss, and the topmost Finn tumbled forward in a somersault to land perfectly at the very front of the stage. The audience applauded as if this were the greatest thing they'd ever seen, and then the performance started in earnest.

Bodies flew all over the stage in a blur of lamé and an endless confusion of stray limbs. Every now and then the Finns would stop in some multi-bodied contortion, and the watchers took this as their cue for yet another round of applause. Romford, hands still, thought around the stem of his pipe that team acrobats must have to bath a lot, what with constantly having to stuff their faces up each other's . . .

Mrs Romford interrupted his reverie. "Aren't they grand?" she whispered.

"Very grand," he agreed.

"You should steer clear of celery seeds when you're pregnant," she added significantly, then turned back to her peanuts.

Baffled, Romford carried on watching the spectacle.

The Family Brød's performance was far too short or far too long, depending on the way you looked at it. So far as Romford was concerned, he was glad when it was finally over: sounds, patterns and the inevitable bursts of applause made him feel as if someone had been using his head as a punchbag. Rather like when Mrs Romford put Wagner on the CD player.

There was a short interval, during which they drank warm orange squash from Mrs Romford's thermos and ate their sandwiches, and then the lights dimmed once again.

If the tension had been palpable before the Family Brød's performance, now it was as if you could have grabbed handfuls of it from the air and used it for chewing gum. Romford's knuckles whitened around his pipe-stem. Mrs Romford dropped her crème caramel and it lay unnoticed at her feet. The silence was like an encaged beast, pacing the confines of its hated cell, until . . .

Blue lightning coruscated over the audience's heads as a blast of thunder shook the floor. One moment the stage curtain was there; the next it was replaced by a blaze of brilliant illumination that almost blinded Romford. A flock of snow-white doves appeared from nowhere and circled cacophonously around the ceiling. Somewhere in the midst of the mêlée there was a haunting strain of music that could have been Egyptian, could have been Korean, could have been just the tape had stretched.

There was a sudden puff of green smoke in the middle of the stage, and out of it stepped the cadaverously imposing figure of The Mighty Thrombosis. He threw his arms wide as if to welcome himself to the proceedings; the inside of his full-length cloak was golden with, embroidered on it, white doves in representation of those that still wheeled and whirled above.

"Greetings from the world of the unknown," the figure intoned. "People will tell you that what you see tonight is mere trickery, but in truth it is a lifting of a veil – the veil that lies between our humdrum lives and the magical kingdom, where truth is falsehood and falsehood truth."

As if to prove the point, he pulled out a cauliflower from behind his ear.

The audience gasped.

Smiling and nodding briefly in acknowledgement, the Mighty Thrombosis proceeded to yank a string of the flags of all nations from behind the other.

The applause was deafening.

The Mighty Thrombosis bowed more deeply this time, then looked to his left, focusing the audience's attention on the emergence from the wings of a statuesque blonde wearing about three carats of gold and very little else. She too bowed, her unbound hair falling in front of her like a bolt of yellow gauze.

And then the serious magic began. Packs of cards turned into flocks of wrens; baseball bats turned, mid-juggle, into spitting kangaroos; streamers turned into bunches of chrysanthemums complete with little plastic tags displaying the watering instructions. (At this point Romford checked his pipe nervously to make sure it hadn't turned into anything.) A casket with the beautiful assistant gagged and padlocked inside it was pierced by swords, cut in half with a chainsaw and finally incinerated using a flame-thrower, and yet she stepped out of the ashes unscathed. The Mighty Thrombosis himself took an iron bar that had been tested for authenticity by half a dozen randomly selected members of the audience and bent it easily into a passable imitation of his own signature. A bucket of water was covered with a red cloth and then, when the cloth was removed, was seen to have become a perfect representation in miniature of the Niagara Falls – whose waters continued to flow despite the fact that there was *no visible water supply*.

After an hour or more The Mighty Thrombosis spoke again, for the first time since his brief introduction.

"And now, ladies and gentleman . . . and others—" there was a little ripple of tamed laughter "—for the finale to my act. Many false magicians the world over have perfected the illusion of pulling a rabbit from a top hat, but I – I, The Mighty Thrombosis – am the only one to use genuine magic to perform the same feat . . . and with, not a rabbit, but a live tyrannosaurus rex!"

There was a roll of drums and the luscious assistant, bearing a perfectly ordinary-seeming black opera hat, insinuated herself across the stage by dint of controlling muscles that Romford had never even known existed.

The Mighty Thrombosis took the hat with a grave little nod of thanks and, using both hands, held it aloft.

Silence fell.

He turned it this way and that, showing the entirety of his audience that it was indeed empty. He flipped open its lid so that they could see right through it. He pressed it flat and then straightened it out again. He pulled a revolver from his trouser pocket and fired a couple of shots through it. There could be no doubt about it: the thing was as empty as an Aberdeen street on a flag day.

Again the drums rolled as with his right hand he held the hat out in front of him, so that the audience could see it was well clear of his body. With his free hand he waved a blue-spotted handkerchief so that everyone could see that it, too, was guileless. Next he lowered the handkerchief down over the upturned aperture of the hat.

Pause.

Then, every eye glued on his hand, he slowly drew away the handkerchief.

The assistant simpered but was ignored.

Dragging out the seconds for dramatic effect, The Mighty Thrombosis reached into the hat and produced . . .

. . . a severed hand.

Someone screamed. Blood dripped. The gorgeous assistant collapsed pneumatically, unnoticed by all save Romford, who was sitting forward in his seat, staring intently.

The Mighty Thrombosis himself looked utterly aghast. "This . . . this was not . . . intended to happen . . ." he stuttered in an Essex accent, quite unlike the voice he had earlier projected.

Then the curtains closed swiftly.

It was the first orthodox event since the start of the wonder show.

"I was on my mobile phone immediately, as you can guess," said Romford, looking pointedly at his empty glass. Obediently I picked it up, went to the bar and replenished it with Old Peculiar. Once we were settled again he looked up at me; his hands were clenching and unclenching.

"Sergeant Mutton had lads there within seconds – the hall's just round the corner from the nick, as you know. Even before they'd got there I'd had the staff seal the whole place up. A mouse could have got out of there without our knowing about it, but not a very fat mouse."

He took a ruminative gulp.

"The Mighty Thrombosis – Albert MacGregor as he really is – was still standing on the stage looking at the thing when we got him," he continued. "Hadn't even gone to help his assistant up off the floor – Missus R had to do that."

"Whose hand was it?" I said.

"That was, of course, a problem – but not such a problem as we'd have thought it might be." Another gulp. "Thrombosis – MacGregor – told us himself. There was a ring on its finger that he recognized: made out of cast bronze and showing a dragon eating its own tail."

"Yes?"

"He said he'd recognize that ring anywhere, and his wife – his assistant – confirmed it as soon as she was feeling properly herself again."

"And?"

"The hand was that of The Even Mightier Spongini – a.k.a. Gerald Dukes – the greatest of all MacGregor's rivals. There was some palaver in the upper – inner, I s'pose – echelons of the Magic Circle five years back, you may have read about it in the newspapers, MacGregor claiming Dukes was stealing the secrets of his tricks, in particular something called The Collapsible Hippogryph, you know the sort of thing. The two men hated each others' guts. And there was more to it than that."

"Oh?"

"Dukes was messing around with MacGregor's wife, Zelda. Common knowledge backstage, we was told. That was what the *real* argument was about – not the tricks, stolen or otherwise."

This time it was me gulping down beer. So Thrombosis had offed Spongini and was creating an elaborate smokescreen to muddle up the coppers, eh? Still seemed it was an open-and-shut case, if Romford was to be believed.

"But all they did was identify the ring," I said, just for something to say. "That doesn't mean it was Spongini's hand the ring was actually *on*, does it?"

Romford looked at me in disgust. "We thought of that. Took fingerprints. Faxed 'em to the Yard. Asked 'em if they were Dukes's. Answer came back within the hour. They were Dukes's, all right. No doubt about it. He was on file because of a bit of pot twenty years ago when he was young and foolish."

He looked down at his flexing hands, then up again.

"And all this time, mark you," he said, "we had the whole place locked up tighter than a nun's . . . well, you get the drift. We had trained men searching it from top to bottom, rafters to basement. Because, you see, there was something missing . . ."

"A body," I said. Even if I hadn't known this already – that empty hopper – it'd have been pretty obvious.

"Precisely. Or even a man with one hand missing, 'cept people tend to make a hell of a lot of a fuss if someone chops a hand off of them, you know. And that hand was *fresh* – it was still bleeding when MacGregor hoicked it out of the hat. So it was really a body we was after. A corpse. A stiff. *Anything*. But not a whisper."

"You interviewed everyone, I assume?"

"Everyone. Started with the Finns – they're from Belfast, by the way, Finns ain't what they used to be, I said to Sergeant Mutton – and worked our way on downwards. Me and Mutton tackled all the interviewing ourselves, we did. Had to let them go in the end, every last one of them. No one knew nothing. Well, maybe . . ."

"There's a lot of room in that 'maybe', my friend."

"Well—" he let the word hang for a few moments, shifting his gaze towards where two drunks were trying to get it together to score a game of darts "—maybe, on reflecting on it, there was something. Zelda."

"The Mighty Thrombosis's wife?"

" 'Xactly. The lady herself. She seemed to be in shock – *seemed* to be – so it was no picnic trying to get much sense out of her, but the missus told me afterwards over the cocoa that Zelda appeared a deal less disorientated than you'd have expected when she came out of her faint. If it *was* a faint."

"So you think she might have known something about it? Might have been warned it was going to happen?"

"Yes. Except that only makes matters worse. 'Cause Dukes was her hanky-panky merchant. So if she'd known about things aforehand she'd have done her best to stop 'em, and if she *didn't* know about them then she'd have been *more* in shock, not less."

"Maybe she'd fallen out with him? You know, when the slap and tickle has to stop sort of thing?"

"She said she hadn't. She was totally open about the whole affairs, said her husband was—" Romford's eyes glazed briefly, as if he were reading from invisible notes "—was a right bastard, brute and utter plonker, used to play practical jokes on me when he'd got a few inside him, which was most of the time, wish it was his *head* came out of that hat, not Gerry's hand, no wonder I looked elsewhere for virile masculine affections, officer, and found them in the brawny arms of my svelte-thewed lover'." He looked glum. "Or words to that effect. Quite a lot of 'em."

"Which means that the only person you know about with a motive to kill Dukes was The Mighty Thrombosis? The whole business with the severed hand was just a smokescreen, a bluff? The only person who could have got the hand into the hat was MacGregor himself?"

" 'Sright." He looked gloomier than ever. I wondered how many pints he'd sunk before I'd got to the Heart & Sickle. "So we did the only thing we could do."

"Took him into custody?"

"Yup."

"For further questioning?"

"Yup."

"And he's not talking." This time it wasn't a question.

"Yup. And you know . . ." His voice trailed off on a meditative note.

"Yes?"

He rallied. "You know, I think the reason he's not talking is that he hasn't got anything to tell us. Unless he's the best actor in the world – and you never can tell with these stage johnnies, of course – he's every bit as mystified as the rest of us." Romford suddenly grinned, wearily. "Seems a bit ironical, if you get what I mean: the mystifier mystified, the conjuror out-conjured, the prestidigitator presti—Um. Oh, hell, anyway."

"What about Mrs Thrombosis? MacGregor, I mean."

"The pheromone-packed wife? Tell you, Victor, she's got—"

"Zelda."

"—Like bleeding prizewinning marrows, and an—"

"The assistant."

"—On her that'd give even Billy Graham a—"

"Get back to the point, Romford."

He shook his head, as if dazed, but soon his eyes refocused. "Ah, yes, current whereabouts of the suspect's missus. Yes." He wiped his sleeve across his mouth. "Well, we had to let her go, didn't we? Nothing to keep *her* in for. No way we could book her as an accessory or anything. 'Sides, the way young Mutton was looking at her I reckoned putting her in the cells overnight might mean the end of things between him and his Sabrina."

"Or you and the Missus?" I said quietly.

He flushed angrily and snorted. "Never any question of that, my lad," he said emphatically. "I've had me chances, I can tell you, but me and her we're just like lickety-split when it comes to malarking on the side, so it's none of your how's your father 'sfar as I'm concerned."

"Leaving that aside, where is she?" I persisted.

"I imagine she's still at the Old Bull Hotel," he said, clearly glad to change the subject. "That's where the concert party was booked in – her and him and the bloody Irish Finns. Finns ain't what they—"

"You said that."

"Yes, I did. How'd you know? To Sergeant Mutton, in point of fact . . ."

The beer was beginning to take its toll. Most of the people who live and work in Cadaver-in-the-Offing flinch if I as much as go near them, but Romford didn't react at all when I put my hand over his and leaned forward to look him close-up in the eyes.

"I'm willing to bet you a month's salary that you won't find her in the Old Bull," I hissed. "You ask me, she's hopped it. Her and The Even Mightier Spongini together, is my guess."

"You think he's alive?"

"I *know* he's alive. Unless he got run over by a car or gored by an escaped bull afterwards, he's as alive as you or me. Probably more alive than you, right now."

"But that doesn't make sense! If he'd a been there we'd have found him. I tell you, we searched the whole of St Boniface's Church Hall until there wasn't anything left to search. And no one could have got out of there – we'd got it sealed off tighter'n a nun's—"

"He walked out in full view of your officers," I said.

"*Im*possible! We interviewed every single member of the audience! I even had Sergeant Mutton interview the Missus, just in case there was charges of favouritism afterwards. She didn't like that much, but the ibuprofen's doing wonders."

"You interviewed all the stage staff as well?"

"Course."

"My friend," I said, standing up and preparing to leave, "it's not my job to solve your cases for you. I'm not a character, like everyone else in Cadaver-in-the-Offing, so I can't even give you useful leads. All I am is the sweeper-upper

– dirty job but somebody's got to do it, sort of thing. But what I *will* do, what I'm *allowed* to do, is offer you a hint that might prove useful to your life in general."

"Wossat?" he slurred. He'd drunk enough beer to be reaching the point of tearfulness.

"I can remind you, my friend," I said, patting the back of his hand, "of the importance of temperance."

It was quite late that evening when Romford, all traces of the beer gone from his voice, phoned me. He didn't waste any time in telling me what I already knew.

"Temperance," he said.

"Yes. And a very good thing it is."

"Makes a man think of an old sixties/seventies pop group, it does."

"That's what it made me think of, too." I blew on my fingernails.

"They were called the Temperance Seven. But the great gimmick about the name was that there were actually nine of 'em."

"Yes."

"The family Brød got the nickname. 'The Seven Deadly Finns' because someone liked the pun, and they kept it – used it in their advertisements – on the basis it made folk remember them."

I breathed out smugly. "When you were describing their performance to me, I realized that in fact there were only six of them. Three on the bottom row of the pyramid, two on their shoulders, and one more on the top – that makes six, not seven."

"And me a trained observer. I just never noticed it myself. Doubt you would of, either, if you'd been there. It was a hell of an act. Apart from that bit at the beginning, when the curtains opened, I couldn't rightly have told you *how* many of the buggers there were – it was just arms and legs and other bits everywhere. One of those cases where it's easier to see something if you're *not* an eyewitness."

I grunted agreement. Whoever said seeing is believing was talking out of his elbow.

"We weren't much interested in those bloody Irish Finns, so Mutton just interviewed 'em in a bunch. 'Seven Deadly Finns', he was told, so he made sure there was seven of 'em and let 'em go. Never thought anything of it, until I asked him after I left the pub, but, yes, a couple of 'em had kept their hands in their pockets the whole time."

"Except that one of them, we now know, was a hand short."

"Precisement, as the Frogs say."

"Where did you catch up with Spongini . . . Dukes?"

"At the Old Bull Hotel, done his packing and sitting on the suitcase, all neat and ready to do a runner from the country with Zelda tonight, after dark. It was him and her planned the whole thing. She cut off his hand for him while The Mighty Thrombosis was doing all his puffs of smoke and things, then they cauterized the stump on the backstage stove. They'd already cold-bloodedly killed, cooked and eaten the tyrannosaur. She was the one got the hand into the top hat – stupid of me to think that MacGregor would be the one to set up his own props. The idea was to make old Thrombosis look bad in our eyes for just long enough that we'd keep him in the nick until safely after the young lovers had fled the coop. The Finns were in on it as well, of course – Zelda and Dukes ain't the only folks on the circuit who can't stand The Mighty Thrombosis: he's made enemies all over the place."

Romford paused, then: "Here! How did you know we found him?"

"I sneaked an extra look in the hoppers just now."

"Oh, um, yes, well, Dave Knuckle was still in town for *Smack My Butt, Babe* so I took him along with me to help make the arrest. And he, er, got a bit carried away during the interrogation . . ."

Ho hum. After all this time, I could read the marks of Knuckle's knuckles like an open book, and this particular book hadn't been in his handwriting. Romford had obviously been very angry indeed: the worst he could have charged Spongini with was conspiring to waste police time, or something – same as Zelda, same as the Family Brød. A man can do what he wants to with his own hand. But I let it pass.

"Dukes must have loved Zelda very much indeed," I said ruefully.

"A lot more than she loved him," Romford said forcefully. "He told us before he . . . um, before Knuckle got out of hand, as it were . . . told us that she'd been due back at the hotel to pick him up a couple of hours before we got there, and he was beginning to think she wasn't coming for him after all. So we hung about another couple of hours after that, and still no sign of her. Reckon she's scarpered – double-crossed him, got rid of both the men in her life in one swell foop—" hm, still a trace of the day's drinking "—and then scarpered over the hills and far away. I've put an alert out to the ports and airports, but I think we've missed her. And no one's going to issue an extradition order for what she's done – not for that. Bloody women."

We said a few more things on that subject before he finally put the phone down. I noticed he hadn't at any point said thanks to me for sorting his case out for him.

So I didn't feel at all guilty about not telling him the rest of it – not that I would have, anyway.

"Is he convinced?" said Zelda behind me just as I lowered the receiver.

"Yes. Case closed, darling. He's satisfied – is washing his hands of the whole thing." I turned to kiss her.

"Poor Gerry," she said. "Poor, foolish Gerry."

She'd liked Spongini well enough, but he'd been yesterday's news for quite a while now . . . ever since I'd met her the last time The Mighty Thrombosis had been doing a gig in Cadaver-in-the-Offing, in fact, during the course of Miss Grimthorpe's *The Kat who Killed the Konjurers*. I was sorry that he'd died, but – hell – he'd be as good as new again in a few days. The plan had been that Romford caught up with him, all right, then took him into custody for a couple of days until he, too, proved to be only a minor player in the game. Meanwhile, of course, Zelda wasn't to flee the country but to come to the one place nobody in Cadaver-in-the-Offing would ever dream of looking.

The cottage of the man they all walk around as if he were a dog turd on the pavement. We could live here together all the rest of our lives, if we wanted to, and no one would ever know. In a few years' time, though, I reckon we'll up sticks and go somewhere else – I mean, my job has its advantages. but I've always dreamed of trying out my chances in the movies . . .

So I take Zelda in my arms. We're free at last, and there's a traditional way of celebrating things like this . . .

Gigglings.

Snoggings.

Strokings.

Kissings.

Gropings.

Fondlings.

Fumblings.

Pretty soon:

Unzippings.

"Oo, Victor," she says. "Oo."

Hands quicker than the eye, that's me.

THE ABSOLUTE AND UTTER IMPOSSIBILITY OF THE FACTS IN THE CASE OF THE VANISHING OF HENNING VOK (A.K.A. THE AMAZING BLITZEN) (R.N. JACK RALPH COLE)

Jack Adrian

I don't know where to begin in talking about the multi-talented novelist, researcher, reviewer, editor, and collector, Jack Adrian, specialist in A.M. Burrage, E.F. Benson, Sapper, Edgar Wallace, Rafael Sabatini, and author of many crime, mystery and adventure stories and novels. So I won't.

The facts were these: in the bathtub, shifting gently under eighteen inches of rust-coloured water, lay the fully clothed (even down to his overcoat and Oxfords) corpse of Herman

Jediah Klauss, the Moriarty of Manhattan, a large ornamental
ice pick sunk in his skull. Never personable (especially in the
matter of nasal hair) he now gave the impression of a dead
dugong.

That (that he was unequivocally dead) was one fact. A
second fact was that his murderer was not in the bathroom
with him. A third was that he ought to have been.

There were other facts. The apartment was in a building in
the low West 70s, a spit from the Park, half a spit from the
Dakota. It was on the 11th floor. It was b-i-g. It had been built
at a time (maybe the 1900s) when architects had grandiose
dreams and clients with money to fuel them. To Commings,
the bathroom looked about as spacious as a side-chapel in St
Patrick's. The bath itself was a vast boxed-in affair, fake (or
maybe not) ivory with a dark mahogany trim. The toilet, next
to it, could easily have doubled as a throne. You could almost
certainly have bathed a Doberman in the bidet.

Over by the door, which was at least three inches thick and
might well have withstood the full blast of an RPG-7 anti-
personnel rocket, Trask bellowed, *"It's impossible!"*

Which, of course, it was.

Commings thought through the sequence of events for what
seemed like the fiftieth time.

Klauss had entered the apartment closely followed by patrolmen O'Mahoney and Schwaab (flagged down outside the
building and invited in because, in Klauss's words, "There's a
guy up there wants to ice me"). They were met by an English
butler (hired for the evening, it now transpired) and a black
maid (idem). They were escorted up the long hallway, past
shelfloads of books (mainly mystery fiction: Carolyn Wells,
H.H. Holmes, Carter Dickson, Hake Talbot, Clayton Raw-
son, Edward D. Hoch, Joel Townsley Rogers, a raft of others),
past cabinets full of rare Golden Age comicbooks (mainly from
the Quality group: *Police Comics, Smash Comics, Plastic Man,
The Spirit, National Comics, Doll Man*, many more), and past
a series of framed posters featuring a preternaturally rangy
man clad in, first, evening dress ("The Amazing Blitzen:

Unparalleled Feats of Legerdemain and Prestidigitation!"), second, vaguely Arabian robes ("The Sultan of Stretch, the Emir of Elongation – see the many-jointed Blitzen zip himself into a carpet-bag!"), and, third, a skin-tight black costume akin to what bathers wore two generations back ("Blitzen! Illusionist *extraordinaire*!"). Smaller bills showed him peering out from a cannon's mouth ("The Shell Man!"), being lowered into a swimming-pool by a gantry with what looked to be a half-ton of ship's cable cocooning him ("The Man With the Iron Lungs!"), and chained spread-eagle to a vast target ("Can he escape before the crossbow bolt pierces his heart?!").

Henning Vok (or, as his real name now seemed to be, J.R. Cole) had emerged from a doorway at the far end ("skinny as a beanpole," as Schwaab said later, "but looking kind of flushed . . . like he'd been running") and welcomed, in open-armed fashion, his visitor, who'd turned to the two cops and warned, "Don't trust the sucker an inch."

Vok/Cole had laughed distractedly and said, "You want the cards or not, dammit?", gesturing at the half-open door. Klauss had walked in and said, "This is a bathroom." Vok/Cole said, "You catch on fast", and then, reaching behind the door, had produced the ice pick, with which, to the consternation of the witnesses, he had proceeded to poleaxe Klauss, Klauss toppling into the tub (full) and sending a tidal wave of displaced water spraying over Vok/Cole, the toilet, the oxygen machine next to the bidet and the floor. Vok/Cole had then jumped for the door, slamming it shut and locking it.

It took the two patrolmen (not having an RPG-7 launcher) twenty minutes to break down the door. When they finally entered, the room was empty. Apart, of course, from the now defunct Herman Jediah Klauss.

"Im-poss-i-*bul*!" said Trask now, through clenched teeth. "And bull's the operative word." He clutched at a straw. "What if they were all in it?"

Commings said, "The butler and the maid, maybe. And could be Schwaab's on the take. But hell, Lieutenant," his voice rose a notch or two, "O'Mahoney?"

"The Prize Prepuce of the Precinct House," groaned Trask. "The only totally honest man on the roster. *God*!"

This last profanity was spat out not only on account of O'Mahoney's notorious incorruptibility, which hinted at stupidity on a serious scale, but because, at that moment, a figure of surpassing bulk, clad in a fur coat and brandishing an unsheathed swordstick in a hamhock-sized fist, came barrelling into the apartment.

"Trask!" bawled the newcomer. "The Commissioner called me! It's a demented dwarf, depend on it!"

Trask shot him a look that could have split an atom.

"Now see here . . ."

"Don't interrupt! Show Professor Stanislaus Befz an Impossible Crime and he'll show you a deranged midget with an ice pick. They never alter their *modus operandi*, the little devils." He surged through the hall like a resuscitated Golem, cutting a swathe through cops, photogs, morgue-men in white coats, and only coming to a halt at the bathroom door. Here he yelped triumphantly. "William Howard Taft! An ice pick! What did I say!" He jabbed the swordstick at the corpse, the blade parting Comming's hair as the detective ducked to the floor. "You've already snapped the gyves on the hunchback, I take it?"

"Professor, there *is* no hunchback . . ."

"Balderdash! Out of the three thousand thirty-three Miracle Problems I've investigated, analysed and catalogued over the past quarter century, crazed mannikins hidden in the false humps of ersatz hunchbacks account for well over half." He glanced down at Commings. "What are you doing down there?"

Trask was snapping his fingers urgently as the behemothesque Befz, not waiting for a reply, strode towards the tub. Commings scrambled to his feet and handed to his chief the packet of antacid tablets kept for times like this. He wondered miserably why amateur detectives specializing in Miracle Problems were invariably fat. And loud. And . . . and *eccentric*.

"Aaron Burr!" oathed the man-mountain, jowls quivering like a turkey's wattles. "Herman Jediah Klauss, the Moriarty of Manhattan!" He spun – or, rather, lurched – round, the swordstick scattering various detectives. "So where's the hunchie?"

Trask was holding his stomach and wincing.

He muttered, "Tell him."

Commings explained about the lack of counterfeit hunchbacks in this particular case. This took some time owing to Befz's innumerable interruptions. Commings finished, "In any case, there were four witnesses who saw Vok, or Cole, do it."

"Mass hypnosis!" thundered Befz. "The oldest trick in the book! I have three hundred forty-eight cases in my records, of which probably the most illuminating was the Great Hollywood Bowl Pickpocket Scam. This Vok, or Cole, undoubtedly flapdoodled the witnesses into thinking he was skinny then flipped open his false hump and let the demoniacal pixie out to do its fell business. The man was clearly a master-mesmerist."

"The butler and the maid, sure," agreed Commings. "And Schwaab, too. But," his voice pitched up, "O'Mahoney?"

Befz glanced at the patrolman. "You may have a point there," he grudged. "Well, there are plenty of other Impossible Murder Methods to choose from . . ."

"Sweet galloping Jesus!" screeched Trask. "The murder method is not in question! We know how he did it! The guy even admits to it himself!" He gulped down three or four more antacid tablets. "Show him the note, Commings."

The note read:

Dear guys,

I have decided to retire on my well-gotten gains, which over the years (due to judicious investment) have made me a millionaire many times over.

Before I go, however, I believe I can do you a couple favours.

Primus: *Attached is a list of robberies which should*

*feature heavily in your "Unsolved" files. Strike 'em. I
plead guilty on all counts;*

Secundus: *I also plead guilty to the expunging of
Herman Jediah Klauss, murderer, shylock, fence (who
invariably paid bottom-dollar: hence my hatred of him)
extortioner, blackmailer, procurer, rabid collector and generally worthless scoundrel. Having inveigled him here on
the pretence of selling him a rare set of "Woozy Winks"
bubble-gum cards (circa 1948), I split his head with an ice-
pick.*

*I mourn the fact that I leave behind my vast collection of
interesting artefacts.*

*That's a lie. Where I'm going, I have duplicate copies of
everything.*

Hasta la vista!

Henning Vok, a.k.a. The Great Blitzen

(r.n. Jack Ralph Cole)

P.S. There are plenty clues.

"Hmmm," larynxed Befz. "So the problem is how he escaped
from the bathroom. That shouldn't prove too tricky. As you
probably know if you've read my *magnum opus* on the subject,
there are precisely one thousand three hundred fifty-two ways
of getting out of a locked room, only seven hundred eighty-six
of which depend on a reel of cotton. And out of that, only one
hundred thirty-five need a new pin and split paper-match.
Walls?"

"Solid brick," Trask grated.

"Ceiling?"

"Same."

"Window?"

"Hasn't been opened in fifty years."

"Floor?"

"Forget it."

"Oh."

Befz absently tapped the blade of his swordstick on the
oxygen machine next to the bidet. It made a tanging sound.

His eye was caught by the large old-fashioned air-extractor fixed into the wall, high up.

"John Quincy Adams! The fan!"

"To get up there," growled Trask, "you'd need to be able to fly."

"*Precisely!*" Befz triumphantly whacked the swordstick against one of the oxygen cylinders. The blade shattered into several shards. "Damn! That's the one hundred twenty-eighth this year. The blessed things cost a fortune too. Never mind. Vok, or Cole, inflated himself with oxygen and floated up to the fan, where . . ."

"Where he'd slice himself up in the extractor blades, yeah. You're losing your touch, Befz. I might just as well ask O'Mahoney if he's got any bright ideas."

"Oh sure," said O'Mahoney. "I mean, it's transparently obvious, Lieutenant."

Numerous pairs of eyes focused on him. He hitched up his gun-belt self-consciously and began to walk around the room, slapping the tip of his nightstick into the open (gloved) palm of his left hand.

"It's an interesting problem sure enough, Professor. Uh . . . and Lieutenant. Oh, and . . ." he glanced at Commings ". . . Sergeant. But there's really only one exit. Although, as Vok/Cole pointed out, there are plenty clues. See, I asked myself, why the bath? But we'll get to that later. I'd like you all to follow me."

Numerous pairs of shoes and boots tramped after him into the hallway. He gestured at the posters.

"It's all there. He was a contortionist. Skinny as a rake. This is an old building. Way back, they built things bigger. Follow me."

They followed him. Back into the bathroom.

"You very nearly hit it, Professor. The oxygen machine was crucial to his plan. Possibly not many of you know that in 1959 a technician in California hyperventilated on oxygen and then created a world record for remaining underwater for thirteen minutes forty-two seconds. Vok/Cole, as we know, had 'iron lungs', but the oxygen gave him that extra edge. As you'll recall, my partner described him as looking flushed, as though he'd been running. Fact was, he seemed semi-hysterical. But like I said, it was the bathwater that tipped me. Way I figured it, water splashed from the tub would hide the tell-tale subsequent splashes of water from quite another source."

He used the nightstick as a pointer. Numerous pairs of eyes swivelled towards the mighty throne-like structure next to the tub.

"That's right," said O'Mahoney. "He flushed himself down the toilet."

MILORD SIR SMIHT, THE ENGLISH WIZARD

Avram Davidson

Avram Davidson (1923–1993) was one of the most idio-
syncratic talents to write science fiction and fantasy. He was
at his best writing short stories, and some of his best have
been collected as The Avram Davidson Treasury *(1998).*
Also well worth tracking down are Peregrine: Primus
(1971) and its sequel Peregrine: Secundus *(1981), plus*
the collection of stories about a wizard detective, The
Enquiries of Doctor Esterhazy *(1975), from which the*
following story comes.

The establishment of Brothers Swartbloi stands, or squats, as
it has done for over a century and a half, in the Court of the
Golden Hart. The inn, once famous, which gave its name to
the court, has long since passed off the scene, but parts of it
survive, here a wall, there an arch, and, by sole way of access, a
flight of steps (so old had been the inn, that Bella, Imperial
Capital of the Triune Monarchy, had slowly lifted the level of
its streets around about it). The shops in the Court of the
Golden Hart are an odd mixture. First, to the right of the worn
three steps, is Florian, who purveys horse-crowns, though the
sign does not say so. (All, in fact, that it says is *Florian*.) There

is nothing on display in the window, the window being composed of small pieces of bull's-eye glass set in lead, a very old window, with the very old-fashioned idea that the sole duty of a window is to let light in through a wall. What are horse-crowns? Has the reader never seen a funeral? Has he not noticed the crowns of ostrich plumes – black, for an ordinary adult, white for a child or maiden-woman, violet for a nobleman or prelate of the rank of monsignor or above – bobbing sedately on the horses' heads? Those are horse-crowns, and nobody makes them like Florian's.

To the left of the steps is Weitmondl, who makes and sells mother-of-pearl buttons in all sizes. However great must be the natural disappointment of the fisher in the far-off Gulfs of Persia when he opens his oyster and finds no pearl within, he can still take comfort in the thought that the shells, with their nacreous and opalescent interiors, must find their way to the great city of Bella, where Weitmondl will turn them into buttons: all the way from the great buttons which adorn the shirts of coachmen down to the tiny buttons which fasten children's gloves.

Facing the steps in the Court of the Golden Hart is the shop of Brothers Swartbloi, who are purveyors of snufftobacco.

There are other shops, to be sure, in the Golden Hart, but they are of a transitory nature, some of them lasting a mere decade. Florian, Weitmondl, and Brothers Swartbloi are the patriarchs of the place; and of them all Brothers Swartbloi is the oldest.

The shop contains one chair, in which scarcely anyone dares to sit, a wooden counter, and, behind the counter, a wooden shelf. On the shelf are five stout jars, each the size of a small child. One is labeled *Rappee*, one is labeled *Minorka*, one is labeled *Imperial*, one is labeled *Habana*, and one is labeled *Turkey*.

Should anyone desire a snuff of a different sort, some upstart sort of snuff, a johnny-come-lately in the field of snuff – say, for example, *Peppermint! Wintergreen!* or *Cocoa-Dutch!* – ah, woe upon him, he had better never have been born.

Words cannot describe the glacial degree of cold with which he will be informed, "The sweet-shop is across the Court. *Here we sell only snuff-tobacco.*"

One day comes Doctor Eszterhazy to the shop in the Court of the Golden Hart. He is not walking very fast, in fact, as he has been following someone, and as that someone was taking his own good time, it may be said that Engelbert Eszterhazy, Doctor of Medicine, Doctor of Jurisprudence, Doctor of Science, Doctor of Literature, etc., etc., was walking decidedly slowly. The man he was following was tall and heavy and stooped and wore a long black cloak lined with a dull brown silk. Now, long black cloaks were not then the fashion, and Lord knows when they had been. It would be supposed that anyone who wore one did so in order to create a certain impression, to draw upon himself a certain amount of attention. In all of Bella, so far as Eszterhazy knew, there were only two other men who went about in long black cloaks. One was Spectorini, the Director of the Grand Imperial Opera. The other was Von Von Greitschmansthal, the Court Painter. And both had their long black cloaks lined with red.

To wear a long black cloak and then to line it with brown . . . with *brown* . . . this indicated an individualism of the very highest order. And, as he could scarcely in good manners stop this strange man on the street and confront him with his curiosity, therefore he followed him. Down the Street of the Apple-pressers (no apples had been pressed there in decades), left into the Street of the Beautiful Vista (the only vista there nowadays was that of a series of dressmakers' shops), down the Place Maurits Louis (containing six greengrocers, two florists, a French laundry, a café, and a really awful statue of that depressed and, indeed, rather depressing monarch), and thence into the Court of the Golden Hart.

And thence into the establishment of the *Brothers Swartbloi*, SNUFF-TOBACCO.

One of the brothers was behind the counter. He looked at the first newcomer, from as far down as the counter permitted him to observe, all the way up to the curious hat (it was made of black velvet and bore a silver medallion of some sort; and, while it did not exactly appear to be a cap of maintenance, it looked far more like a cap of maintenance than it did like anything else). And he – the Brother Swartbloi – permitted himself a bow. The first newcomer drew from his pocket an enormous snuffbox, set it down, and uttered one word.

"*Rappee.*"

The brother took up a brass scoop, reached it into the appropriate jar, removed it, set it on the scales, removed it, and emptied it into the snuffbox.

The quantity was just enough. One hundred years and more in the business of estimating the capacities of snuffboxes gives one a certain degree of skill in the matter.

The tall man placed on the counter a coin of five *copperkas* (the snuff of the Brothers Swartbloi does not come cheap) and a card, allowed himself a nod of thanks, and turned and left.

His face was craggy and smooth-shaven and indicative of many things.

When the door had closed behind him the Brother again bowed – this time more warmly. "And in what way may I help the August Sir Doctor?" asked he.

"By supplying him with four ounces of Imperial."

Small purchases at Swartbloi's are wrapped in newspaper, when not decanted into snuffboxes. Larger purchases are wrapped in special pleated-paper parcels, each supplied with a colored label. The label shows a gentleman, in the costume of the reign of Ignats Ferdinando, applying two fingers to his nose; his expression is one of extreme satisfaction. These lables are colored by hand by old Frow Imglotch, whose eyesight is not what it was, and the results are more than merely curious: they are proof of the authenticity of the label and of the product.

"I had the honour of seeing the August Sir Doctor some months since," said the Brother, "when I was at Hierony-mos's" – he named Eszterhazy's tobacconist, the source of the famous segars – "obtaining of our usual supply of Habana clippings for our famous Habana snuff-tobacco. I am wondering if the August Sir Doctor is giving up segars in favor of snuff . . .?"

He was a dry, thin sort of man, with a few dark curls scattered across a bony skull. Automatically, Eszterhazy took a sight reading of the skull, but it did not seem very interesting. "Ah, no," he said. "It is for one of my servants – a saint's-day present. However, were I to take to taking snuff, be assured that it would be the I-have-no-doubt-justly-famous snuff of the Brothers Swartbloi. Who was that gentleman who was just in here?"

The brother, with a bow at the compliment, passed the card over.

MILORD SIR SMIHT
Wizard anglais
Specializing in late hours & By appointment

In a very elegant copperplate hand had been added: *Hotel Grand Dominik.*

"One does hear," the brother said, "that the British nobility are of a high and eccentric nature."

"So one does. Often," Eszterhazy agreed. It might not have been high, but it would certainly have been eccentric for a member of the British aristocracy to put up at the Hotel Grand Dominik. He reflected, not for the first time, he knew, and not for the last, he expected, on the persistence of the Continental usage of *milord*, a rank not known either to Burke or Debrett. As for the name Smith, no one to the south or east of the English Channel has ever been able to spell it right, nor ever will.

He put down his money and prepared to depart; now that he knew where the stranger was to be found, it was no longer necessary to dog him about the streets.

He looked up to find a familiar, if not a welcome, expression on the face of the brother, who proceeded as expected: Might he take the very great liberty of asking the August Sir Doctor a question? He might. Ah, the August Sir Doctor was very kind.

But still the question was not forthcoming. Eszterhazy decided to help him along; most such silences, following such questions, followed a certain pattern.

"If the question involves past indiscretions," he said, gently, "I should represent that Doctor LeDuc, who has a daily advertisement in the popular newspapers— It is not that? Well. If the question involves a failure of regularity, I should recommend syrup of figs. What? Not that, either? Then you must come right out with it."

But the man did not come right out with it. Instead, he began a sort of history of his firm and family. The first Brothers Swartbloi were Kummelman and Hugo. They were succeeded by Augsto and Frans. And Frans begat Kummelman II and Ignats.

"I am the present Kummelman Swartbloi," he said, with an air of dignity at which it was impossible to laugh. "My brother Ignats – he is at present in the mill, salting the Turkey – has never married, and it does not seem that he ever will. My wife and I – she is the daughter and only child of my late Uncle Augsto – we have been wed for fifteen years now. But there have been no children. After all, no one lives forever. And how would it be possible, Sir Doctor, for there to be no Brothers Swartbloi in Bella? How could we leave the business over to strangers? And . . . and . . . there are so many medicines . . . One hardly knows where to begin. Could the August Sir Doctor recommend a particular medicine, known to be both safe and effective?"

The August Sir Doctor said very, very gently, "I should instead recommend my colleague, Professor Doctor Plotz, of the Faculty of Medicine. You may mention my name."

The Hotel Grand Dominik has come down in the world since the days when it formed a stop on the Grand Tour. Long after having ceased to be fashionable among the gentry, it retained an affection on the part of the more prosperous of the commercial travelers. But it was at that time near the East Railroad Terminal. It is still, in fact, near the East Railroad Terminal, but since the completion of the Great Central Terminal, the shabby old East only serves suburban and industrial rail lines. Consequently, the commercial travelers who stop at the Grand Dominik either are very uninnovative or very old and in any event very unprosperous, or else they are merely unprosperous by reason of such factors as not selling anything worth buying. In fact, for some several years the Grand Dominik has stayed open solely because its famous half-ducat dinner, served between eleven and three, is deservedly popular among the junior partners and upper clerks of the many timber firms who still hold out in the adjacent neighborhood. The rooms are thus ancillary to the hotel's main business. So the rooms are, in a word, cheap.

They are also – no management having been vigorous enough to undertake architectural changes – rather large. Milord Sir Smiht sat in a chair and at a table in the middle of his room, lit by the late afternoon sun. The rear of the room was dim. One caught glimpses of an enormous bed, hugely canopied and reached by a small stepladder, of an antique clothes press, a washbasin of marble and mahogany, a sofa whose worn upholstery still breathed out a very faint air of bygone fashion – and a very strong odor of present-day Rappee snuff – although it was actually rather unlikely that this last came from the sofa, and vastly likely that it came from the *wizard anglais* himself.

Who said, "I've seen you before."

Eszterhazy said, "You left a card in the Court of the Golden Hart, and so—"

"—and so that was why you followed me halfway across Bella, because you knew I was going to leave my card in a snuff shop. Eh?"

The conversation was in French.

Eszterhazy smiled. "The *milord* is observant. Well. It is certainly true. My interest was aroused by the distinctive, I may say, distinguished appearance—"

The *milord* grunted, took out an enormous watch, glanced at it, shoved it across to where his visitor could see it. "My terms," he said, "are two ducats for a half-hour. It has just now begun. You may ask as many questions as you please. You may do card tricks. You may spend the entire time looking at me. However, if you wish the employment of the odyllic force, then we should commence at once. Unless, of course, you are willing to pay another two ducats for any fraction of one-half-hour after the first."

Eszterhazy wondered, of course, that anyone so seemingly businesslike should find himself a wanderer in a country so distant from his own – let alone a lodger at the Hotel Grand Dominik. He had learned, however, that the role which people see themselves as playing is not always the same role in which the world at large perceives them.

"To begin with," he said, taking one of his own specially printed forms from his pocket, "I will ask Sir Smiht to be kind enough to remove his hat for the length of time which it will take me to complete my examination—"

The Englishman gazed at the forms with the greatest astonishment. "Good God!" he exclaimed. "I did once, long ago, at Brighton, to be sure, pay a phrenologist to fumble and peer about my pate – but I never thought that a phrenologist would pay *me* for the privilege!"

"Ah, Brighton," Eszterhazy said. "The Royal Pavilions – what an excursion into the *phantastique!* Do you suppose that the First Gentleman of Europe might have been the first gentleman in Europe to have smoked hasheesh?"

Smiht snorted. Then his face, as he began to take his hat off, underwent a certain change. he completed the gesture, and then he said, "Brighton, eh. I suppose you must speak English, although I don't suppose you *are* English?"

"As a boy I often spent my holidays with the family of my aunt, who lived in England."

"Then let us cease to speak in French. Much better for you to struggle than for me. *Furthermore* – if you have been in England you ought to know damned well that the title Sir never precedes the family name without the interposition of the Christian name, although in such instances as that of Sir

Moses Montefiore one would employ another terminology – a point which I can*not* get across to the Continental mind, confound it! I consent to *milord*, because it is, I suppose, traditional, as one might say; and I submit to S-M-I-H-T because I realize how difficult the T-H is to speakers of any other language except Greek and I suppose Icelandic . . . speakers? spellers . . .?"

Here he paused to draw breath and consider his next phrase, and Eszterhazy took the opportunity to approach him from behind and gently place his fingers on the man's head. He was slightly surprised when the other went on to say, "Anyway, the baronetcy absolutely baffles the Continent of Europe – small wonder, I suppose, when every son of a baron here is also a baron and every son of a prince here is also a prince. No wonder the Continent is simply *crawling* with princes and barons and counts and grafts – no primogeniture, *ah* well . . . Now suppose you just call 'em out to me and I'll write 'em down, can't read this Gothic or whatever it is, so you needn't fear I'll get me back up if you decide I'm deficient in honesty, or whatever, Just say, oh, second down, third over – eh?"

"First down, first over," said Eszterhazy.

Without moving his head, the Englishman reached out his long arm and made a mark in the first column of the first row. "I was christened George William Marmaduke Pemberton," he said. "Called me *George*, was what me people called me. Marmaduke Pemberton was a great-uncle by marriage, long since predeceased by the great-aunt of the blood. Made *dog*-biscuit, or some such thing, grew *rich* at it, or perhaps they were digestive biscuits, doesn't matter. As he'd never gotten any children on Aunt Maude and never remarried after *she* died, couldn't get it *up*. I suppose, rest of me people they thought, well, let's name this 'un after him and he'll leave him all his *pelf*, you see, under the condition of his assuming the name of Smith-*Pem*berton. Baronetcy was to go to me oldest brother. *Well*, old Marmaduke left me *beans*, is what he left me, rest of it went to some fund to restore *churches*, sniveling *par*sons had been at him, don't you see.

"Second down, fourth over, *very* well. Tenny rate, say what you will, always tipped me a guinea on me birthday, so out of gratitude and because I couldn't *stand* the name George, have always used the style Pemberton Smith. Can I get *any* Continental printer to spell Pemberton correctly? Ha! Gave up trying. *Now*, as to the odyllic force or forces, in a way it began with Bulwer-Lytton as he called himself before he got *his* title – ever read any of his stuff? *A*wful stuff, don't know how they can read it, but he had more than a mere inkling of the odyllic, you know. What's that? Fourth down, first over, dot and carry one. And *in* a way, of course, one can say, 't all goes back to Mesmer. Well, tut-tut, hmm, of course, Mesmer *had* it. Although poor chap didn't know what he *had*. And then Oscar took a Maori bullet at a place called Pa Rewi Nang Nang, or *some* such thing, *damn*-able is what I call it to die at a place called Pa Rewi Nang Nang, or some such thing – sixth down and four, no five over, *aiwah, tuan besar*. Next thing one knew, Reginald had dived into the Hooghli, *likely story*, that, and never came up – 'spect a croc got him, poor chap, better mouthful than a hundred scrawny *Hin*doos, ah well."

George William Marmaduke Pemberton Smith fell silent a moment and helped himself to two nostrils of Rappee snuff.

"And what's the consequence? Here is my sole remaining brother, Augustus, heir to the baronetcy. And here's *me*, poor fellow, name splashed all over the penny press, because *why*? Because of a mere accident, a Thing of Nature, here am *I*, as I might be *here*, demonstrating the odyllic forces before a subcommittee of the Royal Society, one of whom, Pigafetti Jones, *awful* ass, having kindly volunteered to act as subject, dis-a-*pears!* – leaving nothing but his *clothes*, down to the last brace-button, belly-band, and ball-and-socket truss – Well! *After all*. *Is* this a scientific experiment or is this *not*? Are there such things as the hazards of the chase or are there *not* such things as the hazards of the chase? *First* off, laugh, then they say, very well, bring him *back*, then they dare to call me a *char-la-tan*: ME! And then—"

Dimly, very dimly, Eszterhazy remembered having read,

long ago (and it had not been fresh news, even then), of the singular disappearance of Mr. Pigafetti Jones, Astronomer-Royal for Wales. But what he was hearing now provided more details than he had ever even guessed at. It also provided, if not a complete explanation for, at least an assumption as to why "Milord Sir Smiht" was and had long been wandering the continent of Europe (and perhaps farther) a remittance man, as the British called it. That is, in return for his keeping far away and thus bringing at least no fresh local scandals to his family's embarrassment, the family would continue to remit him a certain sum of money at fixed intervals.

It was still not clear, though, if he were already a baronet or was merely assumed to be because his father was one. Or had been.

And as for the odyllic force . . .

"Forces," said the tall old Englishman, calmly. "I am quite confident that there is more than one."

And for the moment he said no more. Had he read Eszterhazy's mind, then? Or was it merely a fortuitous comment of his own, in his own disjointed manner?

"*Or*, for that matter," the latter went on, in a generous tone of voice, "take Zosimus the Alchemist, if you like. *Come in!*" The hall-porter came in, bowed with ancient respectfulness (the hall-porter was rather ancient, himself), laid down a salver with a card on it, and withdrew. "Ah-hah. Business is picking up. Fifteen down, three over . . ."

Eszterhazy had not stayed beyond the half-hour, but made a semi-appointment for a later date. The card of the further business awaiting Milord Sir Smiht was facing directly toward both of them, and he could hardly have avoided reading it.

And it read: *Brothers Swartbloi, Number 3, Court of the Golden Hart. Snuff-Tobacco.*

Third Assistant Supervisory Officer Lupescus, of the Aliens Office, was feeling rather mixed, emotionally. On the one hand, he still had the happiness of having (recently) reached the level of a third assistant supervisory official; it was not every day, or even every year that a member of the Romanou-speaking minority attained such high rank in the Imperial Capital. On the other hand, a certain amount of field work was now required of him, and he had never done field work before. This present task, for instance, this call upon the Second Councilor at the British Legation, was merely routine. "Merely routine, my dear Lupescus," his superior in the office, Second ASO on Glouki had said. Easily enough *said*, but, routine or not routine, one had to have something to *show* for this visit. And it did not look as though one were going to get it.

"Smith, Smith," the Second Councilor was saying, testily. "I tell you that I must have more information. *What* Smith?"

All that Lupescus could do was to repeat, "Milord Sir Smiht."

"'*Milord, Milord*,' there *is* no such rank or title. Sir, why, that is merely as one would say *Herra*, or *Monsieur*. And as for Smith – by the way, you've got it spelled wrongly there, you know, it is S-M-I-T-H – well, you can't expect me to know anything about anyone just named *Smith*, why, that's like asking me about someone named Jones, in Cardiff, or Mac-donald, in Glasgow . . . Mmm, no, you wouldn't know about those . . . Ah, well, it's, oh, it's like asking me about someone named Novotny in Prague! D'you see?"

Lupescus brightened just a trifle. This was something. Very dutifully and carefully, he wrote in his notebook, *Subject Milord Smiht said to be associated with Novotny in Prague* . . .

With his best official bow, he withdrew. Withdrawn, he allowed himself a sigh. Now he would have to go and check out Novotny with the people at the Austro-Hungarian Legation. He hoped that this would be more productive than this other enquiry had been. One would have thought that people named Smiht grew on trees in England.

Eszterhazy's growing association with the white-haired Eng-lishman took, if not a leap, then a sort of lurch, forward one evening about a month after his first visit. He had sent up his card with the hall-porter, who had returned with word that he was to go up directly. He found Smith with a woman in black, a nondescript woman of the type who hold up churches all around the world.

"Ah, come in, my dear sir. Look here. This good woman doesn't speak either French or German, and my command of Gothic is not . . . well, ask her what she wants, do, please."

Frow Widow Apterhots wished to be placed in communication with her late husband. "That is to say," she said, anxious that there be no confusion nor mistake, "that is to say, he is dead, you know. His name is Emyil."

Smiht shook his head tolerantly at this. "Death does not exist," he said, "nor does life exist, save as states of flux to one side or other of the sidereal line, or astral plane, as some call it. From this point of view it may seem that anyone who is not alive must be dead, but that is not so. The absent one, the one absent from here, may now be fluctuating in the area called 'death,' or he or she may be proceeding in a calm vibration along the level of the sidereal line or so-called astral plane. We mourn because the 'dead' are not 'alive.' But in the world which we call 'death' the so-called 'dead' may be mourning a departure into what we call 'life.' "

From Widow Apterhots sighed. "Emyil was always so healthy, so *strong*," she said. "I still can't understand it. He always did say that there wasn't no Hell, just Heaven and Purgatory, and I used to say, 'Oh, Emyil, people will think that you're a Freemason or something.' Well, our priest, Father Ugerow, he just won't listen when I talk like this, he says, 'If you won't say your prayers, at least perform some work of corporal mercy, and take your mind off such things.' But what I say—" She leaned forward, her simple sallow face very serious and confiding, "I say that all I want to know is: Is he happy there? That's all."

Pemberton Smith said that he could guarantee nothing, but in any event he would have to have at least one object permeated with the odyllic force of the so-called deceased.

The Frow Widow nodded and delved into her reticule. "That's what I was told, so I come prepared. I always made him wear this, let them say what they like, he always did. But I wouldn't let them bury him with it because I wanted it for a keepsake. Here you are, Professor." She held out a small silver crucifix.

Smith took the article with the utmost calm and walked over and set it down upon a heavy piece of furniture in the dimness of the back of the room. There were quite a number of things already on the table. Smith beckoned, and the others came toward him, Frow Widow Apterhots because she was sure that she was meant to, and Eszterhazy because he was sure he wanted to. "These," said Smith, "are the equipment for the odyllic forces. Pray take a seat, my good woman." He struck a match and lit a small gas jet; it was not provided with a mantle, and it either lacked a regulatory tap or something was wrong with the one it did have – or perhaps Smith merely liked to see the gas flame shooting up to its fullest extent; at least two feet long the flame was, wavering wildly and a reddish gold in color.

Certainly, he was not trying to conceal anything.

But *these* were interesting, certainly whatever else they were, and Eszterhazy took advantage of the English wizard's at the moment administering to himself two strong doses of Rappee – one in each nostril – to scrutinize the equipment for the odyllic forces. What he saw was a series of bell jars . . . that is, at least some of them were bell jars . . . some of the others resembled, rather, Leyden jars . . . and what *was* all that, under the bell jars? In one there seemed to be a vast quantity of metal filings; in another, quicksilver; in the most of them, organic matter, vegetive in origin. Every jar, bell or Leyden, appeared to be connected to every other jar by a system of glass tubing: and all the tubes seemed fitted up to a sort of master-tube, which coiled around and down and finally upward, culminating in what appeared to be an enormous gramophone horn.

"Pray, touch *nothing*," warned Milord Sir Smiht. "The

equipment is *exceedingly* fragile." He took up a small, light table, the surface of which consisted of some open lattice-work material – Eszterhazy was not sure what – and, moving it easily, set it up over the born. On it he placed the crucifix. "Now, my dear sir, if you will be kind enough to ask this good lady, first, to take these in her hands . . .? And, to concentrate, if she will, entirely upon the memory of her husband, now on another plane of existence." The Widow Apterhots, sitting down, took hold of the *these* – in this case, a pair of metal grips of the sort which are connected, often, to magnetic batteries, but in this case were not – they seemed connected in some intricate way with the glass tubings. She closed her eyes. "*And,*" the wizard continued, "please to cooperate in sending on my request. Which, after all, is *her* request, translated into my own methodology."

He began an intricate series of turnings of taps, of twistings of connections at joints and at junctions, of connectings; at length he was finished. "Emyil Apterhots. Emyil Apterhots. Emyil Apterhots. If you are happy, wherever you are, kindly signify by moving the crucifix which you wore when on this plane of existence. *Now!*"

The entire massive piece of furniture upon which the equipment for the odyllic force (or forces) was placed began to move forward.

"No, *no*, you Gothic oaf!" shouted the *milord*, his face crimson with fury and concern. "*Not* the sideboard! *The crucifix!* Just the *cru-ci-fix*—" He set himself against the sideboard and pressed it back. In vain. In vain. In vain. In a moment, Eszterhazy, concerned lest the glass tubings should snap, reached forward to adjust them, so that the intricate workings should not be shattered and sundered – the wizard, panting and straining against the laboratory furniture as the heavy mass continued to slide forward . . . forward . . . forward . . .

—and suddenly slid rapidly backward, Milord Sir Smiht stumbling and clutching at empty air, Eszterhazy darting forward, and the two of them executing a sort of slow, insane *schottische*, arm in arm, before coming to a slow halt—

And then, oh so grumpy, wiping his brow with a red bandana handkerchief, of the sort in which navvies wrap their pork pies, hear Milord Sir Smiht say, "I must regard this session as questionable in its results. And I *must* say that I am not *used* to such contumacy from the habitants of the sidereal line!"

Frow Widow Apterhots, however, clearly did not regard the results as in any way questionable. Her sallow, silly face now quite blissful, she stepped forward and retrieved the crucifix. "Emyil," she said, "was always so *strong* . . . !"

And on that note she departed.

Herr Manfred Mauswarmer at the Austro-Hungarian Legation was quite interested. " 'Novotny in Prague,' eh? Hmmm, *that* seems to ring a bell." Third ASO Lupescus sat up straighter. A faint tingle of excitement went through his scalp. "Yes, yes," said Herr Mauswarmer, "we have of a certainty heard the name. One of those Czech names," he said, almost indulgently. "One never knows what *they* may be up to." Very carefully he made a neat little note and looked up brightly. "We shall of course first have to communicate with Vienna—"

"Oh, of course!"

"And they will, of course, communicate with Prague."

Herr Manfred Mauswarmer's large, pale, bloodshot blue eyes blinked once or twice. "A Czech name," he noted. "An English name. Uses the code cypher *Wizard*. Communicates *in French*." He briefly applied one thick forefinger to the side of his nose. He winked. Lupescus winked back. They understood each other. The hare had had a headstart. But the hounds had caught the scent.

One of the bell jars was empty – had, in fact, always been empty, although Eszterhazy had merely noted this without considering as to why it might be so. He did not ask about it as he listened, now, to the Englishman's talk. Milord Sir Smiht, his cap on his head, his cloak sometimes giving a dramatic *flap* as he turned in his pacings of the large old room, said, "The contents of the vessels in large part represent the vegetable and mineral kingdom – I don't know if you have noticed that."

"I have."

"The *an*imal kingdom, now . . . well, each man and woman is a microcosm, representing the macrocosm, the *un*iverse, in miniature. That is to say, we contain in our own bodies enough of the animal and mineral to emanate at all times, though we are not aware of it, a certain amount of odyllic force—"

"Or forces."

"Or forces. Point well *made*. However. Now, although the average human body does include, usually, some amounts of the vegetable kingdom – so much potato, cabbage, sprouts, let us say – undergoing the process of digestive action," *flap* went his cloak, "as *well* as the ever-present bacteria, also vegetative, *still*. The chemical constituencies in our body, now, I forget just what they amount to. Four-and-six, more or less, in real money. Or is it *two*-and-six? One forgets. *Still*. Primarily, the human organism is an *an*imal organism." *Flap*.

Eszterhazy, nodding, made a steeple of his hands. "And therefore (Pemberton Smith will correct me if I am wrong), when the human subject takes hold of that pair of metallic grips, the three kingdoms, animal, vegetable, and mineral, come together in a sort of unity—"

"A sort of Triune Monarchy *in parvo*, as it were, yes, co-*rect!* I see that I was not wrong in assuming that yours was a mind capable of grasping these matters," *flap*, "and then it is all a matter of adjustment: One turns *up* the vegetative emanations, one turns *in* the mineral emanations . . . and then, then, my dear sir, one hopes for the best. For one has not as yet been able to adjust the individual human beings. They are what they are. One can turn a *tap*, one can open a valve or lose a valve, plug in a connecting tube or *un*plug a connecting tube. But one has to take a human body *just as one finds it* . . . Pity, in a way . . . Hollo, hollo!"

Something was happening in the empty bell jar: mists and fumes, pale blue lights, red sparks and white sparks.

Milord Sir Smiht, dashing hither and thither and regulating

his devices, stopped, suddenly, looked imploringly at Eszterhazy, gestured, and said, "*Would* you, my dear fellow? *Awf'*ly grateful—"

Eszterhazy sat in the chair, took the metal grips in his hands, and tried to emulate those curious animals, the mules, which, for all that they are void of hope of posterity, can still manage to look in two directions at once.

Direction Number One: Pemberton Smith, as he coupled and uncoupled, attached and disattached, turned, tightened, loosened, adjusting the ebb and flow of the odyllic forces. Animal, vegetable, *and* mineral.

Direction Number Two: The once-empty bell jar, wherein now swarmed . . . wherein now swarmed *what?* A hive of microscopic bees, perhaps.

A faint tingle passed through the palms of Eszterhazy's hands and up his hands and arms. The tingle grew stronger. It was not really at all like feeling an electrical current, though. A perspiration broke forth upon his forehead. He felt very slightly giddy, and the *wizard anglais* almost at once perceived this. "Too strong for you, is it? *Sorry* about *that!*" He made adjustments. The giddiness was at once reduced, almost at once passed away.

And the something in the bell jar slowly took form and shape.

It was a simulacrum, perhaps. Or perhaps the word was homunculus. The bell jar was the size of a child. And the man within it was the size of a rather small child. Otherwise it was entirely mature. And "it" was really not the correct pronoun, for the homunculus (or whatever it was) was certainly a man, however small: a man wearing a frock coat and everything which went with frock coats, and a full beard. He even had an order of some sort, a ribbon which crossed his bosom, and a medal or medallion. Eszterhazy *thought*, but could not be sure, that it rather resembled the silver medallion which Milord Sir Smiht wore in his hat.

"Pemberton Smith, who *is* that?"

"Who, that? Or. Oh, that's *Gomes*—" He pronounced it to

rhyme with *roams*. "He's the Wizard of Brazil. You've heard of *Gomes*, to be sure." And he then proceeded to move his arms, hands, and fingers with extreme rapidity, pausing only to say, "We communicate through the international sign language, you see. He has no English and I have no Portagee. Poor old Gomes, things have been ever so slack for him since poor old Dom Peedro got the sack. Ah well. Inevitable, I suppose. Emperors and the Americas just don't seem to go together. Purely an Old World phenomena, don't you know." And once again his fingers and hands and arms began their curious, rapid, and impressive movement. "Yes, yes," he muttered to himself. "I see, I see. No. Really. You don't say. Ah, too bad, too bad!"

He turned to Eszterhazy. Within the jar, the tiny digits and limbs of the Wizard of Brazil had fallen, as it were, silent. The homunculus shrugged, sadly. "What do you make of all *that?*" asked the Wizard of England (across the waters).

"What? Is it not clear? The ants are eating his coffee trees, and he wishes you to send him some paris green, as the local supply has been exhausted."

"My dear chap, *I* can't send him any paris green!"

"Assure him that I shall take care of it myself. Tomorrow."

"I say, that *is* ever so good of you! Yes, yes, ah, pray excuse me now whilst I relay the good news."

In far-off Petropolis, the summer capital of Brazil, the wizard of that mighty nation, much reduced in size (wizard, not nation) by transatlantic transmission, crossed his arms upon his bosom and bowed his gratitude in the general direction of the distant though friendly nation of Scythia-Pan-nonia-Transbalkania. All men of science, after all, constitute one great international confraternity.

The saint's-day gift of snuff was so well received by Frow Widow Orgats, Eszterhazy's cook (who had taken his advice to stock up on coffee), that he thought he would lay in a further supply as a sweetener against the possibility of one of those occasions – infrequent, but none the less to be feared – when the Frow Cook suffered severe attacks of the vapors and either burned the soup or declared (with shrieks and shouts audible on the second floor) her intense inability to face anything in the shape of a stove at all. So, on the next convenient occasion, he once more made his way to the Court of the Golden Hart.

"Four ounces of the Imperial."

He peered at the Swartbloi brother, who was peering at the scales. "You are not Kummelman," he said. Almost. But not.

"No sir, I am Ignats," said the brother. "Kummelman is at the moment—"

"In the mill, salting the Turkey. I know."

Ignats Swartbloi looked at him with some surprise and some reproof. "Oh, no, sir. Kummelman always grinds the Rappee, and I always salt the Turkey. On the other tasks we either work together or take turns. But *never* in regard to the grinding of the Rappee or the salting of the Turkey. I had been about to say, sir, that Kummelman is at his home, by reason of his wife's indisposition, she being presently in a very delicate condition."

And he handed over the neatly wrapped packet of pleated paper bearing the well-known illustrated label – this one, old Frow Imglotch had tinted so as to give the snufftaker a gray nose and a green periwig, neither of which in any way diminished the man's joy at having his left nostril packed solid with Brothers Swartbloi Snuff-Tobacco (though whether Rappee, Imperial, Minorka, Habana, or Turkey, has never been made plain, and perhaps never will be).

"Indeed, indeed. Pray accept my heartiest felicitations."

The brother gazed at him and gave a slight, polite bow, no more. "That is very kind of you, sir. Felicitations are perhaps premature. Suppose the child will be a girl?"

"Hm," said Eszterhazy. "Hm, hm. Well, there is that possibility, isn't there? Thank you, and good afternoon."

He could not but suppose that this same possibility must have also occurred to Brother Kummelman. And, in that case, he wondered, would a second visit have been paid to the large, antiquated room in the Grand Dominik where the *Milord anglais* still prolonged his stay?

* * *

Herr von Paarfus pursed his lips. He shook his head. Gave a very faint sigh. Then he got up and went into the office of his superior, the Graf zu Kluk. "Yes, what?" said the Graf zu Kluk, whose delightful manners always made it such a pleasure to work with him. More than once had Herr von Paarfus thought of throwing it all up and migrating to America, where his cousin owned a shoe store in Omaha. None of this, of course, passed his lips. He handed the paper to his superior.

"From Mauswarmer, in Bella, Excellency," he said.

The Graf fitted his monocle more closely into his eye and grunted. "Mauswarmer, in Bella," he said, looking up, "has uncovered an Anglo-Franco-Czech conspiracy, aimed against the integrity of the Austro-Hungarian Empire."

"Indeed, Your Excellency!" said von Paarfus, trying to sound shocked.

"Oh yes! There is no doubt of it," declared Graf zu Kluk, tapping the report with a highly polished fingernail. "The liaison agent – of course, in Prague, where else? – is a man named Novotny. The password is 'wizard.' What do you think of *that?*"

"I think, Your Excellency, that Novotny is a very common name in Prague."

Graf zu Kluk gave no evidence of having heard. "I shall take this up with His Highness, at once," he said. Even Graf zu Kluk had a superior officer. But then, long years of training in the Civil Service of Austria-Hungary cautioned him. "That is," he said, "as soon as we have had word on this from our people in London, Paris, and Prague. Until then, mind, not a word to anyone!"

"Your Excellency is of course correct."

"Of *course*. Of *course*. See to this. *At once!*"

Von Paarfus went out, thinking of Omaha. Not until the door had closed behind him did he sigh once again.

Oberzeeleutnant-commander Adler had had a long and distinguished career in the naval service of a neighboring power. "But then," he said, stiffly, "I – how do you put it, in English?

Than I copied my blotting-book? I of course do not desire to go into details. At any rate, I thought to myself, even if I shall not be actually at sea, at any rate, at least I shall be able to put my finishing touches on the revision of my monograph on the deep-sea fishes. But the High Command was even more loath with me than I had thought; ah, how they did punished me, did I deserved such punishments? Aund so, here I am, Naval Attaché in Bella! In *Bella!* A river port! Capital of a nation, exceedingly honorable, to be sure." He bobbed a hasty bow to Eszterhazy, who languidly returned it. "But one which has no deep-sea coast at all! Woe!" For a moment he said nothing, only breathed deeply. Then, "What interest could anyone possibly find in a freshwater fish, I do enquire you?" he entreated. But no one had an answer.

"Mmm," said Milord Sir Smiht. "Yes. Yes. Know what it is to be an exile, myself. Still. I stay strictly away from politics, you know. Not my pidjin. Whigs, Tories, nothing to me. Plague on both their houses. Sea-fish, rich in phosphorus. Brain food."

But the commander had not made himself clear. What he would wish to propose of the Milord Sir Smiht was not political. It was scientific. Could not Sir Smiht, by means of the idyllic – what? ah! – thousand pardons – the odyllic force, of which one had heard much – could not Sir Smiht produce an ensampling of, say, the waters of the Mindanao Trench, or of some other deep-sea area – here – here in Bella – so that the commander might continue his studies?

The *milord* threw up his hands. "Impossible!" he cried. "Im-*pos*-sib-le! Think of the pressures! One would need a vessel of immensely strong steel. With windows of immensely thick glass. *Just to begin with!* Cost: much. Possibilities of success: jubious."

But the Naval Attaché begged that these trifles might not stand in the way. The cost, the cost was to be regarded as merely a first step, and one already taken; he hinted at private means.

"As for the rest." Eszterhazy stepped forward, a degree of

interest showing in his large eyes. "At least, as for the steel, there are the plates for the *Ignats Louis* . . ."

The *Ignats Louis!* With what enthusiasm the nation (particularly the patriotic press) had encouraged plans for the construction of the Triune Monarchy's very first dreadnought, a vessel which (it was implied) would strike justly deserved terror into the hearts of the enemies – actual or potential – of Scythia-Pannonia-Transbalkania! A New Day, it was declared, was about to dawn for the Royal and Imperial Navy of the fourth-largest empire in Europe; a Navy which had until then consisted of three revenue cutters, two gunboats, one lighthouse tender, and the monitor *Furioso* (formerly the *Monadnock*, purchased very cheaply from the United States after the conclusion of the American Civil War). Particular attention had been drawn to the exquisitely forged and incredibly strong steel plate, made in Sweden at great expense.

Alas, the day of the Triune Monarchy as one of the naval powers of the world had been exceedingly short-lived and more or less terminated upon the discovery that the *Ignats Louis* would draw four feet more than the deepest reaches of the River Ister at high water in the floods. The cheers of the patriotic press were overnight reduced to silence, subsidies for the dreadnought vanished from the next budget, the skeleton of the vessel slowly rusted on the ways, the exquisitely forged and incredibly strong steel plating remained in the storage sheds of the contractor; and the two gunboats and the monitor alone remained to strike terror into the hearts of, if not Russia and Austria-Hungary, then at any rate Graustark and Ruritania.

The downcast face of the foreign naval commander slowly began to brighten. The countenance of the English wizard likewise relaxed. And, as though by one common if semi-silent consent, they drew up to the table and began to make their plans.

"Qu'est-ce qu'il y a, cette affaire d'une vizard anglais aux Scythie-Pannonie-Transbalkanie?" they asked, in Paris.

"*C'est, naturellement, une espèce de blague*," they answered, in Paris.

"*Envoyez-le à Londres*," they concluded, in Paris.

"What can the chaps *mean?*" they asked each other, in London. "'*English vizar Milor Sri Smhiti*'? Makes no sense, you know."

"Mmm, well, *does*, in a way, y'know," they said in London. "Of course, that should be *vizier*. And *sri*, of course, is an Injian religious title. Dunno what to make of Smhti, though. Hindi? Gujerathi? Look here. Sir Augustus is our Injian expert. Send it up to him," they said, in London.

"Very well, then . . . but, look here. What can this be about *Tcheque novothni?* They simply can't *spell* in Paris, you know. Check up on the Novothni, what are the Novothni?"

"Blessed if I know. Some hill tribe or other. Not our pidjin. Best send it all up to Sir Augustus," they said, in London.

But in Prague they sat down to their files, which, commencing with *Novotny, Abelard*, ran for pages and pages and pages down to *Novotny, Zygmund*. They had lots and lots of time in Prague, and, anyway, it was soothing work, and much more to their tastes than the absolutely baffling case of a young student who thought that he had turned into a giant cockroach.

They had directed the old hall-porter at the Grand Dominik to inform all would-be visitors that Milord Sir Smiht was not receiving people at present. But Frow Puprikosch was not one to be deterred by hall-porters; indeed, it is doubtful if she understood what he was saying, and, before he had finished saying it, she had swept on . . . and on, and into the large old-fashioned chamber where the three were at work.

"Not now," said Smiht, scarcely looking up from his adjustments of the tubing system to the steel-plated diving bell. "I can't see you now."

"But you must see me now," declared Frow Puprikosch, in a rich contralto voice. "My case admits of no delays, for how can one live without love?" Frow Puprikosch was a large, black-haired woman in whom the bloom of youth had mellowed. "That was the tragedy of my life, that my marriage to Puprikosch lacked love – but what did I know then? – mere child that I was." She pressed one hand to her bosom, as to push back the tremendous sigh which arose therefrom, and with the other she employed – as an aid to emphasis and gesticulation – an umbrella of more use to the ancient lace industry of the Triune Monarchy than of any possible guard against rain.

"And what would Herra Puprikosch say, if he knew what you were up to, eh? Much better go home, my dear lady," she was advised.

"He is dead, I have divorced him, the marriage was annulled, he is much better off in Argentina," she declared, looking all around with great interest.

"Argentina?"

"*Some*where in Africa!" she said, and, with a wave of her umbrella, or perhaps it was really a parasol, disposed of such pedantries. "What I wish of you, dear wizard," she said, addressing Eszterhazy, "is only this: to make known to me my true love. Of course you can do it. Where shall I sit down here? I shall sit here."

He assured her that he was not the wizard, but she merely smiled an arch and anxious smile, and began to peel off her gloves. As these were very long and old-fashioned with very many buttons (of the best-quality mother-of-pearl, and probably from the establishment of Weitmondl in the Court of the Golden Hart), the act took her no little time. And it was during this time that it was agreed by the men present, between them, with shrugs and sighs and nods, that they had beter accomplish at least the attempt to do what the lady desired, if they expected to be able to get on with their work at all that day.

"If the dear lady will be kind enough to grasp these grips," said Sir Smiht, in a resigned manner, "and concentrate upon the matter which is engaging her mind, ah, yes, that's a very good grasp." He began to make the necessary adjustments.

"Love, love, my true love, my true affinity, where is he?" demanded Frow Puprikosch of the Universal Aether. "Yoi!"

she exclaimed, a moment later, in her native Avar, her eyebrows going up until they met the fringe, so pleasantly arranged, of glossy black hair. "Already I feel it begins. *Yoi!*"

"'Yoiks' would be more like it," Smiht muttered. He glanced at a dial to the end of the sideboard. "Good heavens!" he exclaimed. "What an extraordinary amount of the odyllic forces that woman conjugates! Never *seen* anything like it!"

"Love," declared Frow Puprikosch, "love is all that matters; money is of no matter, I have money; position is of no matter, I expectorate upon the false sham of position. I am a woman of such a nature as to crave, demand, and require only *love!* And I know, I know, I *know*, that *some*where is the true true affinity of my soul – where *are* you?" she caroled, casting her large and lovely eyes all around. "*Oo*-hoo?"

The hand of the dial, which had been performing truly amazing swings and movements, now leaped all the way full circle, and, with a most melodious twang, fell off the face of the dial and onto the ancient rug.

At that moment sounds, much less melodious, but far more emphatic, began to emanate from the interior of the diving bell. And before Eszterhazy, who had started to stoop toward the fallen dial hand, could reach the hatchcover, the hatchcover sprang open and out flew – there is really not a better verb – out flew the figure of a man of vigorous early middle age and without a stitch or thread to serve, as the French so delicately put it, *pour cacher sa nudité . . .*

"*Yoiii!!!*" shrieked Frow Puprikosch, releasing her grip upon the metal holders and covering her face with her bumbershoot.

"Good heavens, a woman!" exclaimed the gentleman who had just emerged from the diving bell. "Here, dash it, Pemberton Smith, *give* me that!" So saying, he whipped off the cloak which formed the habitual outer garment of the *wizard anglais*, and wrapped it around himself, somewhat in the manner of a Roman senator who has just risen to denounce a conspiracy. The proprieties thus taken care of, the newcomer, in some perplexity, it would seem, next asked, "Where

on earth have you gotten us to, Pemberton Smith? – and why
on earth are you rigged up like such a guy? Hair whitened, and
I don't know what else. Eh?"

Pemberton Smith, somewhat annoyed, said, "I have undergone no process of rigging, it is merely the natural attrition of
the passage of thirty years, and tell me, then, how did you pass
your time on the sidereal level – or, if you prefer, astral plane?"

"But I don't prefer," the man said, briskly. "I know nothing
about it. I'd come up from the Observatory – *damned* silly
notion putting an observatory in Wales, skies obscured three
hundred nights a year with soppy Celtic mists, all the pubs
closed on Sundays – and, happening to drop in on the Royal
Society, I allowed myself to act as subject for your experiment.
One moment I was *there*, the next moment I was *there*—" He
gestured toward the diving bell. Then something evidently
struck his mind. " 'Thirty years,' you say? Good heavens!" An
expression of the utmost glee came across his face. "Then
Flora must be dead by now, skinny old bitch, and, if she isn't,
so much the worse for her, who is this lovely lady *here*?"

The lady herself, displacing her parasol and coming toward
him in full-blown majesty, said, in heavily accented but still
melodious English, "Is here the Madame Puprikosch, but you
may to calling me Yózhinka. My affinity! My own true love!
Produced for me by the genius of the *wizard anglais! Yoi!*"
And she embraced him with both arms, a process which
seemed by no means distasteful to the gentleman himself.

"If you don't mind, Pigafetti Jones," the wizard said,
somewhat stiffly, "I will thank you for the return of my cloak.
We will next discuss the utmost inconveniency which your
disappearance from the chambers of the Royal Society has
caused me throughout three decades."

"All in good time, Pemberton Smith," said the former
Astronomer-Royal of Wales, running his hands up and down
the ample back of Frow Puprikosch—or, as she preferred to be
called by him, Yózhinka. "All in good time . . . I say, Yózhinka, don't you find that corset *most* constrictive? *I* should. In
fact, I *do*. Do let us go somewhere where we can take it off, and

afterward I shall explain to you the supernal glories of the evening skies – beginning, of course, with Venus."

To which the lady, as they made their way toward the door together, replied merely (but expressively), "*Yoi . . .!*"

Standing in the doorway was a very tall, very thin, very, very dignified elderly gentleman in cutaway, striped trousers, silk hat – a silk hat which he raised, although somewhat stiffly, as the semi-former Frow Puprikosch went past him. He then turned, and regarding the *wizard anglais* with a marked measure of reproof, said, "*Well*, George."

"Good Heavens. *Augustus.* Is it really you?"

"It is really me, George. *Well*, George. I suppose that you have received my letter."

"I have received no letter."

"I sent it you, care of Cook's, Poona."

"Haven't been in Poona for years. Good gad. That must be why my damned remittances kept arriving so late. I must have forgotten to give them a change of address."

Sir Augustus Smith frowned slightly and regarded his brother with some perplexity. "You haven't been in Poona for years? Then what was all this nonsense of your calling yourself Vizier Sri Smith and trying to rouse the hill tribes with the rallying cry of 'No votny'? Votnies were abolished, along with the tax on grout, the year after the Mutiny, surely you must know that."

"I haven't been in Injia for eleven years, I tell you. Not since the Presidency cut up so sticky that time over the affair of the rope trick (all done by the odyllic forces, I tell you). As for all the rest of it, haven't the faintest idea. Call myself Vizier Sri Smith indeed, *what do you take me for?*"

Sir Augustus bowed his head and gently bit his lips. Then he looked up. "Well, well," he said, at last. "This is probably another hugger-mugger on the part of the Junior Clarks, not the first time, you know, won't be the last," he sighed. "I tell you what it is, you know, George. *They let* anyone *into Eton these days.*"

"Good heavens!"

"Fact. Well. Hm. Mph." He looked around the room with an abstracted air. "Ah, here it is, you see, now that I have seen with my own eyes that Pigafetti Jones is alive and playing all sorts of fun and games as I daresay he has *been* doing all these years, ahum, see no reason why you shouldn't come home, you know, if you like."

"Augustus! Do you mean it?"

"Certainly."

The younger Smith reached into the clothes press and removed therefrom a tightly packed traveling bag of ancient vintage. "I am quite ready, then, Augustus," he said.

There was a clatter of feet on the stairs in the corridors beyond, the feeble voice of the hall-porter raised in vain, and into the room there burst Kummelman Swartbloi, who proceeded first to fall at the younger Smith's feet and next to kiss them. "My wife!" he cried. "My wife has just had twin boys! Bella is guaranteed another generation of Brothers Swartbloi (Snuff-Tobacco)! Thank you, thank you, thank you!" And he turned and galloped away, murmuring that he would have stayed longer but that it was essential for him to be at the mill in a quarter of an hour in order to grind the Rappee.

"Do twins come up often in the chap's family?" asked Sir Augustus.

"I'm afraid that nothing much comes up often in his family at all, any more. I merely advised him to change his butcher and I may have happened to suggest the well-known firm of Schlockhocker, in the Ox Market. Old Schlockhocker has six sons, all twins, of whom the youngest, Pishto and Knishto, act as delivery boys on alternate days. Wonderful thing, change of diet . . . that, and, of course, the odyllic forces."

Sir Augustus paused in the act of raising his hat to his head. "I should hope, George," he said, "that you may not have been the means of introducing any spurious offspring into this other tradesman's family."

His brother said that he didn't know about that. Fellow and his wife were first cousins, after all. Sir Augustus nodded, again lifted his hat, and this time gestured to the multitudinous items upon the heavy old sideboard. "Do you not desire to remove your philosophical equipment?" he asked.

Smith the younger considered. He looked at his own hat, the velvet cap of curious cut with the curious silvern medallion on it. He took it in both hands and approached Doctor Eszterhazy. Doctor Eszterhazy bowed. George William Marmaduke Pemberton Smith placed the cap upon the head of Engelbert Eszterhazy (Doctor of Medicine, Doctor of Jurisprudence, Doctor of Science, Doctor of Literature, etc., etc.). "You are now and henceforth," the Englishman said, "the Wizard of the Triune Monarchy, and may regard yourself as seized of the entire equipage of the odyllic force, or, rather, forces. Sorry I can't stay, but there you are."

The brothers left the room arm in arm, Sir Augustus inquiring, "Who was that odd-looking chap, George?" and his junior replying, "Phrenologist fellow. Can't recollect his name. Does one still get good mutton at Simpson's?"

"One gets *very* good mutton, still, at Simpson's."

"Haven't had good mutton since . . ." Voices and footsteps alike died away.

Doctor Eszterhazy looked at the equipage of the odyllic forces, and he slowly rubbed his hands together and smiled.

"PUT BACK
THAT UNIVERSE!"

F. Gwynplaine MacIntyre

*F. Gwynplaine MacIntyre had the audacity to sell this
story somewhere else first. So I'm not going to tell you
anything about him. That'll teach him. (But shush, don't let
him hear. If you want to know more about him check out his
stories in* The Mammoth Book of Comic Fantasy, The
Mammoth Book of Historical Detectives *and* The Mammoth Book of New Sherlock Holmes Adventures *where
at least he had the decency to send me some new stories.)*

"This must be the place," said Smedley Faversham, as he
travelled backwards in time to the very beginning of the
universe, and took a look around.

The vicinity in question was a region of space just over six
feet in diameter: spherical, and consisting of ionic plasma gas
superheated to a temperature of ten *billion* degrees Kelvin. At
this temperature, matter could not sustain atomic integrity, so
the contents of the sphere had obligingly broken down into
subatomic particles, photons, and a few exotic particles such as
bosons, muons, gluons and the occasional quark. Of course, a
plasma cloud of such extreme temperature could vaporize
Smedley Faversham instantly, so he was careful to step back

at least a good ten feet and watch from a safe distance as a steady trickle of protons, photons, neutrons and electrons – attracted by the gravity well of the plasma sphere – continued to be drawn into its subatomic mass.

The sphere was more precisely a *hypersphere*, because it had attained a shape of uniform radius through all the dimensions of Space: it was therefore circular, or spherical, in *all* directions . . . not merely in the three most obvious ones. The hypersphere's radius was dwindling slowly, as the immense mass of the plasma cloud forced its contents into a state of supercompression. As each nanosecond elapsed, the sphere became slightly smaller.

Smedley Faversham, intrepid time-traveller, knew that he had indeed arrived at the correct destination in space-time. The plasma sphere directly in front of him contained approximately 99.99995% of all the physical matter in the entire universe: effectively, this glowing sphere was 99.99995% of the entire universe. And since Time is a coefficient of the unified force which functions as both gravity and electromagnetism, it stood to reason that this glowing sphere also contained 99.99995% of all the *time* in the universe as well: all the time that ever *had* existed and ever *would* exist. Since this single ball of plasma gas, now slightly less than five feet in diameter (it had condensed somewhat during the past few nanoseconds), contained nearly all of the Space and Time in the entire universe, then – as Smedley had already observed – this surely *had* to be the place. Because there was nowhere else – and no *when* else – for him to be.

"Any second now," Smedley Faversham chuckled, "all the matter and antimatter in all the infinite dimensions of the universe . . . except for myself, of course . . . will be, if I may employ a technical term, *smunched up* into a non-dimensional singularity of Space-Time. One nanosecond later, it will burst forth to create the Big Bang. And *that* will be the moment," Smedley chuckled again, "when I shall put my fiendish plan into action."

Smedley watched, greedily, as a few straggling photons and

baryons came rushing to converge upon the dwindling sphere, adding themselves to its mass. According to Smedley's calculations, there were only 217 subatomic particles of matter or antimatter (not including his own constituent molecules, and the molecules of his clothing and equipment) still remaining in the entire universe beyond the hypersphere. When those last few particles had entered the hypersphere's inexorable gravity well, Smedley's task would begin.

"The more the merrier," said Smedley Faversham, nodding his approval as a few more latecomers (a graviton, a fermion and a neutrino) came rushing to join the swirling eddy of the plasma cloud . . . which by now had condensed to a diameter of forty-seven inches. "Soon, the Big Bang will begin. In the first two minutes of Time, the temperature of the plasma hypersphere will reduce by a factor of ten as its volume expands. This will allow the formation of simple isotopes, such as helium, protium, and tritium. From those few simple building blocks, the entire universe will be built. Unless, of course . . .," here Smedley Faversham chuckled again, ". . . *I* decide otherwise."

At this point, the Gentle Reader may wonder how Smedley Faversham was able to stay alive, since the oxygen molecules necessary for breathing (to say nothing of chuckling) had not yet been created by the cosmic aftereffects of the Big Bang. Hence, thus, and consequently there was no air for Smedley to breathe while he was standing at a slight distance in Space-Time from the creation of the universe. For that matter – or *lack* of matter – there was nothing solid for Smedley to be standing *on*, since all of the atomic mass in all the infinite dimensions of the universe (minus 189 subatomic particles which still hadn't arrived yet, and Smedley himself) had already converged into the all-consuming hypersphere. By this same application of pitiless logic, the Gentle Readers may also wonder how Smedley was able to *see* the hypersphere, since nearly all the photons in the universe were now *inside* the gravity well of the sphere, beyond reach of Smedley's optic nerves.

The Gentle Readers should mind their damned business.

For those who spitefully demand an explanation, however, here it is: the rules which govern the structure and function of Space and Time within the matter-energy universe are necessarily a *part* of that universe, and must therefore exist *within* it. Smedley Faversham had positioned himself *outside* the borders of Space, Time and the Universe (having stepped three paces back, and slightly to the left), and so he now existed *outside* Space and Time and all the rules which govern the interaction of matter and energy.

Now are you happy?

Smedley Faversham's stomach rumbled, reminding him that he had not eaten since the year 2193 . . . which was now sixteen billion years downstream in Time, give or take an eon, from his present location. He reached into his tucker-bag and retrieved a double portion of Curry Vindaloo take-away, which he had purchased *en route* to the Big Bang during a stop-over at the Kurry Kebab King all-night restaurant in Stoke Newington. Now he unwrapped the takeaway, and he thoughtfully munched curry vindaloo as he watched the arrival of a few more subatomic particles. The hypersphere by now had dwindled to less than a yard in diameter, and very soon the Big Bang would begin.

"That was delicious," said Smedley Faversham, as he carefully deposited the waxed-paper wrapper of his takeaway dinner into the vortex of the hypersphere (it always pays to be neat), and he fastidiously wiped a few bright-orange stains of vindaloo sauce from his fingertips as the molecules of wax and paper and leftover vindaloo were broken down into their atomic components, and the atoms in turn were rendered to their subatomic smithereens. "Of course, curry vindaloo always gives me heartburn, and sometimes – *urp!* – a few *other* digestive problems as well," added Smedley, stifling a belch as the departed vindaloo made a brief attempt at resurrection. "But I do enjoy a good curry, and the heartburn will keep me warm. Entropy won't begin until the Big Bang gets cranked up, so I'll need a heat source in the meantime. And when it comes to internal combustion, there's nothing like – *urp!* – a good curry vindaloo to keep the home fires burning, digestion-wise. Hello, what's this?"

While Smedley Faversham was rhapsodizing on themes vindalooish, the universe around him (or, rather, the hyper-sphere directly in front of him, and slightly to the right) had merrily continued dwindling. By now it was thirty inches across and still shrinking, while several more of the last remaining subatomic particles in the myriad dimensions of Space-Time flung themselves lemminglike into the vortex. But Smedley's attention was distracted by something else altogether: coming towards him, at a velocity beyond the speed of light, was one particular subatomic particle which somehow seemed quite different from the rest.

Most good little subatomic particles, of course, will never *ever* go beyond the speed of light. (They also look both ways before crossing into another quantum level.) But this parti-cular subatomic particle was neither good nor little. This subatomic particle was the same size and shape as a very stout man. With a potbelly. It even *wheezed*, which is something that subatomic particles seldom do, but which stout men with potbellies do frequently. Also, this subatomic particle was wearing lapels. And pinned to one of those lapels was a small silver badge depicting a balance scale superimposed across an hourglass: the scales of Justice and the sands of Time. The symbol of the scales and hourglass in interchronally recog-nized in all centuries and millennia as the emblem of the Paradox Patrol, and it is worn solely by the valiant officers who walk the beats of Time. It is never worn by subatomic particles. And yet the object hurtling towards Smedley Fa-versham at hyperlight velocity was indisputably a subatomic particle, because its outer surface was neatly emblazoned with the words **I AM A SUBATOMIC PARTICLE. I AM NOT A LAW ENFORCEMENT OFFICER IN DISGUISE**.

"*Hmmmm*," said Smedley Faversham. "I can't help but notice something odd about this particular subatomic particle. It utterly defies classification. I'm positive it's not a positron, and I knew it's no neutron. It's firmly not a fermion, and it's definitely not a proton, boson or muon. It's tacky enough to be a tachyon, but it looks more like a moron. When it gets closer, perhaps I can identify it by the sound it makes."

"*Quark!*" said the oncoming particle, between its own wheezes. "*Quark, quark, quark!*"

"Aha!" said Smedley Faversham. "Something tells me that this is a quark. But which variety? It certainly has no *charm* worth mentioning. It must be a *strange* quark. Let me see if I can counteract its spin."

So saying, Smedley Faversham stuck out his right foot, which was impeccably shod in a crisp white pearl-button spat. The onrushing quark emitted a loud "OOF!" as it tripped across Smedley's foot and fell tumbling butt-over-appetite (perhaps it was a *down* quark) into the empty void between Smedley Faversham and the glowing hypersphere. Having already oofed once, the quark now repeated itself: "*Oof!*"

"I'd know that oof anywhere," said Smedley Faversham, ripping off the newcomer's cheap disguise to reveal the sweaty brow and glaring countenance of a red-faced chrono-constable with a walrus mustache. "Well, well!" Smedley jeered. "If it isn't my favorite fourth-dimensional flatfoot: none other than Nougat Callender of the Paradox Patrol!"

"Must you always mispronounce my name?" asked the stout man, rising to his feet and brushing off a few flecks of dust . . . which hastily added their molecular mass to the vortex of the nearby hypersphere. "The name is *Newgate* Callender, if you please. My parents were in law enforcement, so all of my brothers and I were named for famous prisons: Broadmoor, Pentonville, Leavenworth, Clink, Ford, Colditz, Borstal, Bastille, and so forth. My dear sister is named Lubyanka. There's also a cousin I'm not too sure about, named Strangeways."

"Sorry, Nugget," said Smedley Faversham spitefully. "What brings you to this neck of the space-time continuum? And what's with the quark getup?"

Newgate Callender blushed. "The top brass at Paradox

Central have got me assigned to plainclothes duty. I'm supposed to blend in with the local inhabitants of whichever time-beat I patrol, so that I avoid committing an anachronism. I had to wear a toga at Pompeii in 79 A.D., and I wore galligaskins and a doublet when I handled the Christopher Marlowe murder case. Then I wore a farthingale during the Great Fire of London, and . . ."

"Wait a minute," said Smedley Faversham. "Isn't a farthingale *a woman's dress?*"

"It *is*," said Newgate Callender. He was already blushing; now his red face turned several vermilion times redder. "The research department really screwed up on that assignment. But it gets worse: when I went after a crimelord in the Devonian Period who was manufacturing counterfeit trilobites, I had to disguise myself as a cycad." Callender shuddered at the memory. "Nasty buggers, trilobites! Utterly useless, too."

"I disagree," said Smedley Faversham. "Trilobites are quite useful. I recently wrote a poem about cybernetics, and I needed a rhyme for '*kilobytes*'. But why are you — *urp!* — here at the Big Bang?"

"Several minutes *before* the Big Bang, actually," said Newgate Callender. By now the hypersphere had dwindled to a mere seventeen inches in diameter: in a few more minutes, it should attain absolute nullity as a zero-dimensional point in space-time, and the Big Bang would commence. "We got a report at Paradox Central of unauthorized time-travel in the vicinity of the Big Bang, so I was sent here to investigate. I should have known I'd find *you*, Faversham."

Smedley Faversham lowered his eyes modestly. "You honour me, Nought."

"The name is *Newgate!*"

"Whatever. Still, aren't you a tad premature? I haven't actually committed a crime yet. You don't dare arrest me *before* I commit a chrono-crime: you would violate causality."

"Just your *being* here is crime enough, Faversham," grunted Newgate Callender. "For one thing, how did you even *get* here? I know you're a time-traveler, but Time didn't actually get started until the Big Bang . . . so how did you manage to show up *before* Time began? That's like attaining a temperature *below* absolute zero: nobody can do it!"

"Evidently you never met any of my ex-wives," said Smedley Faversham. He glanced at the nearby universe: by now it had shrunk to the size of a basketball. "You see, my dear Naugahyde . . ."

"*Newgate!*"

"Whatever. Going back to *before* the beginning of Time was quite easy. I merely had to set the controls of my time machine to go *all* the way back to where the tachyons end. Then, after I'd gone as far yesterwards as the time machine would take me, I got out and *walked* the rest of the way. And, of course, as a lifelong criminal and all-around nogoodnik, I'm just naturally a predator . . . so it's easy for me to *pre-date* everything, including Time itself. How about *you*, Noogie: how did *you* manage to arrive on a timeline before the beginning of Time?"

"Well, that's just the thing." Newgate Callender coughed nervously. "By existing *before* the beginning of Time, Faversham, you've automatically extended the parameters of existence to include yourself. You've moved the goalposts of the universe, as it were. And you got here ahead of me . . . so it was easy enough for me to arrive at a Space-Time nexus which – thanks to your trail-blazing efforts – was already defined *within* the borders of existence."

"Again you honour me, Nougat, old boy," said Smedley Faversham, once more lowering his eyes modestly. "Really, though: if I'd – *urp!* – if I'd known that you'd be coming here too, I would gladly have given you the honour of *preceding* me to the beginning of Time. You would have beaten me to it."

"The only thing I want to beat you to is a pulp," said Newgate Callender of the Paradox Patrol, whipping out his truncheon and appraising certain less essential portions of Smedley's cranial region. By this time, the dwindling hypersphere of the pre-Big Bang universe had dwindled to the size of a softball. "Why not just give up whatever time-crime you're planning and come along quietly, Faversham? I've caught you orange-handed."

"I think you mean *red*-handed . . .," Smedley started to say, until he noticed the telltale stains of curry vindaloo still clinging to his fingertips. He hastily dipped his fingers into the super-heated plasma orb of the hypersphere, wiping them clean, while he stifled another belch.

"I've got you dead to rights," said Newgate Callender, taking out his handcuffs. "I don't know what kind of chrono-caper you were planning here, Faversham, but I'll bet it would have been a real doozy . . . *if* I hadn't shown up to stop you. Why not make a full confession? You might get a lighter sentence."

"Very well." Once more Smedley Faversham lowered his eyes, surveying the contours of Newgate Callender's trousers to determine if they contained a wallet or anything else worth stealing. Meanwhile, Callender had whipped out a small notepad and a Number Two pencil, and he began taking down the full text of his prisoner's confession.

"Actually, officer," Smedley Faversham began, "I was – *urp!* – I was biding my time until the precise nanoinstant *before* the Big Bang. At that moment, the universe would have contracted to a pinpoint." Smedley Faversham held two fingers a hair's breadth apart, indicating a minuscule object. "All the dimensions of Space and Time would be compressed into the smallest possible increment."

"*How* small?" asked Office Callender, scrawling industriously in his notepad. "I'll need some specifics."

"Pretty small," said Smedley Faversham. "I'd say teensy-weensy."

"Don't get high-tech with me," said Newgate Callender. "Are you sure you don't mean itsy-bitsy?"

Smedley Faversham reconsidered his verdict. "Bigger than teensy-weensy, but smaller than itsy-bitsy," he conceded. "Better make it teeny-tiny."

"*Now* you're being specific," said Newgate Callender approvingly, and he jotted this down in his notepad. "Okay, so you were waiting for Space and Time to form a teeny-tiny singularity. *Then* what?"

"And then," Smedley Faversham went on, "just before the universe could expand into the Big Bang, I was planning to *steal* it."

"You *what?*" Newgate Callender was so astonished that he dropped his pencil. It hung dangling in the void, and Callender retrieved the pencil just as it was about to be sucked into the gravity well of the hypersphere, which by now had dwindled to the size of a small grapefruit. "Wait a minute! You were planning to steal *the whole universe?*"

"All of it," said Smedley Faversham, looking shame-faced and penitent. "Every last micron of Space, and every single quantum increment of Time. The whole shmear. Of course, after stealing the universe, I was planning to file off the serial number, so that nobody could prove I didn't buy it legitimately. Then I was planning to disguise it for resale."

Callender made a choking noise. "*Disguise* the universe?"

"Sure. I could give it a dye job. Paint the galaxies black, so that they look like dark matter, and then . . ."

"Never mind that part," said Newgate Callender. "How were you planning to steal the universe?" The chrono-constable nodded towards the glowing orb nearby. "That's a concentrated ball of ion plasma, superheated to a billion degrees! Were you planning to pick it up in your *bare hands?*"

"Of course not," said Smedley Faversham, reaching into his cummerbund and taking out a pair of oven mitts.

"But . . . but . . . but . . .," Callender spluttered, "after you decided to steal the universe, *what were you planning to do with it?*"

"Hock it, I guess," said Smedley Faversham. "Or maybe sell it to the highest bidder. I could cut it up into smaller pieces – like a stolen diamond – and sell chunks of Space and Time wherever I could unload them. I could break up the universe into separate galaxies, and sell 'em one at a time. If anybody asks where I got the galaxies. I'll say they fell off a truck. Or else I could – *urp!* – I could hold the whole damned universe for ransom."

Newgate Callender's walrus mustache quivered with indignation. *"Ransom?"*

"Sure, why not?" Smedley Faversham shrugged. "I figure the entire space-time continuum must be worth *something*, even at street value. I could hold the universe for ransom, and threaten to rough it up a little if the ransom wasn't paid fast enough. Surely, in the Milky Way galaxy alone, there must be several hundred intelligent species that would chip in a few bucks to get their universe back safe and unharmed. They could take up a collection, or pass the hat. Although, from what I understand, not all of the intelligent species in the Milky Way have hats. Several of them don't even have heads. But some of them have *multiple* heads, so I guess they all average out to one head apiece, and . . ."

"That's a brilliant plan," Newgate Callender interrupted. By now the still-contracting hypersphere of the universe had dwindled to the size of a greengage plum; Callender stood protectively in front of this as he confronted his prisoner. "But there's just one tiny little flaw in your scheme."

"I think not," said Smedley Faversham. "My seam is schemeless. I mean, my scheme is seamless. *Urp!* Excuse the belch, please. Too much vindaloo. If I keep breaking vinda, I'll need a trip to the loo. Okay, I'll bite, Nougat: what's the flaw in my plan?"

"Very simple," said Newgate Callender. "If you steal the primordial universe, and prevent the Big Bang from occurring, then Time and Space will never exist! All matter, all energy, all stars and planets and life-forms throughout the universe will be nullified retroactively. And *so*, Faversham," the chrono-constable leaned forward and grinned, "if you hijack the universe *before* it comes into existence, then *who would you possibly sell it to?"*

"I never thought of that," Smedley Faversham admitted. "You've given me something to chew on, Nougat: what good is stealing the universe if I can't hock it, fence it, or ransom it?" there was a pause while Smedley ruminated, during which the hypersphere became a few microns smaller. Then Smedley snapped his fingers. "I've got an idea! I can always sell *this* universe to the inhabitants of an alternate universe! They can melt it down for scrap, and recycle the dark matter for . . ."

"Look around, bub," said Newgate Callender, with a genial wave of his hand. "Do you see any alternate universes?"

Smedley looked around. Except for himself and Newgate Callender and the vast infinite void, the only matter or energy or space or time which existed was the single nearby hypersphere, which by now had dwindled to the approximate size and shape of a strawberry.

"There *are* no alternate universes!" Newgate Callender crowed triumphantly. "They won't be created until *after* the Big Bang . . . and they'll be created from the same cataclysmic event which created *our* universe. If you prevent the formation of one universe, you nullify them all." Newgate Callender rocked back and forth on his heels, looking pleased with himself. "I know all about this stuff, Faversham. When I joined the Paradox Patrol, I had to study cosmology."

"Really?" Smedley Faversham looked impressed. "You mean, mascara and lip gloss and . . ."

"Not *cosmetology*, you fool!" Callender harrumphed. "Your scheme has failed, Faversham. You might as well surrender. Give up this mad dream of stealing the universe."

"Never!" said Smedley Faversham. "I'm still convinced that the – *urp!*—the universe is worth stealing, even if it has no resale value. I have a theory: if I change the quantum structure of the universe in the past, I can alter the future so that my relatives will never be born. That's my nonrelativistic quantum theory. And now, if you'll step aside, time-copper, I'd like to . . . hey, what's this?"

Coming towards them at the speed of light was a single electron, glowing faintly. Beyond that electron was nothing but infinite void. Smedley Faversham and Newgate Callender both knew what was about to happen: this single electron represented the very last quantum increment of unclaimed matter or energy (excepting themselves, of course) in the entire realm of existence. And when this final electron joined the hypersphere of superheated ion plasma, the concentrated vortex would attain critical mass. It would rapidly compress even further, dwindling down to a non-dimensional space-time singularity . . . and then the mighty Big Bang would erupt.

Smedley Faversham and Newgate Callender both held their breaths (there was no air left, anyway) as the very last straggling electron entered the gravity well of the superheated ion mass. The hypersphere shrank to the size of a kumquat, then a grape, then a raisin . . .

And then it stopped.

The universe, evidently, had no intention of contracting any farther. The Big Bang had been postponed indefinitely.

Newgate Callender unclipped some sort of high-tech gizmo from his belt, and he proceeded to wave this (the gizmo, not the belt) above the tiny raisinsized and highly concentrated universe. "Well, Faversham, you've done it *this* time," he announced.

"Who, me? Done *what?*"

"The large amount of energy which you expended to time-travel back to the Big Bang has been subtracted from the total amount of matter-energy in the universe," said Newgate Callender. "There isn't enough matter-energy left to begin the quantum interphase reaction. In other words, Smedley Faversham: you have *prevented* the Big Bang. The universe will never happen, and it's all your fault."

"*Oops,*" said Smedley Faversham. "Sorry about that."

Newgate Callender stepped forward, and slipped his hand-cuffs onto his adversary's wrists. "Smedley Faversham, I hereby charge you with the murder of everybody in the universe. I also charge you with the malicious destruction of all public and private property in the universe. In fact, I charge you with the destruction of the entire universe. You're *really* in trouble, Sunshine. Let's go."

"Where do you propose to take me?" said Smedley Faversham. He pointed towards the tiny raisin-sized nubbin of space-time, which had stubbornly refused to Big Bang itself. "If the universe doesn't exist, then there – *urp!* – there aren't any prisons or courtrooms or police stations. There aren't any laws either, I might – *urp!* – I might add. Even the law of – *urp!* – the law of Entropy doesn't seem to be valid."

"I'll think of something," said Newgate Callender, and tugged the chain of the handcuffs. "Let's get a move on, Faversham!"

"Wait a minute," said Smedley Faversham. His complexion had taken on a definite greenish hue. "Wherever we're going, could we stop off at a – *urp!* – at a lavatory on the way there? A certain curry vindaloo I ate for lunch is starting to come back from the dead, and I . . ."

"There *are* no lavatories any more, thanks to you," said Newgate Callender. "You'll just have to hold on as best you can. Oh, I almost forgot." The chronoconstable reached towards the tiny raisin-sized remnant of space-time which was all that remained of the universe. "I'll have to draw a chalk line around this, and rope it off as a crime scene . . ."

"The hell you will, flatfoot!" With a savage thrust, Smedley Faversham shoved the Time Cop aside and leaped forward. "If *I* can't have the time-space continuum all to myself, then *nobody* can have it!"

Cackling like a maniac, Smedley Faversham snatched the tiny lump of matter-energy, brought it towards his mouth, and . . . *swallowed* the universe.

Newgate Callender sighed, and made another memorandum in his notepad. "As if you weren't in enough trouble, Faversham . . . *now* I'll have to charge you with destroying evidence."

"You couldn't charge a battery in a lightning storm, fatso," jeered Smedley Faversham. "I'm – *urp!* – I'm walking out of here, and I'm – *urp! urp!* – I'm taking the universe with me. And there's no way you're – *urp! urp! urp!* – stopping me, so . . ."

Suddenly Smedley Faversham moaned. He keeled forward,

clutching his gut. His face, which had formerly acquired a greenish cast, now turned the precise same shade of orange as a double takeaway order of curry vindaloo. He started to froth at the mouth . . .

At that instant, Smedley Faversham felt as if the entire universe was exploding. Literally. And, since the entire universe was now inside his digestive tract . . .

Smedley Faversham regained consciousness in a hospital bed, spread-eagled face upwards, with his limbs (all five of them) shackled to the bedposts. A face, blurred and indistinct, was swimming through his field of vision. Now the face turned over, did the backstroke, and continued swimming in the opposite direction.

"Where am I?" quavered the intrepid time-criminal Smedley Faversham. "For that matter, *When* am I?"

The face above him resolved itself into the sharp nose and steely gaze of Newgate Callender's nephew Gregorian, a uniformed Paradox Patrolman. "You're in the infirmary at headquarters, Faversham," the young officer informed his prisoner. "Uncle Newgate told me all the details of your latest caper."

"Well, tell *me*, then," said Smedley Faversham. "How did I get here? For that matter, how did the universe regain its existence? Wha' hoppen?"

"Thanks to your time-crimes, the universe didn't have enough energy left to complete the Big Bang," said Gregorian Callender. "But the heartburn inside your gut supplied just enough thermal activity to trigger the matter-energy interphase, and the combustion of the curry vindaloo finished the job. When you swallowed the universe, Smedley Faversham, you created the Big Bang . . . *inside* your digestive tract."

Smedley Faversham shuddered. "But, but . . . obviously *I'm* inside the universe now, instead of the other way around. Did I manage to cough up the universe before it expanded to . . ."

"Cough up? Not *cough*, exactly, and not *up*, exactly, either."

With one thumb in midair, Gregorian Callender made a *downward* motion. "Let's just say that curry vindaloo is notorious for the speed at which it passes through the human digestive system. *Southward* bound."

Smedley changed color again, this time turning red with embarrassment. "Do you mean to say that I . . ."

"Yes, you did. All of it. Every quantum of space-time in the universe went through your intestines and out the obvious orifice like grease through a goose. *While* the universe was expanding, I might add. The lab boys are still cleaning up the mess you made. This will certainly make an interesting addition to your arrest record."

"Speaking of which," said Smedley, stirring impatiently in his shackles, "you've got nothing to hold me for, Callender. My caper didn't hurt anyone – except myself – and I didn't damage any property. So, since my actions had no lasting effects . . ."

"Oh, I wouldn't say that," said Gregorian Callender. "Look at these." He keyed up several files on a nearby computer terminal, and turned the monitor so that Smedley could see the images onscreen.

"I recognize those," said Smedley Faversham. "They're standard radio-telescope charts, charting the borders of the universe."

"And thanks to your meddling, Faversham," said Gregorian Callender. "The universe is now *expanding*. Rapidly."

"So what?" jeered Smedley Faversham. "The universe has *always* been expanding. Stars and galaxies are moving away from each other constantly, towards the longer wavelengths of the electromagnetic spectrum. Surely you're aware of the red shift."

"Not any more," said Gregorian Callender. He moved the monitor slightly closer to Smedley Faversham's hospital bed, and then handed him the keyboard. "Look again . . . and try inputting the rate and direction of Entropy as a coefficient."

Straining against his shackles, Smedley Faversham typed a sequence of commands into the terminal, and then gasped as he saw the results. Yes, the universe was expanding. The stars and quasars and nebulae and galaxies were indeed moving away from each other, their individual Doppler shifts modulating at various speeds towards the red end of the EM spectrum. But none of them ever got there. All the various components of the universe were terminating their Doppler shifts within the *orange* portion of the electromagnetic spectrum. To be specific, they were stopping within a wavelength of visible radiation which emitted spectroscopic lines of a bright orange hue looking exactly like . . .

"Curry vindaloo!" said Smedley Faversham, in a voice tinged with doom.

"Precisely," said Gregorian Callender. "Well, Faversham, you've done it again. Only *this* time, you've left your permanent mark on the entire universe. Some of us here at Paradox Central want to lock you up for this. Unfortunately, we can't." Officer Callender looked slightly embarrassed. "Apparently, Faversham, you were *outside* of Space and Time when you swallowed the universe. And since the scene of the crime was located *outside* space-time, then it stands to reason that the crime never took place anywhere in Space . . . and it never happened anywhen in Time, either." Sighing wearily, Gregorian Callender produced a key and proceeded to unlock Smedley's shackles. "Looks like you've beaten the rap . . . *again*, Faversham."

"I'm free to go?" asked Smedley Faversham.

"Better than that," said Gregorian Callender. "My sister Julie Anne just busted a gang of time-traveling creationists who went back to Olduvai Gorge during the Pleistocene epoch and tried to murder all the hominids. Julie's been recommended for promotion, and she and I and Uncle Newgate have decided to celebrate. Julie likes Chinese food, so we've made dinner reservations in the early Ming Dynasty: my sister says that's the best place for thousand-year-old eggs. Anyway, Faversham, for some reason Julie wants you to join us for dinner. Care to come along?"

"I'm not hungry," said Smedley Faversham.

YOU'LL NEVER
WALK ALONE

Scott Edelman

Scott Edelman has been writing science fiction, fantasy and horror for the last twenty years and was, until recently, the editor of Science Fiction Age. *But I don't think any of his previous stories prepare you for the following. You'll just have to take a deep breath and hit this story running – and you won't stop before the end. Believe me, there's no way anything could follow this story – except maybe a stiff drink.*

"Go away!"

"Don't be silly, Sammy. You don't really mean that. Remember all the fun we used to have?"

"No, George, I don't. I really don't. Now if you'd just—"

"We used to play—"

"George, no, you don't have to tell me again!"

"—Tag all the time. I was never any good at that game when anyone besides you was it. I never found anybody else the way I could find you. At first I thought I was just getting better, but then I realized that you always let me win. What else could it have been? Good old Sammy."

"Look, George. That was a long time ago. Almost twenty

years. There's no need to go into this again. I wish you hadn't looked me up."

"You're touched. I can tell."

"George, I wish you'd leave. Really. I'm trying to get some work done and I need to concentrate."

"I won't make much noise. Promise. You won't even know I'm here."

"No."

"Sammy."

"No."

"Good old—"

"No!"

"—Sammy. Sammy, it's really cold out here in the hall. You should talk to your landlord. First he leaves the lobby doors unlocked—"

"Is that how you—"

"—And then, what, he's got the air-conditioning on in the middle of winter? Think I'm catching cold."

"So go home."

"If you want, I'll talk to him for you. Tell him to turn up the heat. Anything for good old Sammy. Sammy?"

"Here, I'm slipping his phone number and address under the door. I'm sure he'll be glad to talk to you right now."

"Why won't you let me in? It's amazing. I felt a strange urge for cannoli, and I was heading downtown to that little pastry shop, you know the one, and I looked up and saw you sitting by the window. I never knew we lived in the same neighbourhood. Who knew after all these years we'd end up just a few blocks apart?"

"Okay, I've learned my lesson. No more sitting by the windows with the shades up. Listen, George. Take my word for it. You shouldn't be wandering around this neighbourhood at night. Didn't you hear? There's a curfew. Don't you watch TV? The mayor announced it himself. No dropping in on friends unexpectedly once the evening news has begun."

"But Sammy, it's Friday night. You shouldn't be alone on Friday night. The Sammy I used to know wouldn't be."

"Right. Friday night. What made you think I wanted to see you? Something wrong with me? Maybe I have a date coming over and you're being a third wheel, or maybe I *wanted* to be alone, did you ever think of that? Maybe I'd rather be watching goddamned reruns than to have to listen to you tell me over and over about how we used to play tag!"

"Good old Sammy, always a kidder."

"A kidder. A kidder."

"Those games of tag were something else."

"Those games of tag were a nightmare. George, listen to me. I'm being honest. I'm being sincere. I feel like spending tonight alone. By myself. I've had a very tough week. So would you do me that small favour? Let me have the apartment all to myself tonight? Jesus, just one night."

"Okay. Fine. I understand completely. Your buddy George is not without feelings."

"Thank you, George."

"You go back to whatever you were doing, Sammy. I'll wait right here until you're up for company."

"George."

"Oh, so you changed your mind? Great! What should we talk about?"

"My neighbours won't like this, George."

"So I'll whisper. They won't even have to know there are a couple of old pals out here reliving old times."

"I'm going to step away from the door now and go lie down, George. I think I'm coming down with a headache. Do you mind?"

"Oh. Changed your mind about the chat *again*? You're being very wishy-washy tonight, I must say. No, go right ahead. I'll be right here whenever you want me. You know, Sammy, you should get a welcome mat – that'd be a lot comfier to lie on."

"Good night, George."

"George!"

"Ernie, God, who ever thought I'd run into you tonight? This is wild. How have you been? Haven't seen you in, what, how many years?"

"Jeez, I don't remember. Sammy would know. He was there, too, wasn't he? Sammy is good at remembering things like that."

"He's something, isn't he?"

"I'll say. I've missed him these past weeks."

"Oh?"

"Oh, sure, I've been away."

"Out of the city?"

"Better than that. I went to sixteen countries in fifteen days. I never even heard of half of them. I sent Sammy a postcard from each one, but writing about something just doesn't have the same impact as talking about it face to face. I'm sure Sammy wants to hear all about it, so when my plane landed back in the States an hour ago, I hopped in a cab and came right over. So why are you lying on the floor with your shoes under your head? I don't know that the carpeting's been cleaned. You can't be too sure these days."

"Sammy won't let me in tonight."

"Being difficult again? Something's been bothering him lately, but he just won't open up to me. He's been like that more and more lately. I can't tell you how guilty I felt about leaving him behind for this trip. I tried to convince him to come along, but he said he couldn't get too far away from the city with his mom being sick and all."

"I thought his mom died when we were kids. He told me that once, said he wanted to be alone."

"That must have been someone else. Anyway, with you around, maybe he'll spill his guts. He always liked you. You could tell."

"Ouch!"

"Excuse me."

"That's my elbow."

"Sorry. I'll just stand on these suitcases. Good thing I always carry so much luggage. I don't have Sammy's height. He always keeps a spare key taped to the top of the doorsill."

"I'll remember that."

"Just make sure there's no one in the hall watching you

when you use it. With the lunatics wandering the city these days . . . Ah! There we go. Grab a couple of the bags, George, okay?"

"Hey, nice couch! Is that velvet or what?"

"Reading *Robinson Crusoe*, I see. Good old Sammy, always the highbrow."

"What the hell are you guys doing in here? Get out. I told you I wanted to be alone."

"Aw, Sammy, if you'd really meant that, you wouldn't have left this key outside for us to use."

"Give me that!"

"Whoa! Here, George, Sammy wants to play."

"Catch!"

"George! Ernie!"

"Say, this is fun!"

"Yeah, haven't played this game in years. That's good old Sammy for you, always coming up with games."

"This isn't a game!"

"Ooo – no need to be so rough. But I forgive you, pal."

"Don't forgive me!"

"Testy today, aren't we, Sammy?"

"Here, Sammy, take a swig of this. I brought it all the way back from Europe for you."

"I'm not in the mood for any brandy right now."

"Sammy, just taste this and you'll be in any mood you want."

"I don't care if Napoleon bottled the goddamned stuff himself, I just want to be left alone!"

"Gee, you sure curse a lot these days, Sammy. Did he talk like that when he was a kid?"

"Only during those games of tag – he used to pretend he didn't like them."

"They went on all goddamned day long! I'd have given anything to get away from you people."

"You don't really mean that, do you?"

"Yes."

"He's just joking, George. Tell George you're joking, Sammy. You could hurt his feelings if you don't watch out."

"I'm okay, Ernie. Don't worry about me. I know the way good old Sammy really feels about me."

"Hey, do you hear that?"

"I hear a ringing. Is that what you mean? Do you hear a ringing?"

"It sounds like it's underwater."

"Is that a phone, Sammy?"

"Don't answer that!"

"Sounds like a phone."

"I can hardly hear it ringing. Where's it coming from?"

"Don't go in that room!"

"I think – the refrigerator."

"Stay way from there!"

"Whew! Sammy, Sammy, Sammy."

"Boy."

"When was the last time you cleaned this thing out?"

"How did this get in here?"

"Don't answer that!"

"Don't worry, Sammy. I've got it. Hello?"

"Sammy, you should know better than to keep this in here. A phone is a delicate instrument and you could—Are those eggs? I don't think I've ever seen eggs look quite like that before."

"Don't—Don't—Don't you guys ever listen to me?"

"Sammy? He's right here."

"No, I'm not! I don't want to talk to anyone!"

"They look like they're growing hair."

"How can you say that, Sammy? After a person goes to all the trouble of calling you, the least you can do is talk to them. You owe them that much."

"Ernie."

"Really, Sammy, I mean it. It's simple etiquette. Sometimes you seem to forget your manners, not that I'm trying to lecture you. I understand how hard it is to remember your manners in this modern world, but—"

"Damn. Give me that thing. Who is it?"

"I didn't get his whole name. Freddie something or other,

he said. Said he was from your high school alumni newsletter."

"Oh, God."

"Is this cheese suppose to have mould on it?"

"Blue cheese is. I had some in Denmark."

"Hello?"

"Or was that Spain?"

"This is American cheese."

"Anyway, it was disgusting."

"Sammy, remember me? This is Freddie."

"I remember. Where'd you get my new number, Freddie?"

"Everyone has *your* number, Sammy."

"Europeans do not eat like us."

"What does Sammy eat?"

"I didn't know it had gotten this bad. I worry about him all
the time. But what can one friend do?"

"We're *not* friends!"

"Sammy? Sammy, are you there?"

"What do you want? I'm trying to get work done."

"Sounds more like there's a party going on."

"There's no party. What do you want?"

"I thought you'd be happy to hear from me."

"Why would you think that? I'm not. What do you want?"

"Sammy has been so touchy lately. What can we do to make
him relax?"

"I'd normally say let's whip him up a late snack, but . . ."

"I'm putting together the latest issue of the newsletter and I
wanted to include—"

"No!"

"—The funniest story—"

"No more stories!"

"—I just heard about you. Don't be that way, Sammy. I'm
sure when you hear it, you'll love the idea. Sure, it may have
seemed traumatic at the time, but all these things seem
amusing in retrospect, don't you think?"

"Fred, do you think you could put out one issue of the
damned thing without mentioning me?"

"But Sammy, you're a popular kind of guy. Anyway, remember the time you went to buy condoms for the first time?"

"No!"

"God, when you stuttered out what you wanted, your homeroom teacher was supposedly standing right behind you. And while you were waiting, your priest came in for a visit, your uncle came by for cigars, and the entire cheerleading squad came in for make-up. Sounds like a riot! You must have been humiliated! Of course, that was a long time ago. I was sort of hoping that you'd be able to verify the details for me. A good journalist always checks the details."

"You can't be serious."

"Who, Fred, Sammy? Serious? He was always a serious kind of guy, wasn't he, Ernie? You should have read the articles he put in the paper about the games of tag. Pure poetry. Ernie?"

"Not now, I'm trying to find something to eat in here."

"Look, I'd consider it a personal favour if you didn't print this."

"Well . . . considering that it's you, Sammy . . ."

"Thank you, Fred."

"Considering that it's you, Sammy, how can I drop this? I have a responsibility as a journalist—"

"Arrgh!"

"Sammy, don't do that. Sammy, please, these things are expensive."

"He ripped it right out of the wall."

"Should have done that a long time ago, too."

"Do you have any idea what those things cost?"

"Doesn't matter. I won't be replacing it."

"Hey, I didn't know there was a party going on!"

"Christ."

"That stuff smells great. Chinese?"

"Richard. Richard, not you, too."

"China? Hey, Sammy, maybe *next* year we'll go there! Boy, fried rice would have beaten frogs' legs any day."

"Gee, Sammy, you should have told me you were having company and I would have picked up enough for four."

"Sammy, you devil, so that's why you wanted me to go. You wanted to hog all the food to yourself."

"I didn't even know—"

"Don't worry, Sammy, there should be enough for everyone if we just ration it out properly."

"I'll get some plates."

"Thanks . . . what was that name again? I didn't get it."

"That was because I didn't introduce you."

"I'll do it, Sammy. I'm George, this is Ernie, and you were Richard, right?"

"Right, and any friend of Sammy's is a friend of mine."

"We are *not* friends."

"There you go, Sammy, kidding again."

"When you get those plates, I'll need a knife, too, George. See, if I cut the egg rolls, we'll each get half. They only gave me three pancakes for the Moo Shoo Pork, so sharing that will be a tad more difficult."

"Don't throw the plates like that – oh, why do I bother?"

"What the heck, Sammy can have mine."

"No, he can have mine! What do you say, Sammy?"

"Does it really matter what I say to you guys?"

"Does it? Does it, Dick?"

"Richard. We love you, Sammy. You know that."

"And I love spare ribs. And what's in this one?"

"Wait! Don't open it. Smells like shrimp. Shrimp in, oh, lobster sauce."

"Good nose, Ernie. And that foil bag over there is shrimp toast. What's the matter, Sammy? You're not eating."

"I'm not hungry."

"Whoa, what's going on in here?"

"And you didn't invite Janet and me, Sammy, how could you?"

"Don't worry. Sammy, darling, I'm not hurt. And Herb isn't hurt either, are you, Herb?"

"I'm not worrying."

"Herb? Janet? Do you mind if I call you Herb and Janet?"

"Why, no."

"Then we'd better all get acquainted. Any friends of Sammy, you know."

"You're not—!"

"Janet, Herb, George. George, Herb and Janet. Richard, Herb and Janet. Herb and Janet, Richard."

"Charmed."

"Pleased to meet you."

"Hello."

"And I'm Ernie. I've just seen fifteen countries in sixteen days. Or was it the other way around?"

"Isn't that interesting? Ernie, George, why don't you two guys stand and give Janet and Herb your seats. You've eaten enough. Let someone else have a comfortable shot at the food. Sammy, how does a popular guy like you get by on so few chairs?"

"What happened to your phone, Sammy? I do a little amateur electrical work, and I think I could fix it for you."

"Don't bother, Herb."

"No problem, guy."

"Hey, we can go shopping for some tomorrow, Sammy. I know a restaurant supply house where we can get some folding chairs wholesale."

"I'll go see if I can borrow some. It's getting crowded here. A nice lady next door once hardly yelled at me at all when I set up a pup tent in the hall."

"She moved out the next day."

"Really, Sammy?"

"Sammy, what do you do when there's a party here?"

"What I'm doing now. Good-bye."

"Sammy, how are you? I thought I'd drop in and see—"

"I'm on my way out, Jerry."

"Out? But you don't like to go—"

"Sammy, stay and eat with us."

"Sammy! The phone! It's ringing again!"

"And I didn't even get the chance to give him that miniature

of the Eiffel Tower. It's got a thermometer in it and everything. I flew with it in my lap so it wouldn't get scratched.
Sammy's been getting picky, you know."

"Look, he didn't eat a thing."

"I just can't eat if Sammy's not eating."

"I once got him a small replica of the Empire State Building
with a digital clock in it, but I don't think he likes the Empire
State Building. I've never seen it around."

"He's getting thinner, did you notice? That isn't healthy."

"Pack up the food quick. Sammy's got to eat something."

"His cheeks looked so hollow."

"You don't think he went and got himself a disease or
something, do you?"

"Sammy is a popular guy."

"Should we answer the phone?"

"No time for that."

"Throw all the food in my suitcase. Hurry. No time for
eating if we want to catch him."

"He took the elevator. Look, it's still on its way down."

"Quick! The stairs!"

"Ooops!"

"Damn!"

"One at a time! One at a time!"

"Don't spill the soup!"

"Sorry."

"Only three more flights."

"Watch it! That stuff burns."

"You should have put that in Ernie's suitcase with the rest
of the food like he said."

"But I wanted it to stay warm for Sammy."

"I knew I shouldn't have worn heels."

"Here's the lobby."

"Which way did he go?"

"I don't see him."

"Let's ask the doorman."

"Where'd the doorman go?"

"He was asleep when I got here."

"Quick! Outside!"

"There he is. And the doorman's running after him."

"Mr Sammy! Mr Sammy!"

"Doesn't he realize how foolish he looks?"

"Sammy, wait up."

"Now he's starting to run, too. Sammy, slow down, if I spill any more soup there won't be any left for you!"

"To hell with your soup!"

"Sammy!"

"Didn't I tell you that his language had deteriorated?"

"He's just tired and hungry."

"Stop making excuses for me. Stop following me around. Damn you, when are you people going to leave me alone?"

"Here, Sammy, have the last piece of shrimp toast."

"To hell with your shrimp toast!"

"Sammy, that was a new jacket."

"He's been like that all evening. I wish I could figure out what's bothering him."

"He should have gone away with me. I told him he needed a vacation. I told him he needed to relax, needed to get away from it all. I even offered to pay his way. But I couldn't convince him to come. When he saw me off at the airport, he had the strangest expression on his face. I think he was sad."

"I was so happy, you buffoon!"

"I was really surprised that he came to see me off. Sammy had never done anything like that before. It made me realize even more what a friend he is."

"I know, I'm touched."

"You're not—Look, the only reason I came to the airport was to make sure that you got on the plane and left the country and would goddamned leave me alone for two weeks!"

"Oh, Sammy, you're not fooling anybody."

"Sammy always does that, tries to belittle his noblest feelings, as if he's ashamed of them."

"That's natural for a lot of men, Sammy, no need to beat yourself over the head about it. Herb used to be that way, too, before we got together."

"But not any more, cupcake. Sammy, you know, Janet's changed my life, she really has. You wouldn't act that way if you could only find yourself a good woman like Janet here and settle down."

"And how am I supposed to do that? When do I ever get a chance with you guys? You haven't left me alone with a woman since the day I was born."

"Sammy, I think you're mistaken. I don't think any of us knew you when you were that young."

"I wouldn't be too sure."

"Excuse me. I don't mean to interrupt, but is there anyone here named Sammy?"

"That's him!"

"Is this, er, is this some sort of convention?"

"No, mister, this is my life."

"Or is it a tour? I mean, I've never seen thirty people just standing in a circle like that. Are you a tour guide?"

"Not by choice. Look, who are you?"

"Don't blame me, I was minding my own business, okay? I've got no problems with you people. You can do whatever you want to in the privacy of your own street corner. Hell, you all look like consenting adults. But I was talking to my wife on the phone and this pay phone next to me started ringing. I guess I shouldn't have picked it up, but I did, and a woman asked for Sammy."

"A woman?"

"The second pay phone from the left."

"Did she say who she was?"

"No, but she sounded like she knew you real well."

"Hello?"

"Okay, okay, so I'm curious. What are you guys doing out here? Is this some sort of cult? It's cold!"

"Sammy? Sammy, is that you? I was worried that nitwit had hung up on me."

"We're with him."

"Ma? I'm standing on a street corner, ma. How did you know where to find me?"

"What do you mean, with him? Is he your guru? Is he a movie star or something? He must be famous, you all look at him as if he was. Be honest with me, should I get his autograph?"

"I did."

"What! He wouldn't give me one! Said he was tired of people selling them."

"Well."

"I'll give you fifty bucks."

"Fifty bucks! You guys would pay fifty bucks for his autograph?"

"Okay, a hundred."

"Wow. To look at him, you wouldn't think he was anything special."

"Hey! That's Sammy you're talking about."

"Yeah, watch it, mister!"

"Whoa! No offence, no offence. You know, now that you mention it, there's something about that guy, but I don't know . . ."

"It's simple. He's our friend."

"I am not your friend!"

"Sammy?"

"Ummm . . . are you guys sure about this?"

"I don't have any friends."

"Sammy, are you there?"

"Your friend Sammy doesn't sound very happy."

"I'm not—"

"He can be like that sometimes."

"Do you think he'd be my friend, too?"

"Sammy!"

"I'm here, ma."

"I've been thinking of you, Sammy, and . . ."

"What happened this time, ma? Did you knock the phone off the hook, and when you were hanging it up just accidentally pushed this number with an elbow? Did the cat use the phone as a scratching post?"

"Nothing like that, dear."

"Or did this number just pop into your head while you were taking a nap?"

"Not this time, son. Fred, you know, the boy who keeps trying to interview me about you for that newsletter of his, well, he just called and gave me this number."

"Fred? How would Fred get this number?"

"Don't yell at me, son. I don't know. He just said he was worried about you. He said you sounded depressed. So he told me he thought it would be a good idea to give you a call to cheer you up and gave me this number."

"Ma, ma, ma, I can't live like this much longer. How were you able to do it? How were you able to protect me for so many years?"

"What's going on? Someone giving out free samples?"

"Shush, we're trying to hear this."

"Hey, this is my mother, guys, this is private stuff."

"What? What? What is it? Gum? Cigarettes? Did I miss all the good stuff?"

"Quiet down, we're trying to hear Sammy."

"Who is that there with you, Sammy? Are you having another one of those parties of yours?"

"Not intentionally, ma. I've got to give you credit, ma. You pulled it off. You kept me shielded from all of this. It took me years before I realized I had a magnetic personality."

"You were always a little slow, dear."

"Ma!"

"It's true, Sammy. You were like this from the very beginning. I didn't do *that* good a job. You just didn't want to realize it."

"Tell me about it, ma."

"No. This is your story, Sammy, not mine."

"All right, all right, who's in charge here?"

"What do you mean, officer?"

"Ma, I can't take much more of this. It's getting worse all the time. It's totally out of control."

"What's getting worse? What do you think he's talking about?"

"Whatever it is, we've got to figure out a way to help him."

"Hey, I'm talking to you. I want an explanation and I want it now!"

"Ssssh!"

"Maybe you should see Dr Friedlander again, Sammy. You used to think he could help you."

"All right, enough of this crap! Who's got the permit?"

"What permit, officer?"

"Wise guy. You people should know by now. No permit, no protest. You're blocking traffic with this little demonstration of yours. You're supposed to have a permit, you're supposed to have police for crowd control. You're certainly not doing a good job of it. People keep walking into the street to get around you. Your cause is not going to be helped if someone's hit by a truck."

"Sorry, officer."

"We didn't mean any trouble, officer."

"Friedlander's a quack. He's just as bad as the rest of them."

"He can't help it, Sammy, it's beyond his control. But maybe he can help you."

"Yeah, yeah, yeah."

"Sammy?"

"I've heard it a million times."

"Sammy."

"Okay, ma. I'll do it for you."

"What's your cause, anyway?"

"Cause? Do we have a cause, George?"

"Bye, Sammy. Love you."

"Love you, ma. Bye."

"A cause, a cause! God, I've never seen a group so confused! Where are your armbands? Where are your signs? How will people know what you're protesting against? You'll never get any press coverage this way. Do I have to write you a blue-print? Geez, not even one lousy sign."

"What's going on here?"

"Nothing, Sammy. Go back and keep talking to your mother."

"Is there something wrong, officer?"

"Are you the leader of this march? Don't you know you've got to have signs? Wait . . . haven't I seen you somewhere before?"

"I don't think so, officer."

"And you don't have the permit, either."

"I was just—"

"You seem like a bright guy. Look, next time, do this right. Get a permit. And for God's sake paint up some signs. What's the whole point of the thing without signs? STOP this, BAN that, FREE so and so. Wise up. I'm going to let you off this time without a citation, 'cause . . . I don't know *why* I'm going to let you off, but next time . . ."

"Signs."

"Right."

"And confidentially . . . get rid of these losers."

"Hey! What is he whispering to you?"

"Guys!"

"Speak up!"

"Sammy, they can't hear you in the back."

"Okay, move in close, guys! There's a paint store down the block. Let's go!"

"He's running again."

"Wait up!"

"Don't worry, he won't get away. I used to be on the track team in college."

"He's slowing down."

"Maybe we wore him out before. Maybe we won't lose him. Maybe—"

"Hurry up, guys! Come on!"

"What is he doing? Damn it, will you watch it with that soup?"

"But I want Sammy to have it!"

"Here we are, fellas. After you!"

"What is this?"

"The signs! The signs!"

"But, Sammy!"

"Get in there, George, we've got to have signs!"

"I don't under—"

"Keep moving, Ernie."

"But what about you?"

"I'll hold the door, folks. You all always tell me about my bad manners—"

"But—"

"—Well, I'm finally shaping up!"

"What's going on?"

"Ah, always good to see a new face. Step up, step up. Step up, Janet! Step up, Herb! Hello, officer."

"Good to see you're taking my advice. I thought I'd give you a few tips."

"Step right in. Is that everyone?"

"Everyone but you, Sammy."

"Yes, everyone but me."

"Wait, what are you doing?"

"Sammy, where'd you get the rope?"

"He's tied the door shut!"

"See you later, guys!"

"Wait. Wait! Let us out!"

"Sammy, get back here."

"Sammy, wait – I still didn't give you the British Museum pencil sharpener!"

"Now for the really hard part. How am I going to find a cab at this time of night?"

"Taxi, mister?"

"What?"

"Taxi, mister? Seeing as you had your hand out like that I thought you might have wanted a taxi."

"I was just scratching my head, but—"

"Okay, hop in!"

"What? Where did you come from? It's time for the theatre to be letting out. Shouldn't you be cruising midtown?"

"Funny you should mention it. And you know, normally I would be. But today is my thirtieth wedding anniversary, and I was heading home early with a dozen roses and a box of candy when I saw you standing there looking lost, so I just had to turn the corner."

"But your off-duty sign is still on!"

"Sheesh! Most people wouldn't be so picky this time of night. There, it's off. Hop in!"

"But—"

"Wait a second – is there some kind of sale going on in that paint store? The place looks packed! Maybe I should hop in and grab a couple of gallons of coral pink. That'd make the wife happy."

"Never mind! You've got yourself a fare."

"You sure changed your mind fast. I think some of those people are shouting something at us. Did you forget your change?"

"No, it's nothing. Push off. It's just a crazy custom they have here. We go way back. They just want me to feel welcome. Some stores give out free stirrers and painters' caps, here all the help gather by the door and shout goodbye. Drive!"

"Gee, if they like you so much, maybe a few more gallons of coral pink wouldn't be such a bad idea. Do you think you could get me a discount?"

"Just head downtown. I'll direct you when I remember the correct address."

"Okay. God, coral pink. Hmmm, was that the sound of glass shattering back there?"

"No. Drive faster. What's this about coral pink?"

"A few years ago my wife had the whole house done over in coral pink. Every room. That's love for you – that colour gives me the shivers, but what Phyllis wants, Phyllis gets. I've been noticing that it's about time for a touch-up, and I mentioned it to her, thinking she'd let us go back to some normal colour, like white, or brown, but no, she tells me that she wants coral pink again. And you know, she's going to end up getting it, too. Women."

"Women."

"Son, you don't say that like you mean it."

"I don't know what you—How am I supposed to say it? I was just trying to make conversation, that's all."

"You just don't sound like you mean it. Period. When you say a word like that you're supposed to have a growl in your voice covering a lump in your throat. You're supposed to create pictures in my mind. You don't just toss off words like that. I'm supposed to be reminded of every woman who ever walked through my life. Reminded of all the things we do for love. I'm supposed to remember my first girl. My first woman."

"Oh. I see."

"Yeah."

"Here, let me try it again."

"If you insist."

"How's this? *Women*."

"Not much better."

"Women. Women."

"If you say so. How much experience have you had, anyway?"

"Hey! That's getting too personal!"

"Not for a cabbie. We've heard it all. Forget bartenders. *This* is the confessional of the people. And just like the booths in churches, we even have a divider between us with a little door, so you can feel intimate, but not exposed. Talking to me is like talking to yourself. So what's your problem?"

"I'd rather not discuss it. Just keep driving."

"Where are we heading?"

"My psychiatrist."

"Oh. You'd be better off cruising with me and putting the hundred bucks on the meter."

"Just drive."

"But what I mean when I asked you where you're heading was you still haven't told me how to get where we're going. You didn't have to tell me you're seeing a shrink. You must be feeling a need to spill your guts to me. Understandable. I'm here for you, son."

"Just keep heading south. I'll recognize where to turn when I see it. It's been so long."

"Oh?"

"I didn't mean it that way!"

"Okay, okay. So you're going to a psychiatrist."

"Yeah."

"Women?"

"Women? No, not women."

"You don't say that as if you mean it, either. Let me tell you something I've learned in this life, son. As a cabbie, you see a lot. This little rectangular mirror is a screen on which I've seen it all. Love and death, sometimes even at the same time. People argue in the back, saying things they never thought they'd be able to say even in front of their partners, people screw in the back, moaning words I didn't think could be moaned, it doesn't matter, I'm invisible. Maybe it's the glass divider. People open up to me."

"Not everyone. Not me."

"People open up to me. The stories I've heard. And what I've learned is that it all comes down to the same thing."

"Women."

"Right. Unless you happen to *be* a woman, in which case it could be a man. But not necessarily. Like I told you, I've seen a lot. Women."

"Not this time. I haven't been able to be alone with a woman for more than five minutes in my life."

"Oh. Well, son, you're not the first with that problem. I understand there are things you can do about it, though. Not from personal experience, you see, but I read a lot. Exercises, creams, lotions, surrogate therapy—"

"That isn't what I mean! I'm not talking euphemisms here! When I say I haven't been able to be alone with them I mean I haven't been able to be alone with them. That's all."

"If you say so, pal."

"You should take a left here."

"You don't sound too certain about that. Are you sure you know where you're heading?"

"No! I mean, yes! I mean – it never mattered before! Damn."

"Calm down, son."

"It's funny. You're making me think things I haven't thought about in years. I guess a part of me has been trying to forget them. If I forget the past, maybe it won't bother me so much that I haven't been able to be alone with a woman."

"Uh-huh."

"No! Not uh-huh. This is what I mean. I remember the first time I got to be alone with a girl. I was thirteen years old. Her name was Barbara. We'd gone for a walk in the woods together, and I remember my palm was sweating so much her fingers kept slipping from mine. We found a dark, quiet place where we made a bed of pine needles and started to neck. I could hardly breathe. My entire body trembled as I started unbuttoning her blouse—"

"Don't move! Keep your head forward and try not to act nervous."

"What? I'm opening up about something seminal here and you try to give me directions? I thought this was a confessional!"

"It is, son. A confessional on wheels that picks up and delivers. Sorry about interrupting you, son, but I think we're being followed."

"There's a car back there?"

"There's a whole goddamned bus back there. And I know this city inside out – no buses run on this street. Do you have any enemies with the transit authority? No, wait a second – the bus is packed and I can recognize a few of them. They're the guys who were by the door at the paint store."

"Oh, no."

"Must be over a hundred of them that are squeezed in there, and a lot of them are leaning out the windows. That is not safe. How smart are these guys from the paint store? Some of them are carrying sings. I can just make them out in the rear-view mirror. Let's see. WE LOVE YOU, SAMMY. GOOD OLD SAMMY. SAMMY 4 EVER. Sammy, that's your name? This is amazing! They do this for all their valued customers? I think I'd have preferred the free painter's cap."

"Speed up! You've got to lose them!"

"What? But they're practically your fan club!"

"Fifty bucks."

"All right. Sit back and relax, Sammy, you don't have to worry. We'll lose them. They're history."

"Yeah, history. I don't seem to have any history. All I've got is the present. I can't believe they commandeered a bus! At least they won't be able to bother me from jail. Hey!"

"Sorry, Sammy. You'd better put on your seat belt or you'll bounce off the walls back there. And hey, can you hold onto the candy and roses? I don't want to get them crushed. So what happened with the girl?"

"*This* happened! I can't ever be alone, one on one. Just as I caught a glimpse of bare flesh, that tender nipple, her sister showed up."

"You think that shocks me? Hey, I could get into that. I told you, I've seen everything."

"Her sister was out with her whole brownie pack for a nature walk. Barbara buttoned her blouse, and smiled at me sickly. Damn! If the brownies had only shown up five minutes later they would have *really* seen nature! But goddamn it, that's what always happens. I am being haunted. If I should happen, through some miracle, to get alone with a woman, before anything can happen, a second will show, and then a third, and a fourth."

"Not in the back of my cab, son. I don't think the shocks would stand it."

"Once, I even thought I was going to have an affair with a neighbour of mine in the building I live in now. We met down in the laundry room on a day when it seemed as if everyone in the building had decided to do a wash. We hit it off as well as we could with the blare of the machine masking every word we said. She's a married woman, and she invited me upstairs for coffee while her husband would be off at work. She brought the coffee pot to the table, and as I began to pour, she placed a hand over mine. I looked up. She was licking her lips. I started to lick them, too. We rolled to the floor, and then the doorbell rang. I begged her not to answer. It was an encyclopedia salesman."

"Kinky."

"She got rid of him quickly enough, and we moved to the couch. I was undoing all her buttons and zippers with my teeth, and as I dropped her slacks to the floor, the bell rang again. I pleaded with her this time. She said she had to answer it, everyone knew she was home, someone might get suspicious. She looked through the peephole. It turned out to be her mother-in-law. We rushed to get dressed and get back to the table and I had to listen for an hour while they discussed drapes and the mother-in-law looked at me funny."

"You might have missed yourself an opportunity there, son."

"When she finally left, we didn't waste any time. We stripped off our clothes and ran for the bedroom. She threw herself down, legs spread, glistening, and I thought—"

"This is it!"

"What?"

"This is it! This is it! That's why I hate coral pink so much. I feel like I'm living inside of a giant – Aha! I think we've lost them."

"And as I lowered myself on top of her, I heard a noise behind me, and we turned to see her husband, standing there naked, home for a surprise quickie for the first time in the four years they'd been married. I ran from the room and back to my apartment without even stopping to pick up my clothes and I got to my door and couldn't get in because I didn't have the key and I had to go back upstairs passing all my neighbours and smiling like an idiot and oh, God! See what I mean when I say I've never been alone with a woman?"

"Women."

"No, not women! It's most definitely not women. It's me. Me! I'm the one that's the problem."

"You think that's the reason Phyllis likes coral pink so much?"

"Wait! Here we are!"

"I wonder if it has anything to do with those consciousness-raising groups she goes to down in the Village each week?"

"Stop! You just drove right past it! This is it!"

"This is what?"

"My psychiatrist's office! All your twists and turns brought me right to his door. This is where I wanted to get in the first place. See what I mean? If my personality doesn't bring people to me, it brings me to them. It just can't be believed. What's the fare?"

"This one's on me. You'll need that money more than I will, son. Especially at a hundred bucks a pop. I have a feeling you'll be needing to cough that dough up for quite a while."

"Here. Take it. I insist. I promised it to you for shaking that bus. You can't let me renege on a promise."

"Forget it. Hey, you can pay me double next time."

"Next time? How do you know there'll be a next time?"

"'Cause I'll be waiting down here when you get through upstairs, son, that's how."

"God, what am I saying? Why did I even bother to ask? But – what about your anniversary? Your wife?"

"She can wait. Coral pink. Jeez."

"Why, Sammy, I can't tell you how happy the doctor will be to see you!"

"Cynthia!"

"It's funny that we should run into each other like this."

"Here, let me get the door. Did the doctor ever tell you what we used to talk about?"

"Oh, no, Sammy, he would never betray a patient's confidence."

"Believe me, if he had, you'd know it definitely isn't funny."

"Oh, Sammy, but it is. This is the first time I've stepped out since lunch. I was only out for five minutes getting the doctor some coffee and a doughnuts. These Friday evening hours really take a lot out of him, but what can he do, his patients need him. He really needs that sugar rush, though, to make it through the evening. Come on, let's get inside before the coffee gets cold."

"Do you think the doctor will be able to see me tonight?"

"Here we are. Let's just have a peek at his appointment book. Hmmm . . . doesn't look good, Sammy. He's booked solid until midnight. Oh, Sammy, could you be a dear and get that phone while I bring this into the doctor?"

"Doctor Friedlander's office."

"Sammy?"

"No."

"Sammy, it's you. Don't try to weasel out of it."

"Fred?"

"Sammy, what are you doing there?"

"I've been seeing Dr Friedlander for years. How did you manage to track me down? I didn't know I was going to come here myself until an hour ago."

"It's funny, Sammy—"

"It's not funny."

"—'Cause it's your fault I called though I didn't track you down at all. I was just calling to say I couldn't make my appointment I had with the doctor tonight. Too busy working on the newsletter, too busy working on that anecdote of yours. When I picked Dr Friedlander's name out of the yellow pages last month, I had no idea that he was your doctor."

"Groan."

"Now that we know, we better make sure we don't talk about each other too much, eh, Sammy? I guess there's a conflict of interest or something. Boy, sometimes it seems that's all I can talk about to the doctor. Good old Sammy."

"I've got to go, Fred . . ."

"Sammy, you look white. Why did you hang up the phone like that? Who was that?"

"Just someone cancelling an appointment. Maybe I should go. Suddenly I don't feel much like seeing the doctor any more . . ."

"But that's perfect. Which patient was it?"

"Fred."

"Fred? The doctor was supposed to see him next. Oh, and thanks for recommending him. The doctor says he can always use the business. Though with all these doughnuts he's been popping with these evening hours he's got to start watching his weight. Go right in."

"But I didn't recommend—"

"Sammy! So good to see you! Sammy, Sammy, Sammy. Long time no see, eh? You look tired, Sammy. Maybe you should have been in to see me a long time ago, eh?"

"Hello, Doctor Friedlander."

"That you should come in after all this time. Well. It pleases me. It really does."

"I'm glad that you're pleased, doctor, but actually, my mother—"

"What a time for you to come in. What a perfect time. This couldn't have been better if we'd planned it, for you see, I've been thinking about you all week. Oh, one doesn't forget about a patient like you so easily, Sammy. I've been doing some research into your condition, and finally, this morning, I think I found an answer to your problem."

"If you've been doing research all week and coincidentally I show up just in time to get the benefit of it, I'm sorry, doctor, but I doubt that you have the answer to my problem."

"You've got to be more positive about these things. That's one of your problems, Sammy. Negativity. Now repeat after me. Hypnosis."

"Hypnosis?"

"That's a statement, Sammy, try not to make it sound like a question. Because hypnosis is what will cure you of your paranoia."

"Doctor!"

"All right, all right, my enthusiasm got the better of me. But even if we won't be able to cure you completely, I'm sure we'll at least make you better able to handle your paranoia."

"That's not what I meant! Doctor, of all the people I know in this world, you should know that I'm not paranoid. You're objective, you've heard my story, seen evidence of it. These are not fantasies. What about Fred?"

"Yes, Fred. I wanted to thank you for the referral. I was surprised, though, that after your not having seen me for so long you still cared enough to hand out my name, Sammy."

"But I didn't recommend him."

"Oh, but you must have. Every other word out of his mouth seemed to be about you. Sammy's such a good friend, let me tell you about what Sammy and I did when we were kids, and if I ever move out of my parents' house I want Sammy to be the best man at my wedding. What am I supposed to think he did, pick my name at random out of a phone book?"

"Actually—"

"But enough about Fred, let's talk about you. Lie down, Sammy."

"I don't think I'm in the most receptive mood for this today, doctor. Maybe I'd better come back some other time."

"Nonsense! There could be no better time than the present. This has to be the perfect appointment. I was ready for you, and poof! Here you are. Who are we to argue with such a coincidence?"

"It wasn't a coincidence."

"Besides, the meter's already running, Sammy, so you might as well lie down and make the best of it. Good, Sammy, good. Just maintain that positive attitude and sanity is just around the corner. Now keep your eyes on this."

"Doctor, why are you waving your fist in front of me like that?"

"Look at the watch, the watch! Not the hand."

"I can't help it, doctor."

"Try, Sammy. There's supposed to be something to it. All the books keep talking about a watch."

"I think you're supposed to remove it from your wrist, doctor."

"Is this better? Inhale. Exhale. Watch the slow sweep of the second hand—"

"I can't."

"Don't be difficult, Sammy, I've told you about curbing those negative thoughts."

"It's a digital."

"Damn! The books I got from the Psychiatric Book Club didn't say anything about this. Well, just close your eyes and we'll wing it. Try to relax as you listen to the sound of my voice."

"I'll try, doctor."

"Think positive. Concentrate, Sammy, concentrate. Take a deep breath. We're all alone here. There is no world outside these doors. There is no one about to rush in to slap you on the back shouting, 'Tag! You're it!' There is no crazed party waiting to build itself around you. There are no insane crowds hungry for your presence. There are no—"

"Doctor! I thought I was supposed to relax!"

"All that exists is you, Sammy, and the sound of my voice. You can feel your whole body relaxing. Your hands and feet are floating as if in a salt sea. Your arms and your shoulders are loose. Your torso is silly putty. You forget you have legs, a penis, toes. Your body is drifting in a pool of relaxation, and your mind follows. Your consciousness is all that is, and you feel yourself going back, Sammy, back to your childhood. You are now Sammy, Sammy the child, yet with the mind of an adult, looking at yourself, watching your young world with the perspective of a god, able to interpret. Have you come to any awareness yet, Sammy?"

"Yes, doctor, I have."

"And what is that, Sammy?"

"You're still smoking too many cigarettes, doctor. Your voice sounds more like a frog than ever."

"Are you coming to any *other* awarenesses? You are now ten years old. Describe what is happening around you."

"I'm in gym class. It's the first day of the new school year. We're about to play volleyball. We've never played volleyball in school before. Sides are being chosen for our first game. The coach picked Billy and Mark to be the two captains, and they were to alternate picking the rest of us."

"And whose side did you end up on, Sammy?"

"There never got to *be* any sides! Billy had the first choice and picked me, and Mark started arguing that it wasn't fair, that *he* wanted me. They started to punch each other and ended up in a clinch rolling all over the gym floor. And they didn't even know if I could play! When the gym coach tried to break it up, Mark and Billy started fighting with him! And then all the other kids started getting into the act as well, saying they didn't want to play if I couldn't be on their team. The school principal had to come down with the whole custodial staff to break up a riot. After that, my mother got a note from the doctor to excuse me from gym class for the rest of the term."

"Let's go back a bit farther, Sammy. Take a deep breath. Drift backwards until you are seven years old. What is happening now?"

"We have just moved again. This time we live only a few blocks from my public school. Mom has decided that since we're so close I'm old enough to walk home from school by myself. I was very proud. The first day I had permission, two other kids followed me home. The next day two more walked along with me. By the third day a dozen came with me for my afternoon snack. My mother was going broke buying milk and cookies."

"Cynthia! Will you try to keep it down out there! I don't see how you and the next patient can make so much noise!"

"But, doctor—"

"No buts about it, Cynthia, tell the patient it isn't a zoo out there."

"But—"

"Enough, Cynthia. This is very delicate work. Go on, Sammy. What happened then?"

"When?"

"The children who followed you home."

"I don't remember."

"How did it stop?"

"Stop?"

"Stop. Why didn't half the class show up the next day? Why wasn't the whole school camping out in front of your house by the end of the month?"

"We moved. We moved. Again and again we moved. Whenever the build-up got to be too much for me and Mom to bear, we ran. I've spent a lifetime on the run, but I can't take it any more! I run, but I can't run fast enough, they keep catching up with me. I've got to settle down. I've got to, but they won't let me. I wake up in the morning and forget where I am, I—"

"Enough, Sammy. Enough. Calm down. Go back one more year, two. You are now in kindergarten."

"I am finger-painting. The whole class is finger-painting. All I can remember about it is Mrs Bartholomew leaning over my shoulder. I couldn't slide a finger through the paint without her leaning closer to see it. She seemed to be haunting me. Whatever she did, there she was beside me. And whenever she asked a question, she wouldn't accept answers from any of the other kids. They would raise their hands and call out her name and she would continue to call out, 'Sammy? And what do you have to add?'"

"Let's go back, Sammy, back all the way to the moment of birth."

"I can see it, see what is happening even before I am born. I can picture her there in the hospital, with me still inside her. My strange magnetic emanations, whatever they are, are growing stronger inside of her. She can sense it, though she doesn't know what it is, for she is being badgered by every nurse in her shift."

"Cynthia!"

"Sorry, doctor, I'm doing the best that I can."

"They all come to her as her labour intensifies, making soothing noises, bringing candy and flowers lifted from other patients in an effort to bribe her . . . for what? I don't think they even know why they are doing it. She sits in her room, wondering at her popularity, both amazed by it and also slightly disturbed. I can hear her thoughts. 'So this is what motherhood is all about,' she thinks, as the labour courses through her body."

"I think it's time to move in a little, Sammy. Let's get to the birth, shall, we?"

"My feelings of always being watched, these feeling you call paranoia . . . I see myself, hours old—"

"But what about the birth? The books say you're supposed to talk about the birth!"

"—And it turns out I *am* being watched all the time. I can see that big glass window in the nursery for all the proud relatives to look in, I can see them staring, eyes wide, hypnotized. Every father who showed up to see his firstborn watched me instead, absorbing every gurgle. Grandparents stared at me, forgetting those who were to carry on their line. Sometimes there were dozens of them . . . and sometimes just one. But every moment during visiting hours, some father, ignoring his own child, some friend, forgetting to take part in the eternal debate of friends, about whose nose had been inherited by the offspring of their friends, had eyes wide staring at my crib. When I dream, I see them. Eyes, hungry, hungry eyes."

"Cynthia, what is your problem out there?"

"Doctor, there are just so many of them, I can't—"

"I'll be out there in just a minute, Cynthia, once Sammy and I are through. Ah, this is getting us nowhere, Sammy. Your fantasy is even more deeply ingrained than I'd thought. Bringing up your past may only make your obsessions worse. Let's try something else, okay, Sammy? You will soon awaken. And when you do, your fantasies of being at the centre of the universe will be gone. Galileo cured the Catholic church and I shall cure you. You will no longer feel this life-threatening paranoia. You will no longer feel chased by demons. This insanity will be abandoned, and you will be able to have a productive life, settle down, hold a job. Do you hear me, Sammy?"

"Yes, doctor."

"When I snap my fingers, you will snap out of your trance, feeling very refreshed. Feeling like a new man. For indeed you will *be* a new man. Your problems will be but memory, your fears will be but dream. You are coming out of your trance, your trance is ending . . . now!"

"Yawn! Sorry about that, Doctor Friedlander. I guess I must have fallen asleep."

"Don't worry about it, Sammy. I know how comfortable the couch is. I've napped on it myself. But the important question is, how do you feel, Sammy?"

"How should I feel, doctor?"

"Dare I say, rested?"

"Maybe, doctor, maybe."

"Dare I say, refreshed."

"Maybe, doctor. Maybe."

"Dare I say . . . cured?"

"Hmmm."

"Hmmm?"

"Cured? Why – yes! I *do* feel different. I no longer feel a shadow behind me. Thank you, doctor! I feel like a new man. How can I ever thank you enough?"

"Are those tears in your eyes, Sammy? I'm touched. Just sign a few forms on the way out, and that will be thanks enough. I've left them with Cynthia. Nothing major, just a release giving me publication rights in your case. It's a standard procedure, but in this case I will accept it as a . . . token gesture on your part."

"Anything, doctor. I am *so* happy! I'll go sign right now."

"Sammy, Sammy, Sammy. There's no rush. Sit back down. Have a drink. Are you sure you have to be going so soon?"

"Doctor!"

"What? What did I say? Did I say something wrong?"

"For a moment . . . you actually had me believing it. See you later, Doctor Friedlander."

"Wait, Sammy! Get away from the door! Don't leave yet!"

"Sammy!"

"Yea, Sammy!"

"It feels like we've been waiting for ever."

"What took you?

"Oh, no!"

"Honestly, Sammy, I don't know where they all came from."

"That's all right, Cynthia."

"They started marching in here with their signs not ten minutes ago. At first they started dribbling in in threes and fours, but now, now they can't all fit in here! And there are even more out in the hall. The doorman called just a moment ago to complain that they have all the stairways blocked."

"Sammy, here, have some soup, there's only a sip left, but it's all yours! See, I saved it all for you!"

"Sammy, here, take my miniature of the Vatican. See, this one has a built-in microscope!"

"Sammy, I was right, wasn't I? Don't I know how to organize a rally? Didn't the signs add a perfect touch?"

"Sammy, boy, this even beats out the old games of tag!"

"Sammy!"

"Sammy!"

"Sammy!"

"Arrggghh!"

"Sammy, what are you doing?"

"I can't face these people any longer! If I have to spend one more minute with them I'll have a complete nervous breakdown, I know I will."

"But, Sammy, not the window—"

"I've just got to get away from these maniacs. The fire escape is the fastest way out. Apologize to the doctor for me. I didn't mean to leave an army in his office."

"But, Sammy—"

"Don't worry, Cynthia. See, I'm shutting the window behind me. Maybe I'll see you again sometime. Too bad it wouldn't do us any good."

"Sammy, there is no fire escape out there!"

"Uh-oh."

"Sammy, come back inside – if not for yourself, think of the great trip to China we're going to take next year."

"Sammy, I thought you were going to let Herb and me help you pick out more chairs for you. Our treat."

"Sammy, how can you leave your friends all alone in here?"

"You're not my friends!"

"Come on inside, Sammy. The ledge is only eight inches wide."

"I can't, Cynthia. I can't move."

"You mean you won't move."

"No, I mean I can't. The thought of going back into the mob again . . . it just paralyzes me. I need some peace, and this is where I'm going to get it. You can shut the window again, Cynthia. I'm just going to sit here where it's quiet. Looking out in the still, near-deserted streets . . . I can imagine for at least a moment that I am part of that solitude."

"Look – there's some nut up on a ledge!"

"A jumper!"

"Don't do it! It can't be that bad!"

"Jump! Jump!"

"What are you, a moron? Don't say that!"

"Hey! *He's* the fool on the ledge!"

"Don't worry, fella. Help is on the way. What's your name?"

"Ummm . . . this isn't exactly what I intended."

"Don't do it!"

"This is the police – stay calm. I repeat. Stay calm."

"Go away."

"You're creating quite a circus down here. How about coming down and letting these good people go on their way? There is no reason for you to hurt yourself."

"Get those helicopters out of here! I'm not planning to hurt myself!"

"Then what are you doing on the ledge?"

"I'm trying to get a moment by myself – leave me alone!"

"Sammy, here, move over a bit and let me get out there with you."

"George, no."

"Yeah, Sammy, you shouldn't be out here all by yourself. It must be lonely."

"Er, guys, I don't think this ledge can hold all of us. Guys?"

"Sammy!"

"Sammy!"

"Sammy!"

"This is the police again. I don't know how you did it, fella, but you can't kill yourself – there are hundreds of your friends down here, hoping for you to live."

"Oh, my God. They're there, they're all there. I want to live! Leave me alone."

"I'm afraid I can't do that. I'm a police officer. The others may just be freelancers, but I get paid not to leave you alone. I can't go."

"You can't go! They can't go! No one can go!"

"Now, don't get yourself worked up. It can't be that bad."

"What do you know?"

"Hey, up there! Isn't your name Sammy?"

"Sammy! The soup! The soup!"

"Sammy, don't do anything rash until I get your autograph."

"Sammy, remember me?"

"Sammy, I still haven't given you the Stonehenge paperweight!"

"Sammy!"

"Sammy!"

"Sammy!"

"Sammy, before you jump, sign these papers! We'll make psychiatric history together!"

"Sammy, don't do anything you'll regret. Janet's got a lot of single girlfriends – maybe you'd like one of them. We could double date."

"Sammy, one more game of tag! Just one more!"

"Sammy, your problem is that you spend too much time by yourself."

"Yeah, you have too much time to think. You should get out more."

"Hey, why don't we all go see a movie together!"

"Let's"

"What's playing?"

"How about—"

"Why not—"

"I know a theatre downtown with great popcorn!"

"Wait! We're doing this for Sammy after all. Let Sammy decide where he wants us all to go!"

"Sammy!"

"Sammy!"

"Tell us! Tell us!"

"Choose, Sammy, choose!"

"Tell us where to go!"

"Sammy!"

"I can't take this any more! PLEASE! GET! OUT! OF! MY! LIFE!"

"Well . . ."

"Okay, Sammy."

"Bye."

"If that's what you really want."

"See you later."

"Excuse me, Sammy, you're blocking the window."

"Wait – what are you all doing?"

"Why, we're going, Sammy. Just like you asked us to so nicely."

"If you really wanted us to go, you should have told us before. None of us want to hang around if we're being a bother to you, Sammy."

"But I've been telling you to go for years! I've been spending my entire life telling you to go. I've been—"

"You never said please before."

"I never said . . ."

"You have terrible manners, Sammy. We've been telling you about them for years."

"Please?"

"Your only flaw. Who knew to believe you?"

"Please. I never said please."

"He's right, Sammy. All you ever had to do was ask."

"Yeah, we would never have wanted you to think we were pushy."

"Please. Please. Please. Oh, my God. Please. I'm free. Thank you! Thank you, world! They're gone. They're all gone. As soon as I get down from here I can begin to live! The first thing I'm going to do is—Uh-oh. The window. It's stuck. Hello? Anybody? Can you come and unjam this thing? Cynthia? George? Herb? Come on, is anybody there? Guys? Where the hell is everybody? Please? Please!"

"Well, if that's really the way you feel about it."

"We're back!"

"Ummm . . . I didn't quite mean that."

"Here, I can wedge the window open with my Prado letter opener."

"Thanks, guys, but you didn't all have to come back. Now get lost – please?"

"You didn't really believe all that *please* stuff, did you? Not when I still have soup for you."

"We'd never leave you, Sammy. We were just trying to cheer you up."

"But—"

"Yeah, we were just joking!"

"April Fools!"

"But this is October, damn it!"

"April Fools!"

"No!"

"April Fools!"

"Please – leave me alone!"

"April Fools!"

"I can't take this any more!"

"Oh, no!"

"Look out! He jumped!"

"Someone catch him!

"The net! Get the net under him!"

"SPLAT!"

"Uh-oh."

"Er – Sammy?"

"Come on, Sammy, get up! The night's early yet."

"Sammy!"

"A fine time to take a nap!"

"I don't think he's going to get up."

"Maybe he's just tired."

"Yeah, that's it. What's left of the hot-and-sour soup will perk him up, though."

"I guess he's not thirsty. It's just dribbling down his chin."

"Ingrate!"

"Sammy just doesn't know how to treat his friends."

"Wasn't that always the way."

"Let's get out of here, everyone – I think we've humoured him long enough."

"I don't think I ever liked him much in the first place."

"Gee, George – since Sammy doesn't seem to want it, would you like this Albert Hall egg timer?"

"Aw, shucks, Ernie – thanks. You know something? It's at times like these when you learn who your real friends are."